FOR BRIANA NOW, THERE WAS NO TURNING BACK . . .

Briana pressed closer, moaning deeply when Colt caressed her breasts through the thin fabric of her gown. There might as well not have been any material covering them, for their tautness quivered eagerly against his touch. All the while their tongues mingled, mouths pressing together in an endless kiss.

Briana fell back on the sofa, arms tightly around Colt. Her hips began to undulate beneath him, and she was astonished by the urgings of her body as it sought its fulfillment.

Colt lifted his mouth from hers, and in the gentle light, she could see the torment in his eyes . . . torment mingled with desire . . .

Other Avon Books by
Patricia Hagan

GOLDEN ROSES
LOVE'S WINE
PASSION'S FURY
SOULS AFLAME
THIS SAVAGE HEART

The Coltrane Saga

LOVE AND WAR
THE RAGING HEARTS
LOVE AND GLORY

LOVE AND FURY

PATRICIA HAGAN

AVON
PUBLISHERS OF BARD, CAMELOT, DISCUS AND FLARE BOOKS

LOVE AND FURY is an original publication of Avon Books. This work has never before appeared in book form. This work is a novel. Any similarity to actual persons or events is purely coincidental.

AVON BOOKS
A division of
The Hearst Corporation
1790 Broadway
New York, New York 10019

Published by arrangement with the author
Library of Congress Catalog Card Number: 86-90748
ISBN: 0-380-89614-1

First Avon Printing: September 1986

AVON TRADEMARK REG. U.S. PAT. OFF. AND IN OTHER COUNTRIES, MARCA REGISTRADA, HECHO EN U.S.A.

Printed in the U.S.A.

K-R 10 9 8 7 6 5 4 3 2 1

For Sally and Branch . . . who were *always* listening, with love. . . .

Chapter One

New York
April, 1889

THE Metropolitan Opera House was ablaze with thousands of glittering lights as the excited throng crowded through the entrance doors, eager for the festivities surrounding the Centennial celebration.

Kitty Wright Coltrane stood apart from the crowd, by herself, lost in reverie. She was oblivious to the admiring stares of elegantly attired gentlemen and envious looks from their female companions.

Time had been kind to Kitty. In maturity, she was even more beautiful than she had been in youth. Golden-red hair reflected the shimmering hues of a brilliant sunrise. There was no fading, no hint of gray. Her skin was as smooth as the richest cream, and her lavender eyes, fringed with long, dusty lashes, still held strange, glowing fires.

She was adorned that evening in a stunning gown of shining emerald satin. Threads of genuine silver were woven through the fabric, and the gown sparkled elegantly in the light. Large diamond earbobs adorned her ears and a diamond and emerald necklace circled her long, slender throat. Her red hair fell in cascading curls, caught here and there by silver combs studded with emeralds. High, firm breasts strained provocatively against the décolleté, banishing any notion that her voluptuous body might have withered with time.

The people in that milling crowd who marveled at the woman's sublime beauty would have found it difficult to believe that she had ever known a day of poverty or misery in her entire life. She was, after all, the wife of one of the richest and most respected men in the state of Nevada, Travis Coltrane. She looked pampered, and she was as beautiful as a goddess.

Travis had inherited a large silver mine twenty years past, the grateful gift of a prospector whose life Travis had saved, and the Coltranes enjoyed a life of luxury.

But it had not always been like that for either of them. Like thousands of other Southerners, Kitty's heart bore the scars of that terrible, bloody War Between the States. She had tried to erase those times from her memory, and as the years rolled by, she succeeded in embracing the joy of each new day, but she could never wholly dismiss the awful memories.

She drew an impatient breath, letting it out slowly as she directed her gaze once more to the entrance of the magnificent building. Guests were still arriving, but where was Travis? A message from President Harrison, delivered to her hotel suite that morning, had advised that the ship carrying her husband would arrive in mid-afternoon and that he would certainly be at the gala that night. There had been no further word.

A smile touched her lips, and she felt the familiar, warming rush that happened each time she thought of the man she loved so deeply . . . so fiercely.

Their love had not been born easily. She recalled with humor the dislike that sparked between them at their first meeting. He, a Union Cavalry officer, had forced her, a Southerner with knowledge of nursing, to minister to Northern troops. He had kept her prisoner.

The four years of that grueling war saw many personal battles between the two lovers, but romance had triumphed . . . after the birth of their child, their son, John Travis, named after her beloved father and Travis.

Their eventual marriage had not ensured eternal bliss. After miserably attempting to become a farmer and work the North Carolina land Kitty inherited from her father, Travis succumbed to his unquenchable wanderlust. In his absence, Kitty fell prey to an old adversary from the war years, an unscrupulous villain who kidnapped her and forced her to endure horrors which her mind could not accept, forcing her into a state of oblivion. She lost her memory, her identity, for several lost and lonely years.

Her return to reality was met by the discovery that Travis, believing her dead and desperate for solace, had married. The gentle woman died giving birth to his daughter, Dani.

Overcome with pain, Kitty silently admonished herself for opening the old wounds. Now was not the time. *Never* was the time. There was too much love between Travis and her to allow the intrusion of all that hell.

A glance at the entrance doors caused Kitty's heart to leap with joy, but her joy wasn't a woman's love for her husband, but a mother's pride in her son.

Colt, as John Travis had long ago been nicknamed, strode through the entrance, looking around for her. Tall, well built, Colt had inherited Travis's dark, French-Creole coloring. His hair was as black as a raven's wing, his eyes a smoldering silver-gray.

His searching gaze found her, and he made his way across the room. For an instant, Kitty could believe she was seeing Travis.

Colt gave her a fond kiss on the cheek, then took her hands, gazing down at her with an apologetic look. "I'm sorry, Mother. There's still no word."

Kitty glanced in the direction of President Harrison, who stood talking with guests, and murmured, "And we still have to worry about what his next assignment will be. I'm sure the President won't let him rest," she sighed.

Colt grinned. "That's the price Dad pays for having fought so valiantly in the war, Mother. He earned a lot of respect, and that's why every time the government has a special assignment, they call on him. Haven't you learned to live with that yet?"

With mock severity, she said, "I've learned to live with a lot more from your father than you would ever dream, John Travis Coltrane. If he lives to be a hundred, he'll still be looking for adventure and challenge. I've never met a man with a wilder spirit."

"Would you have him any other way?" Colt prodded, grinning.

Her eyes mirrored deep love. "No, I don't suppose I would, John Travis, but I would like to have him home for a while. He's been away three months now, and this time was a nightmare, not knowing for weeks whether he was dead or alive."

Colt nodded with grim understanding. Travis's latest commission had taken him far from home, to Samoa, in the eastern Pacific Ocean. The islands there had been fighting their own civil war for ten years. When it appeared that Germany was going to become involved, overthrowing King Malietoa, America and England stepped in to back the king. Warships congregated in Apia harbor.

Travis was on board one of those warships, requested by his government to attend the negotiations with Germany. But then a hurricane struck the islands.

Kitty knew depthless terror. What little communications they received said that all but one of the ships had been smashed to bits. For a long, ghastly time, Kitty went nearly insane with worry as she waited and waited for further word.

Then, mercifully, they learned that Travis had been

on board the ship that managed to avoid the reefs and sail to the safety of the open sea.

President Harrison sent a personal emissary to Silver Butte, Nevada, to inform Kitty that Travis was too valuable to be subjected to further dangers on behalf of this assignment. He would not be required to attend the negotiations with Germany and was, in fact, en route back to the United States already. The President invited Kitty and Colt to journey to New York to meet Travis and enjoy the Centennial celebration, which coincided with Travis's arrival.

Kitty regarded the invitation warily. Was the President softening her up in preparation for another assignment for her husband? She had long ago come to terms with Travis's wanderlust, but she needed to have him to herself sometimes, too.

She blinked, realizing that her son was speaking and she hadn't heard a word. "I'm sorry, dear. You were saying . . . ?"

"That I'm ready to go home," he repeated. "You know I've never liked fancy parties, and I'm already tired of all this—this *show*." He looked around the room, disgusted.

Kitty followed his gaze, understanding perfectly. A large champagne fountain dominated the center of the main room, and champagne flowed down into a pool, the surface of which was covered with hundreds of floating pink and purple orchids. Guests laughed merrily as they leaned over to hold out their crystal glasses and fill them with the sparkling champagne.

The women wore gowns of every color imaginable, casting a rainbow hue. Fantastic jewels sparkled in the lights. There were string ensembles positioned in every corner, and music wafted over the murmur of conversation and delighted laughter.

The floor was covered by thousands of rose petals, their sweet fragrance rising to vie with the odors of perfumes and cigars.

"This is some celebration," Kitty commented, then saw that her son was now lost in his own world. She touched his arm gently. "Could your mood have anything to do with Charlene Bowden?"

Colt barely managed to restrain his disgusted grimace. As usual, his mother saw his innermost feelings. He saw no reason not to confide, "Exactly. No one was more surprised than I was when she showed up at the train station with trunks and her aunt Jessica, and announced she was coming with us."

Kitty had been more than mildly surprised herself, but had carefully refrained from asking questions. Colt was a grown man, and his life his own. She yielded to maternal curiosity only when she thought he wouldn't feel that she was prying. "Had she asked if she could come along?"

"Yes!" His eyes flashed. "When I told her about our invitation, she said she wanted to come along. I told her no. She wasn't invited. Well, you saw what happened." His nostrils flared ever so slightly, a trait inherited from his father, signaling either anger or agitation.

Kitty caressed his cheek with her fingertips and murmured, "You had no choice but to accept her coming along. If you had made a scene, it would have been unpleasant for everyone concerned. You did the only thing you could do."

He shook his head. "I've never met a girl with so much nerve."

Kitty chose her words carefully. She knew her son had no intention of settling down soon, but Charlene Bowden was the only girl with whom he kept company—the only one Kitty knew of, anyway. If Charlene was destined to become her daughter-in-law, Kitty wanted to say nothing about her that might one day be regretted. "She is a lovely girl," Kitty said hesitantly, "but Carleton and Juliette have spoiled her terribly. Being an only child, she's used to getting anything she wants. Right now, you are what she wants.

"You are probably her first real challenge in life," Kitty continued, "so don't be too angry with her, son. She's obviously in love with you. That makes a woman do things she wouldn't do otherwise."

Colt gave her a grateful look. "You always manage to make a situation more tolerable, Mother. You know you were every bit as angry as I was when you saw Charlene at that train station, but you still haven't said one unkind word about her. And I *know* she gets under your skin."

"Only if I let her," Kitty explained with a smile. "Sometimes I think that's the real secret of coping with life, John Travis: being wise enough not to let unpleasantness penetrate."

Colt took to heart every word of criticism or advice his mother ever gave him, for he had the utmost respect for her. During long, intimate conversations with his father, he'd learned much of what his mother had endured in her life. Travis had not only confided his love for Kitty, but had told with burning pride of the way she had survived all the anguish inflicted on her. For Colt, his mother stood on a pedestal that would never crumble.

"You know," he said finally, "if I were lucky enough to find a woman like you, maybe I *would* settle down and get married."

Kitty laughed and shook her head. "John Travis Coltrane, you know as well as I do that you were born with the same wandering spirit your father has. Heaven help any girl who marries you before you get at least some of it out of your system."

Colt laughed with her, but joviality quickly faded as he saw Charlene Bowden coming determinedly toward them.

Kitty braced herself. She did not actually dislike Charlene, but sometimes the girl's snobbery and vanity were too much to endure. Charlene was a younger version of her mother, and Kitty had tried to avoid Juliette Bowden for years. Recently, due to their new station in life, and by virtue of their wealth and Travis's importance to the government, Travis and Kitty were the recipients of invitations to every social function. And Juliette Bowden, wealthy and the most socially minded woman in Silver Butte, was in charge of functions in that city. Kitty was well acquainted with the difficult Juliette Bowden.

As Charlene approached, Kitty noted that if not for the disapproving expression on her face, Charlene would easily have been regarded as the loveliest young lady there. She did not, thank heavens, look like her mother. There was a ripe freshness about Charlene. Her hair, the color of sweet honey, bounced about her heart-shaped face with natural curls. Wide blue eyes were framed by long, silky lashes. Her saucy, turned-up nose would have given her an appealing gamine look except for her snobbish nature. As it was, the nose only emphasized her uppity attitude.

Charlene was tiny, petite, and her gown, in a brilliant shade of red taffeta, with short puffed sleeves, tufts of lace and white bows scattered all over the billowing skirt, made her appear even more daintily doll-like.

Flashing Kitty a smile of greeting, Charlene then turned all her attention on Colt. Her voice was tight as she said, "I've been looking for you all evening. You brought me here, and then went off and left me. I think you are being very discourteous to me."

Colt regarded her coolly, and Kitty was aware of another of his inherited traits. Travis never justified himself to anyone. Colt could easily have explained to Charlene that he had, at his mother's request, gone down to the docks to see if there was any word from his father, or whether Travis's ship had docked. But, just like Travis, Colt offered nothing by way of explanation.

Charlene tapped a satin-slippered toe in exasperation, arms folded, as she stared up at him. What, she wondered, was it going to take to bring him to heel?

"Don't you have anything to say for yourself, Colt?"

He raised an eyebrow, drew in his breath, and let it out slowly. "My dear, it was your idea to come to New York, not mine. It is not my responsibility to see that you enjoy yourself."

With a curt nod and a bow to his mother, Colt turned on his heel and left, disappearing quickly into the crowd.

Charlene whirled on Kitty. "Did you raise your son to be so impudent, Mrs. Coltrane? You've seen the way he treats me, and—"

"Charlene," Kitty was quick to interrupt, "perhaps John Travis has reached the limit of his endurance. Though he was blunt, you must agree that you are not here by his invitation. Perhaps you expected too much of him."

The tears that glimmered in Charlene's blue eyes were genuine, as was the tremor in her voice. "Mrs. Coltrane, I'm sorry if I've caused you any distress, but I really do need to talk to you."

Kitty pitied the urgency in the girl's manner, and she was about to respond to her plea, but at that moment a man nearby remarked loudly, "I do believe that's Colonel Coltrane coming in now. You know who he is, don't you? The President holds him in the highest regard and . . ."

Kitty heard no more as, with pounding heart, she turned and saw her husband, the father of her son, her man. All the love she had for Travis went rushing through her and she thrust her way toward him, pushing through the crowd, calling to him.

Travis heard and turned toward the sound of her voice. As he spotted her, his heart thrilled. She was still the most beautiful woman he'd ever seen. Rushing toward her, he reached out with those strong arms and folded her against his chest, awed by the overwhelming love that never waned, but grew even more intense with every passing day.

For long moments, the two embraced in silence, oblivious to the stares of those around them. Time stood still, and there was no other world but theirs.

Travis was the first to break the spell as he whispered, lips warm against her ear, "God knows I've missed you, Kitty."

She pulled away, tilting her head to gaze up into the eyes that shone with deep, abiding love. Her lips parted, but before she could make a sound, a man exuding authority and efficiency approached, clearing his throat pointedly.

With a polite acknowledgment to Kitty, he addressed himself to Travis. "Colonel Coltrane, I'm Malcolm Preddy, aide to the President. President Harrison requests a private audience with you now, before dinner. Will you come with me, please?"

Travis gave him the crooked, almost arrogant smile that Kitty knew so well. Then, eyes devouring Kitty, he murmured, "Sorry, Mr. Preddy, but the President will have to wait. I'm about to have a private audience with my wife."

He took her arm to lead her away, but the aide said firmly, a hint of annoyance in his tone, "The President is waiting, sir."

Travis chuckled. "So am I. I have been waiting for about three months now."

He started to move away, but Kitty held back. Hesitantly she said, "Travis, maybe you'd better go with him. I'll wait for you here."

"No," Travis said shortly. "I will speak with the President, but I'm not letting you out of my sight, so you'll have to come along." He kissed her cheek and hugged her against him, then looked at the aide.

Malcolm Preddy, wondering about protocol, nevertheless sensed, as people quickly did, that Travis meant what he said. "Very well," Preddy sighed, "I'll take you both to him."

Again Kitty held back, realizing that *her* presence had not been requested. She knew she would feel quite uncomfortable forcing herself into the meeting. Squeezing Travis's hand, she said, "Let me wait for you. I prefer it this way, really."

"As you wish, my dear," he said. "I won't be long."

As she watched him go, she saw the admiring stares of the women he passed. Dashing, handsome, Travis was even more striking that night in an elegant white velvet suit and pale-blue ruffled shirt. His dark hair curled softly around his neck, nearly to his collar.

Yes, she mused, taking a deep breath birthed of pride and love, Travis Coltrane was a handsome man and a joy to live with, satisfying her in every way.

Colt appeared at her side a few moments later. "So he's back," he said. "And I just missed him. Is everything all right?"

Kitty explained that Travis had gone to speak with the President. "Maybe it's about his new assignment, though I hope there won't be one for a while," she said worriedly. Then, remembering her son's distress, she quickly changed the subject. "Where is Charlene? I'm afraid I was very rude, running off and leaving her that way, but when I saw your father . . ."

"No ruder than I was, Mother. I suppose I should go find her, smooth things over." He looked around the room as he spoke. "But I don't see her."

People were starting to move toward the dining rooms. "Maybe you should look for her," Kitty suggested, "while I wait for your father."

Colt nodded. "I think it's time I had a long talk with Charlene. If," he added irritably, "she can hear me at all over the wedding bells ringing in her ears."

Kitty laughed, and Colt shook his head ruefully as

he walked away. She couldn't blame Charlene for wanting to rope Colt in and brand him, but she doubted he'd be branded for a long time to come. Travis had been well into his thirties before he married, and had never truly settled down, married or not.

Twenty minutes passed, and Kitty found herself standing alone, her only company the waiters moving around retrieving discarded champagne glasses and napkins.

She took a deep breath, let it out slowly. Travis was with the President, she reminded herself, and that was important. But she was having a hard time being patient, because she wanted to be with the man she loved.

At last Travis appeared, his expression one of thoughtful resolution, and Kitty grew anxious. Without a word, he wrapped his hand around hers and led her outside, into the night.

"Where are we going?" she protested. "We're already late for dinner, Travis, and John Travis is expecting us—"

He silenced her with a deep, smoldering kiss, then hurried her along.

A short distance away was a small park, with many clumps of high shrubs. The city had not yet brought street lights in this far, for the government officials did not feel it was justifiable to bring the expensive Edison tube, a copper conductor wrapped with jute and placed in an iron tube, to so little-used an area.

Travis started to enter the shadowed, dark park, and Kitty balked. Stamping her foot, she demanded, "Travis Coltrane, just what are you up to? You drag me away without a word of explanation, and now you're heading into the woods. I'll snag my dress on something and—"

"And you talk too much." Travis picked her up, easily tossing her over his shoulder, and continued on his way. "To hell with your dress. We can afford a thousand new dresses."

Kitty continued her litany of complaints and queries, kicking her feet and beating on his back with her fists, but they both knew she wasn't really angry. Finally, when they reached a secluded spot far from the street, Travis set her on her feet. He pulled her close to him.

Kitty continued to feign indignation. "Have you taken leave of your senses? Walking out, missing dinner—"

"You are all the food I need, Kitty."

Tilting her head to one side, lavender eyes shining seductively, she murmured, "Will you ever grow up, Travis Coltrane? We aren't newlyweds anymore."

He gently scooped her breasts from the bodice of her dress in one swift movement. Kneading the firm flesh with gentle fingertips, he huskily whispered, "When we've been married fifty years, I will still want you every night."

Kitty thrilled to the memories of ardent lovemaking they had experienced every night they'd ever been together. Never had she denied Travis, for to have done so would have been to deny her own hunger.

He bent, kissing each nipple to taut erectness. Then he pulled her down to the grass, lying beside her. He removed her gown expertly, continuing to kiss her nipples as he maneuvered her gown away from her body. Soon she was naked, her china-white skin glistening in the faint moonlight.

He unfastened his trousers, releasing his manhood and rubbing it against her enticingly. She felt the pulsating strength of his desire and moaned softly. She longed to tell him of her great need but knew Travis had never wanted words when making love. His body was all the communication he offered.

He spread her legs, bending her knees at the same time, and pushed himself inside the velvet recess of her waiting womanhood. She gasped as he filled her with his massive rod, marveling that she could take all of him. Her hips began to undulate, matching his steady rhythm. Release would come soon, she knew, for it had been so long. Travis did not attempt to prolong the ultimate ecstasy. He knew just how to drive and move within her to take her to sweet joy, and then he allowed himself to explode furiously.

It was, in that brief moment, two hearts, two souls, melding into a single entity. Both gasped as the magic flowed through them, entwining their very beings.

They lay in silence, arms and legs around each other, until their breathing quieted. Only then did Travis roll to the side, still holding her close against him.

"It never ends," she whispered, awed.

"It never will. Not until we die," said Travis. "And who's to say we won't find our own little cloud in heaven and spend eternity in passion?" He chuckled softly. "Maybe that's what heaven is, anyway—one long peak of ecstasy."

Kitty playfully cuffed his chin. "Travis Coltrane, you are going to burn in hell for being so . . . so *blasphemous.*"

"And you will burn with me, princess, because you made me this way."

They lay quietly for a time. Finally Kitty couldn't suppress her curiosity any longer, and asked, "What did the President want you to do?"

She felt him stiffen slightly.

"Travis, tell me," she begged, suddenly alarmed.

He released her, lying on his back and gazing thoughtfully into the star-studded night.

Kitty, with great effort, restrained her anxiety, knowing that Travis would speak when he was ready to. That was his way, and no prodding would hurry him.

After several moments, Travis came out of his reverie and announced softly, "Kitty, we're moving to Paris."

She stared at him, openmouthed.

"Paris," he continued. "We'll be moving to Paris. The President feels I could be of some use there as a diplomat. With the monarchists and the Bonapartists and the radicals all keeping things stirred up, he thinks America had best keep a close watch on things."

He paused to take a deep, tense breath, then finished. "He wants us to leave by the end of the month."

Kitty couldn't speak, couldn't think. A hundred emotions were surging through her. Paris? The end of the month? But what about the mine, the ranch, Colt? What about *home?* Why didn't Travis ask if she *wanted* to go? Maybe she ought to've been consulted, for pity's sake!

He sat up to embrace her, understanding well enough what she was feeling, for he had felt the same way an hour ago. "It will be a new life for both of us, Kitty, an exciting life. I'll never have to leave you again, don't you see? The President promised he wouldn't ask, and I told him it wouldn't do him any good if he did.

"John Travis can run things at home. It's time he took some responsibility for the family interests. Besides, the mine is such a big operation now, it practically runs itself."

He held her close. "We're going to have a good life there, princess. And just think," he added with a chuckle, "there's enough to see and do in Europe that my wanderlust—which you've always found so annoying—will be satisfied for years."

Kitty did not share his humor. It was all too much to be absorbed at once.

Travis's smile faded, and he lifted her face to meet his imploring eyes. "Tell me you'll go with me, Kitty. Please."

That did it. She spoke for the first time. "You don't think I'll let you go without me, do you? But . . . I need time, Travis, to think about all of this. I can't just leave my home as though we were taking a two-week trip. I'm not sure I want to leave, Travis."

He nodded sympathetically, and she went on, laughing nervously, "Oh, Travis Coltrane, you have outdone yourself this time. You've just handed me the biggest shock of my whole life."

His eyes searched hers, and Kitty understood that there was more to come. She knew well though what it was. Sure enough, Travis confided sadly, "We may just get another chance with Dani if we go to Paris."

Kitty felt his pain through the misery in his voice. Although they had not discussed it for a long, long time, she knew the agony was always there for Travis, the disappointment and the heartache over the estrangement of his daughter, Dani.

The girl was in her late teens, and neither Kitty nor Travis had seen her since she was six. Kitty had tried to raise her, to love her as her own, but when Dani's mother's sister, Alaina, moved to Silver Butte, trouble started. Alaina undermined everything Kitty and Travis did. She delighted in Travis's anger, and Kitty, no fool, understood intuitively that the real reason for Alaina's bitterness was something that had happened between her and Travis in the past, something Kitty knew nothing about. Kitty asked no questions, for she wanted no answers.

Alaina's scheme to disrupt Travis's home and take Dani away from him succeeded after a year of hell for everybody. Within that year, Dani changed from a sweet, happy, obedient child to a willful, spiteful, complaining brat. Kitty was at her wit's end. Their lives had become unbearable, and the day Kitty scolded Dani for something and Dani slapped her, Travis sent word to Alaina that she had won. Perhaps, he reasoned to Kitty, the child would be better off growing up around her mother's people in Kentucky.

The day Alaina came to the ranch, gloating, to take Dani away, John Travis's temper exploded. It was a powerful temper, even at his young age. He screamed at Alaina that she was taking his little sister away and he hated her. He told Alaina that she was the reason Dani had turned into such a hellion in the first place. Dani, protective of the aunt who had spoiled her so terribly, turned on John Travis in a rage, kicking and screaming. Kitty and Alaina had to pull the two apart, and John Travis's last words to his sister were, "I hate you! I hope I *never* see you again!"

"I hope you die, John Travis!" Dani screamed in return.

John Travis still carried a tiny scar at the corner of his left eye, the result of that fight, and to the present day, Kitty could not recall his ever mentioning his sister.

The painful memories tore at her, and everything she was feeling showed on her face, as it always did. Travis pulled her closer as she said, "Maybe Dani would like another chance, too, Travis. It's been a long time. Maybe she grew away from Alaina's influence."

"If she had, we'd have heard from her," he said grimly. His eyes narrowed as he mused, "She's living in the South of France now, but that's all I know. When Alaina married that French count she'd been stalking, she and Dani went to live on his estate. I know no more than that about my own daughter."

"Can you get an address? You can write and let her know when we'll arrive in Paris."

He nodded. "The bank in Silver Butte has it. You know I've sent money all these years, though Dani never once acknowledged it."

Kitty squeezed his hand. "Maybe things will be different. She's older now. She must have seen through Alaina by this time."

He said nothing to that, and she knew he was trying not to hope for too much.

"Now then," she said jovially, dressing quickly and

getting to her feet, "let's make ourselves presentable and go tell our son the news."

Travis reached for her hand and roughly pulled her down beside him again. Rolling on top of her, he whispered huskily, "That was just the appetizer, my dear. Now let's devour the main course."

Kitty succumbed once more to the love and passion she felt with every beat of her heart.

Chapter Two

France
July, 1889

STARING, mesmerized, into the gilt-edged mirror, Gavin Mason studied his reflection.

He liked what he saw.

Average height, a physique accented neither by obesity nor by thinness . . . he could find no fault with his body.

Gavin smoothed his blond hair back from his forehead, frowning. Curls. Little-boy curls, tousled and mussed. Damn it, how he hated them. Because of those blasted curls, he hardly looked his twenty-five years, even with the mustache.

He hated the color of his hair as much as he hated the curls. It reminded him of egg yolks, bright yellow. Still, women liked the shade—and the riot of curls. Well, things weren't all bad, he guessed.

He leaned forward to brush a tiny speck from the corner of an eyelid. Blue eyes. Once, one of the many demimondaines he had encountered in his lustful life told him in a fit of anger that he had eyes like a snake—a *blue-eyed* snake—and that he'd surely been sired in hell by Satan himself.

A sneer touched his thin lips. Snake. He liked that, liked it a lot. Some of the men he caroused with had begun calling him "Snake," and that pleased him, too. It made him sound mean, tough . . . like his father. Yes, he recalled proudly, Stewart Mason had been one of the bravest men in all Kentucky, and would probably be alive today if not for that goddamn Travis Coltrane.

Anger mottled his face. He'd been very young, but he remembered all of it, remembered when they brought his pa's body home and laid it on the kitchen table. His mother had screamed and screamed and then fainted, and young Gavin got sick to his stomach and puked all over the floor. Shot right between the eyes, Pa was. Dead center.

Alaina Barbeau had come to the house with the men who carried Pa's body. She'd been the one to tell Gavin the story of how his pa believed in one thing, Coltrane in another. She said Gavin was going to hear all kinds of stories about how his pa had been on the wrong side, a member of the Ku Klux Klan, doing terrible things, but she said he wasn't to believe any of it. Stewart Mason, she said, was the bravest of the brave, because he'd dared to stand up for what he believed in. What he believed in was niggers in their place, and white supremacy. Gavin was never to think any other way . . . and Stewart's son never had.

His mother withered after that, lost all her will to live, and just lay down and died within a year. Gavin's only relatives, an aunt and uncle, didn't want him. He was too boisterous for those childless people. They decided to send him to the state orphanage, but Alaina stepped in, saying she'd never allow Stewart's son to be raised by strangers, or dependent on charity. So Gavin went to live in the big, fancy Barbeau mansion, and nothing was ever the same afterward. He found out what it was like to eat on the high side of the hog, have good clothes, never be without shoes. Alaina went away for a while, and when she came back she had Dani Coltrane with her, and, Lord, did he go into a rage. Live with the daughter of the man who'd shot his pa? Hell, no! He wouldn't do it. He'd rather live in the orphanage, that's exactly what he told Alaina. She slapped him, told him she never wanted to hear that kind of talk again. Dani couldn't help who her father was. She was Alaina's sister's daughter, and a Barbeau, and that was all that mattered.

Well, it had taken some getting used to, but Gavin learned to get along. And as Dani and he grew older, he started to like what he saw. She radiated a quiet, gentle beauty. Her eyes were the color of coffee laced with the richest cream. Her gleaming hair was the color of vibrant cinnamon. Her body ripened into sheer delectability, and Gavin was constantly struggling with himself to refrain from attacking the sweet, succulent fruit.

During their growing-up years, Alaina's father died, and Alaina rapidly mismanaged the family estate until they were almost broke. So when Count Claude deBonnett proposed, they all heaved sighs of relief and moved to France with him. DeBonnett owned a fancy château perched on a cliff along the Maritime Alps, on the Mediterranean, near Monaco.

Those first years, Gavin was terribly homesick. All he wanted was to go home to Kentucky, but he eventually settled down, and even began to see the benefits of his new life. Thanks to Prince Charles III granting a charter thirty-three years ago to build a gambling casino, Monaco—or Monte Carlo, as the Prince wanted it called—became a luxuriously beautiful playground for the world's wealthy. Life there was exciting, glamorous, and Gavin loved it. He stopped thinking about returning to America, and began to dwell on how it would be when he was old enough to indulge in all that was available.

Gavin recalled with a wave of disgust that the Count developed a penchant for gambling at the Casino, and when he got himself killed in a duel, just a year ago, it was revealed that he'd lost most of his fortune. Since then, Alaina had barely been squeaking by on what was left.

Things were so bad that Gavin approached Alaina and asked why she didn't request more money from Dani's father. Coltrane was quite wealthy, the owner of one of the largest and most productive silver mines in Nevada.

Alaina heard him out, then shook her head, explaining that Travis would never agree. After all, he hadn't heard from his daughter in nearly thirteen years.

Gavin found that incredible. "Is Dani crazy? He's one of the richest men in America, and she won't have anything to do with him? How can she be so stupid?"

Alaina regarded his outburst coolly, then confided to him that Dani actually thought it was the other way around, that her father did not want to be in touch with her. "You see," she smiled at him, "Dani has written to him over the years, many letters that I destroyed. Since she never had an answer to any of her letters, she thinks he wants nothing to do with her. She believes he's angry because she wanted to live with me." She shrugged, smiling again.

Gavin exploded, calling her a bitter old fool. Thanks to her stupidity, they were practically penniless. In defense, she sputtered that there'd been no way of knowing the Count was gambling away all their money. She'd thought they were secure.

So Gavin was in a quandary. What could he do? He liked being rich, and he wanted to continue being rich.

He reached for his shirt, hand-sewn of the finest silk in a rich ivory shade. It complemented beautifully the royal-blue suit he chose from the hundreds of suits in his dressing room. Thank goodness the Casino refused to take clothes in payment of debts, he reflected bitterly, or the Count would have left him naked.

A slow smile spread across his face as he met his own gaze in the mirror. Thanks to fate, a wonderful plan had begun to form in Gavin's mind. When Alaina had come running into his room earlier that day, waving a letter and babbling, something had occurred to Gavin, something that took root in his imagination and was already growing.

He grinned as he recalled reading the letter, and Alaina's staring at him, wide-eyed, when he burst into laughter.

"Don't you see what this means?" he'd asked her.

She nodded slowly. "Travis is living in Paris with Kitty. He wants to see Dani, get to know her again."

Gavin dismissed that with a wave. "Not that, the rest of it. He says he's planning to remain in Paris indefinitely. . . ." His eyes scanned the letter hungrily. "Here. He says he's put the silver mine and the ranch in Nevada in her and her brother's name, equal shares for both."

He had waved the letter at Alaina in exultation. "This is it! Dani can sell her share to her brother, or to whomever she wants, and we'll be rich again."

Alaina reminded him that Dani would, no doubt, have her own ideas about what to do with her property. "She might even want to go back to America and live there," she added cautiously.

"Well, she'll quickly get that notion out of her head," Gavin snapped. "Leave everything to me. And *not one word* to Dani about this letter, understand?" he warned. Alaina, knowing his temper, nodded. She assured him that, as with all the letters from Travis through the years, she would pretend it had never arrived.

Gavin finished dressing, elation growing as he developed his plan. Not only was he going to be wealthy again, he was also going to hurt Travis Coltrane.

Gavin laughed aloud as he left his room, beautifully attired and charged with new hope.

Making his way through the house, he whistled softly as he glanced about admiringly at the furnishings. Expensive bric-a-brac, valuable paintings, the very best chairs, tables, and rugs. The château was opulent, but Gavin thought of it as a mausoleum. He preferred simplicity, a feeling of space and light, not this musty gloom. No matter. Soon he would have everything his way. He would have money. Coltrane's money! Ah, revenge was sweet!

Dani's room was at the end of the hall. He always wished he had her windows, and that sweeping view of the azure Mediterranean below, the waves crashing on the rocks. When they had first moved to the deBonnett château, Dani was more reckless, and even mean and haughty at times. She teased Gavin cruelly about being given the best, biggest, prettiest room, declaring nastily that she was a real member of Alaina's family, while he was only adopted. He retaliated by threatening to throw her from the window to die on the rocks below and have her bones picked clean by the crabs and sea gulls. That would send her screaming to Alaina. As the two young people matured, however, Dani mellowed, becoming quiet, even sweet. She changed completely, bewildering Gavin and mystifying Alaina.

Gavin reached her door, but his hand froze before he could knock. There were sounds within. Dani was not alone. Pressing his ear against the smooth mahogany door, he recognized the other voice. It was Briana de Paul's. She had a low, warm, husky voice and only a trace of a French accent, due to Dani's tutoring over the years. Briana's mother was long dead, and her father, the Count's caretaker, had died a few years ago. She and Dani were like sisters.

The beautiful French girl looked very much like Dani, in fact. Her coloring was similar to Dani's, but where Dani's brown eyes were warm, Briana's glowed with the fires of expensive brandy held to a flame. She had a temper to match, Gavin knew, remembering her fiery reactions whenever he patted her nicely rounded bottom as she passed, or brushed against her large, luscious breasts. Briana had told Gavin bluntly that she loathed him, but he wasn't the least put off, knowing she would change her mind once he truly controlled things. After all, with her father dead, she had to support that crippled brother of hers. She desperately needed the maid's job Alaina had given her, and she would find out when Gavin was in charge that in order to keep that job, she would have some very special "duties" to perform.

He could not make out what the two were saying, for they spoke in low voices, but they sounded quite intense, so he leaned closer, curious.

Suddenly the door jerked open. Briana, carrying a tray, ran right into him and a glass of orange juice splattered messily down the front of his shirt and coat.

"Serves you right for eavesdropping," she said coldly, before continuing on her way.

He watched her bottom moving provocatively as she walked down the hall. Soon, he vowed silently, soon those ripe hips would move beneath him, at his command, and the words from her lovely lips would be sweet and cajoling, not cold.

"Gavin?"

He turned away from Briana and entered the room. Dani was seated before the window. Beyond her, the Mediterranean glistened and sparkled with turquoise and blue lights in the late-afternoon sun.

Dani was wearing a simple white muslin dress, and as he seated himself in the wing chair opposite hers, he thought how angelic she appeared, how calm and serene. Lately, he mused, Dani was too quiet. She had withdrawn into herself, and spent more and more time in her room alone, reading. When she did go out, it was to attend Mass or visit with either the nuns or the parish priest.

Some years ago, she had embraced the Catholic faith and, much to his and Alaina's distress, become almost fanatical in her beliefs. Alaina had confessed her horror of the situation, and Gavin heartily agreed. Neither of them, however, had been able to dissuade Dani from her convictions.

He withdrew a linen handkerchief from inside his coat and irritably began to dab at the orange juice staining his clothing. "That clumsy girl," he grumbled. "It's time she learned her place. She's a servant in this household—nothing more. I'm damned tired of her insolence."

Dani ignored that. "I'm glad to see you, Gavin. I've been wanting to talk to you," she said softly, and something in her voice caused him to look up sharply. He noticed the Catholic missal she held so lovingly.

"You spend so much time at your church that neither Alaina nor I see you anymore. You've even been taking your meals in here. I don't like it, Dani. I miss you."

She looked blissful, and he became alarmed. "I've had a lot on my mind lately. There was a decision to be made, one that required much contemplation and prayer. I've made the decision, and now it's time for you and Aunt Alaina to know what it is I've decided."

Uppermost in Gavin's mind was the Coltrane fortune, and he waved his hand impatiently. "Later. We've something important to talk about, Dani. Listen to me."

"This is more important," she protested, leaning forward, wanting him to understand the importance of each word.

"It's my whole life, Gavin, and—"

"My dear," he interrupted, smiling as he removed the book from her hands and held them tightly. Something told him he had to stop her from saying any more. He let the words out in a torrent. "I want to marry you, Dani. I've loved you for a long, long time. I never knew how much until you began to spend so much time alone. I was so worried, because I thought you might have met someone else, but I followed you and found out you were just spending time at the church.

"We have to make plans," he continued determinedly, ignoring her shocked expression. She struggled to withdraw her hands from his, but he wouldn't let go. Her eyes were wide with—what? Fear? Revulsion? He felt a flash of annoyance, but told himself it didn't matter a damn bit. Theirs would be a marriage of convenience—the convenience of making him rich. It didn't make any difference to him whether she loved him or not.

"Surely you know how I feel about you, Dani. I know we grew up like brother and sister, but I always felt more for you. I want us to be married at once! Then we're going to America, to Nevada, to claim what's rightfully yours and—"

"Gavin, stop it!" she screamed, and the sound echoed through the large room, muffled neither by the pink satin-covered walls nor the thick white brocade draperies.

Shocked by her desperate scream, he stared at her in silence.

Dani withdrew her hands from his and leaned back in her chair, contemplating him. What on earth had brought about such craziness? Why, when they were growing up, Gavin had barely tolerated her. He was terribly difficult to get along with—insolent and spoiled. He'd never seemed to like anyone, so the idea that he could *love* anyone was absurd.

Gently, meaning not to hurt him, Dani said, "You don't mean what you were saying, Gavin. We'll just forget this."

"No!" He rose quickly and began pacing the room in frustration. He'd had sense enough to know that she was not going to say yes right away, that he'd have to maneuver her into seeing things his way, but he had not expected such a totally negative response.

He could not tell her about the letter from her father, explaining that she could claim her inheritance. If she knew about that, she'd know why he had proposed to her.

He went and knelt on one knee before her, pretending not to notice when she shrank away. "Look around you," he said quietly, indicating the room. "Beautiful, isn't it? All the luxury money can buy. *This* is the way you deserve to live, Dani, like the princess you are. But it isn't going to stay this way if you don't marry me and let me take care of you. You know Claude left Alaina in extreme financial difficulty, but I'm willing to work hard to take care of us all."

Dani shook her head. If only he would listen to what she wanted to tell him.

"Marry me," he said, so urgently that his whole body trembled. "Marry me, Dani. We'll go to America and claim what's rightfully yours. I'll work on your father's ranch like a common hired hand, if need be. Just let me take care of you. I love you."

He reached for her, and she cried, "Gavin, no! I don't *want* to marry you. I'm not going to marry anyone."

"You might not love me now, but I'll make you love—"

"No!" Touching the crucifix she wore around her neck, she stood up and moved away from him. "This is all I love, Gavin, all I need. Nothing else matters to me anymore."

Gavin had no idea what she was talking about. He knew only that she was being obstinate. He rose from his knees, straightened his coat, pushed back the ever-tumbling curls from his forehead, and said with finality, "We'll talk more about it at dinner. This has come as a shock to you, I understand, but when you think about it, you will see it is the only sensible solution to everything."

Dani stayed by the window where she was, and she put as much emphasis into her voice as she could. "I will not marry you, Gavin. I will never marry. There is nothing to discuss, except—" She stopped, realizing that he wasn't listening to her.

He walked to the door, pausing to say firmly, "We'll make our plans tonight. A small wedding, and we can honeymoon in America."

He closed the door behind him, taking several deep breaths to quell his anger. Damn her, she *was* going to marry him. There was no other way.

As he strode down the hallway, a movement caught his eye, and he saw Briana slipping into a room farther down the hall. He followed her swiftly, wondering whether she had eavesdropped on his conversation with Dani. His eyes flicked over her body. Her high, firm breasts strained against the clinging peasant blouse, and he licked his lips in delightful anticipation.

When he reached the room she'd entered, he went in without hesitation, shut the door, and started toward her.

Briana didn't back away. She stood her ground, dust cloth in hand, and warned, "Keep away from me, Gavin. I'm sick of your grabbing."

He smiled lasciviously. "I'm lord of this household now, and if you want to keep working here, you will learn to serve me . . . and serve me well."

"I won't be working here, if that's the case," she responded matter-of-factly.

"And how will you support your poor little brother?" he taunted, oblivious to the shadow of pain in her eyes. "He'll never be able to support himself, you know, the crippled, twisted—"

"You're disgusting," she erupted, furious. "How *dare* you talk about Charles that way? Now get out of here and let me finish cleaning."

He took a step forward, and Briana grabbed the first thing that came to hand, a heavy brass candlestick from the bedside table. She held it menacingly, eyes cold and unwavering, and he paused, deciding she was, indeed, capable of hurting him. "You will rue the day you lifted a hand to me, you bitch," he growled. Then he turned and left the room, slamming the door so hard that the paintings hanging in the hallway shook. Seeing them shake mollified him somewhat.

Briana sighed and put the candlestick back where it belonged. A tremor went through her as she realized she might have killed him. By God, she'd have done it if she'd had to. She loathed Gavin Mason. He was arrogant, spoiled, evil. She would not tolerate his brazen fondling of her any longer . . . even if that meant having to find another job to support herself and Charles.

Charles.

Tears of sorrow and love welled in her eyes. She had cared for her brother since his birth. Charles was ten years old, nine years younger than she. His poor little body was twisted and gnarled, his legs useless. He could crawl around on the floor, supporting or dragging himself with his arms, but had to be lifted up and down from chairs and bed. When Charles was six, their father had somehow gotten together enough money for a train trip to Paris, where doctors examined Charles and said there was nothing to be done for him. One of the doctors had predicted, horrifying Briana's father, that as Charles grew older and larger, there would be increasing pressure on his spine, which would possibly interfere with his circulation . . . and then kill him. An operation might help, they said, but they knew so little about conditions like Charles's that any attempt at surgery would be strictly experimental and very dangerous. And, of course, very expensive.

There was no money for anything like that, even if they'd wanted to take the risk. They had barely existed on what their father earned as caretaker of the deBonnett estate, and the largest benefit wasn't money at all, but the tiny house on the grounds of the estate where they were allowed to live without having to pay any rent. Since their father's death last year, Briana had been afraid they'd be asked to leave the cottage.

Briana was desolate. What did the future hold for her now? She was going to lose her dearest friend, Dani, and when Dani went away, Briana would be utterly alone. Worse, there was no way she could remain in that household after Dani left. Alaina had a terrible temper, and Gavin would only become more intolerable. She felt like weeping whenever she looked around the worn little two-room cottage. It was all the home she'd ever had. Did she really have to leave it? She guessed she would, sooner or later.

And where would she, a single female with a crippled ten-year-old brother, be able to go?

She reflected miserably that she had no money. Alaina gave her food and a pittance. And there were no other jobs in the area that would pay her even that. She could not care for herself and Charles.

Sitting disconsolately in that room, she realized slowly that there might not be a choice. She might have to yield to Gavin's demands. If there were only herself to consider, she knew she would rather starve. But Charles had no one else. Dear Lord, without her, Charles would be forced to beg for food, and would probably die.

No. She stood up angrily and flicked the dust cloth across the heavy mahogany furniture. She could not let Charles beg. Other women supported themselves by becoming prostitutes, and if she had to, then so be it. Besides, wasn't there more honor in submitting to one man than in bedding many? Gavin would take care of her, and she would take care of Charles. She could stand Gavin's cruelty, and Alaina's, if it meant a decent life for her little brother.

Tears began. Were it not for Charles, she knew she would die before giving herself to a man for any reason other than love. But fate, Briana had learned long ago, dictates a person's morality.

She paused and looked wistfully out the window to the sea, where late-afternoon sunlight rippled through the cobalt waters. The surface danced with diamonds of sparkling light. For her, she mused, the sun was truly setting.

Chapter Three

Carson City, Nevada
July, 1889

COLT sat behind the large mahogany desk, gazing balefully at all the papers in front of him. His mother had always taken care of Coltrane business matters. His father hated what he called "inside chores." Colt concurred. He'd much rather have been outdoors, doing nearly anything else.

He reached for the bottle of brandy and poured another glass, reminding himself that these chores were his now—along with every other Coltrane responsibility, now that his parents had left for France.

He sipped the brandy and looked around the study. The rest of the two-story house reflected his mother's taste, but the study was strictly his father's. It was filled with comfortable sofas and chairs, plain draperies at the long windows, and floor-to-ceiling bookshelves filled with Travis's war memorabilia. A stone fireplace ran the entire length of one wall.

There were trophies mounted here and there, souvenirs of many hunting trips. Colt's mother had hated those, he recalled. She said every time she walked into the study she felt the sad, forlorn eyes of the deer looking directly at her for sympathy.

He leaned back in the soft leather chair and propped

his booted feet on the desk. He'd spent a long day riding the range that bordered the Carson River. He was tired, and after eating the dinner the Mexican cook had prepared for him, would have liked nothing better than to go to bed, but the blasted paperwork awaited him. He'd been putting it off for as long as possible, but it wouldn't go away.

Colt thought about the house, not for the first time. What in the world was he going to do with a fourteen-room mansion? It was a far cry from the two-room cabin they'd lived in when he was a child. There was a sweeping front porch, and there were pillars and marble steps. On the first floor there was, besides the study, a grand entrance foyer, a large formal dining room, and a smaller dining room for family gatherings. There were two parlors as well, a formal one and a family one, each with an ornate fireplace. Also on the first floor was a small room for Kitty to do her sewing and studying. She was forever reading about the latest medical developments.

The kitchen was at the rear of the house, connected by a long, enclosed porch, where Kitty lovingly tended her many flowers and plants. Guiltily Colt reminded himself yet again to water them all.

Upstairs, his parents had large, adjoining bedrooms, each with its private dressing room. They had told him he could move into either one, now that he had the house to himself, but he preferred the room he'd always had, at the far end of the hallway. Between his room and his parents' rooms were three guest rooms. One, of course, was meant for Dani. She had lived there only for a couple of years.

Dani.

He sighed. Colt wasn't sure how he felt about the half sister he hadn't seen in thirteen years. True, they'd had that vicious fight the day she left, but they'd been children, and he held no grudge there. What he did resent was that Dani had been able to turn her back on their father. In all the years of her estrangement, there hadn't even been a letter from her.

Colt thought about the conversation he'd had with his father the night before his parents left for France, when Travis went over the papers the family lawyer had prepared, documents which divided the silver mine and the ranch equally between Colt and Dani. Travis and Kitty had enough money to live on comfortably for the rest of their lives without the mine or the ranch.

Colt figured it was his father's property, to do with as he pleased. If he wanted to give half of it to a daughter who didn't give a damn about him, well, Colt just kept his mouth shut. Still, he couldn't help wondering how long it would be before Dani showed up to claim her share . . . while *he*, Colt, did all the work.

The silver mine was not worth what it had once been, due, in part, to the federal government's limiting the role of silver in the monetary system in recent years. As silver prices declined, a lot of mines had closed down. Bustling mine towns became ghost towns. Silver Butte, once the biggest mining camp in the West, had simmered down and was now a respectable town like many others.

What had kept the Coltrane family from suffering, and also made them very rich, was Travis's wisdom in not depending solely on his silver mine for income. Travis threw himself into cattle raising, building up a large herd, and he'd been very successful despite unpredictable beef prices, high railroad rates, and several severe winters.

All of that had been dropped in Colt's lap. Oh, sure, he knew what to do. He'd worked the ranch and mine since he was old enough to hold a rope or a pickax. But he'd never expected to run it all, far from it. In fact, he'd been planning to hit the trail, travel the country for a few years, try to satisfy an itch for wanderlust.

Well, he told himself grimly, that had certainly

changed. Suddenly he had more responsibility than he'd ever dreamed of. He felt trapped, truth to tell, and there was nothing he could do about it.

Hell, he might as well be married. He poured himself another drink and shook his head adamantly. Charlene had almost quit trying to rope him in after the talk he'd had with her in New York. Then she heard the news about Kitty and Travis leaving, how he'd have to settle down and take care of things, and she'd started right in again. He did not want to hurt her, so he had almost stopped going to see her. Damn it, he didn't want to get married. Not yet, anyhow.

He leaned forward and started looking through the papers. It was the end of the month, so tomorrow he'd have to go into town to draw the payroll for the hired hands. Maybe he'd just stay in town a while. He could use a good time. . . .

He froze, then leaped to his feet, drawing his pistol. Someone was walking in the hall. He doused the lantern on the desk and positioned himself directly in front of the door, waiting.

Two sounds broke the tense silence: the creak of the door opening . . . and the ominous click of his gun hammer.

"Colt?" a soft voice called.

"Damn it, Charlene, you almost got yourself shot!"

Disgusted, Colt shoved his gun into the holster and went to the desk to light the lantern again. He sat down, making no effort to mask his annoyance. "What are you doing sneaking around here?"

She crossed to the desk, perched on the side, and gave him a coquettish smile. Her voice husky, she said, "I wanted to surprise you. I was hoping I would find you already in bed, and I was going to just slip in beside you and—"

"Are you crazy?" he exploded. "You want your daddy to shoot me? How'd you get out of the house this time of night, anyway?"

She trailed her fingertips down his cheek, but he grabbed her wrist and stopped her. "Don't be mean to me, Colt," she said in her baby voice. "Momma and Daddy are away for the night. Momma's sister in Pine Bluff is sick, and Daddy took her there. We've got all night."

He stood up, declaring firmly, "No. You aren't spending the night here, Charlene. I'm not insane."

Her lower lip dropped petulantly, and she blinked her incredibly long, silky lashes, gazing at him with those beautiful blue eyes. "You don't want me, Colt? You don't want . . . ?" She pulled her bodice down, exposing full, firm breasts. Nipples already taut with anticipation looked like ripe berries, just waiting to be savored in his mouth.

Colt felt a quickening of desire. It had been a while since he'd known pleasure with a woman, and Charlene knew how to give him the ultimate. She hadn't been a virgin that first time, that night so long ago in the back of Harley Jernigan's wagon behind the grange hall while the harvest dance was going on inside. But that didn't bother Colt one bit. His father had told him through the years that virgins were trouble. "Stay away from virgins unless you're looking for a wife," Travis had said. "Virgins make a man feel guilty for being the first one. Also, they don't know what they're doing and you have to teach them. Why bother teaching her if you aren't planning on making her your wife?"

Colt hadn't had to teach Charlene anything. She knew it all and managed to teach him a few things. Oh, she was no whore, not Charlene. Like every other male around Silver Butte, Colt figured she'd been broke in by Billy Earl Lassister. They'd courted for over two years when Billy Earl was caught fooling around with a girl in Pine Bluff and her daddy marched him to the parson with a shotgun at his back. Everybody said the baby that arrived six months later was born with hot feet, because he tried to arrive in time for the wedding.

Charlene was hurt and humiliated, and people said she was going to wind up an old maid because she had a broken heart that wouldn't heal. But then Charlene set her sights on Colt, and the gossips had another field day.

The way Charlene was fondling him between his legs, Colt was fast losing his resolution. With every bit of willpower he could muster, he caught her wrist and held it as he said tightly, "I want you to get the hell out of here, Charlene. This is trouble for both of us, and you know it."

Smiling, she stepped back, and Colt released her.

But Charlene had no intention of retreating. She lifted her long skirt, exposing shapely, bare legs. "Tell me you don't want this, Colt," she taunted, giving her head a flirting toss that sent her long blonde hair flying. With one more tug, she jerked her skirt all the way to her waist.

She was naked beneath the skirt.

Colt's gaze fastened on the golden thatch of hair between her legs. He wanted to speak but no words came.

Hands on her hips, she taunted, "It's yours, Colt, all yours. All you have to do is pick me up and carry me to your room. Then you can have me all night long, any way you want me."

He wanted her—hell, yes. With a deep groan, he lunged for her, lifting her easily and cradling her against his chest. He carried her into the hallway, making his way through the house and up the curving stairs. He didn't bother with lights, for he knew the way.

"Hurry, oh, please, please, hurry," she urged, lips and tongue setting his neck on fire. "I want you so."

In his room, he lowered her to the bed and quickly removed his clothing. He settled himself beside her, and was about to pull her close, but she positioned herself on her knees and straddled him, giggling. "My turn first!"

She laughed, her blonde hair blending with the silver light flowing through the windows. She lowered herself upon his rigid shaft, taking all of him and squealing with delight over his size. "See how easily we fit together? We're made for each other, you know." She began moving rhythmically, undulating her hips, grinning at him all the while.

His hands were tight around her waist. The sensation was near torture, as he struggled with the urge to release himself. He wanted the joy to last.

Charlene gasped, nearing her own pinnacle of ecstasy. Her eyes were closed now, her teeth biting into her lower lip, head thrown back, hair tossing like the mane of a bucking bronco. She moaned, as though deep in agony, "So good, my darling . . . going to be . . . like this . . . all the time . . . when we're married . . ."

Then she was caught up in the spasms of her climax, her screams of delight echoing in the quiet night. He held her to him, still impaled as he flung her on her back, rising to his knees to thrust into her deeply, taking himself to his own zenith as she writhed and moaned beneath him.

At last, spent, Colt withdrew and lay on his stomach beside her. Regret washed through him. It had been good. It always was. But he was playing with fire. Her daddy would crucify him if he ever found out.

Charlene was snuggling close to him, fingertips dancing lovingly across the rock-hard muscles of his perspiring back. "You know," she cooed, "we've never slept together, Colt. We've always had to part afterward, but tonight I'm free."

"You're getting out of here, now," he grated, more sharply than he'd meant to. "If your parents come home early and find you gone, they're going to go crazy. I sure don't want them to find you here."

He sat up and pulled on his trousers, urging, "Come

on, Charlene. I'll ride into town with you. I'm not going to send you out alone this time of night. I'll see you to your door. Now, let's get going."

She snuggled back against the pillows. "I'm staying right here. We never get the chance to sleep together, Colt, and we're going to tonight. Relax. It's going to be wonderful. We'll rest, make love again, then I'll fix us a lovely breakfast before dawn and get home long before Momma and Daddy get back."

He stared at her incredulously in the semidarkness. "Stop fooling around, Charlene. We have to get out of here. *Now!*" He held out his hand, but she didn't take it.

Colt was dangerously close to losing his temper. He jerked her out of the bed and stood her on her feet. "Fix yourself, and meet me out back. I'm going to saddle my horse."

Suddenly Charlene burst into uncontrollable sobbing. "If you make me leave, so help me, I'll hate you forever," she gasped.

Colt shoved his hair back from his forehead, exasperated. Women. He'd rather have all the responsibilities of running the ranch *and* the mine *and* a hundred wranglers than attempt to cope with a wife.

The muscle in his jaw twitched. "Charlene, I don't like throwing you out, but you never should've come here and I was a fool to let you stay, even for a little while."

She flung her arms around him and begged, "Please, Colt, don't make me leave. Let me have this one night with you. How can you just throw me out? You just made beautiful love to me . . ." Her voice broke with sobs.

Colt didn't like himself very much right then. She was right. They had just made beautiful love, and he was treating her like a whore. What a louse. Still, his every instinct told him to get her home. "We're taking a big chance," he said helplessly.

Sensing surrender, Charlene stood on tiptoe, raining kisses all over his face. "No, no, we're not," she assured him. "I know Daddy. He won't leave for home till after he's had breakfast. The bank doesn't open till eight-thirty, and it's a two-hour trip to Pine Bluff, so he won't get back till just in time to open up. I can leave here at first light, slip into the house through the back way, and no one will ever know."

As Colt gave in, he promised himself that they were going to have a talk later, and no matter how much she cried, he would make her realize once and for all that he was not going to be pressured into marriage, and further, that if she kept pestering him about it, he'd stop seeing her, period.

She protested again when he left her to return to the work she had interrupted, but he ignored that outburst and went back to the study, flinging himself into his chair. He was angry—with Charlene and, even more, with himself.

He directed his attention to the work before him, vowing that at first light she was getting the hell out of there even if he had to drag her.

Charlene opened her eyes and blinked against the light streaming in through the window. Instantly she was alert, sitting up and looking around wildly. The sun was up. Dawn had come and gone and—where was Colt? Why hadn't he awakened her? "Oh, Lord," she whispered in the empty room, panic welling in her throat, "I'm in trouble now!" Her parents would be home, and would have discovered her missing by then. They would never suspect her of doing something so scandalous as sneaking out to be with a lover, so they would assume something terrible had happened to her. They would call the sheriff, and—oh, what was she going to do?

Grabbing her dress from the floor, she pulled it on, then ran from the room and down the hall, calling

Colt's name. Reaching the stairs, she took them two at a time, almost fell, and grabbed the railing for support.

Colt groggily lifted his head from his desk when he heard screaming, shaking himself as he struggled to clear his mind. What the hell was going on?

Charlene burst into the room, a madwoman, golden hair flying, blue eyes bulging. "Colt! What time is it?" she screamed. "Why did you let me sleep? Oh, God, God, we're in trouble now. . . ." She ran to him and threw herself into his lap.

Colt got shakily to his feet, almost dropping her to the floor. Two things told the story, he realized with a sick feeling: the empty whiskey bottle and the clock. It was nine A.M.

"Oh my God!" He sank back into the chair, his head in his hands.

Charlene paced up and down in a frenzy, wringing her hands as she wailed, "What are we going to do? They're home by now. Daddy's probably called the sheriff, and they've probably got a posse out looking for me. There's no way I can keep him from finding out I've been here all night. He's going to kill me! He'll kill you, too, and the whole town is going to find out. I'm ruined! I'll never be able to face people again!"

On and on she raged. Colt watched, his own thoughts torturing him. There was going to be big trouble, all right, trouble he damned well didn't need. Everyone knew Carleton Bowden adored his only child, and he was not going to look kindly on the man he would blame for besmirching her. Charlene wasn't exaggerating when she said her father would kill Colt. He'd probably try.

A sound in the hall told Colt that the servants had arrived. He got up and called into the hallway that he didn't want to be disturbed, then closed the door. He went to Charlene and gripped her arms, forced her to meet his burning gaze. "All right, now, calm down.

Let's see if we can figure some way out of this mess. Your going all to pieces isn't getting us anywhere."

She searched his face for a miracle, whispering tremulously, "Colt, you've got to believe me. I didn't mean for this to happen. I really was going to leave and get home before my parents did. I swear I was."

He ran agitated fingers through his hair and turned away from her. "I know, I know," he told her absently. Hell, she was cunning, but he doubted that even she would pull a dumb stunt like this.

He walked to the window, stared out at the grassy plain beyond, the sleepy river rolling along lazily in the bright morning sun. Then he turned to face her once again. "We'll say I invited you out here for dinner. We drank too much wine and fell asleep. I'll get the cook to lie and say she was here all night, that we didn't leave the parlor. We'll say we were chaperoned."

Charlene shook her head firmly. "It won't work. Even if Momma and Daddy believed it, there'd be too many busybody gossips that wouldn't, so there would still be scandal."

"Our word against theirs. Let them believe what they want."

She shook her head again. Colt stared at her, realizing suspiciously that the despair and terror in her eyes had gone. She looked—what? Relieved? Triumphant? "That's our story," he said with finality.

She moved to him, touching his cheek with loving fingertips. Voice soft, she proclaimed, "No, Colt, it won't work. We'll just elope. We'll go away for a few days, and send a message home so they won't worry—"

"No!" He grabbed her wrist as he declared icily, "No, we are not getting married, Charlene. I've told you over and over, but you won't listen. I don't want to marry you. I don't want to marry anybody. I'm not going to be roped into marriage because of what happened last night. It was my fault for taking you to bed, but I didn't invite you here, and I'm not going to be suckered into anything because of it. So you just get that fool notion out of your head right now."

He flung her away from him, and she saw how mad he was. It was starting to dawn on him that maybe, just maybe, she had planned the whole thing. It made sense.

Charlene's eyes narrowed and her nostrils began to flare ever so slightly, ominously. Her fists clenched and unclenched at her sides, and Colt realized he'd never seen her look that way before. How could he have thought her beautiful? She looked like a demon, her lips curling back in a snarl, her face contorted with rage.

"You *will* marry me, John Travis Coltrane! You have used me like a wife and so you will make me your wife. I will not have my honor defiled. I will not walk the streets of the town I grew up in with my head hung in shame because of you. You owe me marriage. I will have marriage, or so help me, you will rue the day you were born!"

Colt shook his head slowly. Images flashed before his mind's eye, images of her writhing beneath him, begging him to take her . . . begging him to penetrate her . . . over and over. She had wanted it as much as he had, by God, but he'd never promised marriage, never even told her he loved her. He hadn't used tricks to get her into bed, and he didn't figure he owed her.

Voice icy, he looked her straight in the eye and announced, "No. You can take your honor and go straight to hell!"

He was immediately sorry he'd been so harsh, but it was too late. The scream that ripped from Charlene echoed throughout the house.

"Charlene, wait—"

He held out his hand to her, but she turned and fled

the room. Her sobs were not of pain, he knew, or of sorrow, but were the sobs of rage of a woman scorned.

Colt slammed his fist into the wall, and didn't feel the skin tearing or see the blood. What in hell was going to happen now? There was no telling what she would do. Damn it, it was his fault for blowing up, but she had pushed him over the brink.

He heard crashing hoofbeats and looked out the window in time to see Charlene on her horse, whipping the animal mercilessly into a furious gallop, headed for town. God only knew what she meant to do.

Colt sighed. He knew what he had to do. Face up to it. Be a man. Ride into town and talk to Carleton Bowden. He didn't know what he was going to say, but he knew he couldn't stay on the ranch as though he was in hiding. He'd have to tell the truth, then let the chips fall where they might.

Be a man. That's what his father had always told him. Right or wrong, be a man. That way, no matter what happened, he could hold his head high.

Travis Coltrane, Colt well knew, had never lowered his head in shame in his whole life.

But in that moment, his son was having a hell of a hard time lifting his.

Chapter Four

ALAINA Barbeau deBonnett appeared serene as she sat in her favorite chair, an oval-backed Louis XVI with tapered round legs. But she was not serene. In fact, she hadn't been so upset in longer than she could remember.

She fingered the elaborate tufting, tassels, and braids of the chair arms, absently thinking that no matter what color gown she wore, the warm, ivory brocade upholstering never failed to enhance her and her gown.

Claude had hated the chair as much as she abhorred his taste. He had furnished the rest of the drawing room in the Biedermeier style, in vogue in the earlier part of the century. But Alaina knew that vogue had been confined mainly to middle-class homes. Alaina had never considered herself middle class. She found the classic simplicity of the furniture much too severe, and she detested the rosewood tables with metal inlays, considering them cheap.

Her dream had been to redecorate the entire château in rococo. A beautiful style, it borrowed the curvilinear elements of the French Louis XV, especially the cabriole leg, which was reinstated in heavier idiom. Entire suites were available in walnut, rosewood, and mahogany. The more intricate the carving on the frames, the more expensive the piece, of course.

After Claude's death, she had been forced to sell almost everything of value—paintings, silver, jewelry. Now, with the heavy burden of unpaid taxes, it looked as though the entire château might have to be sold.

"Oh, Claude, I hope you're burning in hell," she whispered to the empty room. She wished now that she had never married him, but his proposal had been the only way out of another desperate situation.

And all because of Travis Coltrane. She hoped one day she could see Travis writhing in fire and brimstone.

She closed her eyes, taking herself back to those golden years when her life had been paradise. The image came to mind of her magnificent home in Kentucky. Oh, it had been the grandest house in all the county. Built of gray fieldstone, it stood four stories high, with a turret at each corner. Even the landscaping had been extraordinary. There were six separate gardens, each laid out in a different pattern. And so many trees—maples, oaks, pecans, stretching regally to the sky. It had been glorious, and remembering it brought tears to her eyes.

Yes, life had been good. But Poppa was involved with the Ku Klux Klan, and had become their secret leader. The government sent Travis Coltrane, a federal marshal, to Kentucky to investigate the Klan. When he finished, a tornado ripped through the Barbeau empire, destroying everything in its path.

Her hands gripped the armrests tightly as she remembered the day Travis killed the only man Alaina had ever truly loved. In a blind rage, she had tried to kill Travis, but she'd blown off her father's arm when he leaped in the way.

God damn you, Travis Coltrane, for all the misery you have caused me in my life!

Poppa lost his spirit, and withered away. She made a mess trying to salvage what was left of the family enterprises after it was discovered that Jordan Barbeau had been the leader of the infamous Klan. To add a final insult to the hell he had already wrought, Travis had married Marilee and taken her off to that godforsaken wilderness in Nevada, where she died giving birth to the child they had conceived before the wedding.

When they married, Alaina recalled with a surge of nauseous resentment, she had hated her sister, hated her because Alaina too had known passion in Travis Coltrane's arms. True, she now believed Stewart Mason was the only man she'd truly loved, but Travis had made love to her in a way that still haunted Alaina. It had been grand, glorious, magnificent. There had never been anyone before him or since who could take her to that pinnacle. Damn Travis.

When Marilee died, Alaina had seized upon a way to make Travis pay for what he'd done. Plotting carefully, she succeeded in stealing her niece's love and loyalty. Oh, how sweet was revenge! Never would she forget the look on Travis Coltrane's face the day she triumphantly took Dani away from him.

Soon afterward, Claude came along and solved her financial woes. Spineless, weak, unattractive, Claude was no real challenge. In a short time, he was on his knees proposing to her. Then they were off to France for what she thought would be a lifetime of opulent luxury.

Now, she told herself dismally, she was right back where she'd started. This time there would probably be no easy solution. True, she was still attractive, still had a shapely figure, but any eligible, wealthy man was seeking a young woman, not a matron.

She pressed trembling fingertips to her throbbing forehead. Oh, dear Lord, what to do? When the château was sold, what did not go for taxes would be seized for Claude's debts. There would be nothing left. Nothing. How could she support herself? Become a servant?

To the very people she had recently entertained so lavishly? She would sooner die. Prostitution? She was too old to command a good price. And, she reminded herself proudly, she'd always felt it was the man's place to service the woman, not the other way around. That would be as degrading as servitude.

There had been one last hope, the letter from Travis informing Dani that she could claim her inheritance. But Dani, damn her, had dashed that hope with her damned religiosity. Where did the girl get such craziness from? Certainly not from Alaina. Religion had never meant a thing to her.

"Oh, damn you again, Travis Coltrane," she cried vehemently. "You're torturing me again—this time through your daughter!" She covered her face with her hands and began to weep. She did not hear the movement at the door, did not know anyone had entered until the soft, hesitant voice spoke.

"Aunt Alaina, please don't cry."

Her head jerked up, eyes narrowing as she stared into Dani's serene face. *She looks like a Madonna,* Alaina thought bitterly. *Why, there's almost an unearthly light around her.* She saw the small bag Dani was carrying, and snapped, "What have you packed? I thought you had to give up all your worldly goods," she said spitefully.

"Just my personal toiletries, Aunt Alaina," Dani replied. "I suppose they'll take them from me when I get there and give me whatever I'm supposed to have. But it's a long trip, and I didn't know what I'd need in the meantime."

Alaina turned her face toward the window, as cold and hard as marble. Dani set her bag down and dropped to her knees before her. She tried to caress Alaina's hands, but Alaina snatched them away. "Please," Dani beseeched her, eyes filling with tears, "don't let us say good-bye this way. Be happy for me, Aunt Alaina. I'm doing what I am called to do. God has spoken to me, and I'm giving my life in service to the church. I've never been happier. Won't you share in the glory of my decision?" She searched her aunt's face hopefully.

Alaina continued to stare out the window. "Just go," she said icily. "You've made your decision, turned your back on me and all the love and care I gave you. If you can find happiness in breaking my heart, do."

"I'll never forget all you've done for me, Aunt Alaina. I love you. Please remember that," Dani begged.

"This is how you show love? By entering an order of fanatical nuns who turn their backs on their families, on the entire world?" She turned around for long enough to give Dani a look of loathing. "You are insane, Dani. You should be entering an asylum, not a convent."

Dani sighed. They had been through all of this before, and she'd tried over and over to explain the deep peace and joy she felt, but Aunt Alaina had not understood, and nothing was going to change her. But, oh, how she hated leaving this way!

She got to her feet and picked up her bag, saying quietly, "I will pray for you, Aunt Alaina."

"And we will pray that you come to your senses," sneered a mocking voice. Gavin stood in the doorway, a glass of whiskey in his hand. He swayed slightly, then downed the rest of his drink. He moved accusing eyes over Dani and sneered, "You selfish bitch! You don't care about anyone but yourself. Doesn't matter that your aunt and I will have to beg in the streets, doesn't matter that you're turning your back on a fortune—to say nothing of my marriage proposal. Just desert us, and spend the rest of your life counting rosary beads. Don't forget to pray for your soul, which," he hiccuped, "I hope burns in hell for your sin of being so goddamn ungrateful."

Dani winced. "The fortune you mention means nothing to me. I won't claim it. If I should die, I've directed that anything meant for me should go to the church." She paused and eyed him carefully. "And as for your proposal, we both know what inspired that." She turned once more to Alaina. "Please. Wish me well, Aunt Alaina. Give me your blessing."

Alaina remained rigid. "You have my *curses,* you ungrateful bitch!"

Pressing a hand against trembling lips, Dani ran from the room, out of the house, and into the twilight.

Alaina began to weep. Gavin took his silver flask from his coat and, not bothering with his glass, drank directly from it. He then slouched into the chair opposite hers.

They sat in brooding silence for a long while, and then Alaina sighed. "Will you stop that?" Gavin snapped. "I'm sick of your making those little noises all the time. You don't hear *me* moaning, for heaven's sake."

Her eyes flashed. "I should like to remind you of your place, Gavin."

"My place!" He barked a laugh. "How long will I *have* a place? Or you, either? Six months? Can we keep the hounds at bay that long? Maybe we can sell the furniture, piece by piece, to keep from starving. Or maybe we should save it to chop up for firewood when winter comes. Shall I take a cup now and go out on the street and start begging? My *place* is about to be taken away, my dear."

"Shut your insolent mouth!" Alaina rose and began to pace the room, speaking more to herself than to him as she railed. "Damn Travis Coltrane! Damn him for getting the last laugh! I am to grovel in poverty, while he and his wife live in splendor in Paris!"

Gavin tipped the flask once more, drained it, shook it, then sent it sailing through the air. It landed against the fireplace hearth, and Alaina jumped, startled. "Don't you ever do anything like that again, do you hear me?" she shrieked. "I won't tolerate drunken behavior. Your father was a man. Why can't you act like one? Can't you go out and get a job? You've never done a thing in your life but live off my money, chase harlots, and—"

She stopped as she caught sight of Briana in the doorway, nervously fingering the hem of her apron.

"What do you want?" Alaina snapped. "You know I hate servants eavesdropping."

Briana stared at the floor, miserable. "I wasn't eavesdropping, madame."

Alaina regarded her coldly. "Well? What do you want? I didn't ring for you. We don't want to be disturbed."

Briana took a deep breath, trying to muster the courage to say what she had spent the past hour rehearsing. Finally she plunged ahead. "I wanted to ask you to please be kind to Dani when she comes to say good bye. Her heart is breaking because of the way you feel about her entering the convent. It will do no good to harbor ill feelings, and her last memories of you should be happy ones. She loves you so much."

Alaina stared incredulously. Who did she think she was, interfering in their personal affairs? She was a *servant!* Alaina knew she should have put her foot down long ago about Dani's treating Briana like a member of the family.

Alaina pointed to the doorway with an angrily quivering finger. "Get out of here! And don't you dare ever speak to me of things that are none of your business."

Briana shook her head. She had to try, just once more. "Please, madame. Dani has talked to me about this. She is hurting so badly. Please, please, try to be kind to her when she comes to say good-bye."

Gavin laughed, a nasty sound. "She's already gone.

Left a while ago, crying her pious little heart out. Too bad you missed it. Quite a performance."

Briana gasped. Dani must have been terribly upset to go without telling *her* good-bye.

"Well, don't stand there with your mouth hanging open," Gavin ordered irritably, holding out his empty glass. "Make yourself useful. Get me another bottle of whiskey."

"Get out of my sight," Alaina chimed in. "You even remind me of Dani."

Briana turned and ran from the room.

Alaina began ranting again, but Gavin ignored her, staring at the spot where Briana had stood. His eyes were narrowed, his brow tense with concentration. Slowly, ever so slowly, a thought began to take shape in his mind. A scheme. It was absurd, of course it was, he told himself. But still, it was something, a light in the darkness.

Would it work? He didn't know, couldn't plot clearly because his thoughts were fuzzy. He'd been drinking all afternoon. The cobwebs had taken over. He remembered what he'd been planning to do to get his mind off his troubles. He needed a woman. A few hours in the loving arms of a hot, eager *jeunesse* was just what he needed.

He looked at Alaina, who was still stomping around, talking. "I need some money," he said.

She turned and looked at him as though he had taken leave of his senses. "What do you think I'm screaming about? Are you so drunk that you don't understand how desperate our situation is, you ninny?"

His temper exploded. Later he would blame his whiskey-soaked brain for his feeling so outraged. But just then, he knew only that she was railing at *him*, God damn it, and he didn't take that from anyone, especially a woman. Leaping to his feet, he caught her wrists, squeezing so tightly she cried out with pain.

And then he was shaking her, hard, until her head was bobbing uncontrollably and she was screaming that he had gone crazy, was going to kill her. He kept shaking her, yelling all the while for her to shut up, leave him alone, stop goading him.

She wrested one hand free and slapped him, but that only incensed him further. He slammed his fist at her in a stunning blow, and she fell backward, knocking over a table. A lamp crashed to the floor in a shower of crystal and glass.

He advanced toward her, maniacal fury in his eyes, and she held up her arms to fend him off. "You stupid bitch!" he roared. "You challenged me to act like my father! Do you think you could ever have slapped him and gotten away with it? I'll show you how a man reacts—"

Suddenly he fell to his knees, unconscious, sprawling forward onto the floor. Behind him stood Briana, holding the footstool she'd hit him with.

Alaina scrambled to her feet, sobbing, looking from Gavin's body to Briana's shocked face.

"Oh, madame," Briana whispered tremulously, backing away. "I didn't know what else to do. I thought he was going to kill you."

"*You* may have killed *him,*" Alaina cried. "Go and get help!

"Madame!"

Alaina and Briana turned toward the stricken face of Gerard, the elderly butler, whose eyes held pity as he looked at Briana and said, "It's your brother." He spoke quickly, nervously. "He's been taken to the hospital. Go at once."

Briana ran from the room, dismissing Gavin from her mind, terror over Charles blotting out everything else.

Alaina beckoned to Gerard, commanding, "Help me get him to his room, then go for the doctor."

Gerard, elderly and frail, bent over Gavin. Just as

he was about to lift him, Gavin moaned and looked around.

"Shall I go for the doctor now?" Gerard asked, relieved that Gavin was alive.

Alaina decided there was no need to bring an outsider in to witness the family's problems. There had been quite enough gossip and scandal about the deBonnett family, thanks to Claude's death and debts. "No. Help me get him upstairs, Gerard. And then bring me cold towels and brandy."

They struggled to get Gavin onto his feet, but once he was standing, he irritably shoved them away from him. Rubbing the back of his neck, he growled, "Where is she? I'm going to kill the bitch. I know it was Briana. I recognized her voice."

"She's gone." Alaina quickly told him of the message that had come about Charles. "Come upstairs and lie down, Gavin. You need to rest."

Gavin told Gerard to forget the towels and brandy, and then he allowed Alaina to guide him up the stairs to the comfort of his bedroom. He lay down, head throbbing, and she sat beside him. "I'm . . . sorry," she began carefully. "I shouldn't have spoken to you that way. It's just that I've been so upset lately."

She bit back tears and shook her head. "What are we going to do, my darling? There's no point in our hurting each other this way."

He trailed warm fingertips up and down her arm, smiling. "Alaina," he murmured, "a thought has been playing with my mind. There just may be a way out. Go see what you can find out about Charles, then come and tell me all you learn."

"Charles?" Alaina blinked, thoroughly confused. "What does that have to do with us? You've never concerned yourself with Charles before." Had the blow to his head deranged him?

"Just do it," he ordered harshly, and with a last,

searching look at him, she rose from the bed and left the room.

An hour later, Gavin was fresh from his bath and sipping sparkling champagne from a crystal glass, feeling much better. Alaina returned and related that there was a great deal of pressure on Charles's spine, caused by his crippled legs. He needed an expensive operation immediately, done by specialists in Paris, and Briana was hysterical.

She settled herself beside Gavin on the divan, accepting the glass of champagne he offered. "Of course," she continued, "Briana could never pay for anything so expensive. Charles will probably die, and I guess it's just as well." She sighed.

Gavin nodded. "Would an operation be successful? Wouldn't it be experimental, at best? He'll always be crippled, won't he?"

Alaina shrugged. Sickness was so depressing, and poor people were always a burden. "The doctors here told Briana that Paris was the only answer. With surgery, they might even be able to make it possible for Charles to get around on crutches."

"Is Briana at the hospital now?" he asked.

"Yes," she said, and her eyes suddenly narrowed. "Why all these questions about that boy? I should think you'd have better things on your mind, Gavin. *We* have troubles, too."

Gavin moved his arm along the back of the divan until it was around Alaina's shoulders. He pulled her close. "I *do* have better things on my mind, my dearest. This."

His mouth covered hers, and she yielded to his kiss, moaning softly. He maneuvered her until she was lying down, and then began sliding her gown away from her shoulders until her breasts were free. Her back arched, and she pressed herself closer to him as her eager fingertips danced down his body, fondling his hard desire.

"One day," she whispered huskily, "we won't have to hide our love, Gavin. One day, we can shout it to the world."

He laughed softly, pulling her skirt up and kissing her bare thighs. "You know I've never thought of you as my adoptive aunt, Alaina . . . only as my lover."

Fiercely, Gavin accepted her love, which she had been offering him freely since he was fourteen years old.

Chapter Five

"How could you? Dear God in heaven, child, how could you do such a thing?"

Juliette Bowden twisted a tear-soaked handkerchief in cold, trembling hands. Her body shook convulsively as she stared down at her daughter. Charlene was huddled miserably on the parlor divan. "Answer me!" Tense with the need to understand the agony being inflicted on her, Juliette demanded harshly, "Tell me what possessed you to throw away your pride, your . . . your *decency*. How could you have shamed your family so?"

Charlene could only shake her head in utter misery. Her head throbbed. Her eyes were swollen almost shut from the tears that would not cease. She'd been crying for hours. What could she say to her mother? It was done, and nothing would undo it.

Pain stabbed her as she recalled the nightmare scene of that morning. People were gathered on the front lawn. Her mother was in hysterics, screaming, and her father was demanding that the sheriff hurry and organize a posse. Then Charlene rode up, unharmed, guilt on her pale, frightened face, and in that moment . . . everyone knew. Without a word spoken, *they knew*.

She dismounted quickly and pushed through the people to make her way, sobbing, into the house. Her parents were right behind her, shouting questions, as she fled to her room. Was she hurt? Who was the villain? How had she escaped her abductor?

The sheriff burst into her room then, and old Dr. Perry, who wanted to examine her injuries. Amidst the babbling of excited voices, Charlene finally pressed her hands against her throbbing head and screamed, "Leave me alone! All of you! I'm not hurt and I wasn't kidnapped. Just leave me alone!"

Carleton Bowden's eyes narrowed as he understood. In a rage, he pushed everyone from the room except Charlene and her mother. Once the door was closed, he towered over Charlene, eyes bulging, face red with fury, demanding, "Tell me the truth, God damn it! Where'd you go last night, Charlene? And don't lie to me, or I'll beat you till you can't walk!"

Juliette, terrified, gathered Charlene in her arms, begging her husband to calm down. Their beloved daughter could do no wrong, she told him. But he waved her to silence and ordered Charlene to talk, and talk fast.

In a choked whisper, barely audible, Charlene met his fiery gaze, her eyes pleading for understanding as she proclaimed, "I was with Colt, Daddy. I love him."

Carleton Bowden had begun to tremble from the tips of his toes to the top of his balding head. He tried to speak, but couldn't force the words past the constricting knot of anger in his throat.

Juliette cried, "We'll announce your engagement. We'll say that's what you were doing last night, planning your wedding. We'll say you were chaperoned, that servants were there the whole time. There will be talk, of course, but then, after your wedding, things will die down. A few months from now, no one will remember—"

"No." Charlene shook her head, unable to meet her mother's eyes. "No. No wedding. Colt doesn't want to marry me."

In the stunned silence that followed, no one was able to look at anyone else. Then Carleton exploded. "He'll marry you, by God, or he'll be pushing up daisies on Boot Hill! No man shames my daughter and gets away with it. I'll kill the son of a bitch with my bare hands. I'm going to see him right now and get this thing settled." He whirled around and stomped toward the door. Charlene ran to clutch his arm, begging, "No, Daddy, don't, please. I'm sorry. I truly am. I never meant to hurt you or Momma. I just love Colt so much. But he doesn't love me, and I don't want him to be forced into marrying me if he doesn't want to."

Carleton looked from her desperate, tear-streaked face to his wife. He shook his head. "What am I supposed to do?" he asked of no one in particular. "My daughter spends the night with a man, and he doesn't want to make a decent woman of her. Half the town is in my front yard speculating about all this, and—just what in hell am I supposed to do?"

Juliette, regaining some of her composure, led him from the room, saying they would talk later, that it was time for him to open the bank. Charlene was distraught and needed to calm down. Later, they would discuss what was to be done about the scandal.

An hour ago, Juliette had summoned Charlene to the parlor, making an attempt once again to understand what had possessed her daughter.

"Why, Charlene?" she cried. "You were raised in a decent home. How could you behave like—like a *whore?*"

Wearily, utterly defeated, Charlene whispered feebly, "I'm not a whore, Momma. I love Colt. I did not mean to stay out there all night. I never meant for you and Daddy to find out. I was going to be home before the two of you got back, but I fell asleep, and when I woke up, it was too late."

"You think that would have made it all right?" Juliette gasped. "Just so we didn't find out? How long has this been going on? How long have you been coupling with him like . . . like an animal? How do you know you aren't in the family way? What then? Who does he think he is? You're no saloon girl. You come from a good family and he can't treat you like this.

"I wish Kitty Coltrane were in town," she went on, wringing her hands. "I can't believe she'd allow her son to get by with this. She'd see to it that he did the honorable thing."

Charlene shook her head. "I don't want to marry him if he doesn't want me. What kind of life would I have?"

"What kind of life will you have now?" Juliette asked, incredulous. "If Colt doesn't marry you, this will be gossiped about the rest of your life. You won't be able to look anyone in this town in the eye. No decent man will have you. You'll die alone, a shameful spinster. Think about it."

At that moment Charlene just wanted to be left alone. She felt sick with an emptiness too miserable to have any end. When her father came home from the bank, he would start all over again. *Damn you, John Travis Coltrane,* she silently cursed him, *why do you have to be so stubborn?*

"Just before your father left, he said he thought it would be best if we sent you to Philadelphia to stay with your Aunt Portia for a while. I agree. It might even be best if you went there to live. No one there will know about any of this, and you'd have a chance to meet someone, get married."

"No!" Charlene sat upright, every nerve in her body tense with rebellion. "I don't want to go to Philadelphia. And I certainly don't want to live with prune-faced Aunt Portia. I'd sooner die. I won't do it."

Juliette Bowden froze. How dared her daughter refuse anything at this point? "You will do as we say, Charlene, and the more I think about it, the more it seems like a good solution. Start packing now, and we'll have you on tomorrow's train. It will be difficult for your father and me, trying to hold our heads up amidst all the gossip there'll be here, but we'll manage."

Charlene stood. Quietly, firmly, she said, "I am not going to Philadelphia, Mother."

"Your father and I say you are."

"I won't go."

Juliette lifted her chin. "He'll put you on that train by force, if need be. I suggest you get off that high horse of yours before he forgets you're grown and gives you the sound thrashing you deserve."

In that moment, Charlene knew there would be no peace for her until she made it clear, once and for all, that she was not going to be made to feel worthless forever for what she had done. Looking down at her wrinkled dress, she thought about changing, then decided it made no difference. People would be staring and whispering no matter how she looked.

She started for the front door.

Her mother blocked her way. "Just where do you think you're going? You can't leave the house today."

Charlene stepped around her and opened the door. "I have to, Mother. I'm going to the bank to talk to Daddy. I want to try to make him understand this isn't the end of the world. We'll all come out of this."

"Talking won't do any good. You've broken his heart. My heart. You've ruined our good name and you've—"

Charlene ran out the door and slammed it behind her. She hurried across the porch and down the front steps, to the boardwalk that led to town.

As she passed the house next door, Mrs. Wilkins deliberately turned her back. Charlene had seen the look of contempt on her face, and a lump rose in her throat.

Farther on, she came face-to-face with two women she had known her whole life, Mrs. Martha Gibson and

Mrs. Ellie Morbane, pillars of the church and respected by all. They looked through her as if she were a ghost. Charlene could feel the chill of condemnation all the way to the marrow of her bones.

Could she live like this, she asked herself? Her mother was right. No man would want her now. Could she live the rest of her life in this town, shunned? Forevermore, she would be "that Bowden woman."

What had she done to her parents, she thought miserably, fresh tears stinging her eyes as she hurried along. They did not deserve this. Perhaps they were right in wanting her to leave town. The furor would die down if she was not around to remind everyone. But . . . live with Aunt Portia? Could she bear that grim an existence? Aunt Portia's house was big and dark and gloomy, a haunted abode for souls in purgatory. Aunt Portia never smiled, never talked about anything but the evils of the world.

Charlene stepped off the boardwalk into the street, heedless of the ever-present mud puddles. Lost in her thoughts, she didn't even feel the cold slime as it oozed inside her shoes.

Absently, she rubbed her eyes. She thought of Colt but felt no bitterness. He wasn't really to blame. He'd never lied, not even in the beginning. That was not Colt's way. He had told her he was very fond of her but not ready to fall in love or marry. Freedom, he had said, was what he craved above everything else. Many years would pass before he was ready to marry.

She smiled a sad smile. John Travis Coltrane was just like his father. He would, in fact, never settle down. Everyone in Silver Butte knew of Travis Coltrane's adventures and exploits. And everyone admired his wife for accepting him as he was.

Once, Charlene had confided to Kitty Coltrane her admiration for Kitty's ability to cope with a man like Travis. She would never forget the surprised look on

Mrs. Coltrane's beautiful face as she responded softly, "That takes no special talent, Charlene. All it takes is love . . . and accepting the man you love for what he is."

Charlene knew now, now that it was too late, that she might have accepted Colt for what he was, too. She herself had ruined everything by being so stubborn. Given enough time, given enough love, perhaps one day she could have been the woman he wanted to marry. Now he probably hated her, for he would have to endure a lot of embarrassment over this scandal. Oh, it wouldn't be as terrible for him, a man. People didn't shun a man for sowing his wild oats. The woman was condemned when she yielded to her desires. But still, he'd be gossiped about.

There was no way to make amends, she thought wearily, no way to undo what had been done.

She stumbled, catching herself just in time to keep from sprawling into the mud.

Daddy was hurt—but Daddy would help her, because he loved her. She would talk to him, and make him understand that she was truly, truly sorry, and would do *anything* to try to make up for all the grief she had caused. But he just couldn't send her to live with Aunt Portia, anything but that.

Maybe she should talk to Colt, too. If she explained to everyone that it was all her fault, that he hadn't invited her to his house, and in fact had tried to make her leave, then maybe he wouldn't be so angry. Charlene knew she couldn't bear it if he despised her, if he had only bitter memories of her.

Her head was down as she made her way slowly to the bank. If she was aware of anything besides her misery, it was only the treacherous mud at her feet, for spring thaws and heavy rains had turned the streets of Silver Butte into a soupy bog.

Lost in painful reverie, she was oblivious to everything else around her. She did not see the gunmen backing out of her father's bank, kerchiefs hiding the lower parts of their faces, their guns drawn.

She did not see the sheriff and two of his deputies take up positions behind the watering troughs, flat on their bellies, shotguns cocked.

Gunfire exploded in the stillness, followed by shouting and screaming. Someone shouted a warning, a warning Charlene didn't heed.

She felt but one sharp, burning sting as a bullet exploded inside her head. And then all the pain and love that possessed her were cast into eternal oblivion.

Colt held his horse to a slow gait as he headed into Silver Butte. Why hurry? Why hasten an ugly scene?

The sun was bright in a cloudless blue sky, and warm, mid-morning winds teased the sagebrush into an undulating dance. High above, an eagle soared, then twisted downward into a spiral before drifting out of sight. A covey of quails sprang suddenly from a clump of mesquite, noisily taking flight.

Colt frowned, thinking about Charlene making this ride at night, when rattlesnakes were out in search of water. When Charlene set her mind to something, nothing could stand in her way. She was that stubborn. That spoiled. But this time she had gotten herself into one hell of a mess . . . and him, too. Carleton Bowden was going to be crazy with rage, no matter that Charlene was to blame.

But was she? he asked himself yet again. He was not guiltless. He should have been stronger, instead of letting lust rule him. He should have made her go home, damn it.

So what was he going to say to Bowden? What *could* he say? Bowden would, of course, insist that Colt "do right" by his daughter and marry her. Quell the gossip. Save the family from shame.

But Colt did not feel guilty enough about the situation to do that. He was not going to be a martyr.

When, and if, he did get married, it would be for love and for no other reason. He was not going to be sacrificed on the altar of respectability. He would not save Charlene's name by giving her his.

When this scene was over with, he was going to get out of town for a few days. Branch Pope was a hell of a good foreman, and if Colt showed him the ropes about the house chores, Branch could keep things running while Colt got away. Maybe he would ride down to Mexico.

But the immediate task was facing Carleton Bowden, and Colt had never dreaded anything more.

Women!

Hell, he didn't like to think of himself as a coldhearted bastard, but more and more he was starting to regard women as something to avoid except when he needed one. Give them pleasure, get his own pleasure, then run like hell.

He thought of the half sister he hadn't seen in almost fourteen years. One of these days she was going to come riding in and claim half of everything—after he'd done all the work! But there was nothing he could do about that, nothing he wanted to do about it, because that was the way their father wanted it. Since everything had been Travis's to start with, Colt figured it was not his place to say anything about the way it got divided up now. Best to keep his thoughts to himself, and his mouth shut.

He was nearing town and could see the houses of Silver Butte. He paused atop a ridge and looked down. It was not the boom town it had once been, but neither was it a ghost town, like so many others that had peaked during the glory days of the Comstock lode. It was alive.

Colt's eyes narrowed. Something wasn't right. He didn't know what had made him tense up, but even his horse was suddenly standing rigid, alert. An invisible shroud of foreboding had suddenly wrapped around Colt.

Then he heard the high-pitched scream ringing in the still air.

He spurred his horse down the incline, taking a quicker path than the road. He moved fast, hard, but the main street was mired with thick mud, forcing him to slow his reckless gait.

Ahead, a crowd was gathered. As he approached, a murmur rippled through them and people began to step back, making room for Colt.

Colt dismounted, and then he saw it . . . the body of a woman lying in the mud. Hair, once golden, was matted with blood.

A man was on his knees beside the body, face burrowed in his hands, sobbing.

Slowly Carleton Bowden lifted his horror-stricken face and saw Colt. His lips quivered as he struggled to speak.

"You! *God damn* you, you killed her! Sure as if you'd shot her yourself!"

His voice broke. He gasped, chest heaving. Reddened eyes, overflowing with tears, bulged at Colt. He struck at the air with his fists and screamed, "I'm going to kill you, Coltrane! Just like you killed my little girl!"

Suddenly Bowden caught sight of the holster at eye level, worn by a man standing a few feet away. He lunged for it, but the man caught his hands and wrestled him away from the gun. Others rushed forward to grab Bowden and lift him to his feet. They half carried him out of the street and back inside the bank.

Colt felt a hand on his shoulder. He didn't move. Vaguely, through the nightmare enveloping him, Colt noted the star on the man's chest. The sheriff began to speak in a barely audible whisper, his voice sorrowful. "It was a bank robbery, Coltrane. We're gettin' a posse together now. Charlene walked right into the shootin', like she was sleepwalkin' or something. Damnedest thing I ever saw. Wasn't my men who shot her, though. They held their fire when they saw her. My deputy says one of the robbers shot her when he was aimin' at us. She just walked into the bullet.

"If it's any comfort," he added softly, "I don't think she suffered. Probably never knew what happened to her."

The sheriff's words were slowly penetrating Colt's consciousness.

"They got away," the sheriff continued angrily. "When we saw her go down, we all just sorta froze, and they got away. But we'll get 'em, by God."

Colt shrugged away the consoling hand on his shoulder and made his way forward. The people who were gathered around Charlene moved out of the way as he approached.

He dropped to one knee beside Charlene, then gently lifted her in his arms. He nearly cried out when her head lolled toward him, so limp . . . so lifeless. He looked into the sightless blue eyes that had so recently burned with passion. With trembling fingertips, he closed them.

He got to his feet, holding her tight against his chest. He staggered through the mud, carrying her out of the street. People spoke to him, but Colt stared straight ahead, hearing nothing.

He took her all the way home. As he carried her up the steps of her house, someone saw him coming and ran to hold the front door open. Inside the house, he passed the parlor, where women were crowded around Juliette Bowden, who lay unconscious on the divan, having fallen into a deep faint.

He moved on up the stairs and when he reached the

second floor, went through the first open door and laid Charlene carefully on the bed.

Then he turned and, wordlessly, left the house and walked back into town. People he passed shrank away from the man whose eyes burned with hatred, and a lust for revenge.

John Travis Coltrane had one thought: Charlene's killers were going to pay. And God help anybody who dared try to stop him.

Chapter Six

BRIANA de Paul sat before the stone fireplace, knees drawn to her chest, chin propped on her hands, staring pensively into the soot and ashes. A warm spring wind blew in through the open windows behind her, bringing the sweet fragrance of lilacs, but she barely noticed. Neither did she glory in the golden sunshine spilling on the floor.

It was four weeks since she'd seen Charles. He had been taken to the Paris hospital by a doctor who was, as great good fortune had it, leaving the Monaco hospital for greener pastures in Paris. If he hadn't pitied Charles and seen to a carriage for the boy, Briana would have had to carry her brother herself, she mused.

Her own journey, a week after Charles left, was a great deal harder than she'd known it would be. She'd begged rides in donkey carts and walked when she was forced to, pausing only for exhaustion or bloody blisters.

Charles was in a charity hospital, in a crowded ward, surrounded by critically ill and dying patients. Her heart constricted when she saw him, lying on stained sheets on a rickety cot, his body crumpled like something broken and tossed aside to die.

When he looked up with pain-filled eyes and saw her standing beside the cot, his face lit up. His sister was the only light in Charles's life. Briana bathed him, begging clean linens from a sour-faced nurse. Charles was even more wasted than when she'd last seen him. The hospital food, he told her, was only scraps, so she went out and begged for centimes until she had enough to buy a pot of soup from a street vendor. Begging was humiliating beyond anything she'd imagined, but she was not going to let her pride stand in the way of Charles's well-being.

The doctors were not unsympathetic to her financial plight. They had arranged, after all, for Charles to be cared for as a charity case. But charity wouldn't pay for the expensive surgery. He could remain in the hospital, and they would try to ease his pain, but, they explained, free surgery was out of the question.

Briana tried to elicit their sympathy. "We are talking about a little boy," she said tearfully, "a little boy who is surely going to die if you don't *try*. Surely you don't need money so badly that you can just turn your back on him."

They emphasized that a principle was at stake. If they gave their services to Charles, how could they charge other people?

She lost control then. She screamed at them, calling them vultures who preyed on suffering. "God gave you your skills, and you use them to live like kings while a little boy lies dying! How can you stand to live with yourselves?"

They turned away from her. They'd heard the same insults, shrieked by hundreds of others who were equally destitute, equally desperate.

Briana had left Charles and gone back to Madame deBonnett, who was still giving her shelter and a job, however meager the wage. To remain in Paris meant attempting survival on the streets, and that was dangerous. It was not uncommon for women to be found in alleyways, raped, throats cut. She had tried to explain to Charles why she had to return to Monaco. She held him close, promising to do everything she could to make money for his operation. He smiled up at her, knowing she'd try, knowing it was hopeless.

From the moment she left Charles, Briana knew utter desolation. How in heaven's name could she get money for Charles's operation? She had no family, no friends of means. Everyone she knew was as poor as she was, with the exception of Madame deBonnett, and that was no help. From what she had seen, the deBonnett fortune was rapidly dwindling away. Besides the fact that Madame deBonnett had money problems, Briana knew she would never loan her money because the woman was as cold as could be, caring about no one except herself and that nasty Gavin.

Despite the warmth of the spring day, Briana shuddered. She loathed Gavin Mason. Lascivious, sneaky, cruel, Gavin had been trouble since the day the Count brought his new family to live with him.

One of Briana's early encounters with Gavin happened when she was twelve. She'd been out in the barn, doing her chores, spreading fresh hay in the horses' stalls. Suddenly she became aware that Gavin was hiding in one of the lofts above, spying on her. When she called out to him, demanding to know what he was up to, he stood up, laughing. Then he exposed himself to her, chortling, "I've got something for you, Briana."

She screamed in horror, dropped the pitchfork, and ran. But he was quicker, jumping from the loft and landing beside her. He wrestled her to the floor and his hands were everywhere at once, clawing at her breasts, grabbing between her legs. "You want it as much as I do," he cried, his breath hot on her face. She twisted from side to side, desperate to escape his wet mouth.

He lay on top of her, pinning her, and in a last wild effort to break free, she smashed her fist into the hard pink thing that was thrusting at her belly. He yelped in pain, clutching himself, and rolled away.

She ran from the barn, sobbing breathlessly, fleeing straight to the little cottage and her father. Flinging herself in his arms, she sobbed and sobbed. Louis de Paul held her against him, his eyes narrowing as he managed to get the full story out of her.

Worse was to come. When her father had heard her out, he gave her a fierce shake and said, voice hoarse, "You will say nothing about this, do you hear me? You will forget this happened. And in the future, be on guard lest he try again." Louis de Paul glared at his daughter.

She stared up at him, stunned. "Papa, you don't mean this! We have to tell Madame deBonnett. She will punish him so—"

He shook her again, hard. "Are you insane, daughter? She wouldn't believe you—or else she wouldn't care. She would send us away, too, and I would have no job and we would have no place to live. No, you mustn't speak of this. Just keep away from him, do you hear me?"

Briana nodded slowly, her heart breaking. Her own father would not protect her.

Ever since that day, she had been on her guard. Gavin had enjoyed their game, becoming bolder through the years.

"One day," he taunted constantly, "you will beg me to pleasure you. You are only toying with me, I know."

It mattered not at all that she bluntly proclaimed her loathing of him; Gavin enjoyed his sport. Even when she declared, "I would rather die than have you touch me!" Gavin only laughed, and waited for another chance to fondle her.

She wanted to go back to Paris and be near Charles, but how could she, when there was no way of knowing whether she would find work? She hadn't a centime. At least Charles had shelter, and at least the doctors could ease his pain. She would offer Charles nothing by leaving her job and traveling to a city where she might not be able to get another.

Briana missed Charles terribly, and worried about him waking and sleeping, having awful nightmares about his being sent to an orphanage because she was dead, or going through the pain of the operation and having it not help. But even so, there was one aspect to her visit to Paris, grueling though the journeys to and from Monaco had been, which warmed her.

She had promised herself a visit to the great Notre Dame Cathedral. One afternoon when Charles had fallen asleep, Briana left the hospital, located two streets from the Pont Neuf, and walked to Notre Dame. There, she gazed up at the many spires and then walked, hesitant and nervous, through the main entrance. It was beautiful inside, beyond anything she had ever seen, the stained-glass windows large and brilliant. The choir sang, and she was there to hear the "Ave Maria."

Finally, she tore herself away to perform the act she had come for. Going outside again and finding the door dedicated to Saint Anne, Briana's patron saint, whose name was Briana's own middle name, she prayed fervently for Charles's recovery. The door was richly carved, and as she backed away to look at all the designs, she ran smack into the wrought-iron gate, jumping because she thought she'd bumped into someone.

The door was almost seven hundred years old, and Briana stood there marveling at it, oblivious to time, until it began to get quite dark. She turned away, sad, knowing she would probably never see Saint Anne's door again, and hurried back to Charles.

She was glad, so glad she had made the journey through the streets of Paris and prayed to her patron saint. Saint Anne's door was something she would remember all her life, and the knowledge comforted her.

She ran across the Pont Neuf. It was fully dark by then, and she was frightened. As she reached the other side of the bridge and ran the two blocks to the hospital, she hoped she was in time to see what Charles was being fed for his supper. She had grave doubts about the food, partly because he hadn't even bothered trying to tell her it was all right. It wasn't all right; it was awful. Oh, why was everything in her brother's life so terrible?

The hospital was old and smelled revolting. She scolded herself for hating to be there. Why, Charles had been there for months, and who knew when he would be able to leave? If he could bear the odor of cabbage and ether, the ancient rotting wood and the flies, if he could live there, then she could stay with him until she had to leave for the night.

One afternoon, when Charles was sleeping again and she thought he wouldn't mind if she left for a couple of hours, she walked across the Pont Neuf, asking for directions from gendarmes, careful not to look in the eyes of any men on the way, until she reached the much talked-about Gardens of Luxembourg, with their lovely statues and beautiful grounds. Finding an empty bench, she sat and looked at the gardens, the palace ahead, soothed by the air of peace. How charming it all was!

All of Paris, in fact, had such an ethereal air about it, it seemed that nothing bad could possibly happen in Paris. Was it true? Would Charles be safe here? she asked herself for the dozenth time.

Having lived all her life in either Nice or Monaco, Briana was frankly terrified of Paris. The nights were brutal, or so she had been warned, with thieves preying on the unwary and all manner of men chasing unescorted females into dark alleys.

But the days in Paris were so lovely that she always forgot her nighttime terrors. In the sun, Paris gleamed. Many buildings were made of white stucco, and nearly as many had roofs of red tile. The combination was dazzling, beautiful, and she began to understand why people wanted so badly to live there. There was something unearthly about Paris during the day, especially in bright sunlight, and Briana's heart took flight when she walked through its colorful streets. Would she really be able to live there one day, she and Charles? Surely he would not fail to get better in this magical place.

The sound of light knocking and the door opening brought Briana out of her reverie. She looked up as Marice Clausand stepped into the cottage. Marice, the daughter of a caretaker on an estate to the south, had been Briana's friend for several years.

The sight of Marice, lovely in an elegant yellow satin gown, surprised Briana. "Where on earth did you get that?" Marice was as poor as she was, and Briana had never seen her in anything but muslin.

Marice, face glowing with happiness, grabbed her skirt and twirled around and around. She stopped before Briana, grinning. "Isn't it lovely? And look at this!" She held out her wrist, on which sparkled a thin gold bracelet.

Awed, Briana touched it, shaking her head. "What happened? How did you get these things?"

Marice settled herself on the floor near her friend, patting her skirt smugly. Admiring her bracelet, she smiled and said, "Well . . . let's just say that I got very, very smart, Briana."

Briana knew that she had recently taken work at a bistro, much to her parents' dismay. "I didn't know you were making so much money."

Marice laughed sharply. "I'm not, silly—not serving food, anyway." She leaned forward. "I discovered that I am sitting on pure gold, Briana."

Briana's head moved back as she stared at Marice. Surely Marice didn't mean what Briana thought she meant.

Marice stiffened. "Oh, don't look so self-righteous. Why should a woman give it away if men are willing to pay for it? All this gown cost me was an hour with a man. If I'd had to pay for it myself, it would have taken me forever to save the money. And this bracelet . . ." She held up her arm and shook it. "Two hours of the easiest work I've ever done." She eyed her friend closely, waiting for her response.

Briana began to shake her head slowly from side to side, numb with horror. "Oh, Marice, I know it's none of my business, but—but it's terrible. It's sinful, and—"

"And we've both been giving it away free for years," Marice snapped. "Only *I* got smart. If you were smart, you'd do the same thing."

Briana's ire rose. How dared Marice make such assumptions? "I've never given my . . . anything away. I've never sold anything, either. I've never been with a man."

Marice grinned a nasty grin. "Do you expect me to believe you've kept your job here without pleasuring Monsieur Mason? Everyone knows how he is."

"I don't care what you believe about me," Briana interrupted hotly. "I wish you hadn't told me this."

Marice's eyes flashed. "I told you this, you little fool, because I care about you. What's going to become of you when Madame deBonnett loses everything? What will you do? There is no way I could ever have gotten along on what I was making before I got smart. Now I am going to be moving away from my parents. I'm taking a room above the bistro. And when I've saved enough money, I'll buy lots of beautiful gowns so I can move to Paris and marry a wealthy man and spend the rest of my life in luxury."

"You will become a demimondaine," Briana said furiously, "and your family will disown you. You will break their hearts. No decent man will have you. The best you'll ever be able to hope for is to be a mistress." Angry, and frightened for her friend, she gathered steam. "And what happens when you grow old and lose your beauty? You'll become madam of a whorehouse!" Briana touched her friend's shoulder, finishing, "You're making a tragic mistake."

"Don't you dare pity me, you little fool," Marice sneered. "It is *I* who pity *you*. I came here to try to help you, but I should have known better. You never were as smart as I am."

Briana stared at her in silence. She didn't want to fight with Marice. When had Marice begun to change? she wondered, and why hadn't she seen it? Had she been too absorbed by her own problems?

Finally, she reached out and took her friend's hand. In the kindest voice she could manage, she said, "Marice, give up this kind of life before you can't turn back."

"Oh, shut up!" Marice snatched her hand away. "I did not come here to have you lecture me. I'm happy. And look at you—poor, as you always will be." Marice leaped to her feet, gave her long auburn hair a toss, and stared down at Briana in contempt. "And you're lying when you say you've never been with a man. You're no virgin. You're just too proud to admit you were stupid enough to give yourself away and not get anything in return."

She ran to the door, turning to glare at Briana one last time. "Come to Paris and beg in the streets, Briana. When I see you, I'll give you a few francs for old times' sake." She walked out the door, closing it with a bang.

Briana felt like crying. Marice, she knew, had not really come only to reveal her plans. She had come seeking approval, and, receiving quite the opposite, had become angry. The two would never be friends again, but there was nothing Briana could do about that, or anything she could do to change Marice.

Briana got up, smoothing her worn skirt, and walked to the mirror that hung on the wall opposite the door. She pushed her hair back away from her face. She looked at herself for a long moment. She looked tired. She *was* tired. Madame deBonnett was an ogre these days, making unreasonable demands. It was as though she were trying to get every shred of work out of Briana, in anticipation of the time when she would be forced to dismiss her. She had already dismissed the butler and the cook. Briana was now required to take over those duties. Only by sneaking out of the house while Madame napped was she able to have a few moments of respite.

Briana sighed, knowing Madame would be awake now, and probably screaming for tea and cake.

Preparing to go back to the château, she turned away from the mirror, lifted her skirt, and smoothed her black cotton stockings.

"Nice. But lift the skirt a bit higher, please."

Briana gasped and whirled around. Her fright was at once replaced by fury as she saw Gavin leaning in the doorway, smiling insolently, eyes bright, as usual.

She jerked her garments down and cried hoarsely, "How dare you!" She pointed at him. "Get out of here!"

He kicked the door shut and began moving slowly toward her. "It's time we had a talk, Briana. Strictly business, however. You've nothing to fear."

She lifted her chin defiantly and said clearly, "I've never been afraid of you, monsieur. And we have nothing to discuss. I work for Madame deBonnett, *not for you,"* she added pointedly.

Reaching her side, Gavin touched her bare arm and murmured, "Such smooth skin for a woman of the servant class."

She swatted his hand away and marched to the door. "You have no right to be here. This is my home, and you are intruding, sir."

He crossed the room and slammed the door. The smile left his face, and his eyes narrowed menacingly. Grabbing her shoulders, he pushed her into a nearby chair, towering over her to yell, "Enough insolence.

You will listen to what I have to say, or else I'll mess up that pretty face so badly that you'll be ashamed to be seen. Do you understand me?"

Briana, still not intimidated, tried to get up, but he shoved her back down and pressed his hands against her shoulders, hard. She tried to push him away, but he slapped her, then entwined his fingers in her long hair and pulled on it mercilessly. Held that way, utterly helpless, she had no choice but to hear him out.

"I really don't want to hurt you, Briana. You're of no use to me if you're battered. Now, will you behave yourself and listen?"

Briana hoped her hatred of him was in her eyes as he gave her hair another yank. "Say what you've got to say," she conceded.

He released her so abruptly she toppled to the floor. Before she could scramble to her feet, he picked her up and sat her in the chair again. "Now then, I will talk, and you will listen."

His eyes moved to her heaving bosom, and he sighed. "I must admit it's hard to discuss business when you inspire . . . other thoughts."

"Please say what you came here to say," she requested coldly.

"Ah, Briana, such spirit," he said. "You'd be sheer delight in bed, moving those luscious hips, with me rammed inside you. Certainly you'd be better than that little twit Marice. Oh, yes," he informed her, "I saw her come in. I was waiting for her to leave. I've had many a good tumble with her, but she's decided to sell what she was giving me for free, and, unfortunately, my allowance has been greatly reduced, so . . ."

He sat down across from her. "I suppose," he continued musingly, "that if we are going to be business partners, I shall have to be completely candid with you and say that my allowance is, actually, nonexistent. The deBonnett fortune is gone, as you doubtless know. Alaina has a reprieve from the bank, but unless something is done soon, the château will have to be sold."

"What do you want of me?" she interrupted. "I have my own troubles."

He nodded. "Yes, I know you do, and that is why we need each other, Briana. You are going to help me and Alaina, and you're also going to be able to help yourself and that poor, sick brother of yours."

He lit a cheroot and inhaled, then blew the smoke out slowly before saying kindly, "How would you like to have enough money to pay for your brother's operation?"

She went stiff with shock. She had never known Gavin Mason to do anything charitable, so there had to be something devious in his mind. "You are not going to get me to submit to you. Not even for that kind of money."

He threw back his head and laughed. "Of course not. I can have you any time I want you, you silly girl, don't you understand that? Besides, I'd never pay that much for any woman. No, I've something else in mind, something that will require you to be quite a good actress. Are you desperate enough to do a good job?"

"That depends on what you have in mind. I have my principles," she informed him.

"But you also have a price," he said wearily. "Everyone does. Now, here is the proposition I'm making to you."

"I'm listening," she said warily.

"I will tell your brother's doctors in Paris to prepare for the operation. I will have Charles moved to a private hospital, so he will receive the best of care while he's waiting for the operation. How *soon* the operation takes place will depend entirely on you. It's a question of how quickly you get your job done."

Briana's heart was racing. Was there really a chance

that she could earn the money? Was there really a chance for Charles?

"You will be going to America with me."

"America?" she gasped. "Whatever—"

He held up a hand for silence. "Listen to me. I don't know if Dani ever told you, but her father is a very wealthy man."

Briana shook her head. "She never talked to me about that."

Gavin proceeded to tell her the whole story, finishing, "So Travis Coltrane is now in Paris. He's written to Dani to tell her that she may claim her half of his estate any time. I offered to marry Dani, but she refused. She was determined to enter the convent." He wrinkled his nose in distaste.

Briana smiled to herself. Dani would never have consented to marry Gavin in any case.

"Why do you need me?" she asked.

"Because," he replied, smiling confidently, "all Dani has to do is go to America and claim her fortune."

"Well, she's not going to, is she?"

He sighed impatiently. "No. She's not going to ask for her money. However"—he paused significantly—"Dani *is* going to America to lay claim to her share of the Coltrane fortune, because, you see . . ." He paused again, then continued: "*You* are going to be Dani."

Briana shook her head without a second's hesitation. "No."

"Yes," said Gavin. "It is the only way you can hope to save your brother's life. And," he continued, "my plan will work. Coltrane won't be in Nevada. The only member of the family who'll be there is his son, who has not seen Dani in almost fourteen years. You resemble her closely enough. The coloring is right. And you speak English perfectly, with only a trace of a French accent. Dani would conceivably speak the same way, having lived in this country for so long." He paused. "Thank God she taught you English. The bitch isn't entirely useless.

"It's all quite simple," he went on fluidly before she could speak. "We'll go to America. I will outline my plan for you later. Meanwhile, I'll make the provisions for your brother's care." He sat back and watched her. What he had told her was all she needed to know for the time being. How he planned to use her to get control of *all* the Coltrane money was nothing she needed to know, at least not yet.

Briana's mind raced. It was not right, but it wasn't as wrong as what Marice was doing. Or letting her beloved Charles die. Wasn't it her sacred duty to help that helpless boy? Dani had no need of the money anymore, so who would be hurt? And Charles would have a chance to live. That same thought kept coming back over and over: *Charles would have a chance to live.*

She leaned back in the chair and closed her eyes. The years rolled backward and she recalled all the close times with her mother. How she wished her mother was there to help her now! Was there no other way? Could Briana stoop so low? Was the fact that Charles's life might be saved a pardoning grace in the guilt of this conspiracy?

Yes. Charles had to have a chance.

With a silent prayer, Briana lifted misty eyes to Gavin and said, "I will do it."

His eyes sparkled. "I knew you would. You're stubborn, but you're not stupid."

"One thing," Briana said quickly, her expression grim: "You will not touch me. You will not try to get me into your bed. That is not part of our agreement. That must be understood from the beginning. I want your word of honor," she said solemnly, wondering fleetingly if Gavin had any honor.

"Oh, you have my word," he said airily. "There are

plenty of other women around, Briana. I don't lie awake at night thinking about you."

He stood. "I'm going now to make arrangements for the money to provide care for your brother, and also to arrange our passage to America. We'll leave as soon as I can get everything taken care of. Meanwhile, go to Dani's room and begin packing her clothes. You will fit into them, I'm sure. Alter whatever needs altering."

He went to the door, then paused to warn, "You will not say anything about this to anyone. I demand the utmost secrecy."

Briana nodded agreement. She certainly didn't want anyone knowing. "You have my word."

Gavin left and hurried to the house, relief making him elated. But he knew the next part would be difficult.

He entered the house and went straight to Alaina's room, where he found her seated at her mahogany desk, studying the family ledgers.

He stood behind her, lowering his hands to dip down inside the bodice of her dressing gown and caress her breasts.

A ripple of pleasure went through Alaina, but she refused to yield to desire. "Not now, Gavin. I'm going over the books. I'm in no mood for lovemaking."

He nibbled her ear. "You will be in a very different mood when I tell you that our worries are over, my darling."

She twisted around to stare up at him. "What are you talking about? We're destitute."

He fingered the diamond and emerald necklace she was wearing, one of the last of the deBonnett family jewels. It was her favorite. The Count had given it to her when they married. It had been in Count deBonnett's family for six generations and was very valuable.

He took her hands and drew her to her feet, leading

her to the bed. Holding her close, tilting her face to look up into his, he talked. He told her of his plan. As he talked, her face began to look less haggard, less worn, and he was pleased with himself.

When he finished, she threw her arms around him, exulting, "Oh, Gavin, Gavin, my darling. You're brilliant! Who will ever know? Travis's son surely won't know Briana isn't Dani. And Travis won't be there. Why, it won't take any time at all. When you come back with all that money, we'll live like royalty. We'll send Briana away so that no one will ever find out."

Gavin caught her arms and said gently, "It might take a while, Alaina. Briana doesn't know this—she has no need to—but we are going to come away from Nevada with more than Dani's half of the fortune. We might very well come away with all of it. I'll have to look over the situation when we get there. I can't plan everything until I've seen what's what."

Alaina nodded. "There's one thing more," he went on, fingering her necklace. "I need money right away. For passage to America. And to take care of Briana's brother. She's not stupid. Unless she knows I've started carrying out my part of the bargain, she won't cooperate."

Alaina's elation faded. "There is no money, Gavin. You know that."

He gave the necklace a tug. "There's this."

Alaina clutched the jewels possessively as she shook her head wildly. "No. Gavin, this is almost all I have left, all that's worth anything. And it has sentimental value. And—"

"And we can buy a dozen just like it once we have the Coltrane fortune," he snapped. "Hand it over."

Here eyes filled with tears, but he wasn't moved. Tears never moved Gavin. With trembling hands, she unfastened the necklace and let it slip into his outstretched palm.

He gave it a playful toss, then put it on the bedside table.

"Now then," he whispered huskily, pushing her down onto the bed. "I want your other jewels, my lovely bitch . . . the jewels that belong only to me."

Chapter Seven

FLAT valleys, ringed by buttes and mesas, framed by rugged mountains—this was the world the posse from Silver Butte and Colt became a part of as they tracked the bank robbers who had killed Charlene Bowden.

For five grueling days, the men rode, senses keenly alert for any sign. The Indian scout Marshal Booth procured fell by the wayside on the second day when it became clear that Colt was a better tracker. Like his father, Colt did not depend solely on signs like horse tracks and broken brush, but trusted his instincts, putting himself into the mind of his prey. He thought as the prey would think. It worked. They were on the trail of the gunmen, and not far behind them.

The trouble was, they were in rugged country, with many places men could hide in ambush. The posse moved slowly, lest they become an easy target for the outlaws.

Except for Colt, who took chances and refused to listen when Marshal Booth told him to be careful. Booth and his deputies were all eager to catch the men who'd murdered Charlene and robbed the townspeople of their hard-earned money. Yes, they were eager. But they were careful not to jeopardize their lives or the lives of the others.

They stopped on the fifth night to camp on the top

of a jutting butte. It was a good place for keeping an eye out all around them. Marshal Booth helped himself to some rabbit stew, then walked over to where Colt was sitting next to a clump of mesquite. Colt wasn't eating, wasn't doing anything except what he'd been doing ever since they'd ridden out of Silver Butte—keeping to himself in frigid silence. He had thrown an impenetrable wall around himself.

Booth knew Coltrane and the Bowden girl had been seeing each other for a while, and he knew there'd been some trouble. Hell, old man Carleton Bowden had pitched a fit out in the street, saying it was Colt's fault his daughter was dead, threatening to kill Colt.

The marshal sat down a few feet from Colt. Colt didn't acknowledge him. He stared into the distance, eyes narrowed.

The marshal ate his stew, keeping his eyes on Colt, who didn't even glance his way.

"Okay," Booth began, intent on having his say. "We need to talk, Coltrane."

Colt regarded him coolly, then averted his gaze.

"You got me worried, boy. I don't like the way you're acting. You charge straight ahead, knowin' any time you could be ridin' into a hail of bullets. It's like you're wantin' to get yourself killed. Well, that's no good, especially if you take me and the other men with you. Now, I don't know what went on back there in town between you and old man Bowden. But whatever it is, settle it when you get home. And, Coltrane, truth is, I'd as soon you headed on back to town now anyway, 'cause you're makin' us all jittery as mules in a lightnin' storm. The way you're actin' is spooky."

Colt murmured, "I know what I'm doing. You have no reason to worry, Marshal."

The marshal's eyebrows shot up. "No reason to worry, when you charge ahead without lookin' left or right?"

Colt smiled. He knew exactly what he was doing.

But he wasn't ready to explain. "You want me to leave the posse, I will," he said.

The marshal's head bobbed up and down. "I think that'd be best, Coltrane. I can send somebody to get that Indian scout back. We might go slower, but it'd be safer. I'd feel a lot better if you'd just head back to Silver Butte."

"I'm not going back to Silver Butte." Colt got to his feet. He reached for the saddle he'd taken off his horse, then started toward where the horses were tethered.

"Hey, wait!" The marshal got to his feet. "Where do you think you're going?"

Colt stopped and turned, staring at him with eyes suddenly flashing. "Don't worry about me, Marshal. You've got a job to do. I've got a job to do. It's best we split up and each do things our own way."

The marshal ran to block his path. "Now, you wait a minute," he ordered, anger rising. "I ain't havin' you ridin' outta here thinkin' you're the law. That ain't the way I run things. If you ain't goin' back to town, you can just fall in with the rest of the posse and start takin' orders and actin' like you got some sense."

He lowered his voice, suddenly aware that others were listening. Placing a gentle hand on Colt's shoulder, he said, "Look, boy, I know you're hurtin', but you gotta get hold of yourself."

Colt turned his head ever so slightly and eyed Booth's hand with such hostility that the marshal withdrew it. "Marshal," Colt said coldly, "just keep out of my way."

He pushed by the older man and continued on toward the horses. Moments later he had his horse saddled and was riding out into the night. They could hear his horse as it moved down the hill.

Branch Pope was sitting near the campfire. He didn't like having a fire. It was a dead giveaway to the outlaws. But many of the men were whiners, saying they were cold, needed hot food once a day.

Branch shook his head in disgust. He was only there because Coltrane was his boss, and he wanted to do whatever he could to help him. He knew about him and the Bowden girl, had also heard about the strange confrontation between Colt and Bowden in the street. There was big trouble. He didn't know what it was, but the big boss, Travis, had asked him to keep an eye on things, and that's just what Branch was doing.

Booth went to Branch and said, "Maybe you'd better go after him. Try to talk some sense into that hard head. He might listen to you."

Branch snorted derisively. "I know when to stay out of his business. Colt is just as stubborn and feisty as his daddy, and he sure ain't one to rattle when he's mad about something. And he's madder'n I've ever seen him. Gives me chills, it does."

He paused and spat tobacco juice into the fire. There was a sudden sizzle of flames. "He's gonna kill the men that killed Miss Charlene. There ain't nothin' you or me can do to stop him, Marshal."

Booth stiffened, aware that all the men were watching him. "Well, he can't take the law into his own hands," he snapped. "I can't allow that." He squared his shoulders and glared at Branch as though Branch were causing all the trouble.

Branch leaned back against a rock, folding his arms across his chest. There was just nothing Branch liked better than seeing a pompous know-it-all make a jackass out of himself. "Well," he drawled, keeping his face impassive, "since you're the marshal, it's your place to ride out and stop him, huh?"

A ripple of snickers went through the men. Booth's face began to redden. Branch Pope was trying to make him look foolish, and he didn't like that one little bit. He squirmed uncomfortably and said, "Hell, he'll get himself killed, that's what. There were five of 'em, and he's one man. I tried to talk some sense into him. I done my duty by him, so if he gets himself killed, it's not my fault."

Branch wasn't worried about Colt, but he knew the marshal was, and he decided to let him stew. He knew Colt would purposely leave a trail, so if Branch didn't hear anything from him in a day or two, he'd just follow along after him and see what was going on. There was, he knew, no problem.

Colt had been trailing the outlaws since leaving the posse. He knew exactly where they were. He'd had them in his sight since dawn. All he'd had to do was remain at a discreet distance, careful to make sure *they* didn't spot *him*. Years of tracking with his father were paying off.

He knew precisely what he was doing, and, he reflected grimly, the bastards ahead of him apparently knew what they were doing, too. Since leaving Silver Butte, they had been riding at an angle, southeast, a route that would take them into the Esmeralda salt marshes, on into Death Valley, and eventually to Mexico. They were counting on the posse giving up and turning back.

The outlaws had made camp for the night in a large crevice, shrouded by mesquite and sage, near the top of a jutting butte. There were five of them: four inside, one outside on lookout. They were not worried about the posse; Colt knew that. They had been careful, circling around, crisscrossing their own trail, taking to streams and creeks whenever possible to hide their tracks. The posse was as confused as they had wanted it to be.

Colt knew all the tricks, however, and had, from the beginning, been aware of every ploy. He had allowed them to become overconfident, and smug. "Think like your prey," his father had told him over and over again, hammering it into his memory. "Think like they think. Anticipate every move they might even remotely consider making. Don't think like the hunter. Think like the hunted."

The sound of drunken laughter reached Colt on the gentle night wind. Yes, they were just where he'd known they would be.

It was a dark night, moonless. He left his horse tethered and walked half a mile. The horse might have made a noise, especially if he was spooked by a coyote. Very carefully, Colt climbed the butte, taking his time, careful not to make a sound.

The outlaws were not as cautious, and he heard them continuously. Finally he sat down and waited, giving them time to get good and drunk.

Closing his eyes, he found the image floating before him, as it always did when he was alone. Charlene lay in the mud, her golden hair red with seeping blood, the bullet hole in her head visible. Then the living Charlene, vivacious, contrary, fiercely passionate, appeared to him, laughing at something he'd said. And then, again, came the vision of Charlene in death.

He had thought it all through carefully. He understood himself. It wasn't that her death made him realize he'd loved Charlene. No. He wasn't confused. He hadn't loved her, not loved her in the way a man needed to love a woman if he wanted to live with her the rest of his life. But he had been very fond of her, exasperating though she was. He saw no reason why he shouldn't feel guilty over her death, for he was sure he had caused it. They said she'd walked right into the gunfire, heedless to shouts of warning. He knew she'd been lost in thought over what had happened between them.

That was his fault.

He had treated her callously. She was caught up in a scandal, her reputation ruined. Her world had been destroyed.

And then her life was over.

The only way he could live with himself was to exact revenge for her death.

He waited in the shadow of the jutting rock, and then, it was time to move. They were passed-out drunk.

He reached inside his boot and withdrew the knife. A wicked weapon, Travis had used it in the war. Some called it a Bowie knife, invented, they said, by the infamous Jim Bowie. His father called it an "Arkansas toothpick." It was one of Colt's proudest possessions, for it had served his father in the war. Now, for the first time, it would serve Colt.

He moved as stealthily as a bobcat after prey. There was no thought, only deadly purpose.

Colt could just barely make out the guard in the darkness. He sat dozing, slumped against the ragged stump of a tree that had tried, and failed, to grow there. The guard came awake at the sudden touch of cold steel against his flesh, but it was too late. "For Charlene," Colt whispered, and, with one savage slash, slit his throat.

Blood gurgling was the only sound.

Colt shoved the body sideways, stepped over it, and climbed slowly up to the crevice that led into the side of the butte. Wiping blood from the knife onto his trousers, he returned the knife to his boot and drew both his pistols from his double holster.

A small fire burned inside the crevice, and the four outlaws were lying near it. He stepped into the soft glow of light provided by the flames and spoke quietly. "This is for Charlene, the woman you murdered five days ago."

His guns blazed simultaneously, felling one man with a shot between the eyes and a second with a bullet under the right eye. The third man turned and scrambled for cover. Colt shot him in the back of the neck.

The fourth drew his gun and fired. Colt felt the burning blow to his shoulder but kept on shooting until the last man fell dead into the fire.

It had been a small fire, and it was smothered quickly by the dead body. Colt found himself in sudden darkness. He stood still, listening as the silence began to rise about him, screaming until it became a giant roar. Five men lay dead by his hand. He felt—what? Guilt? No. Vengeance had been achieved. What he felt was a void, an emptiness that went on and on. Suddenly, there seemed no purpose to anything, no reason for anything.

The pain in his shoulder was deep and burning. Holstering his guns, he pressed his fingers against the wound, felt the profusion of his own blood. It was not, he knew, a clean wound. The bullet was still in him and had to come out. He knew he must have help or he would bleed to death.

He stepped out into the crisp freshness of the night air, breathing in deep gulps. He kept his hand pressed against the wound as he started down the incline. He had to get to his horse and find the posse.

Yet he moved slowly, for fast, reckless movements would only make the blood flow faster. There was a deep roaring in his ears, a roaring that matched the silence. The pain was being replaced by numbness, but the bleeding continued. He was beginning to feel dizzy. Gritting his teeth, pressing his hand harder against the bullet hole, he forced his wobbly legs to continue plodding forward, downward. He hoped to God he'd remember where the horse was.

Suddenly, his foot slipped and he went to his knees. Too weak to stop himself, he fell forward and began rolling down the steep incline, rolling over and over, the pounding of the rocks against his body sending excruciating pain through his wounded shoulder.

Then he felt nothing, fainting into oblivion as he continued to roll down the rocky incline.

* * *

The sound of gunfire in the still night, ricocheting through the mountains and valleys, woke Branch Pope instantly. Scrambling to his feet, he understood what was happening. Colt had found the outlaws.

"Let's go," Branch called to everybody in general and no one in particular. "That's got to be Coltrane and them."

The men shifted uneasily, exchanging anxious glances in the soft glow of the dying campfire. They were weary of riding day after day in the heat, and their eagerness had waned. One man had given up that day, heading back to Silver Butte, saying he had crops to tend.

Branch had been sleeping with his head on his saddle, and he stooped to pick it up, balancing it on his shoulder He scowled at the men, demanding, "Let's ride. That was a damn short gunfight."

Hank Burich spoke up. "We're not crazy, Pope. In case you ain't noticed, it's dark as shit out there, and we ain't got no idea where the gunfire came from. You want us to charge outta here in the dark and ride right into the lot of 'em?" He shook his head and settled back against his saddle. "I say wait till daylight."

The others grunted agreement, and Branch looked to Marshal Booth, who had risen and was standing a few feet away, listening. "Well, since you're in charge," he said, "what do *you* say?"

The marshal cleared his throat and shifted his weight from one foot to the other. Without looking at Branch, he replied, "Well, I—reckon I agree with Burich. I don't see how we'd find anything out there in the dark. We'd just be risking our lives for nothing."

Contemptuously, Branch spat a wad of tobacco juice, landing it directly between the marshal's feet. "Well, *I* reckon you're a bunch of gutless sons o' bitches." He strode angrily to where the horses were tethered and, within moments, was saddled and on his way.

Branch rode slowly. All was silent. Branch allowed

his horse to pick his way along as he steered him toward where Branch thought the gunfire had come from: southwest. There was a valley in front of him and it stretched toward a small butte, maybe two or three miles ahead. The robbers wouldn't have camped out in the open, so Branch figured the shooting had come from that butte.

Branch rubbed his big stomach, a gesture he was not aware of when he was in deep thought. If Colt was dead, then the outlaws were going to know the posse couldn't be far behind, and they would naturally figure that the sound of gunfire would bring the posse riding hell-bent for leather. So they would do one of two things: They'd either take off, trying to put as much distance between them and the law as possible, or they'd dig in, take cover, and wait in ambush. In which case, Branch realized, he would get killed.

Branch kicked his horse, urging him to move faster. A plan was starting to formulate. He'd be a fool if he just rode along yelling out to Colt. But if he waited till he got a little closer to where he thought the gunfire had come from, then fired his own guns, the outlaws might figure they were being fired on and shoot back. He would then have a fix on their location and do his damnedest to keep them pinned down till it got light. Surely even that chicken-shit posse would ride out at first light to see what was going on.

He rode on, the butte growing into a hulking shape as he got closer. He wasn't moving as fast as he'd have liked for fear the horse's hooves would give him away.

Branch rode with one hand on the reins. The other hand held his drawn gun. There were two kinds of varmints he was concerned about just then, the outlaws and sidewinder rattlesnakes. He preferred the legless varmints but intended to be ready for either kind.

About an hour later, Branch drew close enough to the butte that he figured it was safe to fire off a volley of shots. He dismounted, then did so.

Nothing happened.

Why didn't they shoot back? Were they smart enough to figure what he was up to? Were they going to sit and wait for him to ride in on top of them? Damn it, he didn't know what to do.

A quarter of a mile ahead, lying at the bottom of the sloping butte, Colt stirred and moaned. It had been a rough roll down the gradient, and he'd finally been stopped by a large, prickly mesquite. The sound of gunshots penetrated the numbing fog, and he lifted his head, opening his eyes to see that it was still dark. How long had he been unconscious? Who was out there in the night? He knew the outlaws were dead, so there was nothing to fear. Still, you never knew. It didn't do to be careless.

With stiff fingers he reached for the gun on his right side but felt only an empty holster. Fresh anguish shot through his shoulder, and then there was a flutter of panic. If one gun had been lost in the downward roll, then had he also lost the other gun?

His hand closed around the gun on his left side, and he breathed a sigh of relief. Drawing it, he forced his bruised body to roll onto his back. He fired once, twice, then lay very still.

Branch heard two shots. Surely not someone firing at him. Was it a signal? Hell, he was going to take a chance that it was. He couldn't continue to crouch there forever, or even till morning. He fired off two shots in response.

Colt heard and shot two more times.

Branch swung his large body up into the saddle and began riding, suppressing an urge to hurry, forcing himself to go warily in case it was a trap.

Colt pulled himself to his knees and braced his back against a rock. Straining to hear, he was soon rewarded by the distant sound of hooves. He told himself sternly that hope was making him giddy. He must take no chances. Holding his gun cocked and ready, he took a deep breath, mustered what was left of his strength, and hollered, "It's Coltrane."

Branch Pope was not a religious man. But just in case somebody up there was listening, he offered a quick thanks, then kicked his horse into a gallop.

"Here!" Colt yelled as the rider approached. He waved his good arm and fired off one more shot.

Branch closed the gap between them and leaped off his horse. As he reached Colt, his friend fell into his arms. "You're hit," Branch cried, lowering him carefully to the ground. "Where is it? How bad? How many of 'em are left and where are they?"

Colt ground his teeth together, because it was hurting like hell to have Branch touch him. He bit out the words to tell him he was hit in the shoulder, the bullet was still in him, he'd lost a lot of blood, and the bastards were all dead.

At once, Branch knew relief over the outlaws' deaths and fear for Colt. "It's a couple miles back to where the posse's camped. Can you make it there? We've got to get that bullet outta you, or you're gonna bleed to death."

Colt told him there wasn't time to ride back. "We've got to do it here."

Branch gave a low whistle. "I've taken plenty of bullets out, and I'm damn good at it, but I sure ain't never cut one out in the dark."

"Get a fire going," Colt said, his voice barely audible as he struggled against the dizziness and pain. "Either you try or I bleed to death."

Branch gathered dry sage and twigs. In moments, flames were licking up toward the sky. They could see each other in the yellow-gold light. Branch ripped Colt's shirt open, prodded the wound, and shook his head. "Hell, that's deep. I ain't got a good enough knife. I'll gouge you to dog meat."

Colt told him to look inside his boot, and in a moment Branch triumphantly held up the knife. "Hot damn! Your pa's old Arkansas toothpick. This'll do it!" He went to his horse, muttering, "Just one thing more . . ."

He found his bottle of whiskey in his saddlebag and held it out to Colt. His usually gruff voice was filled with pity as he instructed, "Take a big drink, boy. You're gonna need it."

Colt took several long swallows, coughing at the deep, burning sensation but welcoming the instant comfort.

Branch looked at him in silence for a moment, needing to steady himself as much as he needed to reassure Colt. "You ready?"

Colt hesitated. "Cut off the end of one of your reins," he said. "It'll give me something to bite down on."

A minute later, Colt had the length of leather in his mouth, his teeth clamped tightly, and he nodded to Branch to begin.

Taking a deep breath, Branch began probing into Colt's flesh, wincing as he felt the contortions of agony in Colt's body. He moved quickly, wanting to get it over with as soon as he could. The tip of the knife struck lead. Forcing himself not to hurry, Branch scooped, dug, gouged, then maneuvered the blade upward, grasping the bullet eagerly. "Got it!" Immediately he turned to the fire and held the knife blade in the licking flames, crying, "Hang on. Gotta stop that bleeding."

He pressed the red-hot steel against the wound, smelled the nauseating odor of burning flesh. The leather fell from Colt's mouth and he screamed once, then mercifully passed out.

Branch sat back gratefully, and found he was shaking. He stared at the bloodied piece of lead in his hand. Now he had to get Colt somewhere to rest.

He gazed back toward the posse's camp, but Colt was too weak to be moved that far just yet, Branch decided. He could sleep where they were until the next day.

Then they'd go due south, skirting the Esmeralda salt marshes and riding on into California, where there was a small mining camp, Golconda. Not much in the way of a town, it was mostly just a place where prospectors could come in from their digs and raise hell. It would be a good place for Colt to rest up.

Branch smiled as he thought about Golconda. Candy and her girls would be there. Candy ran one of the best bawdy houses in the West, and Branch had friends there. They'd be happy to look after Colt while Branch went back to Silver Butte to look after the Coltrane place till Colt could take over again.

Branch chuckled. Why, some of his best friends were whores, and he was proud of it. They made *nice* friends, and he figured that's just what Colt would be needing to pull him out of his grief—some nice friends.

Chapter Eight

EACH time his horse set a hoof against the rough, rocky terrain, a jabbing pain shot through Colt's shoulder, but thanks to constant sipping from Branch's bottle, there was a cushion against the agony. Soon they would be in Golconda, where he could rest while Branch returned to Silver Butte with the money stolen from the bank. The plan suited Colt just fine. He was in no hurry to go home to the memories . . . and Charlene's father.

Branch frowned as Colt drank again. "You better watch that stuff. You've been guzzlin' since we started out, and you're already weak from all the blood you lost."

Colt grinned. "We aren't far from Golconda now." Then he muttered, "Wonder if Candy is still around. Fine woman."

Branch looked more than a little surprised. "*You* know Candy?"

Colt hiccuped. He felt god-awful, but he'd be damned if he'd give in to misery.

"Well?" Branch prodded.

With false heartiness, Colt responded, "You don't know all my business. I've been riding down to Golconda since I was fourteen."

"Yeah?" Branch growled. "I'll bet your pa didn't know about it."

"Oh, I imagine he did," Colt said fondly. "Never was able to slip much by my father, you know. But he never said anything."

Branch knew Colt was hurting, hurting bad and putting up a front. He decided to help by coaxing his mind away from the pain. "Tell me," he urged, "which one of the girls do you like the best? Rosie? Tilly? Jennylou? Candy's got some fine-looking women."

Colt shook his head feebly. "I haven't been there for over a year." His words were becoming slurred and the buzzing in his head was getting louder, but he was determined to keep going. They could see the shanties and tents of Golconda, but he was having difficulty focusing.

"Well, tell me," Branch pressed on. "Which one did you like best?"

A wave of warmth moved through Colt that had nothing to do with the liquor. "Becky. Sweet as honey. Eyes that make you think of violets, and hair the color of sunrise, all red and gold."

Branch was confused. He knew all Candy's girls. He didn't boast about it, keeping his personal life to himself, but he made three or four trips a year down to Golconda, and he didn't know anyone named Becky. "You sure you ain't fevered? I don't know Becky."

Colt was locked in pleasant reverie. Several moments passed before he explained, "Becky is Candy's niece. She's not one of the *girls.* She just works at the place—cooking, cleaning, you know."

Branch cried, "And you been foolin' around with her? Are you crazy? Candy might seem like an easygoin' woman, but you get her riled and she can be a hellcat. I don't think she'd like you foolin' around with her niece. If she's still in Golconda, you forget about her, you hear? You ain't in no shape for that anyhow. I don't want Candy on my neck, understand? Leave her niece alone."

Colt didn't answer. He was having a hard time remaining upright, and he didn't want to waste his strength trying to explain. Branch had jumped to conclusions about how it was between him and Becky. No matter. It was not important that Branch be told the truth, that nothing had ever happened. Becky was sweet . . . special . . . untouched. Colt stayed away from virgins, just as his father had advised him. But there were times with Becky when Colt wished things could be different.

They rode in silence the rest of the way into Golconda.

The town, if it could even be called a town, consisted mostly of shanties and a few tents, temporary shelters for the prospectors and drifters who came and went. The only permanent structures, besides Candy's place, were a store and two saloons, both constructed of wood, both yielding to the ravages of time and the desert.

There was almost no vegetation. Tumbleweeds danced in the ever-present desert winds. Here and there a mesquite grew, brown and scraggly. There were no trees or grass, just rocks and sand, and a scattered cactus.

Golconda was in fact right in the middle of nowhere.

Candy's place was at the end of the town's only street. Easily the nicest thing to look at in town, it was kept whitewashed, and it sparkled in the brilliant sun. The shutters and trim were pink, as was the picket fence surrounding the yard. The house was two stories high, and a wide porch wrapped around the front.

Men standing in the street and outside the saloons did no more than glance at the duo as they rode in. No matter that one of them was slumped forward in the saddle, a blood-soaked bandage wrapped around his chest. Folks in Golconda minded their own business. It was a rough town, a rough life. Everyone tried to stay out of everyone else's business.

All appeared quiet at Candy's, but then, it was mid-morning on a weekday. Nights, especially weekends, would find men coming and going like small armies on parade.

Colt was nearly blinded by pain. He was dizzy and terribly weak. He felt warm—too warm. It was not the alcohol. A fever was spreading through his body. The wound was infected.

They drew up at the gate. Branch dismounted, tied their reins to the hitching post, and turned just as Colt fell from his horse. As he bent over him, Branch felt the burning heat radiating from his body and knew he had a raging fever. As gently as possible, he lifted the unconscious Colt and hurried up the steps to the house.

Candy Faro had rushed to the window in response to her servant's cry of alarm, and by the time Branch reached her front door, she had wrapped a pink satin robe around herself and was scurrying down the steps. "Hurry, let him in," she commanded the frightened Negro maid.

Branch stepped into the dimly lit foyer, glad to see Candy. On his pleasure visits, he always paused to admire the red velvet wallpaper and the big vases of ostrich feathers. It was a beautiful house. "Where can I put him?" he asked Candy. But before she could say anything, he ordered the maid, "Go get the doc. Fast."

Her mistress nodded for her to obey, and the girl ran from the house.

Candy led Branch down a narrow hallway, to the rear. They entered a dayroom in the back of the house. Six girls, in various stages of undress, stared curiously as they passed. Reaching a small room at the very back of the rambling house, Candy pointed to a sofa. "There. It's quiet here." She watched as Branch laid Colt down, then went over to get a better look at the wounded man. She whirled about, exclaiming, "That's Coltrane! What happened?"

Branch's eyes flicked over her appreciatively. She was a fine-looking woman—tall, slender, with large breasts that spilled provocatively from her plunging neckline. Her hair was flame red, obviously dyed, and her bright green eyes were framed by thick, long false eyelashes. Lavender shadow was smudged in the lines around her eyes. A little age on her, yes, but she was still most appealing. Branch was sorry that she never offered her own services, but she reserved herself for her long-running romance with a married lawman who came to town about once a month.

"Well, are you going to tell me?" Her arms were folded across her bosom, for she had seen the lust in his eyes. "I'm doing you a favor letting you bring him here, so I've got a right to know what happened."

Deciding it was all right, Branch told her everything except about Charlene Bowden. That, he felt, was Colt's business.

"It was too far back to Silver Butte," he finished. "He'd lost a lot of blood already. So I brought him here."

He walked to a side window and peered out, but he couldn't see the front of the house. "Where's that damn doctor?" he snapped.

Candy scowled. "Probably sleeping off a drunk, as usual. Poor excuse for a doctor, he is, but if he were any good, he wouldn't hang around here. Still, he's better than nothing. Luly will bring him as soon as she finds him. Meanwhile I'll take a look at that wound myself."

She went to the door and yelled, "Someone get Becky. Tell her I need hot water and three or four bandages. And whiskey." To Branch, she said, "He'll need that for cleaning the wound and for himself."

Branch grunted. "That's partly what's wrong with him now. He's been suckin' whiskey the whole way."

Candy pulled up a chair and sat down beside Colt. Very gently she removed his bandage, wincing at the sight of the ugly wound. "Goddamn, Branch! What'd you try to do? Burn him to death? Look at that mess."

"It's not as bad as it looks," Branch said huffily. "All he needs is lookin' after—and rest."

"He'll get both here."

Suddenly Branch realized how tired he was. "Any chance of getting some coffee and a bite to eat?"

She nodded toward the door. "Luly probably has something set back. Help yourself. We'll settle up the bill when he's on his feet."

Just as Branch started out of the room, a young woman rushed through the door. He was stunned by the sight of her lovely face, framed by curls in a sunburst of color. Her eyes were wide, bright, and beautiful. Their radiance could put a lilac to shame. She was tiny, but well proportioned, and he marveled at the peach softness of her complexion.

When she approached Colt, her hand flew to her lips, and a broken sob came from her. She rushed to the sofa and dropped to her knees, reaching out to touch his brow. "Colt," she whispered tremulously. "Oh, Colt, what happened to you?"

Candy looked at Branch and murmured, "This is Becky, my niece. They're old friends—but it's not what you think."

Branch merely nodded and left the room, finding the kitchen easily. Against a wall was a cabinet called a "pie safe," where leftover cooked foods were stored so that flies couldn't get to them. He opened one of the wooden doors and found a pan of cold cornbread. He crumbled several chunks into a bowl, then found a pitcher of buttermilk on the table and poured that over the cornbread.

He was just finishing his third bowl when Luly returned with Doc Maltby, so he pushed away from the table and went back to Colt. He was still unconscious. Doc Maltby's hands were shaky, and his eyes were puffy and bloodshot. He had a hell of a hangover, and Branch was glad the bullet was already out of Colt. Damned if he'd trust that old drunk to cut Colt.

Doc Maltby removed the bandage Candy had just put on. He made no comment when he saw the burned flesh, assuming it had been an emergency cutting to stop the bleeding. It had not succeeded fully, but the flow had been lessened. "Clean wound?" he asked. "The bullet is out?"

Branch stepped forward. "Had to cut it out, but it's out now."

Doc nodded. "It's a bad wound, but he should be all right. Keep him quiet. Keep him warm. Lots of broth. No solid food till he asks for it. I'll leave some quinine. That will bring down the fever.

"No booze," he ordered, getting to his feet and opening his leather bag to search for the quinine. "He's drunk now."

"You should be right on *that* diagnosis, Doc," Candy said.

He scowled at her, then went back to rummaging in his bag until he found what he was looking for. He handed her the vial of medicine, then picked up his bag and left.

Becky saw him out of the house, then rushed back, her face flushed, eyes glimmering with tears. "Would it be all right if I took care of him?" she asked her aunt. "Please? He knows me, and—"

"You have plenty around here to keep you busy," Candy interrupted, regarding her suspiciously. "Luly can care for him fine."

Becky shook her head, face set with determination. "You have to let me, Aunt Candy. Colt knows me. We're friends. He'll feel better having me look after him, I know he will. Please."

Branch glanced away uncomfortably. Now he knew

who Becky was. He'd recognized her when he'd first seen her. He also understood now why he hadn't known who Colt was talking about earlier. Like the rest of Candy's girls, Becky didn't use her real name. She was known as Bella, and the last time he'd been there, men were standing in line for her. She was one of the most popular girls at Candy's place. Young. Fresh. Pretty. Angelic. The men really went after her. He hadn't, and was he ever glad now that he hadn't. There were two or three who were his regular choices, had been for years, and he seldom tried anyone new. Oh, hot damn, he thought with a shake of his head, was he ever glad he hadn't had the urge to visit Bella.

He looked down at Colt and shook his head with pity. He was sure as hell not going to be happy when he learned the truth about the woman he thought was an angel. And Branch did not want to be around when that happened. Suddenly Branch couldn't wait to get back to Silver Butte and stay there.

Candy was studying her niece's imploring face, and Branch broke into her contemplation by saying, "I'm heading back, Candy. If I don't get back this way to check on him—and I probably won't, with all I'll have to do back home—just send him on when he's able.

"You know you'll be paid well for doing this," Branch added as he strode to the door. "Just take good care of him."

Candy absently called out that he was not to worry, then turned her full attention to her niece again. She placed a gentle hand on Becky's arm and murmured, "We should talk about this somewhere else, in case he wakes up."

Obediently Becky followed Candy upstairs to her private office. Once inside, with the door closed, Candy went to sit behind her Louis IV desk. From a crystal decanter she poured them each a small glass of cognac, then settled back in her blue velvet chair.

"Now then," she began, after sipping the cognac, "let's be candid with each other, honey. You're in love with Coltrane, and you're only going to torture yourself by hanging around him. You're much better off—and so is he—if you just stay out of sight. Let Luly look after him. This is no good for you."

Becky shook her head. "No. I want to take care of him."

"And when he finds out? What then?" Candy raised an eyebrow. "I remember the last time. I was the one who heard you crying when Colt spent the night with another woman. I was the one who held you and let you cry when he rode out of your life. It can't work, honey, you know that by now. Let it be. You have a future here, and as the rest of the girls will tell you, you're a fool to fall in love—ever. Men are for one thing only, and that's for paying. They're not for anything else. Remember that. That way, you won't wind up with a broken heart."

Becky was used to her aunt's beliefs. She wasn't shocked. She even agreed with some of her philosophies, but not where Colt was concerned. She recalled with total clarity those magical days when she and Colt grew to know each other, to become so close. It was wonderful, and, yes, she had sobbed like a baby when he took one of her aunt's girls to bed, but she consoled herself by deciding that he had been driven by the desire she had kindled. She had been a virgin, and he hadn't wanted to take her innocence. She loved him for that kindness, that tenderness.

"Becky."

She glanced up and saw the hard expression in her aunt's eyes.

"When you knew Coltrane before, you were not a prostitute. You were a dewy-eyed little girl from back East, sent out here because your mother died and your father couldn't raise you alone. Your father had no idea I was a madam, that I run a brothel, for God's sake. Like everybody else back there, he believes I'm a schoolteacher at a mission for Indians. I was wrong to take you in and I see that now, because, heaven knows, I never intended to take you into the business. That was an accident."

Becky lifted a hand in protest, fresh tears stinging her eyes. She didn't want to be reminded, but Aunt Candy was all fired up now.

Teeth clenched, Candy growled venomously, "I could kill Jake Wingate. If he walked through that door, I'd take my gun out of the drawer and shoot him right in that damn dick he's so proud of. If I'd been here that night, it *never* would've happened. I don't let drunks in. You know that. But I *wasn't* here, and he *did* come in, and he forced his way into your room and raped you and there was nobody to stop him."

"Aunt Candy, please!" Becky screamed, covering her face with her hands. "I can't stand it. Stop, please! We can't undo it and I can't stand thinking about it."

"I should have found a way to stop you from getting in the business," Candy sighed. "I should've sent you away. But you said you knew what you wanted, and I figured I'd best let you deal with it your own way. Until now, I thought maybe it was the right way, because you're a natural." She paused to gulp down the rest of her cognac, eyeing Becky critically. "That angelic face, big bosom, tiny waist, curvy hips—men drool over you. Why, you make more money than any of—"

"Stop it!" Becky leaped to her feet and leaned across the desk, pressing trembling fingers against the smooth surface. She knew very well what her aunt was up to. "I won't listen to any more of this. I know why you're reminding me of what I am, but I want a chance to be with Colt one last time. He doesn't have to know the truth."

Her voice broke. "I love him, Aunt Candy. I know I can never have him, but I love him. I never knew how much till I saw him lying there hurt. Just let me get him back on his feet, and I'll never speak of him again."

Candy had known the true depth of the girl's pain, had tried to put a stop to this nonsense, but her own eyes filled with tears and she ran around the desk and gathered her niece in her arms, cradling Becky as she sobbed. "Honey, honey, I'm not going to say no," she soothed. "I just wanted to remind you who you are now, so you don't get impossible dreams. I don't want to see you get hurt any more than you already have been. It'd be different if he was a customer, somebody you pleasured and then fell in love with. That might work out for you. But you aren't what he thinks you are, and if he finds out, what happened between you before you came into the life won't mean a damn thing. You know that. Don't you think you'd better just leave it? Keep the good memories. Don't see him while he's here."

But Becky wouldn't budge. "If you refuse," she warned, "I'll do it anyway. So you might as well make arrangements for my regular customers. I'm going to take care of Colt until he can take care of himself."

Candy sighed. "All right. I'll tell the other girls to stay away from both of you and keep their mouths shut. And I'll tell your regulars that you're out of town. Just hurry and get him out of here. I don't like this situation at all."

Becky left the room and hurried to the back room downstairs where Colt was. She did not like the situation, either. She had decided on the life she had. It helped ease the pain of the rape. And she made lots of money. One day, perhaps, she would do as some of the other girls did: marry and have a home, and children. She was not what they called a "hard-lifer." She hated the life, and she hated the men who paid to fondle and slobber over her body. Her becoming a prostitute had been the tragic result of Jake Wingate's defiling her. She felt that, by taking money for her body, by making it clear that she held all men in contempt, she was making men pay for Jake's cruelty. She took out her hatred of Jake on all men.

All men, that is, except Colt. Gentle, tender, kind, he was the only man she'd ever loved. She had thought she might never see him again.

Now he was back. Wounded. She was going to take care of him, and she was going to savor every moment of it.

Then, when he was gone from her again, she would go back to work. She bit her lip to hold back fresh tears. All she could hope for was to thicken the wall she had built around her feelings.

Entering the back room, she found Luly watching over Colt, who was sleeping. She settled herself in a chair next to the sofa and told Luly she could go. Doc Maltby had put a fresh bandage on Colt's wound, and there were blankets tucked around him.

Becky began to apply cold cloths, provided by Luly, to Colt's head in an attempt to lessen his fever. Now and then he stirred slightly, moaned, and she hoped he was waking up, but he always fell asleep again.

Morning faded to afternoon, and then evening shadows began to fall. Luly came in to light the lanterns, filling the room with a mellow, golden light.

Becky held Colt's hand and squeezed. Her heart felt warm, full, happy. Fate would part them once again, so she knew she had to make the most of every precious moment.

She dozed. A little later she was awakened by the sound of his mutterings. She leaned closer, wincing as he spoke a name: "Charlene." Who was that? Had he found another love?

He stirred. His lashes fluttered, and then his dark

eyes attempted to focus on her. His voice was barely audible as he teased, "I see an angel."

She laughed softly. "No, it's only me—Becky."

He closed his eyes and nodded sleepily. "Yes, I do see an angel." Then he slept again, and her tears fell on his face.

Chapter Nine

BRIANA fell in love with the Coltrane mansion. Though not as opulent as the deBonnett château, it was much more spacious and there was an air about the place that was definitely alluring. She could close her eyes and feel the love, the happiness. It was, she decided, as though the house was smiling.

It was sad that Dani hadn't spent her childhood there, Briana decided. Of course, Briana didn't know the Coltranes, but she felt that they must be good-hearted people, or else their house wouldn't feel so loving.

Certainly the cold and arrogant Madame Alaina wouldn't fit in here, she thought. It was remarkable that, after growing up in such a dismal atmosphere as Madame Alaina's household, Dani had the spirit necessary to dedicate her life to the church.

Briana sat on the back steps, staring out at the stable and the rolling plains beyond, plains framed by distant mountains. It was a warm day, and the butter-gold sun felt good as it melted across her bare arms. She was wearing one of Dani's dresses, a pale-green cotton that revealed far too much of her bosom. She gave it a tug upward, but the deep décolletage still revealed too much of her large breasts. She had that problem with all Dani's clothes, and when she'd tried to alter them, Gavin had angrily ordered her not to, saying he wanted her bosom displayed. She had argued, and he had reminded her that he controlled her brother's fate. Their arguments always ended like that.

She breathed deeply of the sweet air. Yes, it was beautiful here, peaceful and serene. But she would be glad when the deed was done and she could go home to France—and be free of Gavin Mason.

How she loathed that man! The voyage to America had been terrible. He had insisted that they spend every moment together so that he could tutor her. Over and over, he forced her to talk, teaching her to enunciate with only a trace of a French accent. He told her every kernel of information Alaina had passed to him about Dani and the Coltrane family.

"But the best thing for you to do," Gavin said repeatedly, "is just keep your mouth shut. The less you speak, the less chance for making a mistake, and the less chance for anyone to become suspicious. When I am around, I will do the talking."

She had frequently begged him to tell her his whole plan, and that always made him angry. "You have no need to know," he shouted. "I'll tell you what to do and when to do it. Meanwhile, just be charming to your brother. That's all you have to worry about."

Thus far, Briana hadn't even had to do that. She had yet to meet John Travis Coltrane, though nearly three weeks had passed since their arrival in Silver Butte.

She recalled the events of the day they arrived by stagecoach from San Francisco, having taken the route Gavin wanted to take. Weary from the rugged ride, she had wished only for a place to lie down, but Gavin had led her directly to the first bank he spotted.

"We have to get horses and then find our way to the Coltrane ranch," he explained brusquely. "I'm sure the bankers will know exactly where it is. Hell, the Coltranes probably *own* the damn bank," he laughed greedily.

So Gavin had approached a bank officer and introduced Briana as the daughter of Travis Coltrane, and himself as her stepbrother.

Briana hadn't missed the strange expression that passed over the man's face as he informed them that the Coltranes did not do business with his bank, but that he would help them in any way he could.

Gavin said, "Well, we are arriving without notice, and eventually we'll need directions to the Coltrane ranch, but since we're here now, we might as well introduce ourselves to people we will be doing business with while we're in Silver Butte. Would you be so kind as to direct us to the bank where the family does do business?"

The man gave them directions, and then as Gavin thanked him, he said nervously, "Wait. I—I think there's something you should know."

Gavin and Briana waited, and then he said, "Have you been in contact with the family at all . . . recently?"

Gavin's eyes narrowed. "Why do you ask?"

The man gestured helplessly. "I really hate to be the one to tell you about this, but you surely don't know, or else you would not be going to the Bowden Bank."

Gavin began to look wary. "Well? What do you want to tell us?"

The man looked away, then let the words out in a rush. "There was a robbery at the Bowden Bank. Mr. Bowden's daughter was killed." He glanced at Briana before continuing. "She was Colt's fiancée. He went with the posse after the robbers, but he didn't come back with them, and . . ." His voice trailed off.

"Why not?" Gavin asked tensely.

"I . . . I don't like to spread gossip," the man stammered.

Briana knew Gavin was becoming angrier with each moment. But he got a tight rein on himself and said, "Please tell me whatever else you know."

The bank officer confided the gossip, explaining that

Carleton Bowden was bitterly holding Colt responsible for his daughter's death because of an argument they'd had shortly before she was killed. Further, he told them that the Coltranes' ranch foreman had ridden in one day with the recovered gold, and that Colt was wounded during a shoot-out with the bank robbers and was recuperating somewhere south of Silver Butte. "So," he finished, "if I were you, I'd watch what I said to Mr. Bowden. In fact, I don't think I'd even go near him. He probably hates all the Coltranes now." He tried not to look at Briana.

Outside the bank, Gavin was unable to contain his exuberance. "This is even better than I'd hoped for! Young Coltrane has disfavored himself in this town, and that is definitely to our advantage."

Briana was so filled with dislike for the whole business that she said, "Can't we just claim Dani's money and leave?" She knew this would make Gavin angry but wanted to say her piece anyway.

He gripped her arm painfully, jerking her along the boardwalk toward the Bowden Bank. "We'll leave when I say we leave, so don't bring it up again. I've got enough on my mind without having to listen to you whine."

As they made their way down the boardwalk toward the Bowden Bank, Briana pulled her plaid shawl tightly around herself, glad for the cover, such as it was. She wasn't cold, as it was a warm day, but she felt so naked on the occasion of her first performance as an imposter that she needed something to cling to. Dani's bright green-and-red shawl was better than nothing.

Entering the Bowden Bank, Briana stiffened, wondering what Gavin would do. He led her to one of the teller windows and, in a voice thick with counterfeit compassion, said to a pleasant-faced middle-aged woman, "Good morning. I am Gavin Mason, and this is Miss Dani Coltrane. We just arrived from Europe and heard about the misfortune suffered by the Bowden family. We've come to convey our condolences, and"—he paused for emphasis—"to apologize on behalf of the Coltrane family."

The woman appraised him silently, then said, "I will inquire if Mr. Bowden will see you."

She disappeared through a door at the rear of the room and was gone for only a few moments before returning to say that Mr. Bowden would see them.

She escorted them to his private office, where he was sitting behind his desk, waiting for them. Briana was struck by the deep grief etched on his face. Stiffly he listened to Gavin's introductions and condolences, remaining seated behind his massive desk. He did not invite them to sit down. When Gavin finished speaking, he said gruffly, "What do you want with me? Is this visit personal or business? If it's business, you can deal with one of the officers. If it's personal, there's nothing to say."

Gavin took a seat, motioning to Briana to do the same. Ignoring Bowden's scowl, he leaned across the desk intimately. "This is in strictest confidence, sir," he began, while Briana looked on, amazed by his acting ability and his nerve.

"I don't know whether you are aware of this," Gavin continued conspiratorially, "but Dani has been estranged from the Coltrane family since she was a child. We knew nothing about this tragedy until we arrived in Silver Butte. We were shocked beyond words."

Carleton Bowden's expression softened just a little. "Mr. Mason, if you have business with this bank, please let one of my staff assist you. I am still in mourning, even though my responsibilities require me to be here."

Gavin shook his head. "I *have* to deal with you personally, Mr. Bowden. Quite frankly, I had wondered how to approach you about this, but now, in view of the rumors I've heard about your animosity toward the Coltrane family, it is imperative that I deal only with you."

Briana turned her head away, dismayed. She had listened in silent horror as Gavin lied about how he expected resentment from Travis Coltrane's son when he learned his half sister had come to Silver Butte to claim her share of the family money. Carleton Bowden was becoming less forbidding with each word Gavin spoke.

"So," Gavin went on, "you can see that we might need your help if Coltrane proves to be a problem. Dani and I both also hope that we can count on your friendship, because we don't know anyone here."

The bank president actually smiled as he addressed himself to Briana. "Of course. It would be a grave injustice for me to take out my feelings for Coltrane on either of you. You will be staying here, then? Living in Silver Butte? You are not interested in simply selling your properties?"

Briana wanted desperately to say yes, that was just what she wanted to do—sell everything and return to France. But Gavin gave her a warning look. Then he announced that, for the time being, she meant to stay in Silver Butte.

Mr. Bowden nodded. "Very well. When you need my help, come straight to me. I will do what I can."

Gavin said that if all the Coltrane business was handled through the Bowden Bank, then he wanted a financial statement. He added contemptuously, "We doubt that Coltrane would give us an honest appraisal of the estate."

"I will take care of it at once," Bowden agreed. "Is there anything else I can do for you now?"

Gavin asked for specific directions to the ranch. Then, as they prepared to leave, he asked whether Bowden knew how long Colt would be away.

"Forever, I hope," Bowden stated, then added, "I

hear he was shot in the shoulder, but he's getting better."

He glanced apologetically at Briana before finishing, "He's staying at a brothel in a place called Golconda."

Briana and Gavin rode out to the ranch. Gavin made sure that Briana was introduced to all the servants, and he made it clear that she was now in charge of the household. Then he returned to Silver Butte to stay at a hotel there, which was a great relief to Briana.

One afternoon, after Gavin had harangued her for an hour on the necessity of playing her role well, informing her half a dozen times that she owed him everything and that he held Charles's future in his hands, Briana heaved a huge sigh of relief as he departed, bound for the relatively cosmopolitan atmosphere of Silver Butte. How fortunate for her that the ranch bored him!

She went in search of the Mexican housekeeper, Carlota, who had offered to help her let out some of Dani's bodices. Briana had murmured something about gaining weight since she'd bought the gowns. She and Gavin had packed all the clothing from Dani's wardrobe that Briana might need, a few bonnets and all of Dani's gowns and shoes, knowing how lucky they were that things fit. If they'd had to order things made for Briana, the journey to America would have been delayed a month.

The only problem was in the bodices, which were too small by a couple of inches. Dani had good clothes, however, so there was ample material to let things out. A few gowns, the ones made of linen or cotton or silk, would require some ironing to straighten out the alterations so that the gowns didn't show the old stitching. One gown, of gauze, could not be altered at all because the old seams would show.

Briana was grateful that the bustle style had either been played out or failed to arrive yet, for she saw no evidence of it in Silver Butte. She'd hated to think she'd have to wear the silly things and had wondered whether she would. They were still in vogue in France, so Gavin had insisted on her bringing Dani's bustle-style gowns. Having never worn anything frivolous in her servant life, Briana was much relieved when they arrived in Nevada and she saw plain skirts with undercrinolines. She didn't believe she could have worn anything so preposterous looking as bustles, not even to make a good impression in Silver Butte.

All the afternoon after Gavin's departure, she and Carlota worked on the bodices of Dani's gowns. As Carlota lovingly fingered the silks and satins, Briana longed to tell her that she, too, was a stranger to luxury. But she refrained, contenting herself with keeping up a conversation with the woman, glad to have a chance to talk with another female. Carlota was friendly and kind, and Briana was grateful to have her in the house.

As she sat there recollecting, Briana saw someone walking toward the stable. She watched with interest when she recognized Branch Pope, for despite his obvious coolness toward her, she liked him. He was obviously confused as to how to behave around her. Colt, his boss, was away, and since she was half owner of the ranch and silver mine, she was also his boss.

Gavin had told her to stay away from him, but Briana was lonely. She waved at Branch, and he waved back. What harm would it do, she asked herself, to go down to the stables and have a chat with him? She would be careful not to give herself away. It was a beautiful day, and she was bored with being inside and having no one to talk to.

Inside the stable, where she loved the smell of sweet hay and the magnificent horses, Briana found Branch saddling a big black stallion. "He's one of my favorites," she said suddenly, her voice piercing the silence.

Branch whirled around, surprised. "Oh, Miss Dani." He nodded politely, then turned back to the horse, tightening the cinch around his girth. "This here is Janus. He's your daddy's pride and joy. Had him brought over all the way from Arabia when he was just a colt."

She stepped closer and reached up to stroke the great animal's silky mane. He jerked his head, pawing the ground in warning, and she jumped back.

Branch laughed. "Watch yourself. He's high-spirited. Your pa, me, and your brother are the only ones that have ever been able to ride him. I figured I'd better take him out for a run so he won't get fat and lazy, but it'll probably be *him* that gives *me* a run."

She reached to stroke the horse once more, and this time he merely regarded her with those large black eyes. "I would love to ride him," she whispered.

Branch looked her over curiously. "Had much riding experience?"

"Not any," she replied.

"Hard to imagine Travis Coltrane's daughter not knowing how to ride," he muttered.

Briana tensed, wondering whether she'd said something to make him suspicious. Quickly she lied, "Aunt Alaina was thrown from a horse once and almost killed, and she never allowed me near one after that."

He shook his head in sympathy. "That's a shame. Best thing to do if a horse throws you is get right back on again." He pointed to a chestnut mare in the next stall. "That's Miss Kitty's mare. She's pretty gentle, and she's used to riding with Janus. I could put a saddle on her if you'd like me to give you a few lessons."

Briana could hardly contain herself. She clapped her hands together gleefully and cried, "Oh, would you, Mr. Pope? I'd love that. I really would."

"Sure," he said pleasantly, then went to the tack room and came back carrying a saddle. "Just do as I tell you."

He showed her how to mount and how to sit in the saddle, then handed her the reins. "Take it slow and easy. Move with her moves. Relax and don't tense up or act scared. A horse can always tell when the rider is scared, and that makes 'em act sassy. Let her know you're in control—or make her think you are!" He laughed good-naturedly.

Briana was delighted. It all seemed so easy. Branch watched her carefully as they headed out of the stable and across the yard. "Should've known you'd be a natural," he said, impressed by her confidence. "Travis Coltrane's daughter would take to a horse like a duck to water."

She felt a twinge of guilt. He was a nice man. All the people she'd met so far were nice . . . and she was lying to them all. Well, she would try not to think about that, and remind herself that this was for Charles.

They walked their horses across the plain, toward the rolling river. A gentle breeze was blowing, and the sweet air was fragrant with wildflowers that bloomed among the rocks.

Eventually Branch led her horse into a trot, Janus impatient beside the mare. Briana loved it. "Yep, you're a natural," Branch complimented as they rode on into the warm, golden day. "A real Coltrane."

Briana closed her eyes, feeling the cool wind against her face. In that moment she wished she *were* a Coltrane, that this was her real home.

Then she thought of Charles, and felt a pang of guilt. Whatever the future held, she would have to return to France and her meager existence there. She had no illusions that Gavin would give her anything beyond what it took to pay for Charles's medical care. Poverty would once again become a way of life for Briana, and this happiness would become only a bittersweet memory.

But for the time being she could pretend she actually *was* Dani, that this was her real life. She would, she decided in that blissful moment, become completely absorbed in her role. She would truly become Dani . . . and savor the joy for as long as it lasted.

There would be enough time to contemplate the bleakness of her future.

Many miles south, two riders ascended a grassy knoll, then dismounted and stood gazing out at the panorama that stretched in all directions.

Colt clasped Becky's hand and smiled down at her. "I'm glad I talked you into this. I needed the exercise, not to mention getting out of that house for a few hours."

Becky did not speak. Her mind was churning with a maelstrom of emotions. It hadn't been easy to carry out the pretense that she was a maid in her aunt's house. Some of her regular men had made unpleasant scenes when told she wasn't available, and Aunt Candy was becoming more and more irritable over the situation.

Colt squeezed her hand. "You haven't said a word since we left Golconda. What's wrong?"

Becky didn't trust herself to speak, lest she burst into tears. Aunt Candy was right. She was a fool.

He pulled her gently into his arms, cupping her chin in his hand to tilt her face toward his.

Becky struggled to keep from bursting into uncontrollable sobs. The moment had come.

His lips came down on hers, warm, seeking, tender—yet possessive and demanding. He held her gently, his hands moving down her back to cup her firm, rounded buttocks and pull her tightly against him. She felt the hard swelling of his desire and gasped. Drawing his mouth away from hers, he smiled and whispered, "Are you surprised? Haven't you seen it before, beneath the sheets in bed when you were caring for me? Haven't you known how I've wanted you, Becky? Hungered for you?"

She shook her head and tried to pull away, but he held her firmly.

"I've often wished that I'd made love to you the first time we met." His tone was fierce. "You don't know the hours I've lain awake at night dreaming about you, how wonderful it would be to hold you in my arms, to kiss you all over, to come inside you. . . ." His lips pressed against hers once more, their tongues touching in soul-searing thirst.

He drew her gently to the ground, to lie upon the soft grass. The sun was sinking, and the night wind stirring in the desert provoked them.

Becky attempted to resist by saying nervously, "It's late. Aunt Candy will be worried."

"Aunt Candy," Colt laughed, "can go to hell." His fingers worked at the buttons on the front of her yellow muslin gown. "So can the whole world. Here and now, my sweet, I'm going to show you how much I want you . . . how much I care."

Becky could no longer deny her own hunger, and when he bent his head to suckle her breasts, she gasped and cried out, arching her back to press herself closer to Colt. Dimly the taunting thoughts came to her of other men, other lips on her nipples, other hands kneading her breasts. Oh, but never, never like this!

Colt was the only man she had ever truly desired, and she had lain awake countless nights dreaming of being possessed by him. Now there was no stopping her. She wanted him with every beat of her heart. She wanted not only to take what he yearned to give, but to bestow on him all the pleasure she had to offer.

He licked each nipple in turn, his hands making circular movements upon her breasts before moving downward. He kissed her belly, and then he was moving her skirt and petticoats up to expose her legs, her thighs, rendering her vulnerable to his tender assault.

He parted her womanhood with his fingertips, touching her with his seeking, hungry tongue. Becky moaned. It was so sweet as to be almost painful. She had never allowed a man to do this to her.

"Relax," he whispered thickly. "I'm not going to hurt you. I'll be very gentle. . . ."

Becky kept her eyes shut, was glad she couldn't see his face. He thought her a virgin, of course.

Slowly, carefully, she found the pocket of her dress and closed trembling fingers around the tiny vial Aunt Candy had given her, recalling her aunt's words: "When the time comes—and it will—you can make him think you're a virgin. It's chicken blood. Just pop it open and let it dribble between your legs. He'll never know the difference. Women have been doing this since the beginning of time."

Becky felt hot stabs of pleasure, knew that the moment she'd dreamed of, but never experienced, was near. She wanted him inside her, wanted to feel his manhood pulsing deep within, and she reached for him and pulled him upward. "Now," she said, and barely recognized her own voice. Never had she heard herself sound so warm, or so hungry. "Inside me. Please, Colt, I want you inside me."

He was looking at her adoringly, and she was so utterly transfixed by his gaze that she almost forgot the vial. A second before he penetrated her, she slipped it beneath her, pretending momentary pain. He slowed his movements, whispering that she should relax, relax and let him give her pleasure. Once she'd snapped open the vial and emptied its contents, she slipped it back into her pocket and let her love for Colt take over again.

They clung together tightly, and Becky cried out with delight and joy when rapture peaked. This was the ultimate, and she would never know such ecstasy again except with Colt.

His explosion made her as happy as her own, and afterward, they lay quiet, wrapped around each other.

He lay with her face cradled against his face, and

when the tears she could no longer restrain spilled against his cheek, he drew back to gaze down at her quizzically. "Did I hurt you, Becky?" he asked.

"No, no—" She shook her head, her curls brushing against his bare skin. "I don't know why I'm crying, really." She could not go on—the despair was too great to bear—and she burrowed her face against him.

He held her and ran his fingers lovingly through her hair. "You're crying because you know I have to leave soon—and I do. I can't expect Branch to look after things forever."

"When?" she asked, relieved to let him think his departure was the reason for her tears.

He sighed, not really wanting to talk. "A few days, I guess. We'll see. I don't want to think about it, either. But I'll come back, Becky. You just won't know when I might come riding up to your door," he teased.

Becky tensed. The thought was terrifying. What if he came when she was with a man?

She began trembling, and because she was so upset, he decided they needed to talk seriously. "There's something I want to say to you," he told her, eyes intense. "Something you ought to know."

He told her about Charlene. All of it. Her eyes widened with shock, and by the time he'd finished she was almost speechless.

"Did you . . ." She hesitated, fearing the answer. "Did you love her, Colt?"

"In a way, maybe I did. But not enough to marry her. And that's why I told you all this, Becky. I don't ever want to hurt you, so I want you to know how things are with me. I care for you a great deal, but we're going to have to give this a lot of time. Marriage is not in my immediate future, Becky, and you've got to know that." He stared deeply into her eyes, searching for some sign that she understood. "Don't expect more than I can give. I don't ever want to hurt another woman like that, and women think of marriage when they—they care for someone."

She touched his cheek. "It's not your fault, Colt. Not any of it. Stop blaming yourself, please."

He moved a little away and lay on his back looking up at the lavender sky. An evening star glittered just above the horizon, and he fixed his gaze on that. "That's something I'll always have to live with . . . wondering if it was my fault."

They lay side by side for a long time, and then Colt wrapped her in his strong arms once again. "It will be easier this time," he murmured huskily against her hair.

Becky took a long, deep breath. Yes, it was always easier to lie the second time.

Chapter Ten

BRANCH called Dani a natural for ranch life, and Briana secretly, happily, agreed. After only a few riding lessons, she felt at ease on horseback. And her time with Branch was always enjoyable. No longer was he reserved or cold. Why, he was downright friendly.

Briana was everlastingly grateful that Gavin seldom came out to the ranch. When he did come, she had to be careful, for he had told her to keep to herself and have as little as possible to do with the servants and ranch hands. She knew he wouldn't like it that she spent all her time outdoors, learning all she could about horses and cattle and ranching. He would like it even less if he knew how friendly she was with Branch.

Briana fell in love with the desert. Out there, riding with Branch, she was ready to believe the deception didn't exist, Gavin didn't exist, and her own part in the scenario had magically changed from imposter to . . . well, she didn't know just what, exactly, except that she felt as though she *belonged*. Belonged with Branch Pope out there riding the flat terrain, looking up at the majestic Sierra Nevada Mountains. Belonged at the lovely Coltrane mansion, dining with Colt or chatting with Carlota in the kitchen—she, who had so recently been a servant herself!

When she was on the plains, she marveled at the

subtle colors. On the seacoast of Monaco, everything was less dramatic looking, softer, and the sky was a very light blue. On the stark desert, there was sagebrush and rocky soil. The mountains loomed dark brown, altogether different from the Monaco seacoast. The sunsets were different on the desert, too, richer, with glints of yellow and orange besides the mauve and red she was used to seeing.

In those times on the desert with Branch, Briana could be someone other than an imposter, someone new and clean and fresh. She even stopped worrying about Charles when she was riding with Branch, a respite she felt guilty over while welcoming it nevertheless.

She had begun going to the bunkhouse in the mornings to join the men for breakfast. She enjoyed the opulence of the big house, but she so loved the coziness of the bunkhouse. Constructed of rough-hewn logs, it was long and narrow, with double-decker beds lined up on both sides. At the end of the room, opposite the front door, was an open space for long tables and benches, and there was a large stone fireplace to the right of that area. The air always smelled of fresh-boiled coffee and leather, and she loved the odd combination.

Breakfast was hearty, with lots of variety, as were all the meals prepared for the men by Chouyin, the Chinese cook. Briana wasn't able to eat a large steak with two fried eggs on top, but the men did. She was amazed by the quantity of food consumed by the three dozen ranch hands. Not only did each eat at least one steak, some ate two, along with crispy fried potatoes, oatmeal laced with honey, and large, fluffy biscuits laden with fresh-churned butter. There was coffee, and milk was cooled in the nearby stream. Sometimes there was juice made from Muscadine grapes that grew wild along the barbed-wire fences bordering the eastern end of the Coltrane property.

Briana liked the wranglers. Rugged though they

were, these men were gentle with her, treating her with respect, while making her feel welcome.

Branch had found a couple of pairs of trousers that were not too large for her, and she much preferred her new pants to the muslin and cotton day dresses filched from Dani's wardrobe in France. The plaid flannel shirts Branch found for her felt soft and warm. She even had boots, which Branch bought for her in town, and a large felt hat. She felt like a true western woman, besides being happier than she'd ever been.

One morning, after she'd been at the ranch for three weeks, Branch drew her aside after breakfast and apologetically told her that he was going to have to spend a few days at the silver mine. "I'd take you with me, Dani, but it's dangerous there for a woman. Colt wouldn't like it if I did, and that stepbrother of yours," he added contemptuously, "would take a fit. So you just find something to do while I'm gone."

There was more. She listened, disappointed, while he told her he didn't want her to ride alone. "Too many things can happen, Dani. Sidewinder rattlers, coyotes. You might even get lost. Stay close to the house, please."

She hung back that morning, watching Branch ride away, wondering what she was going to do with herself for the next few days. The thought of sitting alone in that big house made her feel blue. The depression led to a mood of great unhappiness, and suddenly she found herself wishing it would all end so that she could go home.

This was, she told herself dismally, turning into a fantasy world. It had become too easy to pretend this was *her* world, to forget the misery that waited for her at home as she struggled to make a living for herself and Charles. The truth was, the longer she stayed on the Coltrane ranch, the harder it was going to be when she had to leave.

"Don't pay no attention to Pope."

She whirled around, nervous, as she saw Dirk Hollister. For some reason, she never felt at ease around him. The way he looked at her, his eyes constantly shifting from her face to her bosom, made her feel as though he could see right through her clothes. He wasn't actually sinister looking. In fact, he was attractive, in a rough sort of way. His dark, unruly hair was too long, but he had a nice face, with finely chiseled features, and his blue eyes were fringed with long lashes. Tall, well built, he could be a handsome man, she realized, if he cleaned himself up and worked on his manners.

His eyes darted to her bosom. "Pope acts like an old woman sometimes. But I've seen you ride, and I know you can take care of yourself."

"He *is* the ranch foreman," she reminded him. Dirk was a new man Branch had hired during Colt's absence. He was a drifter; she knew that much about him and no more.

He gave her a taunting smile. "Don't you own half this place? Well, so that makes you *his* boss, Miss Dani."

Briana nodded. "That's true, but I don't want to make trouble. After all, I've never been around a ranch before. Or that wilderness out there." She gestured to the plains surrounding them.

He shrugged, grinning down at her, standing with his feet wide apart and his thumbs hooked in his belt. "If you'd rather stay in the house on a nice day like today instead of riding out with me to round up strays, okay by me."

He tipped his hat and turned to leave. "Wait," she called out impulsively, her mind racing. Branch took her on pleasure rides exclusively, so she had never seen much of the workings of the ranch.

"Do you really think it would be all right?" she asked hesitantly. "Branch wouldn't be angry with us?"

"Of course not," he assured her. "Come on, Miss

Dani. We'll go get Belle saddled. Pope won't even know about it unless you tell him."

Soon they were riding away from the ranch, the bright morning sun beaming down on the plains. A hawk spiraled in the azure sky high above them, and she wondered how much territory he covered in a day. She'd ask Branch. There was so much she didn't know. She'd learned the names of many plants, though, and she recited them to herself as she rode: greasewood, mesquite, creosote, yucca. At higher elevations there would be sagebrush and Joshua trees, junipers, mountain mahogany, firs, and spruce trees.

A covey of quail darted in front of them, and Briana laughed. "They look like fat baby chickens, don't they?"

"Chickens!" Dirk mocked, not unkindly. "Their feathers aren't as long as a chicken's. But they sure taste better'n chicken when you roast 'em over an open fire."

In the distance, on the southwestern horizon, the Sierra Nevadas rose majestically. In the winter, she'd been told, they would be capped by snow.

"It's all so beautiful," she told Dirk, and he agreed.

"Maybe one day I can take you for a really long ride, out to the Alkali Desert and the Toiyabe Range. That's still wilderness. Of course, Nevada was all wilderness before the Comstock lode was discovered. Prospectors sometimes passed through on their way to California, but not much else happened."

Briana asked him where he was from, and a guarded look came over his face. "Nowhere particular, Miss Dani. I don't know where I was born, and I never knew my parents. It's like all of a sudden I was just *here.*"

"But where did you grow up?" she prodded. "Surely relatives raised you, or—?"

"Nobody raised me," he snarled. "I just got by on my own. I've never stayed in one place. I just keep moving." His voice leveled a little as he finished, "The world is too big to stay in one place."

They rode for a while in silence, Briana embarrassed to have pried.

"What's it like in France?" he asked suddenly. "I'd like to go to Europe when I've seen all there is to see here."

She told him about the south coast of France, about the rocky cliffs and jutting mountains, the endless blue sea with pebble-covered beaches.

He listened, then remarked, "And you think *this* is beautiful? I should think you'd rather be back in France. But I guess a rich person gets bored and restless. Probably nothing satisfies you," he added, a sudden coldness in his voice.

Briana almost laughed. Rich? The deBonnett family believed that a roof over their servants' heads and leftovers from the main kitchen was an adequate wage!

Dirk mistook her silence for acquiescence and glanced at her with contempt.

A moment later, he saw what he was looking for: five stray heifers grazing in the sparse grass along the edge of a stream. "They're peaceful enough," he told her, reining in and dismounting. "Come on. We'll rest here for a spell, then round 'em up and head back."

Briana slid from the saddle and dropped easily to the ground. Stretching, she breathed in the sweet air, delighting in the warmth of the sun on her face. Then, suddenly, she was aware of the way her stretching made her breasts strain against the thin cotton shirt. Too late, she saw Dirk's eyes devouring her. Lowering her arms, she turned away, embarrassed. She kept her back to him, waiting for the moment to pass. She didn't even hear him approach, didn't know he was right behind her until his hands clamped down on her shoulders. As she tried to move away, his lips began nuzzling the back of her neck. "Little rich girl," he teased, "this is probably the only thing you've yearned for and never—"

She jerked away and cried angrily, "How dare you?"

Laughing, he reached for her. She slapped his hand away. "Oh, Dani," he said, exasperated, "don't pretend you didn't know why I asked you to ride out here. You're not that naive."

"I was naive enough to think you could be a gentleman," she declared hotly, turning toward her horse. "I'll find my way back."

"You aren't going anywhere!" He grabbed her around the waist and yanked her back, flinging her to the ground. He fell on top of her, hands moving over her breasts as she screamed. "Stop pretending you don't want it," he commanded, "or I'll have to hurt you. I can be mean . . . or I can be nice. It doesn't matter to me because, either way, I'm going to get what I came out here for."

He ripped open her shirt, and she sank her teeth into his ear, biting down hard. With a yelp of pain, he jerked his head up, and she slapped him. With a fierce snarl, he brought his hand up to crack across her cheek, once, twice, again and again, until she was blinded by pain. Then he clutched her throat and banged her head against the hard ground. "Stop fighting me, God damn it, or I'll have to hurt you bad."

Briana struggled to stay conscious as he yanked at her trousers, jerking them down around her ankles. Pulling at her underwear, his mouth sought hers, moist and hungry. "I'm gonna make it so good," he rasped, "you'll beg for more. I can give you all you want . . ." His tongue flicked against her throat.

Briana twisted her head from side to side, terror welling. She could not let this happen. She would rather die. Mustering all her strength, she brought her nails tearing down his cheek and, at the same time, she threw her body upward, bucking him away from her for just long enough to jerk her knee up into his crotch.

He screamed, clutching one hand to his bloodied face, the other to the excruciating pain tearing through his crotch. "You bitch! I'll kill you!"

But Briana was already on her feet, and in a flash she was hoisting herself up on Belle, landing crossways, lying on her stomach. The startled mare whipped around and started into a trot. Briana clutched the mare's mane, hanging on with all she had, the bumping of the saddle against her stomach painfully knocking breath from her body.

To the side of her, she saw Dirk struggling to his feet. Holding tightly to the mane and bracing herself against the saddle, she swung her right leg up and over the horse's rump. She almost lost her balance, but finally she was able to right herself in the saddle. Tucking her feet into the stirrups, she leaned forward and caught the dangling reins. Then she kicked the mare, urging her into a full gallop, holding desperately to the reins. She had ridden this fast only once before, and that had been with Branch beside her.

"Home, Belle!" she cried against the wind whipping at her face, holding on for dear life.

And Belle obeyed, charging across the plain, head up, tail flowing straight behind her. It was as though she knew the danger, knew that the woman clinging to her was depending on her now for her life.

Though the pain was excruciating, Dirk managed to get to his horse and pull himself up into the saddle. He winced as his crotch pressed against the leather saddle. "The bitch," he snarled, rage driving him. He jerked the horse around and spurred him into a frenzied gallop. "The goddamn snotty little rich bitch. Leading me on. All sweetness and honey. I ain't one of her toys. I'll rip her to pieces then move on. She'll remember me. Oh, hell, yes, she'll remember me, and she'll think twice before she plays some other guy for a sucker."

Briana suddenly heard hoofbeats crashing behind her. Turning her head, she screamed at the sight of Dirk fast closing the distance between them. She clutched at the horse's mane, crying, "Hurry, Belle, oh, *please!*" Tears of terror and desperation ran down her face. She had no weapon, and out there in the middle of nowhere no one would hear her screams.

He was getting so close that she didn't have to turn around to tell where he was, for she could hear his horse. On and on she rode, holding Belle's mane, praying for her to outrun Dirk's horse, praying she wouldn't stumble. Briana's sobs came in great gulps, and it was almost impossible to breathe against the lashing wind in her face and her own terrified sobbing.

The sound of the horse behind her grew closer and closer, and then he was upon her, reaching out to punch her face. She sprawled to the ground, thudding on the rocks. There was a sharp pain across the side of her face, and then blackness surrounded her. Belle kept on going.

Dirk jerked his horse to a halt and leaped off, dropping to his knees beside Briana. Hellfire, he hoped she wasn't dead. He'd let his temper get the best of him, which had never bought him anything except trouble.

She was lying very still, and blood was oozing from three scraped places on her face. He lifted her head and pressed his fingertips beneath her nose. She was still breathing, alive, he realized thankfully. But she was knocked out—and he wanted her awake, so she could know what he was doing to her. He'd wanted to be gentle with her. Lord, she was a beauty, but she'd refused him when he was nice. She'd asked for it this way. She wanted to be taught a lesson, and he was going to give it to her good.

He picked her up and placed her over his horse's rump, then mounted and headed for a cluster of mesquite. Then he got down and carried her behind the bushes, laying her on the ground. Her shirt was open, her underthings torn, her breasts exposed. He fumbled with his trousers, leaning over to suckle at her nipples. Feeling the soreness between his legs, he angrily bit her flesh, glad when she moaned. Oh, she had just begun to hurt. He was going to give her so much pain she'd have to wake up.

He lifted her by the shoulders to give her a rough shake, then saw her eyelashes flutter.

"Come on, bitch," he hissed. "Wake up and see what I've got for you."

His head snapped up at the sound of approaching horses. Three riders were coming—fast. Quickly he adjusted his trousers and then put Briana's clothes to rights. By the time the men reached them, he was cradling her in his arms, feigning anxiety. "Over here," he yelled out. "She got thrown and she's hurt. She's alive, though."

He knew Tom Lucas, Bern Adhop, and Lacy Coley—all wranglers from the Coltrane ranch.

Tom knelt to give Briana a quick examination, then turned to Dirk accusingly. "What was she doing out here with you? Pope is going to have your ass for this."

"Yeah," Lacy agreed. "And so's that prissy stepbrother of hers. We rode out after we saw the mare come in, and we passed him comin' up the road."

Dirk faced the condemning glares. "I had nothin' to do with it. I found out she was gone when I went to the tack room for something and noticed the mare was missing. I rode out to look for her, and this is what I found."

The men exchanged glances. They didn't know Hollister well, but they kept their distance from him.

"Let's get her back to the house," Tom Lucas said.

"Coley, go for the doctor. She's got a bad bump on her head."

Dirk considered bolting, getting the hell out of there, because when she came to, she was going to tell what had happened. But he was broke. A month's pay was due in just two more days. He'd have to hang around for that and take his chances. Besides, he told himself, he could always say she was crazy from her head injury, or that she'd made an advance at him and he hadn't taken her up on it, so she was lying to get even. Hell, he wasn't going to run, not with no money and no place to go.

Gavin Mason rode out to meet them, furious to hear his stepsister had been riding. Haranguing them all the way to the house, telling them where to put Dani and, for God's sake, to be gentle, he ranted about how he'd ordered her to stay inside and swore that whoever was responsible for helping her disobey was going to be punished.

Dirk kept quiet and listened. As he listened, he started wondering what was going on. Mason was acting like a raving maniac. Why was he so protective of the girl? He became even more suspicious when Mason drew him aside and nervously asked him whether Dani had said anything when he found her. Dirk's mind raced. He'd heard all the gossip from the wranglers. Dani was the long-estranged daughter of the *big* boss. All of a sudden, after all these years, she'd shown up to claim her half of the family fortune. Everyone was wondering how her brother, Colt, was going to react when he came home and found her there.

Now, observing Mason's nervousness, Dirk decided to play a hunch. He looked Gavin Mason in the eye and said coolly, "Maybe."

"Maybe?" Mason yelled, then realized the servants were watching and lowered his voice. "What did she say?"

Dirk couldn't stop his gloating smile. His hunch was

right. Mason was hiding something and was afraid Dani had let the cat out of the bag. "Maybe she did, and maybe she didn't."

Gavin began sweating. If Briana had babbled that she wasn't really Dani, if she had said anything incriminating, all hell would break loose. "What is that supposed to mean?" he snapped. How dared this impudent cowboy talk to him this way?

Dirk was enjoying himself and decided to let Mason squirm. Since he was bluffing, he had to be very careful if he wanted to learn what Mason was hiding. He drew a cheroot from the pocket of his worn leather vest and took his time lighting it, then said slowly, "It means, my friend, that I'm the type who minds my own business. Besides, when a person has been knocked out, how can you believe what she's saying?"

Mason's face took on a scared, stricken look, and Dirk became proud of himself. Not only was he on to something, he was also setting up his defense for when Dani screamed to high heaven that he'd tried to rape her.

Gavin swallowed hard, glancing around the room uneasily. They were in the main parlor, a large room, and there were many people around, fussing over Briana, who lay on the divan. Then Gavin studied Dirk. How much did the man know? Damn it, he couldn't take any chances. "Come with me," he said, and abruptly led Dirk from the room.

Dirk followed him upstairs to the guest room Gavin used when he stayed overnight at the ranch. Once the door was closed, Gavin began fidgeting, pacing the floor as he struggled between saying too much and not finding out what he had to know.

Dirk made himself comfortable on the elegant canopied bed, propping himself against the satin pillows, his dirty boots on the lace bedspread. He was enjoying himself immensely, for it was becoming obvious that he had Gavin Mason by the balls, and that the situation might just be worth something.

Gavin continued to pace in silence, and Dirk said gruffly, "I have a job. I can't sit here all day."

Gavin eyed him narrowly, then slowly approached the bed. "I want you to tell me exactly what Dani said."

"Let's just say you don't have to worry," Dirk said cleverly. "I know when to keep my mouth shut."

Gavin's mind whirled, and then suddenly he exclaimed, "How would you like to work for me? I need a man I can depend on."

Dirk smiled. "I'm listening," he murmured.

Gavin couldn't be sure how much, if anything, the man knew, but he was also starkly aware that he could take no chances. "For now, I will triple whatever you are making here. Keep your mouth shut. Ask no questions. Later, when I think the time is right, I'll tell you everything you need to know. There will be plenty of money then." He jabbed his finger in the air for emphasis. "Understand me? Plenty of money."

Dirk pursed his lips, then closed his eyes, pretending to be in deep contemplation. It was a game. He might lose. Then again, he might come out a big winner. Mason was definitely up to something, and he thought Dani had spilled the beans. All Dirk had to do was wait. Eventually he would find out everything.

"All right," he said. "Tell me what you want me to do."

He didn't miss the look of relief that passed over Mason's face.

"For now, go on with your work here as though nothing has changed, and I'll be in touch."

He turned toward the door, but Dirk called out, "One thing more." Dirk spoke without any apology in his voice. "When Dani comes around, she may babble about me attacking her."

Gavin tensed. "Did you?" he asked very quietly.

Dirk gave him an arrogant smile. "Well, Mr. Mason, when someone's suffered a bad blow to the head, she's liable to say anything, and you don't know whether to believe her or not—do you?" With that, he brushed past Gavin and went out the door.

Gavin stared after him, eyes narrowed. The arrogant bastard would bear watching.

He returned to the parlor and found the doctor there. He said Dani wasn't badly injured, just bruised, and would be sore for several days. She needed rest. She was starting to come around, and since there was nothing more he needed to do, the doctor took his leave.

Gavin dismissed the servants. Once he was alone with Briana, he roughly shook her, demanding that she wake up. She opened her eyes and looked at him blankly for a while, and then it all came back. She struggled out of the fog into pure rage. Struggling to sit up, she cried, "That man assaulted me!"

The words came in a torrent. "I got away, but he caught up with me and knocked me off my horse!"

Gavin slapped her, not hard, just sharply enough to stop her frenzied outburst. "Now listen to me," he ordered harshly. "You nearly ruined everything."

"But he almost—"

Gavin raised his hand in warning, and she fell silent.

"As long as it was 'almost,' you're all right, aren't you? Just forget everything. I've taken care of things." Then he informed her that he had finished his audit and was ready to continue with his plans. Pausing to give her a frosty smile, he said, "Rest. As soon as you're better, we will talk about the lavish party we are going to give to present you to Silver Butte society."

Briana shook her head. Why didn't he just take the money? Then they could leave. "I don't understand."

"There's no need for you to. Just do what I tell you to do."

"But how long are we going to be here?" she cried as he got up to leave.

He paused at the door to look at her in that affected, condescending way she so despised. "For as long as I deem necessary, my dear."

Chapter Eleven

"It must stop, Becky."

Aunt Candy was seated behind her desk. Her heavily made-up eyes were compassionate, but her voice was harsh.

Candy lifted a glass of wine to ruby-painted lips before continuing. "You know I'm right. You know you're sitting on a keg of dynamite. Sooner or later Colt is going to find out."

"I haven't actually lied to him," Becky hedged, gazing out the window behind her aunt.

Candy nearly slammed the wineglass into the desk. "You lied to him when you broke that vial to pretend you were a virgin."

Becky looked at her helplessly. "You know I had no choice."

Candy sighed, exasperated. "I was a fool to help you, but I didn't think it would go on and on and get worse. I didn't know he'd keep hanging around here. And *why* is he still here?" Candy demanded accusingly, then rushed on: "Because he fancies himself in love with you, that's why. And you and I both know *why* he fancies himself in love with you."

Becky wished for the thousandth time she had not confided in her aunt all that Colt had told her about Charlene.

Candy's tone became gentler. "Honey, he's trying to

make up for Charlene. He sees you for the gentle, sweet girl you are, and he's fighting with himself to keep from doing the same thing to you that he did to her. He doesn't even realize it—but you do. And you've got to put a stop to it."

Becky shook her head defiantly. "No, I don't. I could walk away from here and never look back. He would never know I'd been a prostitute."

Candy shook her head, knowing that even Becky herself didn't believe that. "And live the rest of your life in fear that some man you've bedded will recognize you? Oh, sure, it might never happen, but you'll never be sure, will you? Are you prepared for how Colt would take it if he found out? No, honey"—she shook her head—"you can't live a lie. Either tell him the truth and let him decide if he still loves you, or walk away now and don't look back."

"But other prostitutes have gotten married, and it worked out," Becky whispered.

"Most of the time the men they married knew about their pasts," her aunt said firmly. "No, baby," she repeated as she reached to clutch her niece's hand, "it's not worth the risk, not worth living every moment in fear. You'd never have any happiness, and Colt would wonder what was wrong."

Becky stood, pulling the yellow satin robe tightly around her. She had been sleeping in Colt's arms when Luly tiptoed in to tell her that her aunt wanted her, so she had obediently come, knowing what Aunt Candy wanted to talk about. After all, Colt had been there nearly two months.

Becky sighed. Nothing had been accomplished by this conversation.

"Well," Candy demanded, also getting to her feet. "What are you going to do?"

"I don't know."

"Has he said anything about leaving?"

Becky shook her head.

"Do you know that there isn't a single night when at least one of your old customers doesn't show up asking for you? I give them other girls, but they want you, and sometimes they get nasty. A few of them know about Coltrane—"

"What?" Becky jerked her head up in alarm. "*How* do they know? You told me you've forbidden the girls to talk."

Candy gestured helplessly. "Everybody in Golconda knows Coltrane is staying here. And since he's here, and you're not available anymore, folks put the story together for themselves. Just be glad Coltrane isn't hitting the saloons, or he'd probably hear comments you wouldn't want him to hear."

Becky nodded. It was true. Only luck had kept Colt from hearing something, and luck wouldn't hold forever.

Candy crossed the room to clasp Becky's shoulders and give her a gentle shake. Softly she implored, "Get rid of him, honey. Send him home. If you don't want to tell him the truth, then tell him you just don't want him hanging around anymore. Or tell him I'm tired of him being here. Anything. But it has to end."

Her hands fell away, and Becky asked, "What if I tell him you want him to leave, and he asks me to go with him? What do I do then, tell him I've got a job here as a prostitute?"

Candy sighed. "Why would he ask you to go with him, when he's hell-bent against getting married? He believes a girl lies dead because he broke her heart, and he's not going to forget *that* soon. No, he might be falling in love with you, but he's not falling that hard.

"But," she rushed on, seeing the pain on Becky's face, "if he does ask you to go with him, bear in mind it's only to be his mistress. Maybe he wouldn't mind having an ex-prostitute for a mistress, I don't know. You'd better think about everything; consider all of it.

But I warn you, he's got to go, Becky. I've got a business to run, and you can't go on like this."

Becky turned to go, and Candy called out, "I mean it. This isn't good for you."

Becky went downstairs, to where she had left Colt sleeping. What was she going to do? The truth was she was helplessly, hopelessly in love with Colt and didn't want to lose him, didn't want him to leave . . . without her.

Colt was asleep, lying on his back, and she stood staring down at him. How handsome he was, how magnificently built. She felt a warm rush, a tremor in her heart fired by love.

How she wished she *had* been a virgin for him!

Colt's eyes flashed open, and he smiled up at her. "Come here."

She went, pausing only to loosen her robe and allow it to fall softly to the floor.

He began to caress her hungrily, and suddenly she knew that, for some reason she couldn't fathom, she wanted to be the giver this time, not the taker. She slid downward, burrowing her face between his thighs. She took all he had to give, delighted by his moans of ecstasy.

Afterward he held her tightly against his chest, stroking her hair lovingly. Abruptly he said, "I want to take you away from here."

She stiffened.

"Becky, you know my situation," he went on. "You know I've got to face up to my past before I can think about a future." He propped himself on his elbow to look down at her. "I can't offer you anything for now except friendship, but it's a beginning."

She let her breath out slowly until she trusted her voice not to falter. "What would you do with me? Where would I live?"

He had thought of that. He had friends in Silver Butte, nice older ladies who would give her a room and help her find a job. Maybe she could be a companion to other old ladies, like a nurse. "It would be a new beginning for you. I can't leave you in this place," he said scornfully.

She trailed her fingertips down his cheek, and he caught them and pressed them against his lips. "Do you love me, Colt?" she dared to ask.

A shadow crossed his eyes. He released her hand and whispered, "No. I don't, Becky. If I did, I guess I'd ask you to marry me. It's as I told you: I don't want to get married and settle down for a long time. That's how I know I don't love you. But I care for you a great deal. I want you around me. I want to look after you, see that you're treated well. For now, I can offer you only my friendship."

Her heart shrank. Silently she screamed at herself, *You fool! You dared think he was leading up to saying he loved you! That he would marry you! But all he offers is friendship! Just who did you think you were?*

A coldness enveloped her, and in a tight voice she challenged, "Then why should I leave here? Candy is my aunt, you know. She's all the family I've got. You can come and visit me. I'll be fine here."

She started off the bed, but he pinned her, looming over her. How intense he looked, almost angry.

"I don't want you here. This is a whorehouse, or have you forgotten?"

"It happens to be my home," she countered, "or have *you* forgotten?"

She pulled out of his grasp, and he let her go. As she yanked on her robe, he gazed at her thoughtfully. "Were you expecting me to ask you to marry me, Becky?"

That infuriated her. "Of course not," she lied. "You aren't the marrying kind."

"But you were a virgin," he said, "and virgins expect a man to marry them."

"Was Charlene a virgin?" she snapped. "Is that why

she was so heartbroken when you refused to marry her?"

He shook his head, then fell back on the bed to stare up at the ceiling. Women. No matter how hard a man tried, he always wound up saying the wrong thing. "Maybe I'd best be moving on, Becky. It's time I went home."

She turned away so he couldn't see her face. "Yes, I think so, too. Aunt Candy was complaining just this morning about you hanging around here for so long. She says you've run up quite a bill, with the whiskey you've been guzzling and all. I told her you'd be good for it. I hope that's true."

Colt could hardly believe what he was hearing. For the first time, Becky wasn't the sweet, angelic girl he'd grown so fond of. She sounded hard and bitter. What could have happened to her, and why had he never seen this side of her before?

While he wondered what to say, she flounced angrily from the room, slamming the door.

He got up and dressed quickly. It didn't take him long to gather his things, because he didn't have much. When he was ready, he left the room and went to find Candy. She was in the front parlor, arranging a vase of her beloved feathers.

"I'm leaving," he said curtly. "Thank you for allowing me to stay here. I'll send you what I owe if you give me a bill."

She didn't look up. "Five hundred should cover it."

Colt thought that was outrageous, but he said nothing. He turned toward the foyer, then felt compelled to say, "Take good care of Becky. I'll be checking on her from time to time."

Candy's back was turned, and she said nothing.

Colt's mind was whirling as he made his way down the street, oblivious to the heat and the dust. Damn, he wished he possessed a little patience. He supposed he was like his father in that way. He simply hated to argue. He believed in stating his position, and if someone wasn't in agreement, he felt it best to just run away rather than argue. But he should have argued with Becky, tried to find a way to make her understand—just as, if he'd made Charlene understand, maybe she would still be alive.

He paused twice on the way to the livery stable, and almost went back to talk to Becky. He didn't want to leave like this. But what was there left to say? True, he was very fond of her. Maybe one day, given enough time, that fondness might grow into love, but he was not going to make her any promises unless he was sure he could keep them. No, he would just go on home. He had been away too long as it was, and plenty of work was waiting.

He had no money on him and told the stablehand he would send some when he paid his bill at Miss Candy's. The boy nodded. He, like everyone else in Golconda, knew who Colt was.

Colt saddled his horse, then led him out into the sunlight. It was a long ride to Silver Butte, and Colt had no provisions, so he found the general store and went in.

He purchased hardtack and a small slab of bacon. "You know who I am?" he inquired of the bald proprietor.

The man nodded. "Yep. Coltrane. Headin' back to Silver Butte?"

Colt nodded, then explained about needing credit.

"No problem. When you pay Miss Candy, just send mine along. She'll see that I get it." He flashed a snaggle-toothed grin. "Happens all the time around here. Men run up bills at her place, then have to send the money. But they always pay. Miss Candy's a special friend of the marshal, and he always sees she gets her money."

"She'll get her money," Colt said. He could have told the man that his bill at Candy's was for room and board, not "services," but, as usual, he saw no reason to justify himself.

He picked up his purchases and strode out of the store, paying no attention to the man leaning against a post out front until the man called out to him. He turned.

"Going home, huh, Coltrane?"

Colt nodded, then continued on his way. The man spoke once more.

"Lotsa men around here will be glad to hear you're movin' on, bein' as you been took up with everybody's favorite over at Miz Candy's."

Colt turned around very slowly. The man's eyes glittered with delight. Menacingly Colt growled, "You're mistaken."

The stranger shifted uneasily as Colt's face darkened, and he struggled to keep from looking scared. "Naw, I ain't. I hear 'em complainin' in the saloon every night about how they can't get in to see Bella 'cause you've got all her time bought up."

"I don't know anyone named Bella," Colt threw at him, "and who I was with is no one's business."

He turned away.

The man hesitated a few seconds. He was scared, but he'd come this far without trouble, so . . . "Hey," he called, nervousness making his voice crack. "Maybe you call her something besides Bella. Maybe you know Bella as Becky—Miz Candy's niece."

Colt took two steps to reach the stranger. He swung once, hard, and the last thing that went through the stranger's mind before blackness closed around him was that the money Miss Candy had promised him had damn well better be worth all this.

Unaware of anything except his rage, Colt strode to his horse, mounted, and galloped out of Golconda as though the devil himself were on his heels, breathing fire.

Deep down, he knew the bastard had not been lying.

Becky. Bella.

Colt stared straight ahead as he rode, every muscle in his body tight.

A woman had had the best of him. He was a fool.

Briana sat in a tufted pink velvet chair before a lace-skirted dressing table. In the mirror she met Gavin's angry stare, retaliating with an angry glare of her own.

"You ignorant little beggar," he sneered. "Where would you be without me? You'd be groveling in the gutter by now, or lying on your back selling what you accuse Dirk Hollister of trying to take."

Briana bolted from the chair and whirled to face him. "Dirk Hollister *did* try to rape me. I don't care what lies he told you. The man is a monster, and I don't want him here. Why are you protecting him?" She paused to take a ragged breath. "As for where *I'd* be right now, what about where *you* would be? You didn't have a chance at getting Dani's share of the estate without me, so you needn't act as though you've done me a favor, Gavin. I'd say it's the other way around. Maybe you'd better start worrying about what *I* can say about *you.*"

His eyes narrowed to slits. Then suddenly he leaped up and grabbed her, squeezing her throat. Her nails tore at him as she struggled frantically, but he only pressed harder. "You shut your mouth, you hear me? I've come too far to have you mess things up now. And if you try, so help me, I'll kill you. And when I get back to France, I'll see that crippled brother of yours dead."

He shook her, saw that her eyes were bulging, but didn't release her. "Don't you say anything about Hollister to anybody. It's important to me that he stay on here, and you will do as you are told. You will help plan your coming-out party. You will obey me. You will not rebel, or you will die."

He released her so abruptly that she fell to the floor.

He stood over her and whispered cruelly, "I can send word that your brother is once more on charity. He will be returned to that hospital, and they will let him die—slowly, of course.

"I can," he continued, "turn you over to Hollister and let him have his way with you . . . after *I'm* through with you. I can make you wish you were dead. I can fix it so you never see your brother again. So heed me well, bitch. You are playing a dangerous game when you defy me."

Feebly Briana got to her feet. The defiance shone in her cinnamon eyes like tiny red dots of fire. Her throat ached, and her head throbbed, but she would not cry, would not let him see her misery. She glared at him in icy silence.

Gavin smiled tightly. "Now then. Fetch me some brandy, and we'll talk about my ideas for your party."

When she returned, Gavin was sitting on the divan in the corner. He took the glass from her and motioned for her to sit next to him.

He smiled patronizingly and said, "My dear, it doesn't have to be this way between us. Why, we can have a lovely friendship if you stop being so difficult. You needn't worry about Hollister bothering you again, either," he said, patting her reassuringly. "He'll answer to me if he does.

"But," he continued after pausing to sip his brandy, "let's talk of pleasant things—your party." He proceeded to tell her that Mrs. Bowden, despite still being in mourning, had graciously provided him with a list of people who should be invited. "She would like to be at the party, but, of course, that is impossible. I would like you to visit her soon, Bri—Dani. She and her husband can be powerful allies for us. Besides that, you need to be seen in town more."

Briana was bewildered and becoming exasperated. "But you finished the auditing, so why can't we claim Dani's share of the money and just go home?"

"You are truly trying my patience, my dear. We will leave when I say we will leave. Quite frankly, if we were not about to present you to society, I would teach you a lesson. If your insolence continues, I will do so. Do you understand me?"

She nodded, fury boiling. He was, she knew, quite capable of beating her.

He explained his plans for the ball, telling her which gown he wanted her to wear, how she was to behave, neglecting no detail. Everything must go smoothly, he warned her.

When he finally left her to return to Silver Butte, she dressed quickly in trousers and shirt, and ran to the stable.

She saddled Belle. No matter that Gavin had forbidden her to ride. He was gone, and the ranch hands were out on the range. No one would even notice, except the household servants, and they wouldn't say anything.

She was smiling as she led Belle across the stable, toward the door and the brilliant gold-and-blue day. To be free, to feel the fresh, sweet wind caressing her face— The thought was sheerest ecstasy.

"Nice day for a ride, Miss Dani."

Her skin prickled as Dirk Hollister stepped out of a stall and blocked her path.

He gave her an insolent grin and mockingly tipped his hat. "Yep. I'm real pleased you want to go ridin'. Told Mr. Mason just as he was leaving that I figured you'd want to. He said for me to oblige you. After all, we don't want you falling off your horse like you did last time—now, do we?"

Trembling with rage, she stepped backward, holding on to Belle's reins. "If you touch me, so help me, I'll kill you, Dirk Hollister," she said.

He laughed, delighted with himself. "Why, Miss Dani, I'd never harm you. The boss wouldn't like it. Now, if you object to my riding with you, well, I think he'd like to know about that. He ain't been gone so long that I can't catch up with him and tell him how unfriendly you are . . ."

Furious with frustration and defeat, Briana turned around abruptly and led the mare back to her stall.

Gavin had triumphed.

Chapter Twelve

BRIANA was already so scared of being caught in the deception she and Gavin had created that the idea of giving a party for two hundred people was just one more terror in what had become a life of continuing terror.

She took a wry delight in being the hostess at a social gathering, since all her life she had been only a servant—unnoticed, deliberately unobtrusive. She had been trained to fade into the background, but now she would have to do the opposite: shine, be the center of attention, the object of everyone's scrutiny.

Would she do something gauche? Say the wrong thing? Gavin had drilled her over and over, covering conversation manners, table manners, everything he could think of. If she made any slips, she knew he would be furious.

Gavin was becoming so dominating as to be unbearable. Not a day went by that he didn't threaten horrors for Charles and misery for her if she failed to obey.

Dirk Hollister was equally obnoxious. Everywhere she went, every time she turned around, he was spying on her, taunting her. She was constantly being watched.

What hurt the most was the realization of how thoroughly she was now trapped. She had allowed herself to become ensnared by Gavin and his plans because she was desperate about Charles. There hadn't been any other means of helping Charles than going along with Gavin's plans. Now she was doubly trapped because she had already perpetrated the deception, had been pretending for weeks to be Dani Coltrane. Even if there was some other way to help Charles, she couldn't back out now. It was too late. She was stuck. There was nothing she could do about it except continue to fall in with Gavin's plans.

This knowledge, combined with Gavin's everlasting abuse, infuriated her and kept her constantly in a nerve-wracking defensive state.

It was all such a mess. Carleton Bowden, according to what little Gavin would tell her, was being as cooperative as he could be, due entirely to his hatred of Colt. Once Briana had signed the legal documents, as Daniella Coltrane, giving Gavin full control of Dani's share of the family holdings, Mr. Bowden had given Gavin free rein. He could withdraw money as he liked, and he spared no expense in preparing the Coltrane mansion for the gala. He wanted to impress everyone.

Briana wandered through the downstairs rooms before the guests began to arrive. Even after all of Gavin's bragging, she was astonished. The party was going to be beautiful.

Roses had been brought in from California by the wagonload, and the air was permeated with the sweetness of the red, white, peach, and yellow blossoms. Satin bunting in pastel shades of green and yellow draped the stair railing, all the sparkling crystal chandeliers, and the gleaming mahogany mantels in each room.

Gavin had procured the services of a French chef, who had come from San Francisco to prepare an array of culinary delights. Tables covered by Swedish lace were laden with duck braised with oranges and orange liqueur, chicken stewed in red wine, and mounds of sauerkraut served with sausages and pork. There were seafood dishes as well, including scallops served in a creamy sauce, and Chef Bénard's specialty, a dish of sautéed, diced lobster, flamed in cognac and then simmered in wine, vegetables, and herbs.

For those not inclined toward French cuisine, there were smoked oysters; chicken fried in honey; shrimp marinated in wine; strips of steak barbecued to perfection; delicate crab claws, and steamed clams in a tantalizing sauce of lemon, butter, and cream.

Briana passed through the dining room as one of the kitchen assistants was setting up the cheese table, and he pointed out the different varieties available, insisting that she sample a few. When coaxed to try the delicate little cheese tarts, she whispered, "Dangerously delicious!"

When she approached the dessert selections, she made a gesture of refusal, smiling her apology. But she paused to marvel at the chocolate mousse and all the pies, tarts, and cakes, some with six layers. Everything was exquisitely decorated.

The house was brimming with the additional servants Gavin had engaged. The women bustling around were dressed identically in stiffly starched white cotton dresses with high collars and long sleeves. Their hair was pulled back in tight, severe buns. Long pink aprons added a gay note to the otherwise severe costume. The men wore white coats and black trousers. Briana thought the pink rosebuds in their lapels looked vulgar, but knew better than to say anything.

As she turned to go upstairs, the violin ensemble arrived, and soon the house was filled with music.

As she dressed in the gown Gavin had chosen for her, Briana was forced to admit that it suited her well, besides being beautiful. Fashioned of white lace, the skirt billowed with rows and rows of cascading ruffles. A wide lavender satin cummerbund encircled her waist, wrapping into a large bow at the back. The sash from the bow fell all the way to her hemline.

She studied the bodice critically, the bustline being the only area of Dani's gowns that gave her trouble. Briana was graciously endowed, while Dani was not. Hundreds and hundreds of tiny seed pearls had been sewn on the bodice, so there was no way to enlarge it. The generous swell of her breasts was emphasized by provocatively deep cleavage. If not for the top row of pearls, her nipples would have been visible. She dared not take a deep breath, for if she did, there would be nothing hidden.

There were no sleeves to the dress, for it was of the recent French design—strapless. She was sure Dani would have worn a shawl, keeping her shoulders covered. Briana made a face as she acknowledged that Gavin wouldn't allow her to do that. He wanted her on display.

One of the servants hired for the evening had a talent for styling hair and had offered to help Dani, which Briana gratefully accepted. The only battle with Gavin that Briana had managed to win was over the matter of her hair. It was long and thick and had some wave, but it was not in style. Frizzed hair was the fashion, and every chic woman had a curling iron heating in the stove or fireplace before she dressed to go out. Briana refused to frizz her hair, and Gavin, apparently deciding it wasn't worth doing battle over, shrugged his elegant shoulders and told her to at least manage to stay clothed like a woman, for heaven's sake. He had seen her in Branch's clothing one morning and been fit to be tied.

Mrs. Morgan and Briana spent a tedious hour curling her cinnamon tresses on a long, slender rod heated in the fire. Then Mrs. Morgan entwined thin lavender velvet ribbons around each curl before sweeping the entire creation up to give the impression of a glorious crown. Mrs. Morgan threaded pearls on a string, then, using a needle, wove the pearls in and out of Briana's hair. The coiffure was a stunning design of shining curls, alluring ribbons, and dazzling pearls.

Briana was just stepping into the new white satin shoes Gavin had brought her from Silver Butte, when he walked into the room—without knocking, as he always did.

He stood before her, eyes coolly appraising, then circled her several times. Briana was annoyed. Was she a horse for sale?

At last he clapped his hands together, delighted. "Absolutely ravishing. The men will drool over you and the women will hate you. But remember"—his tone suddenly became sharp—"concentrate on the women, *not* the men. Do not be flirtatious. It is imperative that the women like you. They must want to cultivate your friendship. With Mrs. Bowden's assistance, I have invited some of the most influential families in the area, and many have accepted out of plain curiosity. They must find you lovely, unblemished, altogether suitable for their social circles. Understand?"

Briana sighed, nodded, and refrained from asking him why it mattered. If they left soon, what difference would it make whether or not people approved of her? But she knew this was not the time to bring up the subject of their departure. As though he'd guessed her thoughts, Gavin said, "One day you will understand the reason behind everything I'm doing, and you will marvel at my cleverness."

He twirled once before her. "How do I look?" he asked eagerly.

He was dressed nearly all in white: white coat and trousers, white shoes, white shirt. His pink string tie and red vest were the only colors. She thought he looked strange, like a dancing fairy, but she kept her expression bland and said, "You look quite distinguished, Gavin. But then, you've always been a very . . . fashionable dresser."

He gave her a smug look. "I know. I just wanted to

hear you say it." He turned to leave, calling over his shoulder, "Remember everything I've taught you, Dani. Be gracious, charming, polite. Every move you make will be appraised and gossiped about later. The guests have started arriving, so I want you to wait thirty minutes, then make your entrance. Understand?"

Half an hour later, Briana made her way to the top of the stairs. Gavin was waiting for her at the bottom and, on signal, the musicians stopped playing. Gavin turned to face the crowd and announced, "Ladies and gentlemen, I am pleased to present to you my beloved stepsister, Miss Daniella Coltrane."

There was applause. Smiling, Briana made her way down the steps, nervously feeling the stares of the crowd. The musicians began playing again, and when she reached the last step, Gavin stepped forward, bowed slightly, and pressed her fingertips to his lips. Then he took her arm and led her into the crowd, introducing her to everyone nearby.

The names and faces became a blur. Everyone seemed friendly, but she hated those curious, probing stares.

A woman drew her aside and began talking animatedly. Mrs. Annabelle Rhodes proudly confided that her husband was *the* Dudley Rhodes, owner of profitable lumber mills not only in Nevada, but in California as well. "I have a nephew I'm dying for you to meet, darling," she gushed. "You'll love Nathaniel. He's as ambitious as his uncle, and one of the most sought-after bachelors in San Francisco. But he's so picky. He comes from a good family, of course—" She paused to breathe, then went right on. The two of them simply had to get together. When could Dani make the trip to San Francisco? The weather was so lovely there this time of year. The two women could make a shopping jaunt of it.

Briana smiled, was gracious, then murmured that there were so many people she had to meet, would Mrs.

Rhodes please excuse her? She made her way through the crowd, toward the table where wine was being served.

Too late, she realized Gavin was presiding over the wine, enjoying the attention he was receiving as he explained all about the different wines he'd imported. Those gathered around seemed suitably impressed.

"And here we have a light, dry white wine, Alsatian," he was saying.

A plump woman wearing a gaudy but expensive gown of sequins and feathers interrupted. "Oh, Mr. Mason, it must be wonderful to know so much about wines." She grinned at Briana. "Dear girl, how fortunate you are to have someone so suave, so worldly, for a stepbrother."

Briana continued smiling and looking pleasant, aching to tell them that Gavin's knowledge of wine resulted from the fact that he consumed so much of it.

Gavin held up another bottle, glorying in having a rapt audience. "This is a full-bodied dry white wine, Côtes-du-Rhone. It goes so well with fish or fowl. Of course," he said airily, "we always drink champagne for festive occasions, and I'll come to that in a moment, but I want to tell you about our reds."

Disgusted with his foppish display of self-adoration, Briana turned away. Immediately she was asked to dance by a pleasant-looking man, but declined when she saw a woman watching with obvious disapproval. His wife, no doubt.

Suddenly she needed to escape the overpowering smell of hundreds of roses, the crush of so many people, the food aromas. Smiling, nodding, exchanging pleasantries, she made her way through the crowd toward the French doors that led to the terrace at the side of the house. There was a row of potted plants just in front of the doors, which Gavin had ordered placed there to discourage guests from mingling outside. He wanted everyone inside, where they could be impressed by the opulence, the grandeur, and Dani.

She stepped around the foliage after making sure that no one was observing her, then quickly opened the doors and moved outside into the quiet night, closing the doors behind her with a great sense of relief.

She walked to the edge of the terrace and took a deep breath. Oh, it was such a lovely night, the creamy white full moon turning the night sky a soft midnight purple. Thousands of stars glittered like bits of shimmering crystal. The air was warm and sweet, and she wasn't the least chilled.

She stood there for only a few moments before she was startled to hear a man's voice call to her from the yard.

"Don't be afraid, Miss Dani. It's only me."

Apprehension disappeared at the sight of Branch Pope stepping onto the terrace. She was glad to see him. "Why are you sneaking around out here in the dark? Why aren't you inside with the others?"

"I wasn't invited," he said plainly, looking at her quizzically. "I probably wouldn't have gone if I had been," he added dryly.

"But," she protested, "you're the foreman. Why was Dirk Hollister invited? He's only a hired hand."

Branch's face tightened. "I might ask you the same question, Miss Dani."

She cried, "I hope you don't think *I* invited him. I detest that—" She commanded herself to be silent. Gavin had warned her about saying anything against Dirk. "I suppose Gavin invited him," she said. "*I* certainly didn't."

Branch's eyes bored into hers. "Seems to me there's lots of things goin' on around here that I don't understand. I'm startin' to get the feelin' that Hollister is bein' pushed in and I'm bein' pushed out. Your stepbrother gives him more and more authority all the time. I can't figure out how Mason got so much say-so, anyhow. You're the Coltrane, and he ain't even your blood kin."

Briana shook her head in dismay. What could she say that wouldn't give her and Gavin away? "Mr. Pope, I'm sorry. I don't know anything about running a ranch, you see."

"Neither does that stepbrother of yours," he lashed out, "and neither does Hollister. It's a bad situation, Miss Dani. I didn't intend for us to get into a discussion about it, but I guess I'd been holdin' so much inside that, when I saw you out here, it all burst out."

He paused to catch his breath, then went on: "When your brother comes home, believe me, things are gonna be different. He's gonna be madder'n hell when he finds out what's been goin' on around here. He's not gonna like the way Mason has taken over what ain't his. And he sure ain't gonna like it if I get fired." He fell silent, letting her absorb his warning.

Briana felt terrible. This man had been so kind to her when the other men thought she was just a spoiled rich girl. Helpless, she whispered, "I'm sorry. I wish there were something I could do, but there isn't. Maybe John Travis will be home soon. I certainly hope so." Oh, what else could she say?

Branch was telling himself to shut up, but it had been building for so long, and this might be his last chance to talk with her.

"Anyway," he went on, sighing, "I sure don't like the way Mason has gotten his nose in things, and Colt won't like it, either. Nothin' that goes on around here is any of Mason's business."

"And certainly none of yours."

Briana and Branch whirled around. Gavin stepped toward them from where he had been eavesdropping, behind a large shrub at the edge of the terrace.

Briana felt a mixture of anger and fright. Anger won out. "How dare you spy on me, Gavin!"

"Shut up and get back in the house," he snapped. "I

saw you sneaking out here and I figured you were up to something. I've been suspicious of you and this bastard for some time."

Branch took a step forward, halting as Dirk Hollister appeared behind Mason. Dirk was carrying a shotgun, which he pointed at Branch.

"Put that away," Branch ordered. "*Now,* Hollister. I don't like guns pointed at me. There's no need for this."

"Oh, there might be, Mr. Pope," Gavin disputed. "You see, as of this moment, you are fired. You are no longer employed here. I won't tolerate insolence from my servants."

Branch burst into raucous laughter, looking unflinchingly at the two men. Addressing himself directly to Gavin, in a deadly voice he said, "Hear me, boy, and hear me well. I'm the foreman of this goddamn ranch. A Coltrane hired me, and it'll take a Coltrane to fire me. I don't take orders from a sissy wetnose that don't even know the difference between a steer and a cow." He shook his head at Hollister, then looked back at Gavin. "I ain't goin' nowhere."

"You might go in a wooden box," Hollister snapped.

"Have all of you gone mad?" Briana cried. She glared at Hollister. "Put that gun away—now."

He made no move to obey.

The cords stood out on Gavin's neck, and his eyes were dark with rage. "I am warning you . . . *Dani* . . ." He bit out the name, pausing before continuing. "Remember our agreement. I am in charge."

Briana lifted her head defiantly. Branch Pope had been kind to her, kinder than anyone else since she'd come to America, and she was not going to let him be hurt. "Mr. Pope stays here. He knows much more about the ranch than you or Mr. Hollister." She met Gavin's fiery gaze, undaunted. "Need I remind you that there is a party going on inside? We are neglecting our guests . . . and a shooting was *not* on the menu for tonight."

"Put the gun away," Gavin snarled to Hollister. "I'll handle her later."

To Branch, he commanded, "Get the hell out of here. We'll talk about this tomorrow."

Branch nodded. "Fine. But I don't think you've got anything to say that I'd be interested in hearing." With a grateful nod to Briana, he turned and walked away.

Gavin leaped forward to grab Briana's arm and twist it behind her back. "Have you lost your mind? If I didn't need you, you insolent little bitch, I'd break your stupid neck here and now and leave you for the buzzards to pick."

Despite the pain in her arm, she returned, "But you do need me, so I suggest you let me go this instant, or I am going to scream and bring everyone running out here."

"Briana, you're trying my—" He saw the look come over her face as her eyes went to Hollister, who was enjoying the scene. Gavin snickered at her expression. "He knows everything, so don't worry about what I say in front of him. I had to have somebody around here I could trust—and it damn sure isn't you."

"Don't worry about me sayin' nothin'," Hollister cackled. "I'm in for a piece of the action now, so I'm gonna be watchin' you every bit as close as he does. One wrong move, and I'll be on you like a coyote on a rabbit."

Briana looked into Gavin's evil, grinning face and knew she could stand no more. "I want out of this. I want to go back to France. I'll put Charles's life in God's hands. I'll find a way to help him without stooping to your filthy—"

Gavin twisted her arm harder, and she yelped with the excruciating pain. "Listen to me, or I'll break your arm. You're in this to stay. Your brother's life is not in God's hands; it's in mine. You try to run away from me before I'm finished here, and I'll see that his miserable life is ended. And you know I mean it. You're in this to the end. You take orders from me and Hollister, and the next time you dare talk back to me in front of someone, I'll turn you over to Hollister and let him finish what he started out there on the prairie."

Briana was trembling, but not with fear. Oh, no, she was far too enraged to cower before those ruthless bastards. "I'll go back inside now," she said, "but I'm warning you, Gavin, you'd better hurry up and get us out of here. And you, Hollister, if you touch me ever again, I'll find a way to kill you."

She fled.

Colt slowed his horse. He had decided not to camp for the night, but to get home as soon as possible, for the closer to home he got, the more something urged him onward. He had been away far too long, had let his heart overrule his good sense.

Never again. He had come out of his time with Becky a smarter man, and more than once during the journey home, he'd recalled his father saying that even if awareness was all that came out of a bad experience, then the experience was worth something.

Now Colt stared at the ranch buildings, all looming ghostlike in the moonlight, except for the big house. Light glowed within the house. He moved his horse on, but slowly. Something was up, and he knew better than to ride into an unknown situation without being cautious.

As he drew closer, he saw there were many carriages and wagons by the house.

He dismounted at the bunkhouse, walking the rest of the way. He hadn't gone far when he saw a man coming toward him. Instinctively his hand moved to his gun.

Branch Pope saw him, stopped only for an instant to stare in disbelief, then ran forward to pound Colt on the back jubilantly. "Hot damn!" he cried. "I ain't never been so glad to see anybody. I was about to come get you. What's kept—"

"What's going on?" Colt interrupted.

Branch followed Colt's narrow-eyed gaze toward the brightly lit house. Faintly, they heard music. "It's a party," he said very slowly, stepping away from his friend in case there was an explosion.

"Who's having a party in my house?" Colt snapped.

Branch let him have it. "A party to welcome your sister."

Colt whipped around to stare at Branch. Had he heard right?

Branch nodded. "That's what I said. Dani's come home—and when you hear all I've got to tell you, you're going to be mighty glad you have, too."

Chapter Thirteen

COLT spent the night in the bunkhouse, listening to what Branch had to tell him, then sorting it all out. He knew he'd better be clearheaded before encountering the half sister he'd not seen in fourteen years.

He was not surprised Dani was there. In the back of his mind he'd wondered all along whether she would take the opportunity to claim her fortune without the tension of having to see their father.

But why had she stayed? Why didn't she just take her share of the money and go?

He had wondered before why his father didn't just send her the money. His mother explained that she and Travis hoped to see Dani, hoped she would come to Paris to visit them once she learned they were there.

Colt was more than a little resentful that Dani could be so cold. She wanted her money, but she was too unfeeling to mend the fences and make peace with his parents. *What kind of a person is she?* he asked himself, truly astonished by her selfishness. Well, selfish or not, she was home. And he would have to deal with her.

But what the hell was her stepbrother doing sticking his nose into Coltrane family business? Who the hell did he think he was, trying to fire Branch and put a drifter in charge of things on a ranch he had no claim on?

Hollister came into the bunkhouse in the wee hours. Colt had taken a cot at the farthest end after instructing the other men to keep silent about his being there. The men were all dying to ask questions, but knew from experience that Colt was closemouthed until he decided it was time to speak. Before they had all turned in for the night, Colt had heard enough from them to know they were very resentful of the situation and hoped he would quickly put things right. He made no comment about Gavin Mason, said nothing controversial.

Early-morning sunlight streamed through the windows. The wranglers had arisen long ago, hitting the range by the time the first shadows of night yielded to daybreak.

All the wranglers, that is, except Dirk Hollister, who stayed behind, eyeing Colt's bunk. He asked Branch why one man remained in his bunk, burrowed beneath his blanket, and Branch told him that it was a new man he'd hired, and that the man wasn't feeling well.

"Great," Hollister said sarcastically. "You hired a sick bum who'll probably get all of *us* sick, too. Wait till Mason hears about this."

As Branch was leaving, Hollister goaded him: "You know your days here are numbered, old man. Mason ain't gonna put up with you. If you were smart, you'd make things easy on yourself. Just get your gear and ride on outta here."

Branch did not reply. He left, and Hollister followed.

When, at last, Colt was alone, he rolled over on his back and stared up at the ceiling. There was, he decided, only one road to take. He'd find out what Dani's intentions were, and then deal with Mason. This was Dani's home, and he couldn't ask her to leave. But he damn well didn't have to put up with Gavin Mason.

He got up, washed, shaved, found some clean clothes

that belonged to one of the hands, and grabbed a couple of biscuits and a mug of coffee.

He was about to go to the big house when Hollister walked in. "Well, well, Sleeping Beauty has awakened," he sneered. "You don't look sick to me, stranger. You look like a goddamn goldbrick. We don't need your kind. Get out of here."

Colt sipped his coffee. "I thought Pope was the foreman."

Hollister snorted. "I'm running things. Now git!"

Colt took his time finishing the coffee, which only infuriated Hollister. Then Colt took his hat from its place on a nail by the door, and started out.

"Maybe you don't hear so good, stranger. I said get your stuff, then get out."

Colt was almost through the door. Hollister clamped a hand on his shoulder, shouting, "Don't get me riled—"

Colt hit him so fast Dirk never saw the movement. One moment he was standing, and then he was crashing backward against chairs, toppling them as he fell to the floor.

Colt tipped his hat and smiled. "Don't get *me* riled." He took a step toward the door again, then added, "By the way, the name's Coltrane."

Colt entered the house through the back door, greeting the startled servants.

He was walking through the downstairs rooms, looking at the mess left from the party, when Carlota, the Mexican woman who'd been in charge of the household staff for as long as Colt could remember, rushed in.

"Oh, Señor Colt, I am so glad to see you," she cried.

Colt nodded, knowing how upset the servants must be. He continued to look around. It had, he noted, been quite a party. Expensive, from the looks of the empty wine and champagne bottles, the hundreds of wilting roses.

Carlota's eyes were wide as she said, "Last night,

Señor Mason gave a big party. I am sorry for all this mess, but it was nearly sunrise before all the guests left, so we started to clean only a little while ago."

Sensing that she was taking his silence for disapproval over the condition of the house, Colt smiled pleasantly at her. "Just take your time, Carlota. There's no great rush. Now, where is Dani? Still sleeping?"

Carlota shook her head. "Oh, no. She was up early, wanting to help us, but I gave her coffee and told her to go back upstairs and just get out of the way. She is nice." She smiled hesitantly. "Not like Señor Mason. He curses at us, and we're not used to unkindness."

Colt nodded. After exchanging pleasantries and reassuring her, he left Carlota and went upstairs. Assuming Dani had been using the room that was once hers, he went to that door and knocked. A soft voice called, "Come in."

She was seated in a chair by the open window, a book in her hands, wearing a yellow satin robe patterned with tiny blue flowers. Her long hair, tied back from her face, glowed like burnished copper in the brilliant sunlight.

At once, Colt silently acknowledged that she was the most beautiful woman he had ever seen.

Briana was wary. What was this stranger doing in her bedroom? But as she looked into his eyes—the warmest, most tender eyes she had ever seen—somehow, she knew she had nothing to fear. "What is it?" she asked quietly.

He did not speak for several moments. In his mind, the years were rolling back. It was difficult to imagine this lovely woman as the same spoiled little brat who had left him her mark on his face the last time they were together. She looked so gentle, so . . . sweet.

He shook his head. Fourteen years was a long time. A lot could happen in all that time to change a person.

Briana waited for him to speak, her gaze sweeping

over him. He was tall and muscular. His complexion was dark, his hair so black as to gleam with blue highlights. The eyes she found so overwhelmingly appealing were gray and fringed by long, thick lashes. He was, she thought, the handsomest man she had ever encountered in her entire life.

Colt crossed the room and stood before her. "I'm your brother."

Briana's hands began trembling. Dear Lord, Gavin had warned her it would happen like this, that one day, out of the blue, John Travis Coltrane would appear.

When she did not speak, Colt settled himself in a chair opposite her. "So," he began, "you've come home."

"And so have you," she managed to counter.

He was able, despite the tension, to smile at her with some fondness. "It's been a while, Dani. Fourteen years, I believe? As I sit here looking at you, it's as though we've never met."

We haven't, she thought, then began struggling to obtain command of the situation. She had to remember all Gavin had drilled into her. "Fourteen years is a long time. I feel the same way about you, John Travis."

"Folks call me Colt, have since I was about sixteen."

"Colt, then," she said. "I realize this is awkward for both of us. You're probably surprised to see me."

He shook his head, the warmth beginning to evaporate. "I figured you'd show up sooner or later. Money can mend a lot of fences."

Gavin had warned her to expect resentment, but she was hurt. This was silly, she admonished herself. *She* shouldn't be hurt. She wasn't Dani. "I would like nothing better than for us to be close," she said awkwardly.

"Close with me?" He laughed, a brittle sound. "What about our father? It's his money you've come to claim, you know. I should think you'd be appreciative enough that you'd want to see *him.* He's been pretty hurt by the way you've treated him."

Gavin had coached her. "I can't expect you to understand why things happened as they did. I never really wanted things to be the way they were."

"Then why were they?"

Briana lifted her chin. She did not, Gavin had told her over and over, have to justify Dani's presence or her claim on the estate. "I have already told you that I do not expect you to understand my feelings, so there is no point in my attempting to explain. Some things, I feel, are better left unsaid. It is enough that I am here. This is my home, Colt. If you resent me then that is too bad, but I have the right to be here."

He sat back in the chair and silently appraised this stranger who was his half sister. Confident. High-spirited. Self-assured. If he wanted to be pleasant, then she would be pleasant. If he wanted to be nasty, he would bet she could be just as difficult. The spoiled little girl who could be goaded into a violent temper tantrum was no more. This was a poised, mature woman.

"All right," he assented, "you're here to claim what's yours. I don't argue with that." He paused, then said, "Let's talk about Gavin Mason and where he fits in."

Not quite sure what to say, Briana shrugged.

"I arrived last night," Colt said frostily, "while your soiree was in progress. I didn't want to intrude, so I spent the night in the bunkhouse.

"By the way," he added pointedly, "I met your Dirk Hollister. I understand he fancies himself the new foreman."

He did not miss the way her expression changed.

"He is not *my* Dirk Hollister, and I assure you he was told last night that I have no intention of seeing Mr. Pope dismissed."

Colt shook his head in disbelief at her temerity. "Well, I'm awfully glad to know that, Dani. I do appreciate your not firing *my* foreman. He's only worked with the family for ten years. I think it's real nice of you not to march in here and kick him out."

Briana was not moved by his sarcasm. Why should she be? None of this, she reminded herself, had anything to do with her, not really. She was playing a role, that was all.

He looked at her carefully, puzzled that she could remain so calm. Nothing he said riled her. "So what about Mason?" he demanded. "Who the hell is he, and why's he here?"

She knew the words by heart. "Gavin is my stepbrother, Aunt Alaina's adopted son. We are very close, and when I announced I was coming to America, he insisted on coming with me because he said it wasn't safe for me to travel alone. He's been a marvelous help to me, especially after I got here and learned of your recent misfortune. . . ."

"My personal life has nothing to do with any of this," Colt snapped, "just as Gavin Mason hasn't got a damn thing to do with what goes on at this ranch. Now, I've heard about how he's ordered the hands around, and the servants. That is going to stop now. He's not to come here unless he's invited. If you don't like that arrangement, then I suggest you move into Silver Butte so you can be with him. Which"—he paused, reminding himself not to let his temper get the best of him—"leads to my next question: Why have you been staying on here? Why didn't you get what's yours and go back to France?"

She shook her head. "It's not that simple."

"Yes," he said, "it is. It's all taken care of. Father explained it to me carefully. You get a sum of cash, and I've already signed papers agreeing to buy out your share of the ranch and the silver mine. Hell, there's a lot of money just sitting there waiting for you. What, for God's sake, isn't simple?"

The next words she had been ordered to say were the most difficult.

"I—I want to live here, Colt. I want to see what my homeland is really like." She kept her gaze on the wall, so she wouldn't have to look at his face.

Colt was stunned. Never had he expected this. He could hardly say, "I don't want you here."

When he didn't say anything, Briana asked, "Do you begrudge my staying here—in my own home?"

He shook his head. She had every right. "If that's what you want, then fine, but," he added firmly, "I run things. Have your parties, sure, but I run the house. Me. Not Gavin Mason. You can tell him to go back to France, but if he insists on leeching off you, then it will be your money he gets, not mine. Do we understand each other on that point?"

Briana was hating the encounter more with each passing moment, but she knew what she had to say. "Gavin can stay in *my* half of the house."

Colt shook his head. "I won't have it."

"You have no choice."

"We'll see about that."

"Fine."

They glared at each other, Colt gripping the arms of his chair to keep from exploding. Briana wanted to cry. He seemed like such a nice man, and oh, how she hated to see those tender, beautiful eyes staring at her with such contempt.

Colt stood. "We aren't getting anywhere, Dani, so I'll get things with Mason straightened out myself. I've already taken care of Hollister, and since you seem to hold your stepbrother in such high regard, I hope the same means won't be necessary with him."

Briana was joyous with relief to hear about Hollister, but she schooled herself to show nothing.

He walked to the door, then turned. "Let's get one more thing straight. If you're going to stay here, you aren't going to be a prima donna. You're to do your share of the work around here, and you can start by getting dressed. I don't know how the genteel ladies of France dress at this time of day, but around here, the womenfolk are up at daylight and ready to get to work. You can start by going downstairs and helping to clean up the mess your friends made last night."

Briana fought the urge to grin. That was exactly what she wanted—to work, to do things, to become a part of this wonderful place.

He went out, then came in again to say stiffly, "By the way, Dani, welcome home." And then he left.

Briana squeezed her hands together, feeling the full measure of her tension. Well, Gavin had met his match; she was sure of that. Once he found out that he wouldn't be able to push Colt around, Gavin would take Dani's share of the money and leave for France. The ruse would be over, and she would be free.

She turned to stare wistfully out the window. She would miss this green and gold and blue world, the wide-open spaces.

She acknowledged sadly that she had a new reason for hating this deception. Under other circumstances, she knew somehow that Colt would be warm and friendly, and thinking about that provoked strange stirrings within her. In that first instant, she had felt something unexplainable, and she wondered whether Colt had felt it also. She had felt drawn to him . . . until those tender eyes had turned so cold.

She shook her head, turning away from the window. It was silly to daydream foolishly. Colt believed she was his half sister, and she could never let him know otherwise.

One more painful thing to try to forget.

One more tormenting reminder of a life that could never be.

Colt left the house. He knew he ought to be in the study, going over finances, but that would have to wait.

He needed to think, because there was a hell of a lot on his mind.

Damn, but his sister was a strange one. He'd never seen a woman so calm in a tense situation. While she had made her position clear, subtly letting him know she wasn't feeling guilty over her long estrangement, she had managed to do so without goading him. If he was angry, if he resented the lack of remorse in her manner, he knew it was due to his own feelings.

Smart. The girl was smart, seemed to know exactly what she was doing. But he was puzzled over her wanting to stay. Why didn't she just take her money and go back to the family she had chosen fourteen years ago? Could she really care about life on a Nevada ranch? He doubted it.

Maybe, he mused as he headed for the stable, she wanted to find a husband here. With the money she was entitled to, she'd have no trouble. Plenty of men would marry her for that reason alone. He sighed. He supposed now he'd have to put up with fortune hunters sniffing around, especially after the big party last night.

He slowed his pace. Dani was a beautiful woman. Did she look like her mother? He had never been told much about that period in his father's life, and he'd never asked a lot of questions, for he understood that that had been a very sad time for both his parents. He knew only that his father, believing his mother dead, had gone to Kentucky as a federal marshal, to put a stop to the mistreatment of the Negroes by the Ku Klux Klan. He had done a fine job, too, Colt recalled proudly, he and his sidekick, Sam Bucher.

Sam Bucher.

A wave of tender feelings went through Colt. He had grown up loving Sam Bucher like a member of the family, even calling him "Uncle Sam." When he died four years ago, peacefully, in his sleep, his death had hurt deeply. It was also the only time Colt ever saw his father cry.

Colt knew well the story of how his father had come by his fortune. He and Sam had saved the life of a prospector, Wiley Odom, who was about to be murdered by claim jumpers. When eventually Odom died a natural death, he willed the mine to Travis and Sam, in gratitude. Sam gave his share to Travis, saying he just didn't want the responsibility. But Sam remained with Travis, having no family of his own, and Travis saw to it that Sam never lacked for anything.

Colt commanded himself to push the memories away. There was enough going on right then without thinking about the past.

"Colt!"

Branch was hurrying toward him.

"Hollister's on his way to get Mason. One of the wranglers saw him on the trail into town, said he had a big bruise on the side of his face. What the hell happened?"

Colt told him, then said, "I'm glad he's gone after Mason. The sooner I set him straight about keeping his nose out of my business, the better."

"And Dani?" Branch pressed.

Colt told him about their brief conversation, confiding that he didn't understand her staying on the ranch.

Branch told him how she'd taken to ranch life right from the start. "Till Mason put a stop to her ridin'. He rules her with an iron hand, he does. She looks like a scared rabbit when he's around."

"You mean she's afraid of him?" Colt asked, bewildered.

Branch shook his head slowly. "Naw, not exactly afraid. The way she looks at him, it's like she can't stand him, maybe even hates him. I get the feeling maybe he's been sent by that woman, Dani's aunt, to keep an eye on her, and she resents it. He sure bosses her around, though, no doubt about that."

They reached the stable, and Colt led his horse from a stall and saddled him. Branch watched in silence for a few moments, and then both men decided it was time to speak of something neither really wanted to talk about. Branch waited, knowing Colt would talk when he was ready, and soon enough, Colt said very quietly, "How come you didn't tell me the truth about Becky?"

Branch shrugged, uneasy. "Not my place to. You never did like anyone messing in your personal business, Colt."

Colt agreed, then said, "Let's just say I came back a little smarter than when I left."

"Good." Branch smiled. "And I hope you didn't get your feelings hurt," he added cautiously.

Colt made no reply, as Branch had figured he wouldn't.

Chapter Fourteen

COLT decided to ride out to the silver mine, to check on operations there. It could have waited. There were other things that needed tending to first, but he wanted a good long ride, and the Coltrane property encompassed over a thousand acres. Not long after leaving the ranch compound, he felt like the only soul in the world.

The talk with Branch, about Becky, had gotten his anger stirring and he chided himself. What was done could not be undone.

He laughed at himself and recalled a conversation he'd had with his father when he was about seven years old. He and Travis had taken a cow to be bred by a bull owned by a neighboring rancher, and Colt had innocently asked how come the two animals would, without the least bit of coaxing, do something that looked so awfully uncomfortable. The expression on his father's face had made Colt feel foolish, without knowing exactly why.

Travis then proceeded to explain to him that while animals coupled for the purpose of creating offspring, the act gave them pleasure, and that was why they needed no prodding. Nature gave them the urge, he had said, the desire, so that, eventually, a baby would be born.

"Humans," his father gently explained, "sometimes

do it only because it feels good, but mostly they do it because they love each other. It's the way a man and woman express their feelings for each other."

Colt thought that over. Then he bluntly asked, "Did you ever do it with Mommy just because it felt good?"

His father's eyes twinkled and his mouth twitched. "Yes, son, I have, and when you grow up and get married, you'll do it lots of times with your wife when you don't care whether you're making babies or not. You'll do it merely because you love her, and that is one of the ways to express that love, by the joining of your bodies."

Colt nodded, straining to understand but feeling that it was a lot to grasp all at once. Then he thought of something else as he gazed toward the bull and the cow. "*They* aren't married."

His father nodded solemnly. "No, son, they're not."

He had gone on to tell Colt that while it was not always wrong, he would feel better if he never used women casually the way some men did. "Remember, son, you are a man, a human being, not an animal. You may have the same instincts as an animal when it comes to sex, but try to have feelings. Try never to let a woman feel that she is being used."

Colt had recalled his father's words the first time he coupled with a girl. He was just two weeks short of his eleventh birthday, and the girl was fourteen. The other boys at school had talked about her. They said that she would "do it." Mindy Hughley was her name, and one afternoon Colt walked her down by the creek behind the school building to see if she would. He didn't know exactly what to do—but she did. She showed him everything. He liked it, liked it a lot. It led to his falling in love with her, and she broke his heart because she never let him do it again. There was an older boy, Ben Wilshaw, and Mindy started doing it with him all the time, or so everyone said. She never played with the other boys down by the creek after school once she paired off with Ben. That was probably just as well, because a few months later, they suddenly got married, and another few months after that, Mindy had a daughter, and she was just past fifteen.

There were other girls through the years. Colt never found himself wanting for romance. This bothered his mother, who was afraid the same thing might happen to him that had happened to Ben Wilshaw, that Colt would have to get married. She never said as much to him, but she talked to his father, and his father talked to him. What his mother did say to him, though, was that he was growing up to be just as handsome and attractive to women as his father, and he should watch out, lest some girl whisk him into an early marriage. She did not mention "having to marry," but he knew what she was talking about.

He rode to the mine that way, awash in memories, and he began to realize that he missed his parents.

When he reached the silver mine, he sought out the foreman, Syd Gillis, and they went over the records, Colt knowing all the while that it was unnecessary. Syd had been in charge of the mine for longer than Colt could remember. Travis trusted Syd, and that was good enough for Colt.

The mine, he was aware, did not produce the quantity of ore it had in the years past, but there was still enough being brought out to make the operation profitable, despite the declining price of silver. When the time came, as it inevitably would, when the mine would not be worth keeping open, it would be shut down, as so many other silver mines had been. Till then, Syd would run it, and Colt would check the books periodically and not worry about it.

He shared a lunch of fried bacon and stewed beans with Syd, and a pot of coffee, then headed home.

Along the way, he met a few of the wranglers who rode the range. These men lived in line shacks, coming in but once a month to receive their pay and have a few nights of revelry in town before returning to their isolated work. Travis Coltrane had always been a fair and honest man to work for, and he'd paid well, so there wasn't as great a turnover as there usually was with other ranchers. Colt intended to follow his father's tradition.

When he arrived back at the house, the sun was just beginning to drop below the western range of mountains, and the sky was ablaze with lavender and pink. He took his horse to the stable, where Branch was waiting, an anxious look on his face. "Mason got here a little while ago. He told one of the stableboys to rub his horse down and put him in a stall, 'cause he's staying for supper."

Colt turned his horse over to Branch and headed for the house. Gavin Mason would not, as a matter of fact, be staying for supper.

As soon as Colt walked into the study, Gavin sprang to his feet, holding out his hand cordially. "Welcome home," he cried. "I feel as though I already know you."

Colt shook his hand, his eyes flicking over Mason. He was nattily dressed in brown leather coat, stiff white shirt, red velvet string tie, gold suede trousers, and knee-high brown leather boots. He presented a fine appearance, Colt noted, but his eyes were snake eyes, suspicious, narrow, mean.

Colt sat down behind his desk. Seeing that Gavin had already helped himself to a drink, he poured one for himself without offering to freshen Mason's. After a long sip, he set the glass down and said tartly, "What do you want here?"

Gavin floundered momentarily. "Well . . . nothing, really. Not for myself, I mean." He took a deep breath. "Actually, I wanted to introduce myself. I'm Dani's stepbrother. No doubt she's mentioned me."

Colt smiled slightly. "Stepbrother? You call yourself her stepbrother, Mr. Mason, yet Alaina Barbeau never legally adopted my sister, so . . ."

Gavin laughed nervously. "Actually, she never legally adopted me, either. My parents died, and Alaina was a close friend of the family, so she took me in."

"Then you're not related to Dani," Colt said flatly. Leaning back in his chair, he crossed his legs and folded his arms across his chest. "So, tell me. What is your purpose here, and—I repeat—what do you want?"

Gavin blinked. "Why are you so hostile to me, sir?"

"Why did you come with Dani?" Colt repeated. "Why are you here?"

Gavin ordered himself to remain calm. His temper was rising. "She needed a traveling companion. A young lady does not travel alone, especially this distance." He smiled, showing Colt that he forgave his rudeness.

"You've been interfering with things here, Mason." Colt's voice cracked like a whip. "Traveling with Dani to look after her is one thing. Butting in where you have no right is something else."

Gavin feigned confusion. "You have the advantage, sir. I don't know what you are talking about."

Colt leaned forward suddenly, his feet hitting the floor with a thud. He looked at Gavin coldly. "You tried to take over while I was away, Mason. You tried to fire *my* foreman and put a new employee, a *drifter*, in charge of *my* ranch. Just what the hell did you think you were doing? Who the hell do you think you are?"

Gavin gestured helplessly. He was on fire with the urge to rage, but he dared not . . . not now. It was not the time. Forcing his voice to be obsequious and coaxing, he said, "I'm sorry about all that. My intentions were misunderstood; I see that now. You weren't here, and Dani knows nothing about running a ranch, so I tried to help."

"Your 'help' is not wanted," Colt stated flatly. "Any decisions made in my absence are made by Branch Pope, not by anyone else. Certainly not by you."

Gavin folded his hands together to keep them from

shaking. "I apologize if I caused anyone any distress. I will also apologize to Mr. Pope, if you wish."

Colt dismissed him with a wave of his hand. "I don't care about your apologies. I want you to leave, Mason. This is Dani's home, but not yours. If I'm being rude, so be it. You haven't earned my hospitality."

"Now, just wait a minute," Gavin snapped. "I'm not leaving as long as Dani remains here. If you find that an imposition, that is regrettable, but that's the way it is."

"Dani can stay as long as she likes, but if you insist on hanging around, Mason, hang around Silver Butte. You are not welcome here."

"Let's not bicker," Gavin beseeched him. "I'd like us to be friends. I'm not asking you for anything. But I care about Dani very much, and I want to be close to her, see that she's all right. Your attitude will make things unpleasant for us all. Can't we work something out? I've told you that I apologize for any offense I may have committed, and I'm willing to do anything I can to make amends."

Colt stared at him silently. The man was a liar. He was pretending conciliation when he wanted to murder Colt. Why was he insisting on remaining? What did Gavin Mason really want?

Gavin got up and reached across the desk to extend his hand once more. "Come on. Let's be friends. That's all I want . . . that, and a chance to visit Dani sometimes, to be sure she's doing all right."

Colt did not take his hand. He waited, and finally Gavin withdrew the hand. "What if Dani decides to remain here permanently?" Colt said. "What will you do then?"

Gavin laughed nervously. "Oh, I'd go back to France, of course, but I don't expect she'll do that. Dani has always been headstrong, of course, thanks to Alaina spoiling her terribly, and right now she thinks she wants to live on a ranch. It's so different from the life she's had in France. She'll get over it, though. Dani never stays interested in anything for very long.

"But," he rushed to emphasize, "as long as she does remain, I want to be close by."

Colt stood up. "Silver Butte isn't far. Dani can ride in when she wants to see you. Later, maybe I'll see that you're invited out here for dinner. Maybe. For the present, I repeat—you are not welcome here."

Colt walked to the door and opened it pointedly. "Good evening to you, Mason."

"I find you rude and insolent, sir," Gavin told him, and Colt nodded his understanding.

Gavin brushed by him. "I'm going to say good-night to Dani," he said, "unless that, too, is forbidden?"

"Make it brief," Colt said, and Gavin strode from the room.

Gavin took the stairs two at a time and burst into Briana's room. She glanced up, alarmed, and he lashed out, "That arrogant son of a bitch won't get away with this!"

In the back of Gavin's mind was something he'd never told Briana, wasn't planning ever to tell anyone. He had to beat Colt, had to triumph over the Coltrane family. Colt's father had killed Gavin's father. Gavin *had* to avenge Stewart Mason's death, *had* to see the Coltranes ruined.

He began to pace up and down the room. "I'm going to enjoy the day when he gets his comeuppance," he muttered. "I'll love every minute of it."

Briana shook her head. There was no reason for any of this. The financial statements had been examined. The documents that would give her the whole of Dani's fortune were waiting to be signed. So why was Gavin wanting them to stay here with all this unpleasantness?

"Let's leave, Gavin," she cried. "I don't want to stay any—"

He whirled around. "Shhh! Just listen to me. I told you that when the time came, I'd tell you my plan."

Briana put her hands over her ears. She didn't want to know any more. She wanted only to leave.

Gavin grabbed her wrists and held them in front of her. "Your brother is not doing well," he informed her. "I waited till now to tell you, because I knew I would need your absolute obedience." He paused, waiting for the news to sink in. "I have received a letter from his doctors. If the operation does not take place soon, Charles will die." He paused again, then went on. "Oh, I know they predicted that there was time, that the spine wasn't going to be crushed for a year or so, but they say now that it's become an emergency. He must be operated on at once."

Briana stared at him, numb. They had visited Charles before leaving France, and she'd seen for herself that Gavin had kept his word. Charles had been moved to a good hospital. He was receiving the best care available in Paris, and the doctors planned to operate as soon as they felt Charles was strong enough for surgery.

She glared up at him accusingly. "You told them to operate as soon as they felt it was safe. You promised they'd already been paid."

He smiled an evil grimace. "I haven't paid them because I haven't told you all you must do to fulfill your part of the bargain."

Briana could hardly breathe. "Tell me what you demand of me, you bastard."

He laughed triumphantly. "A letter to the hospital authorizing Charles's operation has been written, along with a letter to my Paris bank, releasing funds which I have placed on deposit there. These will be mailed as soon as you . . ."

"Go on," she cried, nearly hysterical.

"As soon as you seduce Coltrane."

Briana stared at him, horror-stricken, then cried,

"The man believes I am his sister, so he would never bed me. What could you possibly be thinking of now?"

Gavin released her wrists and sat down. Briana remained standing. "Coltrane is vulnerable right now. He's had a bad experience, what with the Bowden girl being killed. It's common knowledge in Silver Butte that her parents blame him for the girl's death. No matter how arrogant he appears, he's bound to be upset. He is surely aware that he has sullied the Coltrane name. Think," Gavin crowed, terribly pleased with himself, "what it would do to that bastard if he was guilty of bedding his own sister. Incest!" He paused, wanting her to absorb the full meaning of what he was saying. Then he continued excitedly, "He'll be willing to do *anything*, pay any price, to keep something that damning from becoming known, keep people from finding out."

Briana shook her head. "I'll be no party to this."

Gavin smiled. "Then your little brother will die in agony."

They locked eyes, Briana's glittering with rage and Gavin's taunting.

He rose to leave, smirking as he said, "I'd best be getting back to Silver Butte. I've a lot of arrangements to make. I suppose you will want to go to Colt as soon as I'm gone and tell him the truth." He smiled. "I don't want to be here when you do. For your sake, I hope he doesn't become so angry with you that he kicks you out of this house . . . because Hollister will be waiting for you."

She was helpless. They both knew it.

"You know I must do what you ask, you bastard, but Colt is too honorable to bed his sister, so how do you expect me—?"

"There are ways, my dear." Gavin laughed. His gaze moved over her body, lingering on her bosom. "Use them."

He left. Briana stood for a long, long time staring at

the closed door, not really seeing anything through her tears.

She hated herself for having no alternative, and she prayed that somehow, someday, she would be able to let Colt know how sorry she was for what she had to do.

Chapter Fifteen

BRIANA lifted her gaze from the book she was reading and looked at Colt. He was seated across the room, behind his desk. Very handsome, in a pale-blue shirt and soft brown leather vest, he was examining the ranch ledgers.

It had been a pleasant day, and, for the first time, Colt had asked her if she wished to join him in his study after dinner. Briana took this to mean that he was warming to her. Oh, there had been some friendly moments, but inviting her to his study was new, and she was warmed by his invitation.

Colt was, Briana acknowledged, not only the handsomest man she'd ever met, but also most appealing in other ways. He possessed a casual wit and a gentleness that contrasted with his sometimes steely manner.

She sat back in the large, comfortable chair, trying to keep from staring at Colt. She looked around the study approvingly. She liked every room in this house, and that made her curious to know Colt's parents. Warm and loving people had decorated this house; she knew that much from living in it.

It was a big house, however, and wealth was evident. She was used to being a servant, and she had to be careful not to appear awkward, even though, a great deal of the time, she felt that way. She reminded herself to act as though she had been born among these people, for Dani indeed had. No behavior must carry over from her days as a servant, Briana told herself again and again.

She also had to be most careful of her feelings about Colt. She knew what she had to do, but, sweet heaven, she was beginning to like him more and more. She had to be on her guard, she admonished herself. Everything she was doing was being done for Charles, loathesome though the assignment was. She had to be careful not to feel sorry for Colt.

It was hard, though. He was so nice to her, even when he was trying not to be. Why, a couple of days ago, she had ridden out to join him on the range, to see what a branding was like. She knew the wranglers were going to brand a new shipment of cattle, fifty or so, and she'd ridden out fifteen minutes after Colt left the stable, hoping he wouldn't make her go back when he discovered her.

She'd ridden up as he was giving instructions to Branch Pope. When he turned and saw her, she joked, "You never heard me the whole time I was following you. Why, I could have been a fierce Indian and put an arrow in your back."

When he said nothing, merely staring at her, she asked, "Are you angry because I rode out here? I . . . I wanted to see what kind of work you do."

"The house is your territory," he said, "and the range is not. What did you come out here for?"

"Who says a woman can't ride the range," she retorted, "especially when she happens to own half of that range?"

"Are you trying to make a point?" he asked wearily. "Because, if so, I don't—"

"This is my home, Colt, and I should learn all I can about it," she said hotly.

"Your home . . . that you waited fourteen years before becoming curious about?" he said softly. "Let me ask you something, Dani," he went on, his eyes sharp. "Don't you feel the least remorse over turning your back on us all that time?"

Unable to think of anything else to say, she murmured feebly, "Everyone makes mistakes."

"Interesting, isn't it, that you realized this 'mistake' at the same time our father decided to divide his estate? Was that only a coincidence, Dani?"

She felt shame wash over her, and told herself furiously not to be so silly. She wasn't really Dani, so what was there to feel ashamed about? But underneath that, Briana knew all too well what there was to be ashamed of. Everything she was doing was cause for shame.

Keeping her eyes on the wranglers, she made her face as impassive as she could, until, finally, he sighed and said, "Sorry if I'm being rough on you, but that's how I feel."

They sat eyeing each other for several moments, and then, maybe because he felt he'd gone too far, or maybe because it didn't make any real difference, Colt invited her to stay and watch the branding. And when it was time to eat, he asked her to join him and the wranglers around the cookfire. Despite the crackling anger that was still there between them, Briana managed to enjoy the day very much.

After the meal, not wanting to stay longer than Colt would tolerate, she touched him on the shoulder and smiled, saying, "Maybe now you won't think I'm in the way every time I want to see how something's run on the ranch?"

Colt didn't respond. He was asking himself why her touch had jolted him, why having her near all morning had made him feel so emotional. He didn't like the effect she was having on him. And yet, he liked it very much.

He gave her a curt nod in parting, saying nothing. But as he watched her ride away, he considered that touch and the warmth he felt when she was near, musing about it until he forced himself to shake the feeling off. He had work to do, and Dani could not be allowed to interfere—not in *any* way.

Briana knew that something about her bothered him. Sometimes he was so harsh and sometimes he was so nice. He seemed jumpy around her sometimes too, as she felt jumpy around him.

She sat there looking at him behind his desk and sighed. He looked up.

"Something wrong?" he asked.

She shook her head. "I'm a little tired, I suppose. I'll go along to bed soon, but this has been nice. Thank you for inviting me in here. It's so cozy." She smiled at him warmly.

He laughed softly, a friendly sound. "Today was rough on you. How do your hands feel?"

She looked at them ruefully. Despite the leather gloves he had given her to wear, and despite the years she had toiled for the deBonnetts, her hands were still sore. "I'll probably have blisters tomorrow. They won't kill me, I guess."

"Do I need to remind you that it was *your* idea to learn roping?" The twinkle in his eyes was evidence that he was amused.

She shook her head, her beautiful long hair flying saucily around her face. "It was gorgeous outside today, and I enjoyed every minute. I certainly had more fun than I would have here in the house. I'd much rather be with you, learning how the ranch operates."

Colt looked thoughtful. She was trying to fit in. No matter that he thought she ought to take her money and go back to France, the fact was she was here, and she wanted to belong.

He was starting to grow quite fond of her, and that was another puzzling thing. There were times, he grimly admitted, too many of them, when he found himself wishing she were not his sister, that they were not related.

He put down the ledger and stared at her silently. Briana squirmed uncomfortably. "Why . . . Is there something the matter?"

"I just don't understand you."

She got very nervous. What had she done? Had she aroused his suspicions? "What is there to understand?"

"Why weren't you more concerned about seeing Father?" he challenged suddenly. "You could have visited him in Paris before you came over here, but you didn't. Why not?"

Briana lowered her eyes. "It's as I told you before. I have a lot of turmoil, emotions that I must sort out. For now, I want to concentrate on life here; I want to see for myself what it's really like. Later, maybe I will go to visit him and Kitty. Maybe."

"Why does Mason keep hanging around?" Again he caught her off guard.

Taking a deep breath, she told him the best lie she could. "I will be honest with you, Colt. Gavin persuaded Aunt Alaina to allow him to accompany me here because he was afraid I might not want to return to France. You see, he wants to marry me."

Colt nodded. He supposed he had expected as much. "Are you going to marry him?"

She shrugged, hoping she was showing only reluctance, not repugnance. "He cares for me, but I just don't love him. I have no intention of marrying him, and I've told him that over and over—but he won't listen." She looked up at him, then went on: "He says that sooner or later he will make me love him. I don't want to hurt him, so I've just stopped arguing about it, hoping that he'll eventually realize I mean what I say. I don't love him."

A strange undercurrent permeated her tone. Why?

Colt wondered. What was the reason for all that tension?

"He told me," she went on, with no trace of resentment or bitterness, "how you'd asked him to leave and not return unless he was invited. I want you to know that I understand. I am fully aware of how impossible Gavin can be. Aunt Alaina spoiled him terribly."

Colt nodded curtly. "Yeah, she's good at that. I remember what a little brat you were, thanks to her. When you left here, I was glad to see you go. Remember this?" He pointed to the tiny scar beside his left eye.

Briana had no idea what he was talking about. She got up and leaned over to get a closer look at the scar. She touched her fingertip to his face. "A scar," she murmured, then gave a mock gasp. "Surely you don't mean *I* did that?"

Colt was happy with the view he was getting of her bosom, thanks to the low neckline of her dress. Half sister or not, she was graciously endowed.

Briana saw the warm, glazed look in his eyes and knew she was arousing his desire. The realization filled her with shame, for she had never been brazen.

"Tell me," she said, "did I really give you that scar? Is that why you resented my coming here, Colt?"

He shifted his position, looking up at her. "I don't resent you, Dani. I just don't understand how you could ignore your family all these years. You came back now only because of the money, isn't that so?"

She turned away. Dear God, how could she ever carry out Gavin's plan when this was how he felt? "It was time for me to make a change in my life," she murmured, returning to her chair. "I might have come here even without the money. I don't know." She shrugged.

"I do," he said tightly. "You wouldn't have."

She stared at him, not knowing what to say. He picked up the ledger again, shutting her out, and she said, "Tell me about tomorrow, Colt. What are we going to do?"

Without glancing up, he explained that some of his cows had strayed up into the hills near Destry Butte. He and some of the men would be riding up there to try to bring them down. Several were going to be dropping calves soon, and Colt didn't want them straying far away. "It's almost a half day's ride to get there, and it's rough riding up in the high country. Lots of snakes and coyotes. You'd better stay here."

"Oh, Colt, please," she begged, "let me go. It will be a new adventure. I promise not to get in the way. You know I ride well now, so I won't be a bother."

What the hell, Colt told himself. It was going to be rough on her, but maybe that was just what she needed. Then she'd realize once and for all that her place was not here. Let her get her fill.

He acknowledged that there was a new reason why he wanted her to hurry up and leave. He did not like the way she was making him feel. A moment ago, when she was standing so close, leaning over him, he'd seen the rise and fall of her breasts with every breath she drew. . . .

He shook his head. The last damn thing he needed when everything else in his world had gone wrong was his half sister making him feel desire.

"All right," he told her, "you can come along, Dani. But I'm warning you. It's rough going, and no one will have time to coddle you. I don't want to hear any whining."

Briana smiled. "You haven't heard me complain before, have you?"

Colt said nothing.

"You're going to see once and for all that I can do my share around here, Colt," she said emphatically.

Still, he said nothing.

Briana sighed, stood up, and went to him. She gave

him a light kiss on the cheek and said, "I'm really trying, Colt. I'd like for us to be close . . ."

He pushed her away and got to his feet. "Go to bed now. We've got to be up before sunrise."

Briana knew she should be hurt, but she actually felt relieved that he was pushing her away. Perhaps Gavin would see that his plan was impossible and give it up. She desperately wanted not to hurt Colt.

She turned away and started toward the door, quietly saying, "I'll see you in the morning."

As she was about to leave, there was a knock. Colt glanced up. "Who the hell is that? The servants know I never want to be disturbed after dinner."

"There's one way to find out." Briana gave him a cheerful smile, hoping to change his mood, but he continued to glare at the door as she opened it.

A young Mexican servant was holding a tray with a plate of cookies and two glasses of juice. Her dark eyes riveted on Briana's as she said, "The tray you ordered, señorita."

Briana was about to tell the girl she hadn't ordered anything, but the girl whispered, "Señor Mason gave me these orders."

Briana froze. Gavin had sent her, so there had to be something bad behind it.

"Dani? What the hell's going on?" Colt called, and the Mexican girl breezed by Briana and entered the room. She placed the tray on Colt's desk, smiling at him. "You drink this, señor," she coaxed, handing him a glass of juice. "It is good and cold. The jug has been in the spring all day."

"Yes, yes, Ladida, thank you," he said. "Thank you very much. Please leave me now. I don't need you and Dani mothering me."

Ladida left, and a moment later Briana followed suit. Ladida was nowhere in sight, and Briana decided not to seek her out. She preferred to know as little as possible about what was going on.

She walked slowly up the stairs to her room. Opening the door, she gasped, outraged and fearful.

Dirk Hollister lay sprawled on her bed.

"You!" She was barely able to speak, her voice a mere squeak. "What are you doing here?"

"Coltrane ran me off, but I work for Mason. He sent me here with a message for you."

Briana stiffened. "Then give it to me and go. And never come to my bedroom again."

"Oh, just shut up, Briana." He stood. "I'll come and go as I please." He smiled. "That's some stuff Ladida makes. We have her working with us now. She slipped some of it in his juice. She used to work in a saloon in Mexico, where they drugged the customers regularly so they could be robbed easily. They'd wake up the next morning without any memory of the night, and think they'd just gotten awfully drunk. See, I didn't want Coltrane nosing around tonight."

She glared at him. "You tell Gavin that he has no right to do this to Colt. I don't like it and—"

"Nobody gives a good goddamn what you like." His arm snaked out, and his hand wrapped around her forearm in a viselike grip. "Mason is tired of waiting—very, very tired. Understand? He says you should've had Coltrane in your bed by now."

"It isn't that easy," she hissed, trying to twist away. "Please, you're hurting me."

"I'm gonna hurt you worse if you don't shut up and listen to me." He squeezed her arm tighter, enjoying the look of pain on her face. "You haven't *really* tried, have you? You haven't rubbed your tits against him, have you? You haven't tried hard enough, Briana."

He released her suddenly and stepped back.

"Here's the message," he said coldly. "A nurse in Paris wrote you a letter your brother dictated, but you're not going to get the letter until you get Coltrane in the sack."

He paused to enjoy the look of longing and despair

on her face. Cocky bitch. She deserved to be miserable. "He also says that if you don't follow orders very carefully, he's going to have your brother put out of his misery."

Briana's eyes widened. Surely, he wouldn't . . . She shivered. She knew that he indeed would. She had no choice. To disobey Gavin meant death for Charles. Yes, Gavin was capable of carrying out his threat. Charles would die, and heaven only knew what Gavin would do to her.

"Tell him I will do as he asks, as soon as possible." Her voice was barely audible.

"Good. And one thing more." He was moving toward the door. "He says he wants to see you soon. Ladida will tell you when she's going to slip something into Coltrane's drink, and you'll know that's the night. Mason'll slip in here."

She shook her head. "Tell him to find another way, please. I'm afraid. Drugs are dangerous. I don't want Colt hurt."

"Ladida knows what she's doing," he scoffed. "Just do as you're told."

He opened the door and stepped into the hallway. He winked. "One day, we'll have all the time we need, you 'n me, and it's gonna be *so* good. That's a promise." He left, closing the door behind him.

Silently Briana made a promise of her own. Never would she yield to Dirk Hollister.

Crossing to the open window, Briana stood and stared out into the night. Purple and black shadows fell across the grounds. It was a beautiful night. Warm. Mystical. She moved her fingertips up and down her bare arms. The touch of Dirk had made her feel unclean. She was certain that Colt's hands would feel gentle, tender, that she would revel in his touch.

Colt.

She could feel the stirrings of desire within him, yet there was also a fierce restraint, because he thought she was his blood kin. She could sense the maelstrom of emotions churning inside him, awesome in their intensity, overpowering.

On her part, there was, God forgive her, acceptance of the unforgivable. And regret—terrible regret. She could only hope everything here would be over quickly, so she could go home.

As she stood at the window, it began to seem to Briana that perhaps there was another way, a less hurtful way, to carry out Gavin's orders. Maybe Colt could be made to *think* he had been intimate with his sister . . . without the actuality of the act. If he was drugged, his memory shadowed or even obliterated, he could be made to believe he'd done something he hadn't really done.

For the first time in a long while, Briana began to feel less helpless, more independent. Maybe she didn't have to do Gavin's bidding after all. . . .

Chapter Sixteen

COLT was irritable. He had overslept by a couple of hours, which was unlike him. Of all days to do so, he reproached himself.

When he'd dressed and gone out, he found that the wranglers had waited a little while for him to show up at the bunkhouse, figured he'd decided to do something else that day, and scattered to do other chores. That put Colt in a worse mood, because those cows needed to be rounded up before they calved. Which meant, he guessed, that he had to do it by himself.

Carlota had hot coffee waiting for him, and steak and eggs. He waved the food away, gulped down the coffee, and told her, "I won't be back for dinner, and I'll probably be gone two or three days. Pack me some bacon and hardtack. That should do me. I can always shoot a rabbit," he added, speaking to himself.

Then something almost surfaced in his mind, and he asked, "Carlota, is Ladida related to you?"

Looking wary, the housekeeper responded, "My niece, Señor Coltrane. Why? She hasn't done anything wrong, has she?"

Colt shook his head, wondering why he'd brought it up.

In the stable, he frowned at the sight of Dani, grunted a greeting, then turned to see that his stallion, Pedro, was saddled and ready.

"I knew you'd be down sooner or later and want to get started quickly," Briana said.

He nodded, quite taken aback. "Thank you. I'm sorry to be so late, but I overslept."

He stuffed the burlap sack into a saddlebag, then led his horse from the stable.

Briana went to get Belle. She knew very well why he'd overslept. Ladida, whom she'd found early that morning, had been only too happy to brag about how good she was at making sleeping potions. Explaining that she used a mushroom, she emphasized how important it was to know exactly how much juice to extract.

"Too much," she explained, "and the person will have nightmares, visions. When he wakes up, he'll feel terrible, and he'll wonder what has happened. But I mixed just enough juice with the juice of the sugarcane, so he'll wake up feeling . . . just tired."

"Is it dangerous?" Briana wanted to know.

Ladida shook her head. "Not if you know what you're doing, and the amount I gave him last night was just right." She grinned proudly.

Briana hated dealing with her, but Ladida was in Gavin's pay and Gavin wanted her to help Briana, so what choice was there?

She nodded as Ladida slipped her a small packet. "All you have to do is put this in something he is drinking. Remember, it will sweeten his drink, so it is better to put it into something he expects to be sweet. He will become very relaxed, then very sleepy, and you should be able to do anything with him."

Nodding her thanks, Briana had hurried outside to saddle her own horse and Colt's.

Leading Belle from the stable, she called to Colt, "Wait! You know I'm going with you."

Colt reined his stallion about, annoyed. "No, Dani, not now. I'm going out alone. I've got to round up those cows by myself and I won't have time to look after you."

"Who said you'd have to look after me?" Briana flared. "I can take care of myself. Besides, you need some help."

"Help, yes," he snapped, "not a soft-butted woman who'll be screaming about saddle sores by sunset. I don't have time for you now, Dani. Stay here."

"No."

He glared at her, but she was undaunted by his anger. "I have a right to go if I want to. Those cows are half mine now, whether you like it or not."

This was not, she know, endearing her to him. But she couldn't wait until he was in a better mood. Charles's letter was waiting. She had to follow Gavin's orders—and fast.

Colt was in no mood for arguing. Dawn was now history and morning was fading fast. "No, damn it, I don't want you along."

Briana moved her horse to stand alongside his. She faced him, her chin lifted in stony defiance. "You can't tell me what I can and cannot do around here, Colt. Like it or not, this ranch is half mine, and that means I'm as much the boss as you are. We're wasting time arguing, so let's just get moving."

With a haughty toss of her head that sent her auburn hair flying, Briana nudged Belle into a gallop. She did not have to turn to see that Colt was right behind her, for the thudding of Pedro's hooves on the ground echoed all around.

They rode out toward the northeast range. Neither spoke. It was a beautiful day. The sky was as brilliant a blue as the dazzling Mediterranean she so longed to see. Now and then a white cloud puffed its way along the horizon, the only break in a seemingly endless ocean above them.

She turned in the saddle to give him a pleading look.

"I really don't like it this way, Colt. I've told you I want to be your friend. Please believe it's true."

She continued to look at him appealingly for a few moments. When he did not speak, wouldn't even look at her, she reluctantly turned around and let him be.

Colt stared at her back as she rode ahead of him. He watched as her firm, rounded bottom moved up and down in rhythm to the motion of the mare. He glanced away guiltily. She was his sister, damn it, and the sight of her trousers stretched against those perfectly molded hips was making him swell with desire. Maybe, he told himself to assuage the guilt, maybe it wasn't Dani he really wanted. Maybe he just had needs. Perhaps a trip into town on Saturday night would ease the tension.

There was a certain redhead at the Silver Star who was nice for a few hours of fun. She was no prostitute. Derita merely liked a man to satisfy her yen, and if a few dollars were left on the bedside table, fine. If not, she didn't mind. Colt liked Derita because she did not want anything besides lovemaking. She gave as good as she got. She was not interested in manipulating a man into marriage.

He must, he told himself fervently, be forever on guard against any woman's wiles. He had a lot of bad, bitter memories where females were concerned, and he figured he'd best concentrate on a future without complications from the opposite sex.

They rode on in silence, each lost in brooding thought, until they reached the boulders at the base of Destry Butte. Briana looked upward and saw the steep incline that led to the flattened top. "A cow would never try to climb that," she said. "What makes you think they're up there?"

"I never said they were," he retorted, pointing to a distant fissure leading into the rocky slope. "In there. This is one of the largest buttes around. The fissure turns into a ravine, and after that, a large inner cavity. Sort of a small canyon. It widens in the middle to maybe a quarter mile or so, before it narrows into a rock wall at the far end. Cows have a way of wandering in when they're about to foal.

"So do bobcats and coyotes, when they're hungry . . ." he added ominously.

Briana shivered. "I'm not scared. I can take care of myself."

"Good," he said. "You stay out here, and I'll go inside and start rounding up the cows."

"I'm going with you," she cried.

Colt frowned. "Then come on, damn it, but make sure you stay out of my way."

She followed him doggedly, casting wary glances about as they made their way into the fissure. She stared upward, saw the jutting, hanging rocks, and wondered what horrible creature might lurk there.

But then they reached the innards of the butte, and Briana gasped at the wonders before her. Like a painting of a jungle, it was a world of cool greenery, the dampness within encouraging the growth of silky foliage. "It's beautiful," she whispered, drinking in the sweet air.

Colt drew his gun and held it out to her. She shrank back. "What's that for?"

"Take it," Colt snapped.

She shook her head. "I don't want it."

Colt closed his eyes. Women! They could be such a pain in the rump. "Take it, Dani. I've got to leave you here alone, and you need something in case a varmint comes along. You never know what you might run into in a place like this."

Briana had never held a gun, much less fired one, and she wanted no part of it. "You keep it. If I see anything, I'll scream, and you can come shoot it."

Colt found her fear almost amusing, but managed to scowl anyway as he said, "All right, I'll take the pistol, and you can use the Winchester rifle if you need to."

"I *won't* need to," she said firmly.

Colt moved toward the thick growth of scrubs that filled the cavity of the butte. He hadn't gone far when something caught his eye: a hoof sticking out from beneath a clump of bushes. Kneeling, he pushed leaves and branches aside. His nose wrinkled in revulsion at the overpowering stench of death. It was a cow, one of his, and she had died before giving birth to her calf. Starvation? Snake bite?

"Colt, I smell something bad."

"Dead cow, Dani," he said tonelessly and started walking closer to the inside of the cavity.

Twenty yards farther on, he stumbled across another dead cow. Tension began to creep over him like a thousand invisible spiders. He wished he'd waited another day, until he had some of the men along. Something was killing these animals, and the carcasses were being left to rot. They were not being eaten. Out here, it was kill for food, not for sport. So why were the cows being killed?

He looked around carefully, for this would not be the first time he'd stumbled into a snake pit, to find the earth moving with hundreds of wriggling poisonous vipers. But there was no snake pit. There was no sound, either, save for his own breathing, and now and then the gentle whistle of the wind dancing down from the top of the butte.

He moved on. A few seconds later, he froze. To the side, in the stiffened throes of an anguished death, lay a dead coyote. His mouth was turned nearly inside out, as though his final scream had been ripped from his throat in agony.

Something very strange was going on, and the atmosphere within Destry Butte was permeated with an overwhelming feeling of death. Instinct was urging Colt to go back, get Dani, and get the hell out of there. Fast.

He turned, froze stock-still, wondering why he hadn't

sensed its presence as he found himself staring into the glassy eyes of a coyote, probably the mate of the one lying behind him. Its mouth was open in a silent snarl, and there was saliva stretching from upper fangs to lower. Froth and foam bubbled around its sharp yellowed teeth.

The coyote lurched sideways, momentarily losing its assault stance, and in that instant Colt went for his gun.

The animal lunged. Colt jerked to the right. A large rock smashed against his elbow, preventing him from drawing his gun. His body bounced backward, and the coyote missed him, then whipped around as fast as its weakened body would allow. Colt felt the ground sliding out from beneath him and he fell backward, a drop of six feet, landing squarely on his back. As he was falling, he yelled to Dani, "Get the rifle. Get the rifle and shoot!"

He reached for his own weapon, but it had fallen from the holster. Staring upward helplessly, he saw the coyote poised at the edge of the precipice.

At any moment, Colt knew, the beast would jump on him. He would be able to get away from it, probably beat it to death with a rock because it was so weak. But the animal's attack wasn't what he feared. No, an instant death wasn't what would happen to Colt. He knew now what had killed the cows and the other coyote, what killer was on the loose there in the butte.

Hydrophobia.

No doubt, as animals wandered inside the butte, they were bitten by whatever carrier had not yet died. Then they themselves fell victim to the dreaded disease, attacking any living thing that came in.

How many others were there within the cavity? Coyotes? Bobcats? Bats? And if they lived long enough to make their way out of the butte? What then? The disease would spread . . . to skunks and raccoons and wolves. Humans, too, would be attacked and would die in agony, as all victims did. There was no cure for hydrophobia.

The coyote fixed his gaze on Colt, as best he could through the mist of pain the sickness caused. A thin, ragged sound came from within him.

"Dani, for God's sake, bring the rifle and shoot!"

Briana had managed to unfasten the rifle from its straps on the side of the saddle and run through the brush toward the sound of Colt's voice. She stopped when she saw the coyote, its back to her. She crept away from it, to the side, to a place where she could see Colt.

Colt lay on his back, legs bent, arms straight out as though to fend off the attack of the creature above.

She raised the rifle. The coyote didn't see the movement, and hadn't yet seen her.

Colt inclined his head ever so slightly, not wanting to make a sudden movement. Speaking as softly as he could, he called out, "Dani, move *very* slow. Don't frighten him. Aim for his body. You'll come nearer hitting a large target than if you go for his head. You won't have time for more than one shot before he goes for you. When he does, run like hell. I'll be moving—trying to find my pistol."

Briana's throat constricted with fear. She had never fired a gun in her life, never even held one in her hands. What if she missed?

Her lips trembled, and she called, a sob in her voice, "I can't . . ."

Colt saw the coyote take a menacing step forward, his back arching. "Shoot, God damn it!" he yelled, not bothering to keep his voice low. "Dani! Aim the goddamn gun and pull the trigger. *Now!*"

It seemed to take forever to raise the rifle so the shiny wooden butt rested against her right shoulder. Her left hand held the barrel, and she sent up a silent prayer as she found the cold trigger.

She closed her left eye, squinted her right, and fired.

She reeled backward as the gun butt slammed into her shoulder, and the exploding shot echoed around the innards of the butte.

She didn't realize both her eyes were squeezed shut until Colt cried out hoarsely, "You got him, Dani! By damn, you got him!"

She tossed the rifle to the ground and ran to Colt, jumping from one rock to another until she reached the floor of the butte.

Colt stepped over the dead coyote and ran to meet her. He folded his arms around her and pressed her close.

"Hydrophobia," he whispered, unashamed of his trembling. Death had never loomed so close before. "Whoever he bit would have died in agony, just like the cows."

She didn't understand, but she decided she'd ask him later to explain. Right then, she wanted him just to hold her.

He held her tightly. "Most women would have fainted," he said, awed. "Why, you never shot a gun before, yet you saved my life. I'll never forget it."

He gave her an affectionate kiss on the cheek and flashed a broad smile. "Tonight we'll celebrate. Right now," he said grimly, "we've got to set fire to this place and burn these carcasses. Any animal that comes along and eats the diseased flesh will become infected and spread the disease. We've got to get back to the ranch and alert the men, then tell the other ranchers around here that we've got hydrophobia in the area."

He turned away and began dragging dry brush into a pile to make a fire. Briana stood and watched him, then moved to help. As the first flames of the fire began to crackle, she felt a heat of a different kind within, knew how much she really wanted him. If only she could possess him—and be possessed by him—in a normal way, and not through treachery.

Chapter Seventeen

It was late when Colt and Briana arrived back at the ranch house, and the servants had retired. Colt said that the celebration dinner would have to wait until the next evening.

Briana, wanting the companionable atmosphere between them to continue, said, "Oh, but I'm a very good cook. I can put something together for us while you go to the bunkhouse to talk to Branch."

"You know how to cook?" Colt said. "But I imagined you leading a life of luxury, Dani, with servants taking care of everything." He stared at her curiously.

Briana turned away lest he see the guilty look that was surely on her face. Of course she could cook. She was a servant. "I learned to cook when I got bored," she explained nervously. "There was never a lot for me to do. It was a secret. Aunt Alaina never knew. She would never have allowed it because—" She fell silent. Lord, why was she rattling on so, sounding so jittery?

Because you are not who he thinks you are, she screamed at herself, *and because you know what you must do to him.*

She hurried toward the house as soon as she could, anxious to be away from him. On the back porch there was a lantern hanging by the door, and she found matches inside. She lit the lantern and held it before her as she walked across the yard the short distance to the ice pit where food was kept cool.

The structure around the ice pit was made of split logs and was about ten feet square. Pulling the peg from the fastening of the drop door, she was struck by the odor of the close, damp air, and the smell of rotting wood and earth.

She picked what she wanted, then hurried back to the house. She hastily prepared dinner, then went to the study and set the small table in the corner, knowing it would be much cozier than the spacious formal dining room.

She set out candles, then went to the large area off the kitchen where the wines were kept. Selecting a bottle of white wine, she held it to her bosom for a thoughtful moment, then put it back. Ladida had said the elixir was best mixed with something sweet.

She hurried back to the ice pit, where she'd seen a bottle of *blanc-cassis,* a liqueur, and sweet. Made of white wine and black-currant syrup, it was kept chilled for use on special occasions. Well, she mused grimly, this night, if all went according to plan, could hardly be regarded as ordinary.

Walking back to the house from the ice pit, preparing for an intimate supper with the wealthy scion of a Nevada ranching family, Briana asked herself whether she could ever have guessed that this might happen to her one day.

When she was twelve and Charles was three, when their parents were alive, the family had moved from Nice to Monaco, where their father had gotten the job as caretaker for the deBonnett estate. Briana was terribly homesick. She missed her good friend Elise, and her father's old job as caretaker on the Androuet estate. It wasn't as large as the deBonnett estate, but Monsieur and Madame Androuet were a million times nicer and the quarters the de Paul family had been given were small but cozy. True, it wasn't a whole dwelling all to themselves, but there were several other children on the estate for Charles and Briana to play with, and her parents were more cheerful there. Briana missed Nice, too, finding Monaco starchy and stiff.

She sighed, remembering Charles's fifth birthday, when they were well ensconced at the deBonnett estate. The Count had asked Louis de Paul to hire as many gardeners as necessary, three or four, to help with the early spring planting in the large formal gardens to the south of the mansion. Papa had been gone half the day, finding the men, and when he came home and saw the cake Mama had baked and the celebration the family was getting ready to have for Charles, it was apparent from the look on his face that Papa had completely forgotten Charles's birthday. Poor Papa. From the day they left Nice, he hadn't had a moment of quiet. He'd been harried since they arrived in Monaco and he died harried.

Briana shivered. No matter how difficult life caring for Charles all by herself might prove to be, she was not going to let herself be buried beneath life's concerns the way Papa had done . . . or fade away like a dying lily, as Mama had done.

The table ready, the potion mixed carefully with the *blanc-cassis,* which was wrapped in cold damp towels and waiting in a silver bucket, Briana went to her room and bathed hastily, knowing that Colt would be coming in soon.

She selected a gown that had been one of Dani's favorites, of rose satin, trimmed in delicate Belgium lace. However, on Dani's slender body, the fabric had flowed loosely, modestly. Stretched across Briana's curving buttocks and large, perfectly molded breasts, the result was wickedly provocative. Under normal circumstances, she would never have allowed a man to see her in something so revealing. The cleavage was deep and enticing, and she noted in the large mirror that when she walked, every movement of her hips showed sensuous undulation.

She brushed her shining hair back from her face and tied it with a white satin ribbon. Ready, she faced herself in the mirror. Dear God, she couldn't bear to do this to Colt. Why, when he saw her in the skintight gown, they were both going to die of embarrassment.

She went to the study and opened the liquor cabinet behind the large desk. Taking out a bottle of whiskey, she removed a glass from the shelf above the cabinet and poured herself a drink. She drank it down quickly, coughing. Tears stung her eyes. How could anyone like the horrible brew? Wine was nicer, but the calming she sought came much quicker with whiskey.

Colt entered the room a short while later to find Briana standing before a photograph of Kitty. Standing next to her, he announced, "I think Mother is the most beautiful woman I have ever known."

Briana blurted, "Yes, I wish I'd known—" She stopped, terrified. What had she been about to do? Admit she'd never known Kitty Coltrane? Thank God the whiskey had not completely obliterated her thought process, and she was able to cover by saying, "Known her better. I wish I'd had the opportunity to know her *better.*"

She turned to give him a beguiling smile, touching his forearm in an intimate gesture. She leaned forward a little, revealing a good view of her full-sculptured breasts. "Thanks to my being so headstrong and spoiled, my time with your mother was quite brief. I was never privileged to know her in the way I'd have liked.

"Still," she continued softly, fingertips dancing up his arm lightly, "I was always aware of her great beauty—and quite envious, I admit."

Colt laughed, warm and happy to hear her avowal. She was not the insensitive, self-involved little snob he had always believed her to be. He only wished her touch did not arouse him so!

Her perfume, the feel of her so close, her touch . . . Colt needed a drink. Bad.

He went to the liquor cabinet and poured himself a whiskey. Then he noticed that the whiskey bottle was considerably lighter than it had been the previous evening.

Briana was grinning at him, looking quite glassy-eyed.

Colt laughed. Of course she had been drinking. No wonder. "You're a heroine now, you know," he told her admiringly. "The men were quite impressed when I told them what happened."

"A lucky shot," she said with real humility. It *had* been pure luck.

She gestured to the table. "Will you bring in what's being kept warm in the oven? It isn't as nice as I would've liked to prepare for you, but it will have to do on such short notice."

Colt nodded, returning from the kitchen with the casserole dish in a moment. "Dani, it looks just fine to me. Real fine."

They sat down, and Briana reached for the chilled bottle of *blanc-cassis.*

Colt raised an eyebrow. "What made you decide to serve that? It's terribly sweet. I don't think Father ever served it except at Thanksgiving or Christmas."

Briana struggled not to sound desperate. "But, Colt, this is a special occasion, and it's such a nice drink. I *adore* it." Actually, she detested the sickly sweet liqueur, but she'd sampled this bottle after mixing in the potion, and been pleased by how successfully the liqueur masked the flavor of the potion.

Colt gave in, holding out his glass. "Just a little, please. I'm still sipping my whiskey."

Briana hesitated. What effect would the combination

have? Was it dangerous? She prayed not, but she had to go on with her plan.

Colt talked as they ate, explaining that, first thing in the morning, the men would ride out to all the ranchers for miles around and tell them about the hydrophobia at Destry Butte. There was the awful possibility that infected animals had lived long enough to leave the butte, go to other areas, and bite other creatures.

"Is there nothing else to be done?" Briana asked, shivering at the memory of the coyote's glassy eyes, the saliva dribbling from his fangs, the foam caked in the fur around his mouth.

She asked, curiosity getting the better of her, "Have you ever known anyone who was bitten by an animal with hydrophobia?"

"Yes. It was horrible," he replied grimly. "And there's only one cure: death."

Briana reached for the whiskey bottle he had set on the table. "Let's talk of pleasant things, shall we?" She filled her glass again.

"I thought you liked the liqueur," Colt said.

"Oh, yes, yes," she responded hastily, "I just don't want to drink it so quickly. Besides, it's too sweet to go well with food."

Colt agreed, pushing his own glass away in favor of the whiskey.

Briana felt herself becoming more and more mellow. She wasn't used to drinking. Colt, too, was relaxed.

They left the table and, taking their drinks, sat on the sofa before the fireplace. It was a warm night, but Colt lit a fire anyway. He left the doors to the patio open, and a gentle breeze blew across the room.

Briana warily glanced over her shoulder at the bottle of drug-laced liqueur on the table. She had to find a way to entice Colt to drink enough to pass out. He'd drunk a glass of the liqueur, but that wasn't enough. Then she could complete her plan.

It felt good, Colt mused, as he sat beside Dani, to be able to be with a woman and talk easily. After a while, he found himself talking about Charlene. He confessed feeling that he had caused her death, and Dani was quick to admonish him.

"You are entirely blameless, Colt, and you must concentrate on that."

She touched her fingertips to his brow, pushing back a lock of his unruly black hair. She leaned closer to him as she did so . . . and she didn't miss the way his breathing quickened. The flash of longing in his eyes signaled that it was time.

He shifted away from her uncomfortably. "Well, it's over now, and I shouldn't burden you with it." He sighed. "I think I'll call it a day. It's got to be an early morning for me."

Briana clutched his arm. She did not hesitate, knew it had to be now—or never. She slid her arms around his neck and kissed him.

At first, Colt was too stunned to feel anything. Then, slowly, as her mouth worked against his, he awakened. He yielded. His lips melded against hers in a kiss that burned to the depths of him. Liquid fire raced through them, igniting passionate desire for fulfillment.

Briana pressed closer, moaning deeply when he touched her breasts through the thin fabric of her gown. There might as well not have been any material covering her nipples, for their rocklike tautness quivered eagerly against his touch. He scooped her breasts out, to cup and gently squeeze. All the while their tongues touched, mouths pressing together in an endless kiss of rapture.

Briana fell back on the sofa, arms tightly around Colt. She reveled in the sensation of her breasts in his hands. No man had ever touched them before, and the hunger to feel his lips on her nipples was overpowering.

Her hips began to undulate beneath him, and she was astonished by the urgings of her body as it sought fulfillment. For this was, for Briana, the first time.

Colt lifted his mouth from hers, and in the gentle light, she could see the torment in his eyes . . . torment mingled with desire.

Suddenly she was struck with the sudden realization of what was happening to them. If he did wish to make love to her, she could not refuse, would not dare refuse. Charles's life was at stake, and probably her own as well. All she had expected was for him to desire her, then pass out from the drug. That was her plan. But if he didn't pass out?

She could feel the massiveness of his manhood against her thigh, and her fingers, pressing against his strong, broad back, began drawing him even closer to her.

"God, no!"

The cry was torn from Colt. He jerked away, bolted to his feet, and lurched a little, hands pressed to his temples. "God, no! My *sister,* for heaven's sake! My goddamn sister!"

Briana got up off the sofa. "Colt, don't turn away from me."

She went to the liqueur bottle and grabbed his glass. Could she make him drink it? She turned and found him staring at her with wide, incredulous eyes. "Are you crazy, Dani? Have you lost your mind? We can't . . ."

Briana had never seen such wretched despair in anyone's face. She hated herself. Colt did not deserve to suffer this way.

Another pain stabbed her, deep in her soul.

She cared for him.

The admission stunned her. She had never felt that way about a man. How could she go through with this fiendish plan and hurt a man she cared for so deeply?

With great effort, Briana made herself seem light

and gay as she went to him with the glass and the bottle. She poured him a drink, then held it out to him and smiled. "It's over, Colt. It won't happen again and it was no one's fault. Now, can we have a drink and say good-night?"

His muscles relaxed a little. She was right. It was over. Emotions had gotten away from him, but he had stopped in time. No need to dwell on the ugliness of it. "You're right," he said. "Let's say good-night and just forget about it."

He drank the whole glass, then took the bottle from her and poured another glass, drinking all of that, too.

Chapter Eighteen

BRIANA said good-night and left Colt in the study. A short while later, she heard him go to his room. After waiting for almost an hour, she finally went to find that he had succumbed to the effects of the drink before removing his clothes. He lay sideways across his bed, breathing deeply.

She moved quickly, maneuvering him lengthwise on the bed. When he did not wake up, she realized he really was out cold. Pulling the covers back from beneath him, she began to remove his clothing, the shirt and vest first. He slept very soundly.

Unbuckling Colt's wide leather belt, Briana reached for the fastening of his trousers, then hesitated, her heart pounding. Dear God, she was about to strip a man naked!

But there was no time for hesitation. It *had* to be done. Pulling his pants down, and his underwear, keeping her gaze averted, she rendered him completely naked.

Then Briana dared to look at him. Awestruck, her burning gaze swept over his perfectly molded body. She knew she was without the ability to compare him with other men, for she was inexperienced. Nevertheless, John Travis Coltrane was truly a glorious man.

She started to turn away but realized, with only a slight twinge of shame, that she liked the sight of his genitals. Warmth spread through her, and she dared to reach out and caress him.

He stirred, ever so slightly, but enough to make her jerk her hand away. A tremor began, a taunting reminder that she was going to have to take off her own clothes and lie naked beside Colt all night.

Realistically, Briana knew it should not appear that she had gone to bed with him so willingly. It would, therefore, have been better had she been able to get him to *her* room, to *her* bed, as though he had forced her. But that was impossible. He was far too big and heavy for her to move.

Removing all of her clothing, she lay down beside him, rigid. She didn't touch him, but only lay there, her heart pounding.

She had extinguished the single kerosene lantern and lay staring up into the darkness. The night passed with agonizing slowness. She forced herself to think of anything except where she was and what she was doing.

She thought of Charles. How wonderful it was going to be when, at last, they were reunited. Why, one day, he might even be able to walk, however precariously.

Think of the future, she commanded herself.

With the money Gavin had promised, she could afford a room where she and Charles could live decently. She wished to remain in Paris. Charles would be close to the best medical care, and pleasant employment for herself would be easier to come by than in Monaco.

At last, too tired to think but too anxious to fall asleep, Briana closed her eyes and waited for morning.

Colt did not feel good at all. Before he even opened his eyes, he knew it was going to be very difficult to get out of bed. He had done it again, had too much to drink. His head was pounding like a hundred blacksmiths' anvils, and his throat felt like sand.

He tried to raise his arms to stretch, hoping the tight, knotty feeling in his muscles would dissipate. His left arm moved. His right arm did not.

He opened his eyes, then sat bolt upright, jerking his arm out from beneath Dani's head. "Lord, no," he cried hoarsely.

Briana burrowed her face in the pillow.

Colt leaped from the bed, then realized his nakedness, and looked around frantically for his trousers. Finding them, he dressed as fast as he could, exclaiming, "No! We didn't. Lord, tell me we didn't . . ." He was talking wildly, glancing everywhere except at Dani, for he couldn't bear to look at her just yet.

Suddenly he went silent, turning away from the bed and going to the window. He stood there silently for several minutes. Then he turned around very slowly and looked at her.

"Tell me," he begged, voice rasping, "that it didn't happen."

"It did," she cried wretchedly, desperate to have the horrible moment done with. "It did, Colt."

"You asked me to come here with you," she continued in a rush, lifting her face from the pillow but not looking quite at him. "We started kissing, and it just . . . happened. . . ." She dissolved into tears that were not feigned.

With an agonized moan, Colt turned from her again. He was in the midst of a torment from which there was no escape. *How* could it have happened? *How* could he have been so weak? Lord, he did not even remember anything except leaving the study and heading for his room. He didn't even recall Dani being with him in the hallway.

He turned to stare at her. She was huddled miserably on the bed. He tried to feel revulsion for her, but it wasn't her fault.

"I'm sorry, Dani." The cry tore from him. "I'd rather be dead than have this happen. Forgive me. It won't happen again, ever!" He went to the door, stopped, but did not turn to look at her. "Please leave here. Please go back to France. I can't stand to look at you."

He bolted through the door and down the hallway, his footsteps echoing through the house.

Briana continued to lie there, huddled, clutching the sheet to her. After a while, she heard the sound of servants entering the house to begin their day. She scrambled out of bed, then threw on her gown and hurried down the hall to her room.

She decided to dress and ride into Silver Butte to tell Gavin that she had succeeded in seducing Colt. She'd done what he wanted her to do, and he would give her the letter from Charles. They might even leave soon! In fact, she thought wildly, happily, she might not have to return to the ranch at all.

In Silver Butte, Briana rode to the hotel where she and Gavin had stayed when they arrived. Situated at the end of the main street, it was, by far, the prettiest building in town. A large porch swept the front of the neatly painted white four-story building. She saw some of the older, permanent residents sitting in wicker swings and watching her curiously as she dismounted and tied her horse to the hitching post. She felt shy in her men's trousers, but how else could she dress if she was going to ride? She couldn't wear a gown, for she didn't know how to ride sidesaddle.

Nodding to no one in particular and everyone in general, Briana entered the dimly lit hotel lobby, and was at once refreshed by the cooler air within. She asked the young desk clerk for Gavin Mason's room number and was told he was all the way up on the top floor.

Reaching Gavin's door, she heard a woman's voice. She glanced once more at the room number and, satisfied that she was at the right room, knocked hesitantly.

The door swung open, and Briana stepped back. A woman was standing there eyeing her sharply. The woman was wearing a bright-green satin robe. Her lips were painted a red more brilliant than ruby, and her eyes were shadowed in pale blue.

Briana looked beyond her and saw Gavin seated on a yellow velvet divan. At the same instant, he saw her and rushed to the door.

The woman in green looked at them warily.

Gavin placed a possessive arm on Briana's shoulder and steered her into the room. "This is Delia, Dani. The two of you will get along just fine." He pushed Briana onto the divan, his eyes shining. "Well, tell me," he asked. "Is it done?"

Briana lowered her head. "It's done."

Gavin clasped his hands together, as if in fervent prayer. "Wonderful. Wonderful! Now we can begin to think about going home!"

Delia quickly interjected, her voice soft, coaxing, "Don't forget, honey baby, you're taking me home with you." She gave Briana a menacing look, adding, "And it don't matter whether you like it or not. He's mine now."

"*I* certainly don't want him," Briana couldn't help retorting.

Gavin ignored that, too pleased to be angry. "How did he behave? Was he wildly upset? Uncontrollably angry?"

Briana glanced away, unable to bear the gloating triumph on Gavin's face. She assured him that Colt was indeed the epitome of misery, and she told him the lies she'd planned to tell him about seducing Colt. All the while, Delia hovered anxiously near them, trying to hear. Exasperated, Gavin finally stood up and shoved Delia into the bedroom, instructing her to stay put until he called her to come out.

It didn't take Briana more than a few seconds to understand why Gavin had taken up with Delia. Though plump, Delia was angelic looking, with strawberry-blonde curls and light-blue eyes. She had lovely features and a saucy way about her. Briana was worldly enough to know a prostitute when she saw one, and she was certain Delia was one. She had a shrewd look about her, and enough poise that Briana was sure Delia never did anything without being in control of herself, saucy and fun-loving though she appeared to be. That appearance was all contrived, Briana was sure.

Did Delia know that Briana wasn't Dani? If Gavin had told Delia any of the facts, he must have been confident that she wouldn't blab.

At that point, Briana was too exhausted from their deception and too heartsick over Colt to worry about either Delia or Dirk betraying her and Gavin. Gavin would have to handle both of them.

The one good thing was that Gavin now had a pretty woman he could bed—someone whose presence would take his mind off Briana's body, for which Briana was deeply thankful. Gavin was the kind of male who needed someone in his bed all the time, and Delia would surely know how to satisfy a man.

When Gavin joined Briana again, she pleaded, "Colt is so hurt over what's happened that I can't bear to face him. I'm going to stay here until we leave for France."

"What?" He shook his head firmly. "Absolutely not. I want you to get back to the ranch now and get ready to bed him again tonight. We have to move fast, before he decides to leave town to avoid you."

Astonished, Briana jumped up and cried out in angry protest that she wouldn't do it. Gavin grabbed her shoulders and shook her. He pushed her down on the divan and sat beside her, holding onto her arm. "You've already proved what a whore you are," he said, smiling the cruel smile she had hated for what seemed like an eternity. "What difference does it make to you whether you sleep with a man once or a hundred times? Get back there, Briana. Use your body all day and all night if necessary, but turn Coltrane into your slave." His eyes riveted hers, and she found she couldn't look away. It was as she'd suspected, but not quite allowed herself to believe. Gavin wasn't just ruthless, wasn't just cruel; he was mad. And he would make her do what he wanted, as he'd made her come here in the first place, impersonate Dani, seduce Colt. . . .

"Fine, Gavin," she said evenly, knowing better than to rile him, "and may I have the letter from Paris, please?"

She hardly dared to breathe. He watched her for a moment, then stood up and disappeared into the bedroom, appearing again in a minute with the letter. She tore it open, read that Charles sent all his love, was feeling stronger, was looking forward to the operation with only a little fear . . . and begged his sister to come back. Most of all, he wanted his sister to come back.

Unwilling to let Gavin witness her reaction to the letter, Briana merely folded it hastily and held it tightly in her hand, to be read again later, when she was alone.

He stood and motioned her toward the door, away from the bedroom. When they were far enough from the bedroom so that Delia wouldn't overhear, Gavin said, "She is going back to France with us, but keep your mouth shut around her because I've told her only so much and no more. She thinks you're really Dani; remember that. We don't want anyone in Silver Butte to know the truth, for God's sake. It's bad enough that I had to tell Hollister, but I had to."

"But why is she coming home to France with us?"

"I'll explain when the time is right," Gavin growled.

"I always do things when the time is right and not a moment sooner."

Briana left him as soon as she could, and rode Belle back to the ranch. Back to Colt.

Dear Lord, she reflected, the truth was that, far from being disappointed that Gavin had forbidden her to stay in town, she was thrilled. Now that the awful thing had been done to Colt, now that the man surely hated her, now that it was too late for him to feel anything for her except revulsion . . . now she could at last admit the truth: She had fallen in love with Colt.

And there would never be anything she could do about it. In breaking Colt's heart, she had also broken her own.

While Briana was riding back to the ranch, Gavin was learning some surprising things about his playmate.

"Gavin," she called to him as he was closing the door after Briana.

He turned, puzzled by the strange tone of Delia's voice. Then he saw that her eyes were glassy, the way they looked when she was making love. Was she wanting him *now?* he wondered. "Yes?" he responded quietly.

Delia stared at him fixedly. "Keep Dani with us," she said firmly, "and don't worry about her being rebellious. I know how to deal with her, Gavin dear."

Gavin chuckled. He began to understand what Delia wanted with Briana, and that suited him just fine. Delia was one hell of a woman. Gavin considered himself one hell of a man, but there were times when she wanted more than he cared to give. Maybe Briana could ease things for him. As he looked at Delia, he felt a warm rush in his loins. It might be fun, the three of them. Besides, he had no intention of letting Briana go off on her own once they returned to France. He couldn't. She knew too much. He'd have to keep her under control.

Gavin looked at Delia. Their eyes met and held. "Very well," he said.

Gavin held his arms open, and Delia ran to be folded in his embrace. In a moment they were naked in bed, caught up in their passion. As they made love, each had Briana in mind.

Chapter Nineteen

BRIANA returned to the ranch to find that Colt had moved out, taking his clothes down to the bunkhouse, declaring that he would be living with the hands from then on.

The next day, Briana waited for Branch by one of the barns, and hurried to ask whether there was evidence of the hydrophobia outside Destry Butte. It was a chance to hear news of Colt without having to inquire directly.

Branch told her that it appeared there were no other instances of the dread disease. "Plus," he said, "now that we burned the whole inside of the butte, it prob'ly won't spread from there. What we're hoping is that all the animals bitten died before they got a chance to leave the butte. We're sure the disease started there, 'cause we found fifty carcasses in there. We shot two more mad coyotes, one bobcat, and—" He paused, giving her a strange look. "Well, didn't Colt tell you about it? That was yesterday. Boy, that was somethin'. We had near a hundred men swarmin' 'round that place."

"I'm afraid I haven't seen Colt since he moved to the bunkhouse," she said as casually as she could.

Branch folded his arms across his large chest as he looked at her thoughtfully. "You two had a fight, didn't you? I should've figured. He was braggin' about you the day you shot the coyote. Then, the next day, he looked snake-bit.

"Don't reckon it's my business," he went on cautiously, "but I am gonna stick my neck out and say life's too short for kin to be fightin'."

Briana started to turn away, and he called out to her.

She turned around.

"Is there anything I can do? I didn't say nothin' to Colt, but he sure looks bad. I don't think I saw him look this bad even after Miss Bowden was killed."

Briana shivered. Oh, how he must be suffering. "No," she said quietly. "There's nothing you can do. It's just something we're going to have to work out."

"Why don't you go back to France?" he asked suddenly, and she was stunned that he would be so blunt. "I'm sorry, Miss Dani, but somebody had to say it. You aren't happy, and he's miserable, so maybe it would be better all the way around if you went."

Briana bit her lower lip thoughtfully. What could she possibly tell him?

By the end of the week, Briana was no closer to setting up another night with Colt. He did not come to the house at all, and was seldom seen around the ranch. Twice, she caught sight of him from a distance, but when she started toward him, he rushed away.

Their behavior was obvious to everyone around. The hired hands, the servants, all talked about it, speculating as to what had happened between Dani and Colt. What was *going* to happen? they wondered. Each owned half of the ranch.

On Saturday night, Briana went to her room early, completely discouraged. She doubted that Colt would ever even speak to her again. Just before dusk, she had gone to the bunkhouse, having mustered the nerve to ask one of the wranglers to go inside and tell Colt she needed to talk with him. How embarrassed she was to have the man return and, looking sheepish, inform her that Mister Colt couldn't see her then, and didn't know when he would be able to. She turned away, tears of humiliation burning her eyes.

She sat in darkness in her room, having watched Colt ride out with six of the men, heading into town for a Saturday night of revelry. Then, not bothering with lights, she began to undress, hoping she would fall asleep quickly despite the tormented thoughts whirling within.

Lost in her misery, she didn't hear the door softly open . . . softly close, didn't know anyone was there until a hand was clamped over her mouth.

"Just relax, little darlin', it's me."

Dirk Hollister! Briana's fear was immediately overcome by anger. When he released her, she hissed furiously, "What do you want? How dare you sneak in here?"

"Our . . . employer is getting angry over the delay out here, so he sent me to fetch you. You're coming with me. Into town."

Briana was confused. "What for? I can't walk into one of those saloons and—"

"If you will listen," he interrupted irritably, "you'll find out. It's all taken care of. You're going to have a room at the hotel. You'll tell Coltrane you decided to move out of here because he was treating you so bad. How do I know you'll tell him? Because you'll just happen to see him leaving the saloon, very drunk—drugged, too—and you'll find him coming to your room in that state.

"You see, darlin'," he went on, "Ladida is taking some of her girlfriends into town to make sure Coltrane's buddies are all taken care of, so he'll be on his own. She also knows the bartenders, and she'll make sure everyone gets good, strong drinks. How about that?" He grinned.

Briana glared at him with loathing for both him and herself. How low she had sunk!

His grin faded. Dirk Hollister never liked for anyone to look at him like he was dirt. This snotty bitch was looking at him just that way. He leaned over and stared down at her in the moonlight. She needed to be taught a lesson, but Mason had told him firmly he could not dip his stick in her. First, she was Coltrane's, and next, Mason was going to have her. Later on, Mason would hand her over to Dirk.

Dirk didn't see how that was fair, especially since Mason had that wild thing, Delia, in his bed day and night. She must have some powerful stuff, he figured, because Mason acted like he couldn't get enough. But all Dirk had was Ladida, and the truth was, she made Dirk nervous. She was too strange—and what a temper! She wasn't pretty, either, and her body was nothing like the one he was looking at now. Briana, in a little lacy underthing, that luscious flesh bathed in silver moonlight . . . well, it wasn't fair, asking him to keep his hands off her.

He wrapped his fingers in her long hair and twisted her head back. He placed first one knee beside her, then the other, and was straddling her. He continued to grasp her hair, bending her head back so she couldn't yell.

She choked the words out. "Mason will kill you if you touch me."

He laughed shrilly. "I'll just tell him you needed calming down. Now, you just do what I tell you to do, and you'll be moaning in just a few—"

They hadn't heard the door open, so Ladida's scream of rage startled them both.

Ladida hurled herself on Dirk, beating him with her fists, cursing him. Dirk threw Briana from him and yelled, "Have you gone loco, woman? I'll squash you like a goddamn bug if you don't calm down." He grabbed Ladida and held her firmly.

"Ladida loves you," the Mexican girl cried, wriggling. "I want you to make love only to *me!*"

With a low, guttural laugh, Dirk took Ladida in his arms. "Well, now, I'd much rather have you than that icicle there. Come on, show me how much you want me. We got time."

He yelled to Briana, "Get dressed and get out of here. Wait for us downstairs. As soon as I'm finished pleasurin' this little spitfire, we'll head to town."

Ladida and Dirk began kissing passionately, fondling each other.

Briana, trembling with humiliation, rushed around the room, gathering her clothes. As quickly as possible, she left them and hurried downstairs, not wanting to endure the sounds of their thrashing around.

And all the while she wondered . . . would the nightmare ever end?

It was close to midnight when they reached Silver Butte. Ladida left them and made her way to the saloon where her girlfriends were, she knew, entertaining Colt and his men. Dirk took Briana to the hotel where Gavin was irritably pacing.

"Where the hell have you two been? You should have been here hours ago," he snapped. Hastily, he explained his plan to Briana, then took her to the room where she'd be staying. A few minutes later, Dirk took her to the saloon where Ladida had gone, where Colt was drinking.

She waited in the shadows while Dirk went in to check on things. Soon he came out to proclaim that Coltrane was, indeed, quite drunk, in such a stupor that he hadn't recognized Dirk. "The bartender didn't know what was going on. He's gonna put Coltrane in the alley. Ladida's friends took care of Coltrane's drinks, and he's in real bad shape. The bartender didn't even know what they were doing."

Holding Briana tightly by her arm, Dirk led her

through the shadows, down the alley, across a narrow street, and then they were directly behind the saloon. Seeing a man slumped against a trash barrel, she knew it was Colt.

"Go on," Dirk whispered. "Help him to his feet and get him to the hotel. I'll be watching all along the way in case he passes out completely. Then I'll carry him, but I hope that won't be necessary. It's better this way."

On stiff, reluctant legs, Briana went to Colt and knelt beside him. "Colt? It's me. You can't sleep here. Come with me."

His chin rested against his chest, and at the sound of her voice, he tried to raise his head. "Go away," he mumbled. "Get away. No good for you."

"Come with me," she repeated, tugging on his arm. "You must come with me. Now."

He shook his head, tried to stand, fell to one knee. Then, with her helping, he finally stood. He was so muddled that he let her lead him. Slowly, stumbling under his weight, Briana guided Colt along until they reached the hotel. He said not a word as she led him through the lobby, up the stairs, and into her room.

Reaching the side of the bed, she pushed him onto it as gently as she could. Through the mist of tears that seemed a permanent part of her vision those miserable days, Briana maneuvered him out of his clothes.

Finally he was naked beside her, as he had been a week ago.

She lay all night with her head on his shoulder, arm across his strong chest, feeling that she was, somehow, offering him comfort for what she was about to do to him. The comfort she gave to him comforted *her,* and no one else would ever know she had done it. She lay there listening to his breathing, apologizing to him silently with every breath of her own.

At dawn, the sound of the doorknob turning caused

her to go rigid. Eyes wide, she stared toward the door, pulling the sheet tightly around them both.

The door opened slowly. Gavin appeared, eyes sweeping over the scene before him. A slow grin spread across his face, and Briana squeezed her eyes shut.

"Oh, no, I can't believe it!"

Briana's eyes flashed open at the sound of Gavin's sudden, horrified scream. He slammed the door behind him and came into the room.

"Dani," he screeched, "tell me this isn't what it seems! Oh, Dani, how could you?"

Briana realized, shocked, that Gavin was actually sobbing. His fists were striking the air as he continued to scream, "No . . . no . . ."

Colt stirred, struggling to awaken. Who was screaming?

Suddenly Gavin leaped at him, slapping him, screaming, "Animal! Your own sister!"

His shrieks were silenced as Colt came alive and struck him, knocking him to the floor. Then Colt struggled to stand, shaking his head to fling away the sick fog surrounding him.

When he saw Briana, Colt covered his face and turned away, moaning, "No! I couldn't have!"

"I ought to kill you!" Gavin struggled to his feet. Facing Briana, he commanded harshly, "Get out of here, Dani. Go to my room and wait for me there. *Now.*"

There was nothing she could do except obey. She dressed hastily, wishing Gavin weren't watching, and then moved toward the door.

The room suddenly went deathly quiet, neither man saying anything. Colt was in shock, and Gavin was letting it sink in. Just as she reached for the doorknob, Briana looked from Gavin to Colt. How could she leave Colt this way? Why, he looked like a broken, beaten old man.

Gavin sensed what was happening. "Dani, go!" he thundered, pointing to the door. *"Now!"*

Wretchedly Briana gazed at Colt for what she knew would be the last time. Her heart cried out silently, *"You will never forgive me, but I pray one day you will understand that I had no choice, no choice. And I love you so. . . ."*

She ran from the room.

Gavin faced Colt. "When the people of this town learn what you have done, Coltrane, they'll tar and feather you. You cost the Bowden girl her life, and now you've ruined your sister's life. Maybe they'll go ahead and hang you, Coltrane. Who would blame them?"

And your father murdered mine, Gavin thought savagely. *You deserve this.*

Colt could not speak. There was no defense and nothing to be said.

"Oh, let me out of here!" Gavin cried, moving to the door. "I can't stand the sight of you!"

When he left, slamming the door behind him, Colt was alone. He would, from that moment on, always be alone. He was a pariah, and only he would be able to bear his company.

Chapter Twenty

COLT's head ached so badly that he began to feel it through the numbness. How could it have happened? He remembered drinking heavily in the saloon, wanting to get drunk, needing to get drunk. He needed to forget about Dani, and what he'd done.

But instead of forgetting, he'd let it happen a second time! How?

Things were terribly fuzzy. He remembered a swarm of girls coming in. They were all over his men, who were delighted. He hadn't cared for company, so he'd retreated to a table in a far, dark corner. Someone kept bringing him drinks. He kept tossing them down.

Then came the dream. He was outside somewhere—where? Dani was there, and he told her to go away. It was just like all the other dreams about Dani that had come to him every night since the time of that singular nightmare that haunted him with each beat of his heart.

But in the other dreams, Dani had gone away when he begged her to. This time, she hadn't gone away. And this dream wasn't a dream.

Finding his horse in the stable where he'd left him, Colt mounted and rode out of town. He made his way to a rocky knoll overlooking a creek, where he was sure to be alone.

Colt knew that Gavin Mason wouldn't waste any

time spreading the filthy story about the Coltrane boy. It would be Gavin's way. Gavin wouldn't care that it might also destroy Dani. He wouldn't care that it might destroy the entire Coltrane family. Colt was deeply grateful that his parents were away. Sooner or later, they would find out, but they'd be spared the worst of the gossip.

How could he face them? How could he face anyone ever again? It would just be so much easier to take his gun from the holster and put it to his head.

Coward!

Colt was washed with self-loathing and revulsion, but he heard the cry of his tormented heart. He was not a coward. He would not take his life.

He would simply walk away from it, that was what he'd do.

The sun was hot and the air was sweet with the fragrance of wildflowers. Colt left his sanctuary and rode straight back into town, to Carleton Bowden's bank. As he dismounted and looped his horse's reins around the hitching post in front of the bank, he dared to glance at people passing by. Anyone who saw him nodded and smiled, or even spoke to him. Well, he supposed, word hadn't spread after all. He might have time to do what he had to do, then get out of town without having to face everyone's loathing.

He looked toward the hotel where he'd last seen Dani. Had she been preparing to leave town after all? Yes, that was it, but she'd run into him staggering around drunk, tried to help him . . . and look what had happened.

Why? Why had she allowed it?

She cared for him, he knew. He had seen it in her eyes, had felt it when she touched him. Why, if they weren't kin . . .

But they were.

He stepped from the street onto the boardwalk and went into the Bowden Bank.

The employees all stared at him, and he heard the rustle of whispering, like dry leaves.

Once Bowden was told that Colt wished to see him, there wasn't a long wait.

Carleton Bowden sat behind his large desk, hands folded tightly on the highly polished surface. Everything about him was neat, orderly, for he was an efficient man.

His hands gave him away. He seemed to be clenching them, and he looked at Colt with rage.

"Make your business brief, Coltrane," he said.

There being nothing else he could do, Colt said, "I wish I could undo what was done, Mr. Bowden. No one is sorrier than I am."

Bowden's face remained frozen. "That's not why you're here, is it?"

"No," Colt admitted, "it isn't. But, you know, if you could look at the situation objectively, you'd see that—"

Bowden stood up very slowly. "You think that because you killed the robbers and got our money back you are vindicated? Is that it?"

Colt shook his head slowly, and Bowden went on: "My only child lies in her grave and you suggest I be *objective?*"

Taking a deep breath, Colt said, "I know your bank has always handled the family business, Mr. Bowden. Can we talk about that?"

Carleton Bowden was as relieved to change the subject as Colt was. "If you have business, state it. Otherwise, get out of my bank and out of my sight."

Colt took a deep breath. "I want to sign over all my interest in the ranch, the mine, and all the other family holdings to my sister, Dani. Now."

Bowden was taken aback. "Did I hear you right?" he demanded.

"You did. How soon can you transfer everything?"

"Why, why, very soon," Bowden sputtered. "An hour. Are you sure?"

When Colt had convinced Carleton Bowden of his certainty, the latter said, "The bank will have everything ready in an hour. Then you'll go over to Tom Kirk's office, and he'll be sure the legal aspects are in order."

Still glaring at Colt, Bowden ventured, "Does this mean you're leaving town, Coltrane?"

Colt nodded, offering no explanation, and Bowden said, "Thank God. I can't stand the sight of you."

Two hours later, Colt rode out of Silver Butte. He had only his stallion, Pedro, his rifle and pistol, the clothes on his back, and a few hundred dollars crammed down in his saddlebag. He no longer owned anything.

He headed west. As he rode, heading into the butter-gold afternoon, a soft breeze touching his warm face, he dared think things through one more time.

How could he have let something so despicable happen?

Goddamn, weakening-of-the-flesh-and-mind whiskey hadn't helped. Still, that didn't explain it.

He cared for Dani; that was the truth. Yes, he cared. The feeling went beyond anything he'd ever felt for a woman. What was weird, too, and frightening, was that he could not remember making love to Dani. Try though he did, he couldn't recall a thing about it, either time it had happened.

Shoulders hunched, head lowered, the very picture of a man whose spirit was broken, Colt rode away from Silver Butte to whatever Destiny had in store for him.

Gavin read the message from Carleton Bowden to Daniella Coltrane four times before he allowed himself to believe that it had worked. He had won! The entire Coltrane fortune was his!

Now it was over, except for the transfer of property

into gold. The Coltrane holdings would be sold so that Gavin could take his fortune to France in gold bullion. That's where Dirk Hollister and the five men Hollister had hired for Gavin would come in. They would be the guards he would need for so much money. True, he was going to have to pay them a large salary and pay their passage to France, but Gavin was now a rich man.

It warmed him to think how Coltrane would react when, one day, he learned that "Dani" had sold everything they owned, everything the Coltranes owned! Oh, he would be crazed with fury. And even more delicious, Gavin mused, would be the reaction of Travis Coltrane. All he'd acquired after killing Stewart Mason had been wiped out by Stewart's son.

Delia came in then, and Gavin stared at her in deep contemplation. Delia was not as beautiful as many women, was a bit older than he liked, and her body was on the plump side. But she was the first woman he had ever bedded who agreed to do anything Gavin wanted, no matter how bizarre, or painful, and he appreciated that. Through the years he'd become bored with having to cajole in order to get the kind of satisfaction he craved. Even Alaina, who had once been so hot-blooded, had never thrilled him as Delia thrilled him. So, despite her flaws, he knew he would keep her with him for some time.

He smiled. "It's over, dearest. Coltrane gave everything to his sister. Now we can make plans to leave."

Delia's eyes shone. "You're really taking me with you, Gavin, darling? I'm going to France?"

Gavin made her wait for a suspense-filled moment, then nodded slowly. She screamed and ran to throw her arms around him. "Oh, you make me so happy, Gavin, so happy. . . ." A lusty gleam entered her eyes as she looked up at him. "Let me show you how happy, my darling. Now."

Her voice was husky with desire, but Gavin shook

his head regretfully. "Not now, my sweet. Dani and I have business at the bank."

Delia made a face. "Is Briana—Dani—going with us?" she asked. When Gavin nodded, she said, "She's going to stay with us always, isn't she?"

Gavin nodded again. "I can't let her go," he said. "She could cause me a great deal of trouble if she said the wrong things to certain people." Delia nodded eagerly, and he admonished, "You will say nothing to her about this, Delia. If you do, she'll be too hard to handle."

Gavin smoothed his coat, took his hat from the table, and headed for the door. "Now I have to run along. When I return, we'll play, all right?"

Delia gave him a coquettish smile. He left.

As the door closed, Delia stuck out her tongue. *Slimy bastard*, she thought. How she loathed his touch. How she despised yielding to his perversions and having to pretend she loved it. One day, she would no longer have to put up with him . . . one day when she got her hands on some of that money he had so easily tricked out of the Coltranes.

She locked the door behind Gavin and went back into the sitting room. There was a large box of chocolates on a table by the divan, and she sat down and began to stuff them into her mouth, one after another. Gavin Mason was an insufferable pig. As she wolfed down the candy, she recalled the night she had first met him, in a Silver Butte saloon. She had known he was peculiar, but that made no never-mind. Peculiar men, she'd learned in San Francisco, are always willing to pay more than straight johns, and if the price was right, she would perform any trick a man wanted, no matter how painful. Money was a great healer.

She heaved herself from the divan and went to the corner bar, where Gavin had left an open bottle of wine. She filled a glass and began sipping, reminiscing about meeting Gavin. During those first moments in bed with Gavin she realized that he was absolutely the strangest nut she had ever met. She decided not to see him again. But then he'd mentioned being from France, and when he talked about going back there, teasing that he might take her with him because she was so marvelous in bed, well, that had gotten her attention. She'd been with him ever since—and didn't intend to let him go. She knew what he'd been doing to the Coltranes, but didn't figure she was implicated.

She finished the wine, reflecting on how smart she was to hook a man like Gavin Mason. Devouring the candy, she lay down on the divan and fell asleep.

The next thing she knew, someone was shaking her. She opened her eyes to see Dani—she had to remember to call her that—standing over her.

"Have you seen Gavin? I need to—"

The women heard Gavin's key in the lock at the same time. Gavin dismissed Delia, who grumbled but left. Then he gave Briana a huge smile. Studying her, he prepared to break the good news.

He knew there was only so much leverage he could get out of her brother. Blackmailing her through Charles had kept her in the role of Dani, but once they were home in France, it would take force to keep her in line. Until then, he was forced to pacify her as much as possible to keep her from becoming hysterical and confessing everything to the authorities. Guilt over Colt might make her do that, he knew.

Keeping a happy look on his face, Gavin said, "We will be leaving soon for California, my dear. We'll buy gold bars, and then we'll take the first available ship to England, then go on to France."

She stared at him, waiting for clarification.

"Coltrane signed over his share of everything to you, Dani," he said slowly, proudly. "You see, it was the least he could do after committing the unforgivable sin of incest."

Briana started, then stepped back in horror. He was

lying; he had to be. Her whisper was barely audible. "No. Tell me Colt didn't give up everything he had. . . ."

Gavin reached into his pocket and brought out Carleton Bowden's letter—addressed, of course, to Daniella Coltrane, not to Gavin, who had no legal claim on Dani and was not her guardian. If Briana had really been Dani, she thought for the hundredth time, she would have been furious. But she was thoroughly numbed by the realization of how much they had hurt Colt, and she spared little thought for Gavin's effrontery in intercepting the letter.

After scanning it just enough to be sure Gavin wasn't making this up, Briana threw the letter at him and went to sit down, burying her head in her hands.

"He did," she whispered. "He gave up everything, and gave it all to me."

Gavin was jubilant. "He did indeed. I planned it this way, you silly girl. And I've more wonderful news. Mr. Bowden has already found a buyer for the ranch! So, Dani will sign the papers tomorrow morning, and we'll leave with a fortune in gold as soon as Bowden can arrange for the purchase of so much bullion." He took a deep breath. "Go put on your prettiest dress and prepare to celebrate with me tonight. We are going home . . . and we're going home *rich!*"

Briana closed her eyes. If only she could shut out the horror of what she had done.

Chapter Twenty-one

SETH Parrish sat unsmiling behind his massive oak desk, hands folded across his stomach. He wanted to hear what John Travis Coltrane had to say to him. He'd had an uneasy feeling ever since Carleton Bowden had contacted him about the sale of the Coltrane property. Yes, he'd been eager to buy it, and, yes, he'd also had a lot of questions as to why it was for sale.

Seth had known Travis Coltrane since Travis had first come to Nevada. He respected the man immensely. He liked his son, too. Seth knew nothing about the daughter. He'd heard the girl's mother was a woman Travis was never legally married to, and that the girl had gone away with her aunt some years ago. Other than that, folks knew nothing about Dani. Seth was the kind of man who kept his business to himself and respected other people's right to do the same.

Colt sat in a high-backed leather chair. He ignored the splendid view through the wide glass window that ran the length of one whole wall. The plains stretched toward Coltrane land, and Colt didn't need any reminders of why he was there.

"You know why I came," he said firmly, pushing aside the whiskey that had been set before him. Like Seth Parrish, he was not interested in socializing. And Lord knew he'd had enough trouble from liquor.

Seth nodded slowly, shifting in his chair. He looked

at Colt levelly, face expressionless. "Suppose you tell me what's on your mind."

Colt met his piercing gaze. Seth Parrish was a big, powerful man, but Colt couldn't afford to let himself be intimidated. He said flatly, "I want my family's land back."

Seth's face showed no surprise. He supposed this was what he'd expected. "Then why'd you sell it?"

Colt shook his head. "I didn't. I'd never have given it to my sister if I'd known she was going to sell the land, Seth."

After riding out of town, a defeated and bewildered man, Colt had headed for the desert. There, he agonized over everything that had happened, driving himself mercilessly through each memory until, bit by bit, he'd pieced the truth together—or as much of it as he could uncover. He'd rationalized every possible motive Dani might have had, even considering that she might have been so stunned by his giving everything to her, and also been feeling guilty over what had happened between them, that she'd wanted to turn her back on everything and leave, as he had done. But no, that was being naive. She would have needed a little time to react that way, to make plans. She had made her move the second the ink dried on the papers he'd signed, as though she had known all along what he would do and was just waiting for the chance to swindle him.

Hell, he asked himself, what did she care about the land anyway? She was not a true Coltrane, did not care any more about her heritage than she cared about their father. She and Mason probably had the whole thing planned from the beginning. But that was a secret Colt had to carry alone, for he couldn't let anyone know how things had come to this pass.

"I don't want to talk about her reasons," he admitted. "I came here to find out how much you paid her, how much it will take to buy everything back." His gaze didn't falter.

Seth sighed, then leaned back in the chair as he stared thoughtfully at the young man. Making his voice gentle, he said, "I want you to know that I am willing for you to buy the land back, son. I'm not a greedy man. Certainly not a land-grabber. I never had any inclination to be a land baron. The only reason I jumped at the chance to buy your family's place was because it was right next door, and the price was good. I have three sons of my own, as you know, so I figured, with your land, I'd have plenty to divide up three ways."

He paused and shook his head sadly. "I can tell you never intended for this to happen. Maybe I should have checked with Travis and tried to find out what was going on, but contacting him would have taken a lot of time, and I didn't want anyone else to get that land."

"How much?" Colt urged.

"Carleton Bowden told me your sister put the whole price in gold since she was leaving the country. I didn't have that much."

Colt leaned forward, the tension creeping up his spine. "Tell me how much you want for the land, Seth. Please."

"Exactly what I paid for it." Seth looked him straight in the eye. "I had to borrow a lot of money on this place to raise that much, and I'm not going to lose my land over this. You're going to have to give me back every penny of that million dollars."

John Travis Coltrane leaped to his feet, more rage in his face than Seth had ever seen. The curses came out hoarse, rasping, and Colt's chest heaved furiously. "A million dollars?"

Seth stood up, facing Colt across the desk. "We're talking about a silver mine that's still producing, a fine mansion, barns, stables, horses, livestock. Everything on that land is mine. If you want it back, I'll sell it to you for exactly what I paid for it. I'm a fair man. And I'm a friend of your father's.

"Any other man," he went on, "would tell you to go to hell. A deal's a deal, and it was entirely legal. But I know you been through a lot, and something about all this stinks, so I'll sell the land back." He hesitated. "I take it Travis didn't know anything about this."

Colt shook his head. Why lie? He moved to the window, gave in to the plea of his tormented heart, and looked toward home. There was a stab of awful pain, and he turned away again. Lifting miserable eyes to Seth Parrish, he vowed, "I'll get your money back. All of it. Just give me some time."

Seth nodded. "You wouldn't sell it to someone else, would you?" Colt asked.

Seth said, "No. I'll give you all the time you need. Within reason," he added. He was a businessman, yes, but he prided himself on following the Golden Rule. Not that Seth was a religious man, but he did follow that creed.

Colt walked to the tall oak hat rack by the door to Seth's office and took down his hat. "I'll be back as soon as I can, and I appreciate your being so decent, Seth."

Seth shook hands with Colt. Then, curiosity rising, he followed as Colt made his way through the spacious house to the front door.

From the front porch that stretched the entire length of the mansion, Seth watched as Colt mounted Pedro. Only then did he give in to the question that was bursting within him. "Colt, where do you plan to *get* that kind of money?"

Colt smiled, but there was no warmth in the smile. His eyes were like ice. "From the person you gave it to, sir." He said it as though it were all quite simple. "I'm going to France."

He urged Pedro into a gallop, and dust flew as he rode away.

Seth Parrish stood on the porch and watched until John Travis Coltrane disappeared over the horizon.

Then he turned and went back inside, smiling to himself. Getting back a million dollars was a formidable mission. But this was, after all, Travis Coltrane's son.

As soon as they had as much gold as it was possible to buy in Nevada, they set out for San Francisco.

Gavin warned them on the journey from Nevada that, once they arrived in France, they would have to be very circumspect. It wouldn't do to let anyone learn of their new wealth, because that might lead to undesirable questions. They would take second-class train accommodations and, when necessary, ride in plain coaches. They would have to arrive in Monaco very discreetly.

For that reason, he'd felt they could enjoy their new wealth while in America. If they rode into San Francisco in a huge, fancy coach, what harm could it do?

Anxious to celebrate and to show himself off, Gavin hired an enormous white coach for himself, Briana, and Delia, letting the guards ride behind in plainer coaches, and on flatbed carts, with the luggage and the gold. Once the larger portion of the gold bars was acquired, in San Francisco, all six hired men would have to ride with it in plain wagons.

The white coach suited Gavin's mood. He was elated. He even became sufficiently expansive to tell Delia and Briana stories about his poverty-bound childhood in Kentucky. His face darkened as he related the story of his father's death, and Travis Coltrane's part in it. Briana understood then why it had been so easy for Gavin to defraud Travis Coltrane's son, and why he'd taken such an unholy gleeful attitude toward her seduction of Colt. It wasn't mere greed. Gavin hated the Coltranes. Travis had killed Stewart Mason. Seeing the look in Gavin's eyes as he told of his father's death, Briana realized that Gavin's madness had begun early in his life. And it *had* been a hard childhood; she didn't deny that. But hers had been difficult, too, and her attitude toward life was wholly different from Gavin's. What had warped him? Had it been his adoptive aunt?

Gavin talked on and on, oblivious to whether Briana and Delia were actually listening. He was enjoying his role as wealthy American, recently returned from Europe, a man of great means who had a château in Monaco and would soon be able to buy something much, much larger.

As he talked on, throwing in observations about America and how Kentucky would probably look to him if he paid his home state a visit, Briana's mind drifted from what he was saying. She looked around inside the large coach. The interior was done in deep-brown leather, and the floor rug was red velvet. There was gilt paint everywhere, inside and out. There were lanterns inside and outside, too, and four matched black horses drew the carriage.

She smiled sadly, thinking of how high she'd risen in the world since betraying her friend, Dani, and breaking the heart of the man she loved. How high she'd risen, and how low she'd fallen. Her friend Marice would laugh and laugh, she thought. Some months before, Briana had been horrified to learn of Marice's receiving a gown and a bracelet for her services. How much more horrifying were her own recent deeds, reflected Briana. *Oh, Charles,* she silently begged, *did I do right? Will you live? Are you truly better already?* The possibility that all she had done would mean very little to Charles in the long run was unthinkable, and she shut her mind against the thought.

One night, when they stopped at an inn near Sacramento for dinner before going on—Gavin wanted to make the best time possible—Briana watched covertly as Gavin preened himself before a large ornate mirror in the foyer. Primping his blond curls, smoothing his mustache, he brushed at his favorite deep-blue velvet coat and gazed adoringly at his reflection. *He may seem silly and vain,* Briana cautioned herself, *but in fact he can be cruel, and he's violent. Remember that, because you are under his thumb until you reach Paris.*

They dined on very good food, including fresh brook trout, which Gavin continually disparaged because it wasn't prepared elegantly. There was no wine, only beer, and Gavin rolled his eyes at Delia and Briana as if to say, "See how provincial they are?" His attitude became more supercilious the closer they got to San Francisco, and the greater the distance they put between themselves and Silver Butte, Nevada.

In San Francisco, they had no difficulty getting passage to England. Still feeling quite extravagant, Gavin booked the best accommodations, on the *Pacific,* a luxurious American liner that could sail at a speed of thirteen knots.

The ship boasted the latest in everything including the new electric lighting. There were elegant public rooms, decorated in French and Italian Renaissance styles. In the state rooms there was furniture by notables such as Adam, Sheraton, and Chippendale.

Gavin chose the best room for himself and Delia, and Briana was just across the hall, so he could keep an eye on her. Dirk and the other five hired men, however, stayed in plain cabins on the lower decks.

Briana had been closely guarded throughout the trip from Silver Butte, and the sea voyage was no different. There was not a moment, day or night, when one of Dirk Hollister's men was not posted outside her door. Her meals were brought to her, and once a day, with a guard beside her, she was allowed some walking, for exercise. Finally, Gavin had told her she was not to attempt to speak to anyone.

Being a prisoner suited her, for all she wanted was to be left alone in her misery. She was grateful, too, not to be in the company of Delia, who was arrogant and mean and talked incessantly.

Briana spent her hours agonizing over Colt and trying to be hopeful about the future, about making a life with Charles in Paris. She longed desperately to see him. Had the operation been performed? She guessed so, as Gavin had sent the money.

By day, she stood at the little porthole in her cabin and stared out at the endlessly rolling sea. She felt caught in a void. Nothing ended, and nothing began.

Nights were the worst, for she had no control over her dreaming, and her mind gave way to the tortures of guilt. Colt's handsome, adoring face would drift toward her. She was tormented by that smile, those laughing dark eyes, the two small dimples at the corners of his mouth. Sometimes she could even feel his arms tight around her, holding her close against his rock-hard chest. She awakened sobbing.

She wanted him. Fiercely. She loved him.

She knew she would carry the nightmares to her grave, and she knew she would carry her love for Colt with every beat of her heart.

Finally, mercifully, they arrived in London and went at once to the train depot and boarded the train for Dover. From Dover they crossed the channel to Calais. There they boarded another train for the trip to Paris.

At long last they reached Paris, and though it was still night, Briana ran from the train, exhilarated. She looked toward the glittering lights of the city and hugged herself with delight.

It was over.

Her role as Dani was done with, and her new life would begin now—her life with Charles, in Paris.

A strong hand clamped down on her arm, and she whirled around. It was the swarthy guard, Tom.

"Mason says I'm to take you to the hotel," he said, staring at her chest instead of her face. "Let's go."

Briana tensed, then chided herself for being so stupid. Of course they would go to a hotel for the rest of the night. She could not go to the hospital to see Charles. Not yet. A few hours' sleep, then a nice, hot bath . . . The thought birthed a smile. She wasted it on

Tom, for he returned her smile with a gloating secret look, just as Delia had sometimes done on the train. Tom made her flesh creep. All of Dirk's henchmen made her feel that way.

Tom stood guard outside Briana's door at the hotel. Exhausted despite her exhilaration, she went straight to bed, wanting to be refreshed when she saw Charles. She hoped weariness would keep the nightmares at bay.

Mercifully, sleep came quickly and soundly, and it seemed that only moments had passed when she heard someone calling her name.

Gavin stood over her. "Get dressed quickly. We leave within the hour for the depot. Your brother will be there waiting."

"The depot?" she echoed, mystified. "Why? How? Has he been discharged from the hospital? Why didn't you tell me?" She glared at him.

"Just get dressed," he ordered. "I have no time for questions."

Within a half hour, Briana tapped on the door to let the guard know she was ready. She was wearing one of Dani's prettiest gowns, a day dress of yellow velvet, with a long-sleeved jacket and high collar. Paris could be cold in mid-November.

Dirk Hollister was waiting for her, having replaced Tom as her guard. He stepped forward and took her arm. He smiled down at her and whispered a compliment, but she frostily ignored him as she always did. Her comeuppance was not going to be long in coming, he vowed. When Gavin Mason had his fill of her, Dirk was damn well going to have his.

They rode in silence through the as-yet silent streets of Paris, and when they arrived at the train depot, Briana didn't even wait for Dirk to help her alight. In unladylike fashion, she slid from her seat, grasped the sides of the carriage, and jumped to the cobblestones below.

She looked around wildly, excitedly, and then she saw him, sitting in one of those chairs with large wheels, a thick blanket tucked around him. A poker-faced woman dressed in a stiff white uniform stood beside him, but Charles was smiling joyously, his whole face illuminated with a love too great to be contained. He raised his arms to his sister, shouting her name over and over. Briana called out, "Charles! Charles!" Lifting her skirt and petticoats, she ignored Dirk Hollister's commands to wait, and began running toward the brother she adored and had been so horribly, desperately worried about.

She fell to her knees before Charles, wrapping her arms around him, and he hugged her, their tears mingling. For a long time, neither could speak; then they both began at once, convulsing with laughter.

Then Gavin appeared and dismissed the nurse, explaining to Briana that she would be taking over her brother's care.

As the nurse walked away, Briana called out to her, asking if there were any special instructions she should know about.

The woman looked to Gavin, then turned and left.

As Briana stared at Gavin, waiting for an explanation, he instructed Hollister, "Get the boy on board, then load his chair."

As Dirk started toward Charles, Briana held up her hands in protest. "Why are we boarding the train?" she cried. "I told you, I'm staying in Paris. It will be easier for me to find a job here, and Charles will be near—"

"You are leaving with us," Gavin said smoothly. "Do not cause a scene, Briana."

He barked orders to Hollister: "Get them on the train. Now!"

"No!"

Briana got to her feet and faced Gavin with more courage than she'd known she had.

He had what he wanted: the Coltrane money. And she had her brother. It was time to part. She wanted it done quickly, for she couldn't bear the presence of this despicable man any longer. If he was going to renege on their bargain and not give her any money, then so be it. She would find a way to support herself and Charles. But being in the company of Gavin Mason and his friends was destroying her.

She told him as much, keeping her voice low so the passersby didn't overhear.

He exchanged amused glances with Dirk Hollister, then stepped very close to her and said, in an equally quiet voice, that she would either do as he said—at once—or he would have Hollister take Charles away and kill him. "Don't think I won't do it, my dear." He smiled. Anyone watching would have thought they were having a pleasant conversation. "You will be gagged. That's easily done. And Hollister will take your brother into those bushes over there and choke him to death and leave his body for the crows."

Briana could hardly take it in. "Why?" she hissed at him. "I did what you asked. Now it's time to let me go. Why should I go with you now? What more do you want of me?"

"You're going home with me. To Monaco. But only for a little while, till everything has calmed down. It makes me nervous, knowing Travis Coltrane is in Paris. He might come looking for his daughter when he hears what happened back there, and I cannot have you running around saying the wrong things. So you are going with me. When I feel the time is right, then I will set you free, with ample money for you and Charles."

Briana stared at him long and hard. She did not trust Gavin. "I won't say anything to anyone, I promise," she told him. "Just let us go."

He smiled again. "I cannot do that. There's entirely too much at stake. I also cannot wait any longer. Come along. Charles is well enough for the journey, according to his doctors. We can talk about more treatment later. Some quiet time on the south coast will do him good, you know."

She looked at Hollister, and then back at Gavin. What else could she do except obey Gavin once more? She couldn't take any chances with Charles's life. Later, there might be a chance to escape. Now, she was helpless.

Forcing a smile she went to Charles and told him, "It's all right. We're going to Monaco for a while. You've missed home, haven't you?"

Before Charles could answer, Dirk lifted him and strode quickly toward the train, Briana following close behind. Dirk and Charles disappeared inside the train, and a conductor wearing a black uniform helped Briana step up on a wooden platform. She took the conductor's hand, then hesitated a moment before turning around to face Gavin. Her eyes were almost black with rage. "You have pushed me too far, sir. I yield to you no longer after this day."

She entered the train.

Gavin stared after her. She was in for quite a surprise if she thought she could tell him what was what.

But something in her voice, her gaze, had been so chilling that, despite his contempt for her, Gavin actually trembled.

Chapter Twenty-two

BRIANA and Charles were taken to a small private compartment on the train and locked inside. Narrow wooden benches faced each other. There was a large square window. Charles was situated so that he could view the countryside and the spectacle of the French Alps rushing toward him as the train headed south. After tucking a blanket around his knees, Briana sat down opposite him, filled with the joy of being with him.

She took his hands in hers and squeezed them gently. The train began to chug forward. "Tell me about it," she urged him. "Tell me about the operation, and what the doctors say—everything."

His eyes searched hers, and his lower lip quivered. "Where were you, Briana? Why weren't you there when I was so sick? You were away for so long. . . ." His tone was accusing, and he rushed on to cry, "And who are all those people with Monsieur Mason? I watched them loading big crates onto the train. They look mean. I don't understand . . . so many things."

His eyes were filled with tears, and Briana struggled to control her own emotions. Now was not the time. She lifted her chin, forced a smile, and hoped her lies were convincing.

She had fabricated a story for him, all about traveling to America with Gavin to work for him, cooking for him, to earn the money to pay Charles's doctors in Paris. They had, she told him, gone to America to collect money from the estate of a relative of Alaina's who had died in the past year. "So now Madame deBonnett's money problems are over," she finished, making her voice bright and bubbly, "and so are ours."

"But those rough-looking men—"

"Nothing to fear," she said firmly. "They are just the guards Monsieur Mason hired to look after all his money.

"Now then," she urged, "I want to hear all about *you.*"

Charles tried to appear brave as he told what he remembered about the operation. He said it had not hurt too terribly much, but Briana's heart went out to him, for she knew he had suffered . . . and suffered alone.

"And, Briana," he finished with a triumphant sigh, "there's this new doctor, Richibauld, who says he can fit me with special braces. With training, he says, maybe I can walk one day—without crutches! Isn't that amazing?" His brown eyes were bright.

Briana's smile was as wide as his. "Then I promise we will return to Paris as soon as possible."

He went on to explain that the doctor had said it would take time for his spine to heal completely, and that was the reason he was confined strictly to the wheelchair for several more weeks yet. The doctors didn't want him even attempting to use crutches.

They talked and talked. Around noon, a guard brought a basket of food—cheese, bread, apples and oranges, wine for Briana, and milk for Charles. After eating, they stretched out on the benches and gave way to the sleepiness inspired by the steady rhythm of the train as it rumbled along.

Slumber did not last long, however, for, with a loud screeching and repeated hissing of steam, sparks flying as wheels ground against the track, the train careened to a halt.

Dirk Hollister opened the compartment door to see if they were all right, explaining that the train had stopped just before plowing into a snowslide. An avalanche from the jagged mountain above had sent snow cascading down onto the tracks. It would, the trainmen predicted, take several hours to clear the way.

They passed the time by talking, both Charles and Briana having so much to say. She told him all about Nevada, the ranch, some of her happier experiences there. She talked about riding Belle out on the plains, rhapsodizing over the awesomely beautiful scenery.

She even told him a little about Colt, describing him as a friend she had met on the ranch. As she talked, she became gratefully aware that reminiscences of the happier moments helped assuage the regrets. For a little while, she was able to pretend that nothing ugly had happened. She felt warm all over speaking of Colt so tenderly, so lovingly, and she didn't realize just how clear her innermost feelings were becoming to Charles until he interrupted her with a smile.

"Briana, I think you went to America and fell in love."

Unable to respond, she laughed nervously, feeling foolish. "That's ridiculous. Mr. Coltrane was a very nice man and we had some good times together, but that is all. Besides," she said with mock superiority, "What does a ten-year-old know about love?"

Enjoying the merriment, Charles teased her. "He will write to you, and ask you to marry him, and we can both move to America and live on the ranch. Do you suppose that might happen?" His eyes were dancing, and Briana realized he wasn't merely teasing. He liked the idea, and she couldn't have him daydreaming over such nonsense. She would never see Colt again.

"He has someone," she lied quickly, turning her face

away lest Charles see the pain that was surely there. "He loves her very much."

Despite the effort she was making, tears began. Charles touched gentle fingertips against her cheek. "I understand," he whispered.

Briana prayed to God to forgive her for what she'd done to Colt, for she knew she would do it all over again to save this precious child's life.

It was night before the tracks were cleared and the train could move. How long, Briana wondered through the black night hours as Charles slept soundly opposite her, before Gavin would finally keep his end of the bargain and allow her and Charles to go free?

They reached Lyon as the sun was rising, and took another train to Nice, arriving at night.

She woke Charles and had him bundled in blankets and ready when Artie and Biff came to carry him outside to a waiting carriage. She followed close behind, worrying that the short, slight Biff might drop Charles. The night was cold, and she shivered despite her thick woolen cape.

An entourage of two carriages and three wagons carried them and the gold bars to Monaco, to the deBonnett estate. Briana overheard Gavin telling Dirk that he was glad they were behind schedule, for their nighttime arrival meant that there would not be people around whose curiosity would be aroused by all the wagons and the six men in western American dress. Gavin had left Monaco with only Briana, but had returned with an army of gunslingers.

Charles fell asleep again before they reached the estate. Briana protested when Dirk lifted the boy from the carriage, and headed for the château. She scrambled to follow but was restrained by one of the other men as Gavin gave them instructions. Briana had assumed that she and Charles would go to their little cottage at the rear of the estate. But it appeared that they were to be lodged in the château. It was not a good sign.

She watched, Lem holding her arms, as Gavin gave orders for the wooden crates to be taken around to the rear, where a hatchway led to the wine cellar. Briana shuddered, thinking about that terrifying place. It was icy cold down there, for the catacomblike structure had been dug out of stone, straight through the bowels of the earth. She had hated having to go down there to fetch wine, fearing unknown dangers in those shadows. The steps leading down were long, narrow, and curving. Once, when she was a child, the burning torch she carried had been extinguished by a draft, and she was plunged into devouring darkness. She had screamed in terror, but there was no one to hear her, so she forced herself to calm down and picked her way back up the stairs, groping along the slimy walls. There were spiders down there, and countless rats. It was a memory that still tortured her, and she avoided the wretched place whenever she could.

Gavin signaled to Lem, and Briana was taken into the château with the rest of them. They were met by the sight of Alaina and Delia glaring at each other.

"Damn you, Gavin," Alaina exploded, "I'll not have you ignore me this way! I have waited and waited to hear how things were going, and now you just walk in with this . . . this woman!" she sputtered, nodding toward Delia. "Who is this creature? How dare you bring her into my home without asking my permission?"

Gavin regarded her stormily. He hated scenes, especially when other people were present. "Not now, Alaina. I am tired. I need food and wine. See to both. Bring them to my room."

He turned toward the stairs, but female voices assailed him. Alaina screamed for answers. Delia whined.

"Take me to my brother," Briana said to Dirk. "At once. I don't care anything about any of this."

The ensuing bellow from Gavin struck everyone silent. He repeated his orders for food and wine to Alaina, then told Delia to shut up. "Go to the top of the stairs and turn left. The first room on the right is yours. Wait there until you hear from me, and don't say another word. Go!"

Delia scurried up the stairs, biting back tears of humiliation. She had come to Europe to be treated like a queen . . . not like a slave.

He turned to Hollister. "The cripple is no problem, but she has to be kept under guard. Lock her in the wine cellar."

Horrified, Briana turned to run. Lem wrapped beefy arms around her, holding her hard. Struggling with all her might, she shrieked at Gavin, "You bastard! I did everything you asked me to do. Why are you doing this to me?"

Shaking his head dolefully, Gavin said, "You fool. Do you think I am so stupid as to set you free and allow you to tell the authorities—tell anyone—what we did? I realized you were falling in love with Coltrane. I knew you were getting weak, and I know human nature very well. Your kind, my dear, will keep on stewing over the past, allowing your conscience to get the best of you, until you just have to confess everything, trying to put things right."

He sighed, mourning the idiocy of human nature. Then, signaling to Dirk, he continued up the stairs, oblivious to her shrieking.

Dirk took out a kerchief and stuffed it in Briana's mouth as Lem held her. "I believe," Dirk drawled, "the boss said you were going nighty-night in the cellar, sweetheart, so let's go."

She tried to kick him, but Dirk sidestepped away from her. He and Lem, assisted by Artie, the guard with the snakelike eyes, took her out of the château and around to the side. Dirk's three other men were standing around, and he snapped at Biff to get a torch and lead him down into the cellar.

Thirty-seven steps took them all the way down. When they reached the bottom, Dirk set Briana's feet on the cold, rocky floor but continued to hold her wrists together tightly. He nodded to Biff, telling him to set the torch in a holder jutting from the stone wall. Then he dismissed the guards, and Dirk and Briana were left alone.

Dirk released her, and she pulled the gag away. "You can't leave me down here. It . . . it isn't humane."

Dirk snorted, looking around. He counted six wine kegs, and there were two walls covered in tilting shelves, with places for two hundred wine bottles, though there were not that many in stock. "Seems to me you can have yourself a good time. Just start drinking, sweetheart, and the time will go by very fast."

"Couldn't you just tie me somewhere upstairs? Is it necessary for me to be in this horrible place?" she cried.

Dirk shrugged. "You heard the boss give the orders. I just follow them."

Briana clenched her fists. "You can't leave me down here. Talk to Gavin. Tell him what it's like down here. Tell him I promise not to make any trouble. I swear this on the graves of my parents. . . ."

"Hell, sweetheart, I just don't know . . ." He scratched his chin, pretending to consider it. Actually, he had no intention of asking Gavin to change his mind, for he was enjoying this. She was a haughty little bitch, and he liked seeing her desperate.

Finally he told her, "I'll go upstairs and see if I can persuade him to put you somewhere else. But I can't guarantee anything. You've known him a lot longer than I have. Hell, I don't have to tell *you* how stubborn he can be.

"So," he continued, after flashing her a big grin, "I'll do what I can."

Briana nodded. "That would be very kind of you. And I would also appreciate your finding out about Charles—where he has been taken, who is caring for him. Please."

It was all Dirk could do to keep from laughing aloud. Did she really think he was going to do her any favors after the snotty way she had always treated him? Acting like he was dirt?

He leaned closer, his voice warm with sympathy. "I'll tell you what else I'm gonna do for you. I'm gonna leave you some light down here. I'll find my way up in the dark, so's you can keep the torch. That way, you won't be scared."

Trying to sound as amicable as possible, Briana murmured, "Thank you."

Dirk smiled to himself as he turned to leave. He stared into the ebony abyss. *Lord, it's spooky down here,* he thought.

Dirk had been only too happy to hire on with Mason and travel to France. He damn well didn't want to be anywhere nearby if the Coltranes figured out what had happened. He also didn't think Colt was going to go around for the rest of his life with his head in the sand, ashamed over bedding his sister—or a girl he *thought* was his sister. Sooner or later, he would go home, find out about the sale, and then all hell was going to break loose.

Dirk didn't figure on sticking around Mason for long, either, just long enough to get his hands on enough of that gold to live like a king.

As he gave Briana a final look, he promised himself that she was one good reason to stay around Mason a while longer—her and the gold. Running his eyes up and down her body, he licked his lips.

"Just be nice to me, and I'll be nice to you," he said quietly. "That's the way it works, you know.

You don't get somethin' for nothin' in this life, and you can't expect me to stick my neck out for you unless you're nice to me. Don't you understand the way it works?"

His hands snaked out to clutch her breasts and jerk her toward him, and in that moment his mouth clamped down on hers. She flung her head from side to side, nails digging frantically into his flesh. But she was no match for his strength.

Briana knew sheer, absolute terror. Panic welled up, choking her. Was he going to kill her? Or only torture her? He was a madman; she knew that.

She lifted her face upward to scream as loudly as she could. By some miracle, she might be heard. Someone would come.

The torch flame licked hungrily as the air was whipped by her flailing arms. Bending toward Dirk, she reached over his shoulder for the conelike end of the torch and wrenched it from its holder.

With all her strength, she brought the torch down and laid the flaming end against the side of his head. The acrid odor of burning hair filled the cellar as Dirk released her, screaming in agony.

He slapped at his head, batting at the flames in his hair. The torch fell to the floor, and Briana backed away, out of his grasp, shaking uncontrollably as he ran, screaming, toward the stairway.

In a moment, she was alone in that cold, silent crypt.

Gavin sat in his room, waiting for Alaina. He knew she was furious, and he was braced for a storm.

It wasn't long before she pushed open the door and crossed the room, setting a tray on the bedside table so hard that the glasses of wine sloshed over, spilling burgundy stains on the carpet. "Ingrate!" she hissed through tightly clenched teeth. "Is this how you repay me for a life of luxury? Had I not taken you in, your kinfolk would have abandoned you to an orphanage.

And this is how you repay me? By bringing a whore into our home? Did you really think I would tolerate such—"

"Shut up, Alaina." Gavin sighed, bored. He was exhausted from the endless journey, and he was also hungry and thirsty. But more than that, he needed time to think, to plan.

He went to the tray and picked up one of the two glasses of wine, downing it in one gulp. He looked over the board of cheeses she had brought and sampled one, then cut a slice of another.

Alaina stamped her foot. "Did you hear me, Gavin? That whore must leave. I will not have her under my roof."

Gavin looked up. Cool eyes flickered over her. She still had a nice body, and she was pleasing in bed. He felt a stirring of desire. She rarely protested his requests for bizarre acts and, all things considered, their love affair had satisfied him. But that was history. Was she so naive as to think their passion would last forever? That he would never desire a woman nearer his own age?

He motioned for her to sit opposite him, but she shook her head curtly. He reached out and jerked her down into the seat. "How many times do I have to tell you I am tired? I don't feel like listening to nagging."

Alaina lifted her chin defiantly, eyes cold.

"Aren't you even interested in hearing how wealthy we are?" he asked. "I was afraid to write you all the details, for fear my letter would fall into the wrong hands, but it was all quite . . . interesting. And successful. We have reason to celebrate." He lifted his glass in salute, but she continued to regard him icily.

With a sigh, he reached for the other glass of wine. "Very well. Pout if you wish. Surely you know," he began, "that social position increases with great wealth. Can you imagine the loathing and revulsion there will be if anyone guesses our relationship? You will have to accept Delia as a cover."

Alaina blinked, and the extremely long lashes she had ordered from Paris wavered like tree limbs. "Cover?" she echoed. "That woman is a cover to keep people from knowing about us?"

Gavin trailed his fingertips down her cheek, lying glibly. "Of course. My dear, you know you are the only woman I truly want, but society would shun us for our love. We must keep it a secret, especially now that I am well past the marriageable age."

Alaina frowned. "I don't want her here. And don't lie to me and tell me you aren't sleeping with her, because I know you too well to be fooled. I'm not stupid, Gavin," she added nastily. "And now that we have the money, we can go away together, really be together—the way we should be. Please, Gavin, just get rid of her."

He shook his head. "This is how it is going to be for the time being," he said firmly.

"People will think she is your fiancée," Alaina hotly protested. "Maybe she *is* your fiancée. Maybe the two of you are plotting to take all the money and run away together, leaving me with nothing. Gavin, you can't treat me this way."

She tried to stand up, but Gavin gave her a rough shove back into the chair, towering over her as he shouted, "Now, God damn it, for the last time, I'm warning you to shut up."

Their eyes met, held, blazing with anger and sudden resentment. It was the resentment that surprised them. Where did it come from?

Alaina felt humiliated. Gavin could not love her anymore, she knew, not and treat her this way.

For his part, Gavin was disgusted. Who did she think she was, that he would tie himself to her for the rest of her life? So what if he enjoyed her body? He enjoyed plenty of women's bodies. They were all pleasing, he had found, if you just regarded them as what they were—pieces of flesh to be used at will. It was when they started making demands that they became, like Alaina, a liability.

He did not like the accusing way she was looking at him, so he slapped her. That provoked harsh, broken sobs, and he got up to get a bottle of wine from his cabinet in the corner. When he returned, he told her, "Either shut up and listen to what I have to say, or I'm going to give you a beating that will put you in bed for weeks."

Alaina fell silent. He meant it, this abomination of a man who had returned to wreak misery on her.

She nodded. He flashed a smile, sat down, and poured himself a glass of wine. He began talking, telling her how he had succeeded in bringing back the *entire* Coltrane fortune. Proudly he described every delicious detail, and, after a time, it was as though he was musing out loud, for the pleasure and adoration of his own ears and no one else's. Alaina might as well not have been in the room.

But she *was* in the room . . . and she was infuriated beyond belief by his love for himself. But worse was to come. He announced that he would be going to Greece soon. "I think it is best that Briana and I disappear for a while. We cannot arouse suspicion over our sudden windfall. Also, Travis Coltrane is in Paris, too close for me."

Alaina's eyes grew wide and her heart began to hammer. Risking another blow, she dared ask, "What about me? What will I do while you're away? And why Greece?"

He reminded her of Count deBonnett's relative who lived on the island of Santoríni. "St. Clair left France, if I recall correctly, because he was wanted for a political crime. And when he left, he took the entire fortune of the local government with him. You remember your husband talking about him and his wealthy life in exile? Well, I do believe I will pay dear Cousin St. Clair an extended visit."

"He was a distant cousin," Alaina informed him coldly. "He doesn't even know you."

But Gavin was undaunted. "Money talks, my dear, and I have six guards with me, too. His kind of island isolation is exactly what I need for a time. I'm certain he'll see it my way.

"Now then," he continued as he poured more wine, "I want us—you—to host a lavish dinner party as soon as possible. I want all the gossips invited, because I want the word spread that I am leaving France to return to America to live. We will say that you have received some money from a distant relative, enough to pay all the Count's creditors and give you a nest egg. I don't want anyone to know where I've really gone. When the time is right, I will return to you and we will move away from here, make a life somewhere else—perhaps in Spain.

"I cannot," he concluded firmly, "live in constant dread that the Coltranes will come after their money. Maybe they'll find out the truth about Dani."

Jealous apprehension having gotten its hooks into her, Alaina asked, "Are you taking that woman with you?"

Gavin nodded. "And I'm taking Briana, too, of course. You will keep her brother here and tell people that she went with me as a maid to Delia. After a time, I will send word that Briana is dead, and then you can send her brother to an orphanage."

He gave her a benevolent look. Smart Gavin had figured everything out beautifully, as usual.

But Alaina knew he was lying to her. He would never come back for her. She knew it.

Suddenly the château exploded with screams.

"What the—" Gavin and Alaina rushed to the door, and she flung it open in time to see Al, one of Gavin's men, charging up the stairs, white-faced and shaken.

"Where's the boss? I gotta see him," the man cried.

Delia stepped out of her room, and Al nearly knocked her down as he rushed straight for Alaina.

Gavin stepped out into the hall. "What the hell's wrong?" he demanded.

"Trouble," Al gasped hoarsely. "It's Hollister. The bitch in the cellar . . . she set fire to him."

Chapter Twenty-three

A MAN stood in the narrow, cobbled lane, staring up at the château. A farmer pulling a wooden cart passed him, glanced at him, and quickened his pace. The man's eyes were narrowed to dark, malevolent slits, and his jaw was set grimly.

"Want me to come with you?" his companion asked.

For a moment Colt did not respond to Branch's question. Then he said, "I'll go alone."

Branch didn't like that at all. The way Colt had been behaving was spooky. "I think I'd better come with you, old buddy. You're liable to go berserk and kill somebody."

Colt gestured at him to stay where he was, and without another word, began walking slowly, warily, up the twisting lane that led to the imposing deBonnett château.

Branch stared after him. It had been a long, hard journey, and things were sure to get harder from here on. They had sailed from Norfolk, Virginia, because they'd heard of a German vessel that would be leaving for Europe and was capable of achieving a much faster crossing of the Atlantic than the luxurious passenger liners that sailed from Boston and New York.

Arriving in Southampton, England, they booked onto a smaller ship to cross the English channel. From Calais, they went by train to Nice, then bought horses to get them to the southern coast of France, and Monaco.

Branch was tired, for they'd had little rest since docking at Southampton. But he didn't blame Colt for not wanting to stop. He knew that if he was in Colt's boots, he'd be acting the same way.

Colt lifted the heavy brass knocker, then slammed it against the thick wooden door several times. He waited a second, then knocked again.

"All right, all right. I'm coming," a woman's voice called irritably in French. Once more, he was glad his mother had urged him to study the language. Otherwise, just getting to the château would have been much more difficult.

The door swung open, and Colt found himself staring down into the face of a woman who had surely been lovely once. But had her eyes always been so cold? He wondered whether warmth or tenderness had ever shone within their green depths.

Alaina's hands gripped the doorframe as she swayed. The years peeled away. She swallowed hard, then, in a barely audible squeak, she gasped, "Travis." Then she closed her eyes.

Colt stepped back warily. Was this Dani's aunt Alaina? His father had told him all about that treacherous woman. "I'm his son," he said quietly. "Colt."

Her eyes flashed open.

"I said," Colt repeated, "I am Travis Coltrane's son, and I am here to see my sister, Dani. Where is she?"

Alaina gaped. He was the image of his father: the same color hair—so black it was almost blue when the sun caught it—and eyes the color of steel, with vague glimmers of gold.

Her gaze moved downward, then up again. Yes, the same tantalizing body, too, as though all the gods had joined together to create the perfection of manhood.

In a flash, she recalled that long-ago wonderful night

in Kentucky, when Travis Coltrane had made love to her and made her beg for more.

She had left her own bed, after everyone else in the house was asleep, and had made her way quietly to the guest room where Travis was sleeping. She removed all her clothing and crawled naked into his bed before he even realized she was there.

He had made love to her like no man ever had before—or since.

The dreaminess left as quickly as it had come, and in its place appeared the taunting reminder that no man had ever spurned her as coldly as Travis Coltrane had done.

He had also killed the man who had loved her truly: Stewart Mason.

"Get off my property, you bastard! You no-good son of "

She raised her arm as though to strike him, but Colt grabbed her. He knew she despised his father. Wasn't that essentially what had brought them all to this point? Alaina Barbeau interfering in their lives?

Alaina struggled, but he held her. "I order you to leave," she cried.

"I'm not going anywhere until you tell me where to find my sister."

Alaina glared at him. Oh, why did he have to be so handsome? Why did he have to bring back all those warm memories of a love she had struggled so hard to forget? No woman who had ever been bedded by Travis Coltrane could ever forget him, no matter how brokenhearted he might have left her.

Alaina was no exception.

Alaina and Colt locked their gazes on each other. Colt's was challenging. Alaina's was passionate with remembered love and with hatred, the two emotions warring with each other.

"Ma'am," he said quietly, deciding that maybe humoring her would get him somewhere, "all I want is to see my sister. Would you call her, please?"

Alaina looked thoughtful. It had been a terrible time. First, there was the fight with Gavin, because she had gone to his bed in the middle of the night and found it empty. He had said, when she saw him at breakfast that morning, that he had been doing some work on his ledgers in his study, but she knew he'd been with Delia. They'd fought about that, and over so much else. All they did anymore these days was fight. Her life had been hell since his return, and the only thing that soothed her was vodka in the mornings and whiskey in the evenings.

"Ma'am? . . ." Colt repeated.

Alaina's lips curved into a smile. He was truly just like his father, and it would be nice to talk to him, ask him how Travis was doing.

She opened the door wider and bade Colt enter. "In there." She nodded toward the parlor to the right of the marble foyer.

As he walked through the foyer, Colt decided that the château wasn't really any more elegant than the home his mother had furnished back in Nevada—the home, he reminded himself grimly, that was no longer his. "Where's Dani?" he demanded. "I'm tired of waiting."

"She isn't here," Alaina said as they entered the parlor. She crossed to the bar and poured herself a glass of vodka and orange juice. She offered a drink to Colt, but he shook his head and went to stand near her. Unable to keep the fury from his voice any longer, he hissed, "The fun's over. You know why I'm here. Now tell me where Dani is or I'll turn this goddamn house upside down. Do you understand me?"

She gave him a coquette's smile. "I haven't introduced myself, Colt. I am Alaina, the Countess—"

"Yes, I knew that when I first saw you," he interrupted.

Alaina was glad she was wearing her green satin robe with the white lace around the high collar. It made her breasts look firmer than they actually were, because of the understitching in the bodice. She had also made up her face, knowing there would be a scene with Gavin and wanting to look good.

She gazed at the man standing beside her. Oh, he was a sight to behold. Would he be every bit as good as his father?

"I will give you one more chance to tell me where she is, and then I will start looking for her myself," he told her.

Alaina blinked. The young Coltrane was angry. Why? Oh, yes, it was coming back now. Goodness, it was hard to think when the vodka got to tickling around inside.

"Dani isn't here," she told him coolly. It was the truth, and she looked at him levelly.

"Where is she?"

Alaina shrugged. "She and Gavin returned to France from America last week, but she stayed in Paris while Gavin came back here."

"Where can I reach her in Paris?"

Alaina shrugged. "I don't know." She did not like all these questions, because she didn't know what she was supposed to say.

Colt persisted. "Then where can I find Gavin?"

Alaina reached for the vodka, and poured another drink. "I don't know that, either," she said.

"I will be back." Colt turned and walked out of the room and out of the château. He strode down the path, his thoughts racing. He could have torn the house apart looking for Dani or Gavin, but he sensed, somehow, that neither was there.

Alaina lifted her head from the pillow, groaning as the thudding, throbbing pain in her temples assailed her. She heard the sound of voices, not far away. Where was she?

She remembered coming upstairs, determined to have a discussion with Gavin. She was not going to be relegated to second place by his homely whore. She would have a nice bottle of champagne ready, and when he came into his room, they would drink it, and talk. She would make him realize he couldn't do without her. They would make love. When he was satiated, she would help him figure out a way to get rid of Delia. Everything would be as it had been before he'd gone to America. Oh, she would allow him his indiscretions. She was sophisticated. She knew that men strayed. But she would always be the one he returned to.

Alaina blinked. She was in the little dressing room off Gavin's bedroom, the tiny chamber where he took his baths in the ornate porcelain tub. There was also a dressing table, where he kept his bottles of expensive colognes and talcs alongside his shaving things. Seeing her reflection in the large wall mirror, Alaina realized that she had fallen asleep on the gold brocade divan.

"She's nothing but a baggy-faced old alcoholic, and I don't know what you ever saw in her."

That was Delia's voice, and she was just on the other side of the green velvet curtain that separated the dressing alcove from the bedroom.

"Oh, why look for trouble, Delia?"

Gavin sounded annoyed.

"Trouble?" Delia screeched. "You told me you lived with your adoptive aunt. You did not tell me you'd been screwing her since you were fourteen years old, for chrissake. You didn't tell me she thinks she owns you. If I'd known about this, I wouldn't have come."

Gavin's response was to laugh brittlely and say, "Oh, yes, you would have, my dear, because you knew I was going to be a wealthy man. That's why you've hung on, why you came with me over here, and that is why you will stay. So why don't you just shut your nagging mouth and take your clothes off?"

"Listen, Gavin," Delia snapped, "you can't have your way with me any time you feel like it. I'm not in the mood."

He sighed. "I told you, my dear, we are leaving for Greece soon. You will love it there. You will live like the princess you are, and you will be happy."

"And your old hag? What about her?"

He laughed, a nasty sound that made Alaina cringe with humiliation. *Old hag?* Was she an old hag? "Sooner or later, she'll realize we aren't coming back. By then we'll be living in Spain or Portugal, maybe have mansions in both! Would you like that?"

There was silence, and Alaina knew they were kissing.

She rose slowly, heart pounding. She didn't want to stay and listen to their lovemaking.

She crept out into the hallway, her heart shriveling with self-loathing. *Old hag.* She would never forget those words.

She moved toward her room, her fighting nature coming to the fore. Humiliated she was, and she hurt badly. But, by God, she wasn't going to lie down and die.

When she reached her room, she closed and locked the door as a plan began to form. She would find a way to revenge herself on Gavin, and that way would involve, of all people, Travis Coltrane's son.

Alaina pressed her fingertips against her temples. Her head hurt terribly, but she smiled despite the pain. Vengeance was going to be oh so sweet . . . as sweet as being made love to by Travis Coltrane.

Chapter Twenty-four

COLT and Branch had found a small hotel on a side street and procured two rooms. Colt went to his room without a word, and Branch didn't press him for an explanation of what had happened at the deBonnett château.

Branch took a change of clothes and went to the chamber at the end of the hallway for the luxury of a hot bath. Water was brought to him in large ceramic jugs by a blushing, smiling French maid. Branch promised himself he would seek her out later.

After a much-needed shave and then a hearty meal downstairs, Branch entered the small room at the rear of the hotel lobby which served as a saloon. He was not at all surprised to see a familiar figure in the smoky shadows, leaning against the bar.

"So, why didn't you tell me you were coming to have a drink?" Branch greeted Colt as he stepped up beside him, signaling to the bartender.

"We're going back there tonight," Colt said without preamble. "I'm going to find Dani if I have to tear the place apart, stone by stone."

He told his friend about the encounter with Alaina. None of it surprised Branch. "Yeah, your pa told me about her. Well, you didn't expect to just walk right in and take the gold, did you?"

Colt shot him a look. "I can't take *all* the gold, anyway, Branch. Dani is still entitled to her share, no matter what she's done. I'm going to take my half and that's all."

"Parrish is going to want the entire amount," Branch hesitantly reminded him.

Colt nodded. "I can get a mortgage. I made sure about that. I'm just grateful for the chance to buy it all back. Parrish didn't have to agree to sell it back, you know. He's a good man." The bartender approached to refill his glass, but Colt declined. He intended to be sober and clearheaded when he returned to the deBonnett house. He had learned the hard way how badly whiskey could mess things up.

"What if Dani has no say-so?" Branch asked him, having been afraid to broach the subject during their journey. "What if Mason laughs in your face and says the whole deal is legal, and there's nothing you can do about it?"

"If that happens, I'll just kill him," Colt replied easily. He winked. "No problem, old friend."

And Branch knew there would not be. Colt was too much like his father. If there was a problem, it would be either solved or eliminated. That was the Coltrane way.

They had been in the bar for an hour, and were talking about taking a walk around the tiny municipality of Monaco before heading back to the deBonnett château, when a young man came in and began scanning the shadows. He crossed to them.

"Monsieur Coltrane?" he addressed Branch.

Branch shook his head, and Colt nodded. "I'm Coltrane."

He handed Colt a small pink envelope that reeked of lavender scent. "I was asked to deliver this to you, monsieur." He lowered his voice to a whisper. "From Countess deBonnett."

Colt fished in his pocket for a few coins and handed

them to the messenger. Then he tore open the envelope and read the note.

Without a word to Branch, he slid from the bar stool and strode purposefully, almost angrily, from the room. He supposed it hadn't taken much sleuthing for Alaina to find out where he was staying.

He left the hotel and crossed the street, making his way around the corner to cross yet another cobbled street and enter a narrow alleyway. At the end of the alley was a tiny red door with a hand-lettered sign proclaiming L'HÔTEL. An odd place for a countess, Colt mused.

Opening the door, he entered a foyer that was hardly more than a closet. The tiny square of space reeked of mildew. When his eyes adjusted to the darkness, he began to climb the narrow stairway. There was a hallway to the left at the top of the stairs, and he walked down it until he reached room four.

He knocked.

Almost at once the door opened. His eyes swept over Alaina, who looked nothing like the woman he had met earlier. Her coppery-bronze hair hung loose, curling about her face and shoulders. Her eyes, like dark, rich chocolate, shone with warmth—and desire. Her lips were ruby-red and moist, like dewdrops on a rosebud, and her pink tongue licked her lower lip as though in anticipation of a delightful meal.

His gaze moved slowly downward, taking in the translucent white nightgown. Every curve of her body was visible in the candlelight from just behind her. Colt could see her breasts, the way they rose and fell with every breath. He could see her narrow waist, the gentle swell of her hips, the dark shadow of her pubic hair.

"Come in," she said, standing aside so he could enter. "I do apologize for my rudeness this morning, Colt. I want to make up for it now."

Colt stepped inside, and the door closed behind him.

"Apology isn't necessary, Countess deBonnett. Just tell me where I can find my sister. I imagine you know why I've come so far."

"Of course." She smiled and crossed the tiny room to sit down on the side of the bed. "Money. Isn't money the reason for everything in life?" she asked casually.

Colt glanced around the room at the narrow bed, small dressing table, small mirror. The single window looked down on the alley below.

"So tell me where Dani is," he repeated bluntly.

She patted the space next to her on the bed. He stayed where he was. She smiled, sighed. "Tell me what your father told you about me that makes you afraid of me."

"What my father told me about you isn't anything you'd want to hear. Just tell me where I can find Dani."

Alaina ought to've known he would be stubborn, for he was sure to be just like his father. She decided to spur him with a little anger. "Finding Dani is not going to be easy, Travis—"

"Hold it." He held up his hand. "I'm Colt. Don't confuse me with my father."

Alaina's eyes were at once hard. "I will call you what I wish to call you. I deal the cards here . . . Travis."

Colt shook his head in disgust. She was crazy. "Talk."

"Dani is being held prisoner."

Colt stared at her without saying anything.

Alaina fidgeted. She wanted the conversation to end and passion to begin. "Why?" Colt asked finally.

"Who knows?" She shrugged. "Gavin brought a mistress back here with him. Maybe he keeps Dani tied up because he's afraid she'll kill Delia . . . or maybe Delia wants Dani out of the way. I have no way of knowing."

Suddenly Colt decided that maybe she was telling the truth. He sat down beside Alaina, ignoring the look that came into her eyes as she moved closer to him. "Tell me everything," he urged.

She reached out to trail her fingertips along the line of his jaw and whisper, "You're so like your father. The same smoky eyes . . . the same wavy black hair. And your gorgeous body . . ." She boldly touched his thigh. "Yes. Just like him. In *looks* . . ." Her voice trailed away meaningfully. "What about in bed?"

Colt was just beginning to realize that she was everything his father had said she was when, without further preamble, she looked him straight in the eye and said, "You make love to me, now, and I will tell you where to find Dani. Otherwise," she said flatly, "you'll probably never find her—and you might die trying, because Gavin has hired many men to stay at the house. I have not told him you're here, but once I do, you won't have a chance to get near the château.

"So"—she smiled and leaned against him—"tell me, my beautiful darling, you *do* find me attractive, don't you? Surely you won't mind spending a few moments in my arms? I can take you places you've never been before . . . love you like no woman has ever loved you."

She nibbled his ear, teasing and tantalizing, all the while wriggling her body closer to him, rubbing her breasts against him.

"Make love to me, my darling Travis," she commanded huskily. "Possess me."

Colt knew he would probably wish later that he'd just gotten up and walked away, but he slipped his arms around her and lowered her to the bed. He began kissing her, and once he did, Alaina held nothing back. She clung to him tightly, all restraint abandoned. She had entered a memory, and it was not Colt who held her, but Travis Coltrane himself.

She tore off the translucent gown and, with nimble, anxious fingers, released him from his trousers. "Now. Take me now. Later, when we make love again, there will be time for slow teasing and playing, but now I want you. I've waited so long, Travis, so very long."

She positioned his hard, throbbing member and lifted her hips to receive his mighty thrust. He clutched her buttocks and moved into her as deeply as he could. She clutched his back with one hand, his neck with the other, felt his warm lips against her flesh as she moaned loudly.

"Yes, yes, big and warm and wonderful. I can feel you all inside me, so big, so beautiful. You're part of me now, Travis. I have always loved you. Oh, press harder, darling. Fill me, fill me with your love."

Then her words began coming together in an incoherent babble as her whole body shuddered with ecstasy.

Suddenly Alaina stiffened, and her nails dug into the rock-hard flesh of Colt's back. Moaning sounds emanated from deep within her. Then she slumped in his arms, limp.

Colt reached his own climax, then withdrew and rolled over. They lay there, breathing hard, and then he asked, "Where's Dani?"

Alaina gazed at him coquettishly. "You're every bit the man your father was, Colt. I cannot remember feeling this way since the last time he held me, so many years ago."

She reached for him, fearing that he would leap from the bed at any moment and leave. "I hated him, you know, when he preferred Marilee to me. I loved him so. I had to have my revenge, you see. So I hurt him through Dani, taking her away from him. But now you're here, to take his place, to take away the hurt."

Colt gently pushed her back. The desperate way she was clinging to him was making him very nervous. The woman was crazy, but for the moment she was the only way to Dani. "And you"—the words came glibly—

"are quite a woman, Alaina. I'm sure my father knew a great deal of pleasure in your arms."

"And so shall you, my darling." She began running her hands possessively over his body. "You have no reason to return home. I'm a wealthy woman. We can travel all over Europe, and I can show you sights you've never seen. Forget everything else. Think only of me, of the pleasure I can give you."

Like a pelican diving for food, Alaina darted down, attempting to take him in her eager mouth, but Colt was quicker. His hands fastened around her throat, and he lifted her up.

"No more, my sweet. Half that money your conniving niece brought home with her is mine. I will stop at nothing to get it, and that includes breaking your pretty neck if you don't tell me where to find her. I want to know *now.*"

He squeezed her neck ever so gently to emphasize his intent, and Alaina nodded.

He released her. "Tell me."

"I will have to lead you to her," she told him nervously. Lord, even the anger in his eyes was the same she had seen in his father's.

She hurriedly explained about Gavin's men. "They're heavily armed, and they guard the hatchway to where she is kept. I'll have to make plans before we can—"

"Before you leave this room," Colt told her, "we will make those plans and set a time."

Alaina already knew what she would do. "Tonight I'm giving a party, a large one. I can get the guards distracted by serving them some of the food and lots of wine. The bastards are always hungry, and they all drink. They'll be no problem.

"As for you," she continued, propping herself on an elbow, "come to the house around nine. Go to the little grape arbor on the east side and wait for me there. I will come when the path to the hatchway is clear, and then you can free Dani and take her with you." She suppressed a smile. She kept remembering to say "Dani" rather than "Briana," and she was congratulating herself.

Colt regarded her coldly. "Why are you doing this? No matter why Dani is being held captive, Gavin is going to be angry with you."

She saw no reason not to reveal some of the truth. "I am in love with Gavin," she said plainly, wondering if Colt was shocked. "He brought that whore, Delia, back with him, and that's caused me a lot of heartache. I don't want him lusting after Dani."

He believed her. This was not a woman who tolerated competition.

Colt stood, began putting his clothes in order.

Alaina watched silently for a moment, then gingerly asked, "Was it really good for you? Under . . . other circumstances, could you love me, Colt? Like your father did?"

Colt kept his eyes averted. His father had never loved her, he knew that. Sure, he had probably made love to Alaina. She was appealing, and had probably been a beauty then. But Travis had not loved her.

He smiled down at her. "Tell me, Alaina. Was it good for you? Did I please you?"

Her eyes shone. "Oh, yes, Colt. You make me feel like a real woman. But tell me, could you love me, as your father did?"

Colt nodded slowly. "Yes, I think so," he said kindly. "You said I was just like him."

He turned and left the room. A moment later he was heading out of the sleazy little hotel.

Just like his father? He wondered if he was that much a man. Time would show. . . .

Colt returned to the bar and found Branch sitting at a table in the smoky-blue shadows. Branch had a strange look on his face, and when Colt sat down, he was struck at once by the tension in Branch. He looked baffled, and Colt prodded, "What's wrong? I've never seen you like this."

Branch shook himself, then murmured, "Damnedest thing. Can't understand it." He gave a short, nervous laugh and shrugged.

Colt was impatient, for he had news of his own, was anxious to tell Branch about Dani being held prisoner. "Tell me what the hell happened," he snapped.

Branch shook his head in disbelief. "After you left, the messenger hung around. He wanted a drink, and then he started asking questions about who you were—I guess because he was wondering why Countess deBonnett would be sending a message to you.

"I didn't tell him anything important," Branch was quick to assure, "but I saw no harm in saying we were looking for Daniella Coltrane."

Colt frowned. "And?"

"He said he had known her when she was younger, before the deBonnetts sent her to a school in Switzerland."

Colt waited, then prodded again. "Well?"

"Colt, according to him, Dani is a nun now."

Colt was shocked. But then mystification gave way to understanding. Maybe Dani felt so terrible about what she'd done that she'd given herself to God out of remorse, or penance, or whatever it was nuns did.

But if what the messenger had said was true, that meant Alaina was lying . . . which meant that he was being set up for an ambush in the grape arbor at nine o'clock.

Hurriedly he explained to Branch everything Alaina had told him, finishing by saying, "Now we know it's a trap."

Branch clamped a heavy hand on Colt's arm and said ominously, "No, no. I don't know what Alaina is talking about, but the messenger said Dani'd been in a convent since last spring."

Colt recoiled.

Branch leaned closer, eyes narrowed. "Something real damn funny is going on. If what he says is true, then there's no way Dani could have been to America. So . . ."

Colt felt as though someone had hit him in the stomach. *Yes,* he told himself, his mind racing, *something real damn funny is going on.*

Chapter Twenty-five

ALL was quiet. A slight breeze came in from the Mediterranean Sea, and the night was cold as Colt stood on a narrow crag looking down at the deBonnett château.

Below, Branch was hidden in the darkness, armed and ready for surprises.

Colt had watched as carriages arrived at the château. There were a dozen.

It was too dark to see the two men Colt had spotted earlier, the men walking outside, carrying rifles. They'd stepped back into the shadows as the carriages arrived, and as Colt watched them, he began to believe that Alaina was indeed setting up an ambush.

Nine o'clock was approaching. Colt made his way down the rocky incline, and when he reached the grape arbor, he gave a low whistle. He waited.

A few seconds later, Branch whistled softly, then stepped out of the darkness. "Is it time?" he whispered.

"Just a few more minutes," Colt whispered back. "Keep those guards in your sight. If they make any move toward me, shoot them."

Branch nodded grimly. "Then we'll have a war on our hands. The rest of Mason's hired goons are going to hear the gunfire and come running."

"We've got no way of knowing how many there are,

but there's two of us, old friend. That's enough for our side." He grinned.

Branch watched as Colt moved to the edge of the arbor, only a few feet from where the guards were hidden in the shadows of the house. Branch could just barely make out a wooden hatchway near where the guards stood watching. Was the hatchway where the gold was hidden? And Dani?

"What's *she* doing out here?" one of the guards, Lem, suddenly whispered to the other.

There was no time for Al to respond, for Alaina appeared, struggling with a large tray. "Good evening, gentlemen," she greeted them cheerily. "You must be hungry, and since we have so much food inside, I brought you something nice.

"There's a bottle of wine, too. I left it on the back porch," she added, thrusting the tray at Lem. "You can sit on the steps and eat back there."

She turned to leave, then called over her shoulder, "I hope you enjoy your meal."

As she disappeared around the corner of the house, Lem said to Al, "What was all that about? The old bitch has hardly spoken a word to us since we got here, except to gripe about something."

Grunting agreement, the other man lifted the white linen cover and inspected the offering. "All I know is, this looks damn good, and the thought of some wine is even better."

Al started toward the rear of the house, where the porch was. "Well, what are you waiting for? Come on, and bring the tray. Nobody will ever know if we take a break for fifteen minutes, for chrissakes."

Lem followed hesitantly.

Ten minutes later, Alaina stepped around the corner of the house and hurried to stand before the hatchway, darting an anxious glance in the direction of the arbor.

What Colt had just witnessed did nothing to assuage

his suspicion of treachery. But at that point, he had no choice except to go through with the rendezvous.

He stepped toward her, and Alaina gasped, her hand fluttering to her throat. "Oh! You startled me." She motioned to the hatchway. "She's down there. Hurry. We don't have a lot of time before the guards come back. Gavin keeps a tight rein on everybody."

Colt opened the hatchway and stared down into the dark pit. Beside him, Alaina whispered, "I couldn't risk bringing any light. We'll have to feel our way down. Follow me."

Knowing that Branch was close by and watching, his hand close to his gun, Colt stepped into the void.

"Be very careful," Alaina whispered nervously. "The steps are narrow and curving. Just put your hands on the wall and feel ahead with your feet. You may feel something scurrying around. The mice are terrible down here."

They made their way downstairs very slowly. Around the last curve in the stairway, Colt could see a glow of light just ahead. From directly in front of him, Alaina explained sarcastically, "Gavin sends someone down here regularly to make sure the torch is burning. I suppose he doesn't want her to hate him *too* much, not if he's planning to make her his mistress."

Colt decided the whole pack of them were crazy. He didn't give a damn about Alaina's resentments over her lover, but the intricacies of these relationships might explain how he and his family had been swindled.

Alaina stepped into the cellar, Colt right behind her. As he took in the ghastly sight before him, he gave a low growl and sprang forward.

Briana lay on a pallet on the rough floor, ankles bound with rope, arms stretched above her head and tied. A kerchief was wrapped tightly around the lower part of her face, muffling her cries. Above the kerchief, her eyes were wide with shock at the sight of Colt kneeling before her.

He jerked the kerchief away, demanding, "What in hell's going on? Are you all right?" He slipped his knife from inside his boot and cut her ropes.

As soon as her hands were freed, Briana began to massage her sore wrists to start the blood flowing.

Tears shimmering in her eyes, presenting a misty image of his beloved face, Briana could only shake her head and whisper, "Not now. We must get away from here. Gavin's a madman, and this one"—she nodded toward Alaina—"is his lover and just as mad."

With Colt's help, Briana struggled to stand. Her legs were cramped from enduring her position on the floor for so long. "Believe me," she told Colt, looking into his eyes and shuddering at the loathing she saw there, "I will tell you everything once we're out of here."

He nodded curtly. "Let's move."

"Wait." She stepped away on stiff legs toward Alaina. "I'm taking my brother with me," she declared staunchly. "Where is he? Is he at our cottage?"

"No," Alaina said impatiently. "Get out of here now, before Gavin catches you."

"Where is Charles?" Briana demanded.

"You didn't think *I* was going to tend to a crippled child, did you?" Alaina asked, exasperated. "I had him taken to an orphanage near Paris. Find him yourself."

Briana lunged at her, but Colt grabbed her. "There's no time for this, God damn it."

He slung the sobbing Briana aside, then grabbed Alaina by the arm and threw her to the floor, in the place where Briana had been tied. He yanked her hands up and tied them.

"What are you doing?" she screamed.

Colt put the kerchief over her mouth, saying, "Sorry to have to do this, Alaina, but I'm not sure this isn't a trick. If it *is* a trick, I can't worry about you sounding an alarm.

"If it isn't"—he paused and winked—"then Gavin won't know you betrayed him. He'll think I forced you to take me to Dani, then tied you up. You see, I'm only helping you.

"Let's go," he commanded.

Briana gestured toward the shadowy area beyond the wine kegs. "There! The gold Gavin got for selling your property. It's all there. I watched his men bring down the crates."

Colt decided to take a moment and check. Grabbing the torch, he carried it to where wooden crates were stacked. It took him a moment to examine the contents of one and see that it did, indeed, contain gold—his family's fortune.

He went back to face Briana. "So Mason double-crossed you and decided to keep all the money for himself. I've got a lot of questions, and you'd better come up with some damn good answers." He pushed her toward the stairway. "Move!"

Briana said nothing as they made their way up the stairs, taking the torch with them, leaving Alaina in darkness. Her muffled cries faded as they moved toward the top of the hatchway.

Colt extinguished the torch, whispering to Briana to wait. Then he slowly lifted the heavy wooden door and carefully peered out into the night. There was no sign of the guards. He reached for Briana's arm and gave a tug, signaling that she should follow.

They ran through the night into the sheltering vines of the grape arbor, the decaying foliage rustling in the breeze.

Colt gripped Briana's wrist as he led her all the way through the arbor and out the other side. When they reached a small stone wall that stood between the arbor and a road, she pulled back.

Colt jerked around to stare at her.

Quietly she said, "I must tell you something. Now."

Colt eyed her warily. "I imagine, dear *Sister,*" he said in a voice that chilled her to the marrow, "that you have plenty to tell me. And I want to hear all of it. But I want to put a little distance between me and Mason before we talk. There's no need for anybody to get killed over this."

They jumped over the wall and ran a good distance down the road before he said, "Tomorrow, you and I and the local law will come back and get my share of the gold. Then you and Mason and Charles, whoever he is, can all go straight to hell."

"Charles is my brother."

Colt's hand fell from her wrist. He blinked.

"I said, Charles is my brother," she repeated.

Colt laughed harshly. "Maybe you'd better tell me the rest of it."

Dear God, she cried silently, *help me.*

She took a deep breath and then said simply, "I am not your sister." As he stared down at her, his face unreadable, she rushed on. "Your sister, Dani, is in a convent in the mountains. She became a nun. And I . . ." She couldn't go on.

Colt closed his eyes momentarily.

"As I said," he told her in the coldest voice she had ever heard, "I imagine you have a lot to tell me. And I want to hear every goddamn word. . . ."

He jerked her along behind him, pulling viciously as they ran down the dirt road.

Gavin finally extricated himself from the fleshy woman who had been clinging to him for the past half hour. Lord, how he hated fawning females, especially blubbery ones. But it was important, for now, that he make a good impression on the locals.

For that reason, too, he had ordered Delia to remain upstairs during the party. She was furious, but he was getting better and better at handling women's tantrums. A rough hand once in a while did its share of good, he mused. That brought Alaina to mind. Where the hell was she? *She'd better not be off someplace getting drunk,* he thought furiously.

He left the smoke-filled parlor and made his way down the long hallway to the kitchen, where he found the three women cooks he had engaged for the evening, the deBonnett servants having all been let go when the Count's money ran out. The women were sitting at the long wooden worktable. Kettles of food sat on the big black coal-burning stove, and the air was pungent with the odor of many delicacies. "Where is the Countess?" he demanded, speaking in French.

The two younger women looked to the older one, who was apparently in charge. She shrugged and shook her head. "I don't know. She was here about an hour ago, but I haven't seen her since."

"Well"—he glared—"did she tell you when to serve dinner? It's getting late."

"She took a tray of food and a bottle of wine and left, saying she would return soon, and that dinner would be served when she got back."

Gavin was getting angrier with each moment. "What the hell do you mean? Who did she take the tray to?" Damn, but he was mad. The servants were not to know about Briana being held prisoner in the cellar. Alaina knew that—just as she knew that he, himself, took care of feeding Briana. Twice a day he sent food down, and a guard untied Briana while she ate.

The woman shook her head. "I don't know who she took it to, monsieur."

Gavin strode out the back door and onto the porch. There, on the stone steps leading into the rear courtyard, was a tray with two empty plates on it, and a wine bottle.

What in hell was going on? He hadn't told Alaina to feed anyone, and Alaina never did anything on her own initiative.

He rounded the corner of the house, breathing furiously. Ahead, in the faint light from the windows, he saw the two guards leaning against the hatchway, giggling. Al was picking his teeth with the tip of a knife.

"God damn you," Gavin bellowed, "you aren't getting paid to have a party when you're standing watch. Where's the Countess?"

The two men straightened, exchanging nervous glances. They had heard stories about "the Snake's" temper, and neither wanted to see it. Al spoke first. "We didn't ask for nothing. She came out here with a tray for us and told us to go eat on the back porch, so we did."

"No harm done," Lem assured him anxiously. "We weren't gone over fifteen or twenty minutes."

Gavin was ready to explode. What was Alaina up to? He knew how angry she was with him lately—over Delia, and his plan to leave for Greece without her. He'd tried to coddle her in other ways, such as not raising hell when he found out she'd sent Charles to an orphanage without asking his permission.

His gaze went to the hatchway. *Briana.* Alaina hated Briana almost as much as she hated Delia. "Open it!" he commanded, and the men rushed to obey.

Gavin did not like making his way down the narrow steps without light, but there was no time to stop and get a torch. Just as that thought went through his mind, his foot touched something solid. He bent and retrieved the burned-out torch. He tossed it aside, suddenly terribly anxious. "Hurry up," he urged Lem and Al.

The three took the stairs as fast as they dared. Before reaching the cellar, Gavin heard the muffled sounds.

He groped in the dark, found the struggling woman, found her face, the kerchief that silenced her, knew before he even yanked it away that he would hear Alaina's voice in the black pit . . . not Briana's.

She gasped, then cried hoarsely, "Colt! He took Briana!"

Gavin's scream of rage reverberated along the stone walls like the cries of a hundred demons.

He whirled around, toward the stairs.

"Don't leave me!" Alaina screamed. "Don't leave me down here, Gavin, please—"

But Gavin was scrambling up the steps as fast as he could, his men right behind him.

Panting, he gave them orders. "Round up the others, and tell them to meet Hollister at the stable as fast as they can get there. He will give them further instructions."

Al reminded him, "Hollister never comes out of that shack . . . not since that wildcat burned him."

"Let me worry about that," Gavin roared. "Do as I say!"

He started toward the little cottage where Hollister lived, Briana's family's house. But then he turned back toward the big house. There were guests to be taken care of, and he didn't want them to hear the commotion. How he wished now he had never given the party, had not yielded to the desire to let everyone know the family was no longer destitute.

He called to Al, telling him quietly to return to the cellar and free Alaina and tell her to go to the kitchen *at once.*

He returned, briefly, to the party and apologized to his guests, telling them that something had gone very wrong in the kitchen. Hoping they were all too drunk to care about the delay or his absence, he went to the kitchen, where he was relieved to find Alaina. She was terribly shaken, but he calmed her quickly enough to keep her from babbling in front of the servants.

He dragged her into an empty room and then, stammering with shock, she sobbed out her story. She'd felt sorry for the guards, and taken them a tray. On her way back inside, Coltrane had assaulted her, threatening to slash her throat if she made a sound. He made her show him where Briana was, and he'd tied her up so she couldn't sound an alarm when he made off with Briana.

As she finished her story, Alaina flung her arms around Gavin's neck and pleaded, "Don't be angry with me, please. He forced me."

Gavin endured Alaina's embrace, so as not to upset her further. "Did he know Briana wasn't Dani?" he asked furiously.

She shook her head. "No. At least . . . he didn't say anything to make me think so. But you know she'll tell him everything."

"No doubt," he murmured grimly. He pursed his lips thoughtfully. There was only one thing to do, he knew that much.

He issued orders quickly while Alaina listened, nodding. The guests were to be called to dinner, served, and then ushered out of the house as politely but as quickly as possible. Excuses were to be made for his absence. A sick friend would do.

He left and hurried to the cottage, where he found Dirk Hollister sitting in the shadows before the cold fireplace, his head wrapped in a cocoonlike tourniquet, sunk in misery. A single candle offered scant light.

Gavin drew up a chair and sat down beside him, but Dirk didn't even speak. He continued to sit, huddled, staring into the ashes of the hearth.

Gavin reached over and touched his knee. "Hollister?" Hell, did the man even have his sanity anymore? Gavin had been too busy to visit him. Maybe he was worse off than anyone realized.

Without turning around, Dirk mumbled, "Leave me alone."

"I can't," Gavin was quick to inform him. "We've got trouble, big trouble. I need—"

"Trouble?" Dirk cried in fury. "You think *you've* got trouble? I'll show you trouble . . ." He pulled away the bandage around his head and turned so that Gavin had a full view.

"This," Dirk declared, voice trembling with rage and pain, "is trouble! I've got to go through life looking like this . . . a goddamn dried-up grape!"

Usually, Gavin was hard-pressed to find sympathy for anyone. But in that moment he genuinely pitied Dirk Hollister. Here was a once-handsome man, who'd been turned into a side-show freak.

Dirk Hollister looked like a slab of overcooked bacon. His flesh was red and yellow and shriveled, and the doctor had bluntly declared that it would always be that way. He was scarred for life.

Dirk lifted red-rimmed eyes to Gavin. "I want you to know, you'd better keep me away from that bitch. Because if I ever lay eyes on her again, I'll kill her, and nobody will be able to stop me."

"No one will try," Gavin said.

Dirk was surprised. "You mean that?"

Gavin quickly told him what had happened. With each word, spirit returned to that broken man.

"Your men are waiting for you to lead them," Gavin said slowly. "I am going to make arrangements for a ship to take us to Greece. As soon as we can, we'll load the gold and set sail.

"I want *you,*" he went on, placing an arm around Dirk's shoulders, "to find Coltrane and kill him. Bring the girl to me and—"

"No!" Dirk cried furiously. "*I* want her. I'll make her beg to die for what she's done to me." His body trembled with fury and longing.

"Bring her to me. Don't touch her," Gavin ordered. "When I'm done with her, I promise you can have her.

"Do it my way," he continued emphatically, "and I will see to it that you leave France a rich man. You can do whatever you want with Briana later on. And you'll never have to worry about money again." He paused. "Do we have an agreement?"

Dirk held out his hand and Gavin took it. Their bargain was made.

They left the cottage and hurried out into the night . . . and whatever the night would hold for them.

Chapter Twenty-six

BRANCH met Colt and Briana on the road, and the look he gave her made her cringe. He stared at her with pure contempt, as though she had betrayed him. She couldn't bear it.

Brokenly she whispered, "I did not want it to be this way. I swear I had no choice, Branch."

He stared at her wordlessly

Colt mounted the horse Branch had waiting for him, and then pulled Briana up behind him. "We'd better put some distance between us and Mason," he told Branch. "There will be plenty of time to talk later." He related only that Dani was, indeed, in a convent, and the woman behind him was an imposter.

"It was all a hoax, a swindle," he explained, voice cracking.

Briana dared to speak up. "I will tell you all about it as we ride."

Colt jerked around in the saddle and glared at her. How he wanted to hit her, the lying, conniving bitch. "Just keep still until I tell you to speak."

After they'd ridden for a while, Colt demanded to know where Dani was. "I want to see my sister and find out what, if anything, she knew about all of this."

"She knew nothing," Briana told him.

Then Branch interjected, "Who the hell are you, girl? And how did you get involved in all this?"

"My name is Briana de Paul," she said calmly, grateful for the chance to tell them even a little. "I worked as a servant for the deBonnetts. My father was their caretaker until he died, and we lived in a small cottage on the estate." Then she rushed on to explain about the deBonnett money being lost, and Dani becoming a nun, and Gavin's plan.

"The letter from Dani's father," she added, "came at just the time Dani was to leave to enter the convent. She knew nothing about the letter, so of course she knew nothing about Gavin's scheme to claim her share."

Tentatively, when they didn't stop her from talking, she said, "I did as I was told so as to save my little brother. He's crippled, and . . ." She trailed off, in tears, feeling that they didn't even believe that much.

Colt insisted on riding to the convent, and Briana explained that it was situated on a mountain called *Jaune*, near the Italian border. She didn't bother telling them that the mountain was thus named because in the spring and summer months the slopes were covered with bright yellow wildflowers.

"Going there would be a waste of time," she warned. "It is a severe cloister, an order of nuns who remove themselves from the outside world and never leave the convent. They never allow visitors. Dani told me all of this. It is a very strict sect, and you will probably not be permitted to see her. Besides, she knows nothing about this, I promise you."

Colt was rigid. "Just tell me which direction to head." Nothing was going to stop him from seeing Dani. He was going to hear with his own ears that she knew nothing about this, that she would back him up legally to recover all the gold. And then, God help Gavin Mason.

"East," Briana told him. "It is about a four-hour ride by carriage. I went there once to pray at the fountain outside the walls, where the waters are supposed to be holy. I took Charles with me, in hope of helping him."

"And did it help?" Colt asked her.

"No," she replied. Then she ventured, "Helping Gavin was the only way Charles could have the operation he needed in order to live. His spine was being crushed."

Colt shook his head. It was all a lie, of course. She had been promised a part of the money involved and needed no persuasion. When she started to speak once more, he snapped at her to be quiet. He had other things on his mind besides listening to her attempt at self-justification.

They rode in the darkness for an hour, and then the road became narrow, rougher, as they began their ascent into the mountains. Colt and Branch decided they would stop for the night and leave again at first light.

With the horses tied, Branch discreetly disappeared among the brush to find his own place for the night, leaving them alone to fight.

Briana sat on a rock, staring into the blue and purple night. She heard the inviting sound of water rushing. A stream would be cold, but a bath was too tempting to resist.

She began walking toward the sound.

"Where do you think you're going?"

She stopped but did not turn around. "I need a bath. I was tied in that hell-hole for nearly two weeks. Maybe more, I don't know."

"I'll go with you."

She panicked. "No! I want privacy."

Colt laughed, an ugly sound. "You didn't want privacy those nights you seduced me. You were plenty eager to have me see you naked then."

Briana swayed. She had to tell him the truth, and tell him now. . . .

"Oh, I forgot," Colt growled, reaching her side. "You have to be bought, don't you? There *is* a difference between a prostitute and a whore, isn't there? I imagine you command a very high price.

"Tell me," he continued, "how much of a cut did Mason offer you? I'm curious to know how much it cost me to bed a woman like you. It's a pity I can't remember what it was like because—"

Briana slapped him.

Colt wasn't fazed. He continued to gaze down at her, and when she raised her arm to slap him again, he caught her and slung her over his shoulder. Ignoring her cries, he carried her through the brush, all the way to the bank of the rushing stream, and dropped her into the frigid water.

Briana floundered, struggling to stand on the slippery rocks. The stream was waist-deep, and she couldn't get her footing. She fell backward, the cold water closing over her, and she fought her way to her knees. "You bastard!"

Colt laughed. "Perhaps it's best I *don't* remember it. You're probably no better than the average whore."

Briana stopped shivering. His cruel taunts were like a great warming fire, filling her with deep rage. Yes, she had deceived him. But she had stopped short of coupling with him. He didn't know that, but *she* did. The knowledge that she had outwitted Gavin and spared both herself and Colt that terrible degradation was one thing she could be proud of. And she *was* proud of it.

She had fallen in love with Colt, but now that love was turning to hatred. Despite his rage, he might have allowed her a chance to explain. She had suffered, too, by God. He wasn't the only one.

She decided to ignore him, to keep her knowledge to herself . . . for the time being, anyway.

As the first shadows of night began to succumb to dawn, the trio moved from the quiet forest and on toward the convent. Briana spoke only once, to ask that she be allowed to ride with Branch. Colt grunted assent. He didn't want her anywhere near him.

They rode in dejected silence. Colt attempted to dwell on thoughts other than the ones at hand. France, he acknowledged, was a beautiful country. The northern part was farmland, nourished by the waters of the Loire and Seine rivers. The south, where they were, offered an uninterrupted string of golden beaches fringed with palm trees, olive groves, and orchards.

Kitty had written Colt glowing letters about her life in Paris, describing the city as prosperous and gay. Travis had work to occupy him, and, denied his company much of the time, Kitty had become involved in studying art.

Impressionism, she had written Colt, was Paris's gift to art and had brought an absolute revolution, a renaissance in painting. All the great Impressionist painters—Monet, Renoir, Sisley, and Pissarro—were French, she wrote.

Colt missed his parents very much, but he was glad they'd been given this opportunity to live in Europe. Of course, once this ghastly mess was sorted out, he would go to Paris to see them. And, he realized grimly, he was going to have to tell them the whole story.

He tried to brighten his disconsolate mood by promising himself to see all of France before leaving. The land, he knew, was divided between four great river basins and several mountain ranges. Besides the Seine River, flowing through Paris and winding north to the English Channel, there was the Loire in the west, known for the historic châteaux studding the valleys it flowed through. The Loire flowed all the way to the Atlantic Ocean at the north end of the Bay of Biscay. In the south, also flowing into the Bay of Biscay, was the Garonne River, with its wide tidal estuary known as the Gironde. The Rhône River rose in the eastern Alps and wound its way south through valleys famed for their fine vineyards.

Colt looked toward the mountains in the north, the breathtaking cluster and slopes of the Alps, including the highest peak in all Europe, Mont Blanc, rising to more than fifteen thousand feet.

"Colt."

Branch's sharp voice brought him from his reverie, and he turned around. Branch was pointing straight up. "See what I see?"

There was a formidable wall of rocks ten feet tall and, beyond it, surely, his sister's convent. It looked cold, forbidding. How could Dani . . . But there was no time to think of it just then.

The trail up was narrow and rutted with holes. In some places, the trail was bordered by nothing but a sheer drop down to death against the jutting rocks.

They reached iron gates, and Colt dismounted to peer beyond the gates to a courtyard. The ground was covered by pebbles, and here and there were marble benches and a vast array of marble religious statues. There were no shrubs or trees, and the scene was entirely severe.

Stretching to either side of the courtyard and situated just behind it was the convent. It was rectangular in shape and constructed of stones. The building covered about half an acre. There was a high, tiled roof above the two stories, and there were a dozen windows facing the courtyard, all of them tall and arched.

A squat building stood to the left, connected by a roofed walkway to the convent. There was a belfry at the top of that small building, and remnants of ivy clung in feeble desperation to the decaying rocky structure. Colt, Briana, and Branch could hear the sound of women's voices singing inside it. Except for the singing, there were no signs of activity.

The antiquated lock on the iron gates offered no resistance to the butt of Colt's gun. The iron entranceway opened, grating and squeaking. Colt stepped into the courtyard, motioning to Branch and Briana to follow him.

As though waiting for their entrance, a plump woman appeared suddenly from around the corner of the chapel. She wore flowing white nun's garb. Not a wisp of hair showed from under her wimple. The starched white cloth was pulled tight across her forehead, and the top peaked tall and pointed. A short white train hung to her shoulders.

As she drew closer, the three visitors discerned that a gracious welcome was not in store. Her eyes, behind thick spectacles, were cold. Her lips were tight, and she walked with long, purposeful, angry strides.

She addressed them in French. "What do you want here?"

In the calmest voice he could muster, Colt explained, "I'm looking for my sister, Daniella Coltrane. She's a nun here."

Briana was quick to clarify, "A *novice*, Sister."

The nun's eyes swept over Briana, first with curiosity, then with contempt. Briana felt most uncomfortable in the trousers Branch had given her.

"My sister," Colt prompted. "I wish to speak with her."

The nun glared at him. "I know nothing about this. Did you write to the Mother Superior and tell her you were coming?"

Briana whispered, "She probably isn't allowed to tell you even that Dani is here. Dani will have a new name now, taken from a saint. Her worldly name wouldn't even be known."

Colt nodded solemnly, then addressed the nun. "I want to see my sister, and I'm going to see her even if I have to take this place apart stone by stone."

The nun's eyes widened, and she stepped back. No one had ever challenged her authority in the forty-two years she had been at the Convent of the Blessed Virgin. The convent tradition was to give any visitor as good a meal as possible, and then send him on his way. That was all any visitor could expect. It was, she knew, a five-hundred-year-old tradition.

Sister Marie walked to the gate and pointed at the twining road leading down Jaune Mountain. "Go in peace, my son." She made her voice gentle. "What is done is done. There is no one here who can call you her brother anymore."

Colt muttered an oath. Enough was enough. He pushed by her and headed straight for the chapel.

Sister Marie was right behind him, crying, "No, no! You must leave at once. People of the outer world cannot come in here." Her voice cracked. Why wouldn't he listen? Nuns in this convent renounced the world, all of it, including their families. Christ became their family—their only family. The family each nun left behind had to understand this, hard though it was.

Colt kept on walking toward the chapel, and Sister Marie wrung her hands in frustration. "Why won't you listen to me?" she called to him, and he turned and looked at her. "She cannot speak with you, for to do so would be to break her vows. It is forbidden. You'll be causing her harm if you . . ."

Colt continued his march, and in a moment he reached the wooden double doors of the chapel. He opened them and stepped inside.

Heads turned at the sound of intrusion, and forty pairs of eyes were on him. He couldn't help but be impressed by the hallowed aura of the chapel. Shafts of rainbow light shone delicately through the stained-glass windows, spilling across forty women in white. The nuns were on their knees, hands clasped beneath their chins.

At the front of the chapel were statues of the Virgin Mary and three other saints. Hanging above the altar was a silver Christ on a mahogany cross. The nuns were a sea of white as they continued fingering their rosary beads while staring at Colt.

Colt saw so many faces, knew that he would never recognize Dani. He walked to the front of the chapel, turned, and said quietly, "I apologize for interrupting, but I must talk to my sister, Daniella Coltrane." He searched the curious, frightened eyes, then urged softly, "Where are you, Dani? I need you. Please."

No one spoke.

From the rear, Sister Marie cried, "She cannot answer you. She has taken vows, and she cannot speak with you."

"She owes me something, Sister," he called to her. "I'm her brother, and I *need* her. I figure that's as important as honoring a vow."

The nuns gasped, and there was the faint sound of whispering. Colt looked to his left as a nun stood up and moved toward him.

A ripple went through the chapel.

Cinnamon eyes gazed up at Colt. A voice as soft as a summer breeze said quietly, "Yes, John Travis. How may I serve you?"

Colt stared down at his sister.

Chapter Twenty-seven

THE bitterness of Dani's estrangement from the Coltranes, cobwebbed memories of fighting . . . all these vanished as brother and sister embraced in the shadows of the chapel.

For long moments, they clung together.

Then the magic ended as Sister Marie reached them. "You have committed a sacrilege," she hissed at Dani, "by disrupting this service and communicating with an outsider."

Dani knew she was right. Still, the mission, the duty, of their order was to pray perpetually for the peace of the world and for the salvation of souls in purgatory. Was there not a similar need here? Before her stood her brother in obvious torment. Should she not minister to her own brother?

Sister Marie clutched Dani's shoulders. "Heed me and obey." She gave her a gentle shake. "Turn your back on him, my child, just as you have turned your back on all worldly things."

Dani looked from her to Colt, saw the terrible need in his eyes. Only something vitally important would have brought him here. Beyond him, she saw Briana. Yes, something was very wrong, and she could not refuse to help her friend and her brother.

Dani touched the nun's hands on her shoulders. "I must do what my conscience tells me to do, Sister. I cannot expect you to understand, but I will answer my brother's call." She held out her hand to Colt. "Come with me."

Colt motioned to Branch and Briana to come with them, and Dani led him out of the chapel as the nuns resumed their service.

They entered the courtyard, then walked to a small garden behind the convent. There were marble benches situated around a tiny fish pond, and after embracing Briana, Dani gestured to the three to sit. "Now tell me why you have come," she said. "I know it is terribly serious."

Colt started at the very beginning. When he explained Briana's deception, Dani held up a hand for silence. "You did such a thing?" she quietly demanded. "You went to claim *my* inheritance? And why was I not told of the letter from my father? The first in fourteen years!"

Briana was about to attempt an explanation when Colt quickly interrupted to say that there had been other letters over the years. "He wrote to you regularly, Dani. You never answered."

Dani stared down at her tightly clasped hands. "I never received them," she whispered. "I never knew. I always wondered why he did not respond to *my* letters."

Colt suddenly realized what had happened. His eyes met Dani's, and Colt murmured, "Alaina. She made sure the two of you were never in touch with each other."

Dani sighed. "She has done a terrible thing."

Then she looked at Briana again. "But why did you agree to help with the deception? You were my *friend.* I thought I knew you."

Briana had only to say one word: "Charles."

Dani looked at her carefully, then nodded. "I see. Where is he now?"

Briana explained about the orphanage, and told her briefly about the operation.

"Then some good has come of all this," Dani said, smiling, and Briana was glad to see a flash of the old Dani in this solemnly garbed woman.

Colt cut in to state, "She told me about a sick brother, but I didn't believe any of it."

Dani assured him that indeed the story was true. "Forgive her for the deception," she said. "I would have done the same for you."

That surprised him. "I don't know if I'll ever forgive any of this," he murmured.

"You must." She leaned over and surprised him further with a kiss on the cheek. "It is the only way we can know peace in this life, by being able to forget wrongs committed against us." She paused, then went on, "I came here to find peace, and I have."

Colt looked at the dreary surroundings. He knew it wasn't his right to judge, but what a terrible place to live. He'd never claimed to be religious. He figured that if there was a Supreme Being he would worry about it later. If Dani felt otherwise, then so be it. But did she have to live in such bleakness? He supposed it wasn't important that he understand. It was her life, not his. "I suppose I've ruined this for you. That nun was pretty angry with you."

Dani didn't look at all concerned. "God's will be done. God brought you here, so He meant for me to help you. Now, tell me what you want me to do."

"Nothing, I guess," Colt told her. "I just had to see you and talk to you and—forgive me, but I had to make sure you had nothing to do with any of this. I'll go back to Monaco now and get the gold. I'll deposit your share in a bank for you, if that's what you want me to do."

Dani's eyes widened. "No. It is not necessary that my share go to the church immediately. Take my share back with you and buy back the ranch and the mine. Protect my interest as you do your own, and one day, my share will go to the church. Maybe this way I can make up, somehow, for all that's happened to you. My share should be aiding the Coltrane family."

"You don't have to make up for anything," he told her firmly. "None of this was your fault."

She clasped his hand and gave him a sad smile. "Maybe it was, in a way. Had I been stronger, more like Kitty, Alaina might not have been able to turn my head and take me away from my family. Let me make restitution in some way. Take my share back with you, John Travis."

Branch could remain silent no longer. "That will be a help, miss."

Colt glared at him, and Branch shrugged apologetically.

Briana offered shyly, "Don't worry, Dani. I'll do everything I can to help, too."

Colt stiffened, and Dani asked, "Why were you persuaded to sign over your interest to her? I know you thought she was your sister, but why would you want to give away everything that was yours?"

Branch glanced away uncomfortably. He had pretty well figured out what had gone on between the two. Now, from the way Colt was looking and the way Briana was looking, it didn't take much to figure his suspicions were right.

Dani had spent most of her life around Alaina, and she began to realize why Briana and her brother looked so uncomfortable. She paled.

For a brief instant, Briana almost exploded with the need to tell Colt the truth. But would it make things worse for Colt to find out he had been doubly swindled? She didn't know anymore. She was so confused. Why make him hate her even more? If she told him the truth, she couldn't do so in front of other people.

They all remained silent until suddenly Dani inquired shyly, "Would you like to send for Father? He should know about this. And you might need his help in getting the gold back from Gavin. I know how treacherous Gavin is, and I don't want you hurt, John Travis."

Colt laughed shortly, brittlely. "I'm not scared of Gavin Mason. And the last thing I want is for our father to hear about this before I've settled the score. Allow me that much dignity, please, Dani."

Dani could understand that easily enough.

The four lapsed into silence again, each lost in thought. Dani felt more pain than ever before. All those years, her father had tried to get in touch with her and Alaina had kept them apart. All those wasted years. All that suffering for the whole family. She would pray for Alaina's soul, but she wondered how even God could forgive Alaina for all she'd done.

Branch felt terrible for all of them. He looked from one to the other and longed for this encounter to end so they could be on their way. Get the gold. Head for home. One day, Colt would be just fine again. It wouldn't hurt anymore. He was sure of that. They had to be on their way, though.

Colt stared at the ground, knowing they should leave. By now Alaina would have been discovered. Mason would probably take the gold and run, and they would have to chase him. But Colt couldn't bring himself to walk away, not yet. Here was his sister, and when would he ever see her again? She would never leave the convent, and he would never visit with her again. He wanted to be with her for a little while longer, to drink in the sight of her lovely face, and have something of her to remember.

As Colt sat beside Dani, he was struck by the realization that he would never have been drawn to her *that way,* lovely though she was. There was feeling between them, but that feeling had nothing to do with desire and he was certain it never could.

The feelings he'd had for Briana had been different from the start. Deep down, he had always wanted Briana as a man wants a woman. This realization made him feel much, much better.

Suddenly Dani withdrew her hands from Colt's, stiffening as she looked beyond him. Walking purposefully toward them were two nuns. Colt recognized Sister Marie. The other, he supposed, was the Mother Superior. Her mouth was turned down in a disapproving grimace. He doubted the corners ever moved in the opposite direction. As she drew closer, he could see the pinched lines of her face. The woman doubtless had a sour personality to match her expression.

Dani leaped to her feet. She bowed her head and gave a curtsy as she acknowledged respectfully, "Mother Superior."

The nuns stopped a few feet away, and then Mother Superior took a step forward. Positioning herself directly in front of Dani so that she could send a burning ray of chastisement straight into the novice's eyes, she said, "You have committed a sin against your vows, my child. A report will be filed with the bishop. He will decide what is to be done with you."

She paused, allowing time for this information to impress her victim. Then she continued, "You may be asked to leave, for you have broken your sacred vow to renounce the world."

But Dani was not so easily cowed. "Mother Superior, this is my brother, whom I have not seen in nearly fourteen years. He needed me to help him with a terrible—"

"That means nothing!" The nun's voice was like a cracking whip. "You took vows to leave the world and to spend your life in obedience and humility. When this man came into the chapel and called your name, you were bound by your vows to deny him as you would deny the summons of Satan."

"Sister," Colt interjected, "I don't profess to be a model Christian, but I can't say as I appreciate being compared to Satan. If you want to blame someone for this, blame me, not Dani. She did what any decent human being would have done."

Mother Superior's face turned crimson with rage. For several seconds she sucked her breath in and out, attempting to quell her fury. Finally she cried, "Young man, leave here at once. I do not intend to listen to you."

Colt started a retort, but Dani clutched his arm. "Just go, John Travis. We are only making things worse."

Colt wanted to embrace Dani once more, but knew that would only bring more trouble for her. He said, "I'll tell Pa the whole story, Dani. At least he'll know why you weren't in touch all these years. He'll understand the—"

"You will relay no messages!" Mother Superior exclaimed in horror. "There will be no communication with your sister. Do you understand?"

In a flash, Colt decided it was a real blessing that this shrewish woman had removed herself from civilization. She had, no doubt, saved some man from a life of god-awful misery. Dedication was fine, and religion was a good thing, he supposed, but wasn't there a place for human compassion somewhere in any religion?

Deciding it was futile to try to reason with the Head Dragon, aware that he would only make things worse, he sent Dani a message with his eyes, hoping he conveyed all the love he now felt for his sister.

He turned toward Branch. "Let's go."

The three departed from the convent, each sorry to have to leave Dani, all hoping it wouldn't go too hard for her.

Briana clung to Colt's back as the horse picked its way along the precarious trail. Her head was slumped in despair. She was unaware of the way her breasts moved rhythmically against him. Nor could she suspect how the sensation of her nipples, taut and hard against his back, aroused Colt.

When they reached Monaco, Colt told himself, he would let her go—be damned glad to get rid of her.

His knuckles were white as he gripped the reins tightly, finding himself assailed by a taunting thought: He had made love to her and could not remember a thing about it. He had touched those nipples, caressed those luscious breasts that now jounced against him so provocatively, and could not remember!

And *that*, Colt decided fiercely, she owed him.

Soon they reached a leveling off of the mountain, and he saw, not far from the road, a small stream flowing from somewhere high above.

Colt slowed his horse as he stared toward the mossy bank along the little brook. Then he called to Branch, "We'll catch up with you below. We've got something to settle."

Giving him a wave, Branch rode on, leaving them to their much-needed privacy.

Colt lowered Briana from the saddle and set her on her feet. He held her tightly as he stared down into her russet eyes. Then he kissed her, hard, demanding.

For a few seconds Briana was stunned into passivity. Then she began to fight, pummeling at him. But he lifted her easily, throwing her over his shoulder. He carried her away from the trail, toward the velvety green moss along the bank of the stream.

Briana screamed, but Colt merely chuckled. When he dumped her to the ground, towering above her as he began to remove his clothing, he said harshly, "You made sure I was good and drunk those nights, sweetheart, but you did too good a job. I was so far gone, I don't remember any of it. I figure, after all the hell you put me through, the least you can do is show me how good you are."

Briana flung her head from side to side. "No! You can't! You—"

"Oh, I can." He flashed her a mocking grin. "And I

will. . . ." He undid the buttons of her shirt and pulled it off her.

Briana knew she had but one chance. She cried, "No! We didn't make love, Colt. I just made you *think* we did. I couldn't go that far with you. I couldn't do that to you. . . ." Her voice broke on a sob.

Colt finished removing her clothing, then stood back to feast hungrily on her nakedness. Lord, but she was a sight to behold. He had bedded his share of women, but he'd never known such perfect mounds and curves. How in hell could he have been drunk enough to forget someone so beautiful?

Briana squeezed her eyes shut in humiliation. "Please," she whispered, "you have to believe me, Colt. We never made love. I only made you think we did. Ladida gave me something to drug you, and then I removed our clothes and lay next to you so you would believe we had made love. But we didn't."

Colt shook his head. She was a cunning little wench, the likes of which he had never seen. What havoc this lovely creature could wreak!

He dropped down beside her and threw one leg over both of hers to render her immobile. Then he lowered his lips to the delectable mound of her breasts and took one delicious nipple deep inside his mouth, pleased at the way it rose so hard and impudent against his tongue.

Briana writhed beneath the assault. Despite her shame, spasms of delight shot through her. Never had she dreamed a man's lips could be so hotly consuming, searing her.

She beat on his back, felt the iron muscles rippling as she struggled to move him away. He held her easily, as though her strength was nothing.

She knew she was at his mercy. "Please, Colt, you have to believe me. I have never been with a man."

He paid no attention. His swollen member pressed

against her thigh. Briana gasped. She squirmed, heaving her buttocks upward, trying to shove him away, but he used the movement to thrust his knees between her legs and open them, holding her thighs parted and vulnerable beneath him.

"Now," he panted, "this time we'll both remember."

He thrust his massive organ against her, entering her with a mighty stab. She cried out. Fleetingly he wondered why she was pretending pain. He knew she was aroused.

Then he felt it . . . the resistance. He hesitated. Was it due to the position they were in, the way he was having to force himself inside her? Never before had he forced himself on a woman.

He pushed harder, wincing as she screamed. Why was she persisting?

He gave another thrust, then felt his sudden entrance past whatever obstacle had held him. Again and again he pushed himself into her, and Briana began to feel a quickening deep within her belly. Never had she felt such agony. Never had she known such ecstasy.

She exploded in climax, crying aloud with the sheer wonder of it.

Colt took himself to his own pleasure.

Then he withdrew from her gently and lay beside her, his head on her heaving bosom.

He was about to ask why she had behaved as she had when he looked down and saw blood on himself.

He sat bolt upright, blinking in denial, saw the crimson stains on her thighs and between his legs.

She lay trembling beneath him.

"Briana?" He touched her face gently. "Oh, Lord, tell me this is a trick . . . just another trick. Is it, Briana?"

She shook her head violently and then, unable to stop herself, reached up and wrapped her arms around his neck, pulling him down to her.

"I love you," she whispered brokenly. "I think I always loved you, from the beginning. I knew that what I was doing was terrible. I couldn't go all the way with Gavin's plan, Colt. I couldn't seduce you. Ladida mixed up something to drug you . . . as I told you . . ."

She paused to take a deep breath, then burrowed her lips against his neck. "I did it because I loved you. I still do love you. And even though you hate me, I always will love you."

She clung to him, crying, joyous with relief now that the pretense was over.

Colt shuddered, looking down at her in wonder. Strange feelings were dancing through him, and he didn't have to think very long to understand the new emotions.

Yes, he acknowledged quietly, she had tricked him, but everything she'd done had been born of desperation, the need to save her little brother.

And in the end, she'd been unable to make him party to an incestuous act.

He gathered her in his arms, staring down into eyes that were clearly suffering. What he was feeling, he realized, was the awesome awakening of love. Perhaps it had always been there. But now there was no pretense anymore, and no shame.

His lips brushing hers, he whispered, "Briana, can you forgive me? I didn't know . . . didn't know you loved me . . . until now."

Despite all the pain, she was able to blink back tears and smile at his beloved face. "If this is what it took for you to believe, once and for all, that I never wanted it to happen as it did . . . and that I do love you . . . then the hurting was worth it."

He trailed gentle fingertips down her cheek. "It doesn't have to hurt, sweet lady, doesn't have to hurt at all. It can feel very good. Like this . . ." He moved his hand downward to cup her breast ever so gently. As he lowered his lips, his fingers danced downward, across her belly and down even farther. Slowly, tantalizingly, he parted the entrance to her channel of love and massaged her with teasing strokes.

Briana gasped. The pain was gone, and in its place was joyful anticipation of wonders to come.

He placed his knee between hers, and this time she willingly spread her thighs, opening herself to him. Then he was astride her again, and this time there was no holding back. Briana cupped his strong buttocks and guided him into her. She met his every thrust eagerly, for this was the man she loved with every breath she drew, and she wanted his body joined to hers for all time.

The magic fires spread, and then Briana was exploding with an ecstasy she'd never imagined existed. She clung to him, crying his name.

Colt took himself to his own glory, then burrowed his face in her neck. He whispered that he loved her . . . realized he always had.

He gazed down at her adoringly. So many feelings were welling up in him that he hardly knew what to say.

"Briana . . ." he whispered, and she smiled up at him, a rapturous smile.

A shot rang out, echoing against the mountain rocks.

Colt slumped across Briana's naked breasts, blood trickling from his forehead.

For a moment, she was frozen with horror. Surely this was a nightmare.

In that moment, Dirk Hollister walked out of the brush, a smoking gun in his hand.

Briana saw him, and, mercifully, her world turned black.

Chapter Twenty-eight

DANI had gone with Mother Superior to her office and sat penitently before her as she received another tongue-lashing. Sister Marie was present, looking aghast, watching Dani, hoping to see some sign that the novice understood the depth of her transgression.

But Dani only sat quietly, nodding. Caught up in the maelstrom of her emotions, it was all she could do to keep her face impassive. To think of the evil Aunt Alaina had done, the pain she had caused so many people, was astounding. Dani was numbed by thoughts of what might have been, had the attempted communication between her and her father not been sabotaged by Alaina.

She bit down on her lip till she tasted blood. No, she wouldn't let the two women see her cry. They couldn't understand how she felt. They were older, and long accustomed to the ways of the church. Why, Mother Superior had been away from the outside world for over forty years. She was in touch only with the bishop, and only for business reasons. Never did she communicate with her family. How could someone who had lived the cloistered life for forty years understand Dani's wild surge of emotions? Her life had been thrown into complete chaos in a single hour.

After a stern lecture that had left her red-faced and

gasping, Mother Superior repeated her intention to report Dani to the bishop.

"You will do penance at once," Mother Superior ordered angrily. "Go to the chapel and pray until evensong. You will fast until Sunday, when Father comes to hear our confessions."

Dani lifted her eyes and looked directly at Mother Superior's cold, condemning face. "No," she said softly. "I will not do penance now. I must meditate on what has happened to my family."

She stood up as Mother Superior and Sister Marie exchanged looks of astonishment. No one ever disobeyed a direct order from Mother Superior!

"You . . . you must!" Sister Marie cried. "You cannot just . . ."

Making her voice as soft as she could, Dani addressed Mother Superior. "I mean you no disrespect. I am well aware that I have committed a serious infraction of the rules. When I have come to terms with myself, then I will seek absolution."

She left them gaping after her.

Dani walked across the courtyard. She kept going until she found her special, private place among the shrubs, where she could always be alone with her thoughts.

There she sat, deep in thought, until she heard the shot ring out.

She sat there, wondering. A hunter? But they respected the convent and stayed away, or so she'd been told.

A chill of foreboding began to work its way through her. Quickly she got to her feet, left the sanctuary of the foliage, and started down the road, forbidden though it was to go beyond the gates. As she moved, the fear grew stronger, and she quickened her pace, lifting her long skirt.

Suddenly, in the distance, she heard the sound of a woman screaming, screaming as though the hounds of hell were snapping at her. There was the sound of men shouting in excitement, and then the thundering of hoofbeats. Many horses were moving along the rocky mountain path.

She rounded a curve in the road, then stopped as something to the left caught her eye. She turned, hands flying to cover her mouth and stifle a scream.

Colt lay naked on the ground beside the stream. The water flowing below his body was red with the crimson rivulets coming from his head.

She ran to him and, kneeling, lifted his head gently onto her lap. His blood spread bright-red stains across her skirt.

She called his name again and again, in despair and in supplication.

He moaned—a tiny sound, barely audible, but it was enough. Dani choked on her own sobs as she attempted to rouse him, daring to shake him only very gently.

Others had heard the gunfire, for the shooting had taken place so near the usually serene and quiet convent.

Nuns came running down the trail. Horrified by what they found, they ran back to the convent to summon their port in all storms—Mother Superior.

She did not rush to the scene, but gave directions for bringing Colt to the convent infirmary.

Dani followed as Colt was lifted on a litter and carried gently back up the trail and into the convent.

She waited outside while Sister Mary Francesca, a nun with two years' nursing practice, examined Colt. At long last, Dani was allowed to enter the barren room. The walls and ceiling were white. There were no curtains at the arched windows, which overlooked a bare, rocky slope and an autumn-browned valley below. The floor was wood, and had been scrubbed with bleach and water so many times that there was no color left to it.

There were four beds lining each side of the long

room, narrow cots with iron headboards. Colt was lying very still on a bed near the window, a crisp cotton sheet and a thick wool blanket over him. His head was wrapped in a cocoonlike bandage and propped on a pillow. His eyes were closed, and his chest moved only a little.

Dani looked at Sister Francesca, her eyes begging for good news—but for honesty as well.

"Your brother has not been conscious in all this time," Sister Francesca informed her frankly. "The bullet did not enter his head, or he would be dead. It grazed his skull, and grazed it hard. With my limited medical knowledge"—the nun shrugged apologetically—"I can only assume that the bullet hit hard enough to bruise his brain, causing a concussion."

Dani swallowed hard. "Will he live?" she whispered.

Sister Francesca looked away. "I have done all I can think of. We will just have to wait and see what God wants to do about this."

Dani moved to Colt's bed and, leaning over him, brushed her lips against his cheek. "Live, John Travis," she whispered. "Live. Please."

Then she turned away. It was time, she decided, to send a message to Travis Coltrane that his children needed him.

Gavin Mason strode furiously up and down the area outside the hatchway to the deBonnett cellar. His men were bringing up the crates of gold with agonizing slowness. Damn it, why was this taking so long? The ship he had booked for the voyage to Santoríni was in the harbor, so all they had to do was load the gold and set sail.

Dirk Hollister stood a little ways off, watching the men struggling with the crates. Gavin regarded him warily. How could the blundering fool have been so stupid as to kill Coltrane and Pope so close to the convent? Hollister hadn't admitted it, but the two men with him had told Gavin they'd questioned the wisdom of the shootings, telling Dirk that the bottom of the mountain was a far better place. And at the very least, the bodies ought to've been hidden. But Hollister was hell-bent and wouldn't listen.

Gavin had exploded when they reported to him. He told Hollister what a stupid son of a bitch he was, and now things were dangerously tense between them.

Gavin hadn't liked it any better than Hollister did that Coltrane and Briana had been found naked in each other's arms. When the men brought her back, Gavin saw her virginal blood smeared on her thighs and rage overtook him. Everything was clear now. He knew the depth of her feelings for Coltrane. She had drugged Coltrane, but she hadn't coupled with him, not if she was still a virgin. All this time, Gavin had been deceived.

Well, no matter. It was over, and Coltrane was dead. Briana, bound and gagged, would be hidden on one of the wagons that would transport the gold to the ship. They were going to Santorini. Once they were safely there, he would have Briana whenever he wanted her.

Gavin didn't have to ask what had made Hollister act so crazily. Hollister both desired Briana passionately and hated her savagely for scarring him.

As three men struggled futilely to get a crate through the hatchway, Gavin's tension got the best of him, and he railed, "God damn it, move your asses. You got it down there, so why can't you get it up? We haven't got all day. Hollister blundered the job, and we've got to put as much distance as we can between us and France, because you can believe Travis Coltrane is going to come after us with everything he's got."

"Which is . . ." Alaina taunted softly, "a *lot.*"

Gavin whirled around. What was she doing here?

"Get out of here, you old bitch! I won't listen to your goading. You're looking for trouble."

Alaina flinched. Why must he treat her this way in front of these men?

"Did you hear me, bitch?" Gavin roared, lips turned back in a vicious snarl, eyes glittering. "Get out of here!"

"After all I've done, you ungrateful . . ." Alaina sputtered.

"Ungrateful!" Gavin shoved her away from him, and she sprawled to the ground.

"I warned you I wasn't going to listen to your drunken nagging anymore," he cried.

"You old bat!" he went on furiously. "You're the one who should be grateful—grateful I was able to stay with you so long. You're a disgusting old lush." He gave her a savage kick in the side.

Slowly, gasping with pain, Alaina struggled to stand, falling twice before she managed to get herself up. Her side hurt terribly, and she clutched at it, crouching over.

Gavin took a menacing step nearer. "I will tell you one time: Get out of my sight, or you'll make me really hurt you."

She reached out for the stone wall of the house, leaning on it for support.

The crate was finally through the hatchway.

"Is that the last one?" Gavin asked, and the men grunted assent.

"Get it on the wagon, and let's head for the harbor." He turned to Dirk and said, "I'm going to make sure Delia's ready. Wait for me by the wagons."

He started toward the house, and Alaina called out, "Wait! What about me? How long before you come home, Gavin?"

Gavin turned around very slowly and stared at her. What did it take to make her comprehend? "You brought all this on yourself, Alaina. I am sick of you, and I don't know whether I'll come back or not."

Alaina's spirit had not been crushed despite all the humiliation of the last few weeks. "You bastard!" she screamed, her voice ringing out like a death knell. "You goddamn, no-good bastard! You can't just leave me here to starve while you take everything for yourself. I've got as much right to that gold as you have—more, really. If it weren't for me, you'd never have gotten it."

"I owe you nothing," Gavin growled.

Just then Dirk dared to intervene. "You aren't going to leave her here to starve, are you?"

Gavin sighed. "Don't be dramatic, Hollister. She still has some things she can sell—furniture and so on. Now let's *go*. She's not destitute. If Travis Coltrane catches up with us, *we'll* be destitute."

Alaina had, at last, become too angry to feel humiliated. She was smoldering with a rage so fierce it actually caused a burning sensation in her chest. And she knew just what to do about it.

By the time Gavin finished yelling at Delia for being so slow and rushed downstairs again, heading outside to check the wagons, Alaina had reached the kitchen. She heard Gavin leave, then crept to the big chopping block in the middle of the room. Beneath, neatly positioned in their slitted compartments, were a dozen knives of various sizes.

She chose the longest and largest.

Then she began to make her way upstairs. All was quiet.

She picked her way along carefully, for her side was aching terribly, and it was grueling to climb the stairs. She was also having difficulty focusing. How many vodkas had she had today? She couldn't remember. When she had taken care of the evil in the house, she promised herself, had gotten rid of the demon that had taken over Gavin's will, she would have champagne, to celebrate.

What had happened outside, Alaina told herself, was not Gavin's fault. The man she had loved for so long, treated as a son in his younger years and then as a lover, would never, ever treat her that way. Why, Gavin was Stewart Mason's son, and Stewart had adored her.

No, the Gavin she loved had become possessed by that creature who'd seduced him and come back with him from America.

The door to Delia's room was ajar. Alaina stood very still and peered inside.

Delia was standing in front of her dressing table, humming as she tucked her curly hair inside a wide-brimmed straw bonnet. She was wearing a pink velvet dress made in the newest fashion. She looked fresh and pretty. She twirled, smoothing the long, flowing skirt, delighted with herself. The delicate lace edging at the high collar, framing her face, gave her an innocent, cherubic look.

Delia was thinking about how good Gavin was for her. Oh, he was no great lover, and she didn't much like him *that way.* She also did not love him. But he was rich, filthy rich, and that made all the difference that mattered. She intended to stick to him like a newborn calf to its mother. Nothing would come between them as long as he stayed rich.

She went out onto the small balcony off her room, wanting a last look. Who knew whether she'd ever come back to Monaco? Gavin had said they probably wouldn't. It was a dramatic view. The rocks below were large and jagged, and the azure waters of the Mediterranean lapped lazily among them. Sea gulls darted, crying to each other. It was a lovely view, but Delia resentfully recalled the panorama from Alaina's balcony. There, the sea could be seen in all its splendor, as well as the mountain range to the east.

Delia placed her hands on the waist-high balcony railing, standing on tiptoe and leaning forward, trying to see the yard to her left. Only a tiny corner of the yard was visible. She wanted to see Gavin, to wave to him to let him know that she was on her way downstairs. She knew that she made a beautiful sight, the sea and sky surrounding her for background.

Gavin was nowhere in view. She turned, and in that instant, Alaina brought the knife down in a deadly arc.

With lightning speed, Delia leaped to the side. And then she gazed in horror as the force of Alaina's lunge propelled her over the railing. Dumbstruck, Delia watched the screaming Alaina hit the scrubby brush along the rocks, then tumble on downward to lie at the water's edge. She lay very still.

Alaina's scream died away, and Delia's shrieking took its place.

She was still screaming when Gavin burst into the room moments later. He slapped her hard several times until she stopped screaming and succumbed to broken sobs. "She tried to . . . stab me. I jumped to the side, and she just plunged over the railing. . . ."

Gavin's thoughts raced while he quieted her. As he was weighing the odds against Alaina's still being alive, Dirk burst in.

"Mason!" he called. "She's not dead. She must've hit the bushes first, and that broke her fall. But she won't live long, not the way she's busted up."

Gavin eyed him shrewdly. "Is she . . . very bad?"

Dirk nodded brusquely. "What doc do you want to send for?" he asked. "I told the men not to move her till the doctor got here."

When Gavin spoke next, both Delia and Dirk gaped at him, amazed and disbelieving.

"We'll leave her where she is. When someone eventually finds her body, they'll think it was an accident that happened after we'd already gone. To send for a doctor means answering a lot of questions. See?"

* * *

At last, the horses and wagons began to move down the road toward Monaco, and the ship in the harbor.

Gavin and Delia, in the deBonnett carriage, felt like royalty. Settling back against the smooth red leather seats, Gavin placed a possessive arm around Delia, drawing her close.

Thinking of Alaina on the rocks, dying, was unpleasant, but not intolerable. She had become a lush and a bore. Once, he had enjoyed her. Hell, he'd even been fond of her. But those days were gone.

Gavin smiled as he gazed at Delia. He hoped she was taking a good look at the coastline, because she would not be returning—not with him, at any rate.

He intended to leave her in Greece.

He would return to Monaco with Briana. She would be either his mistress or his wife, whatever he decided was best. He was, by God, going to possess her— No, he was going to *own* her.

Travis Coltrane sat behind the large mahogany desk in his richly appointed office at the American Embassy in Paris. He was wearing a three-piece suit in a soft shade of charcoal-gray. His shoes were black, and highly polished. A gold watch chain hung across his vest. Travis looked important. He *was* important.

And he hated his job.

Tossing aside the document he was trying to read, he rose from the high-backed burgundy leather chair and went to the window. He stood there, hands folded behind his back. Though Kitty had guessed he was miserable with their new life, he had not, as yet, said so to her in plain words.

Travis had never been a desk man, an indoors man, and he never would be. He longed to return to Nevada and his beloved ranch. He longed to work in fresh air and sunshine. Hell, he was so eager to get back in the saddle, he wouldn't even complain when the snows came and the frigid winds blew.

He told himself to concentrate on where he was. The view before him was surely magnificent. The Champs de Mars, a vast parade ground, stretched south for more than half a mile. The Champs de Mars had been the scene of many historical events, including violent riots and celebrations during the French Revolution.

At the far end stood the École Militaire. A handsome military school built in the eighteenth century, it looked more like a palace than a military academy. Initially meant to provide officers' training for the sons of poor aristocrats, the school was later opened to outstanding students from academies outside Paris.

Travis recalled the story he'd heard concerning the academy's most famous student—Napoleon Bonaparte. It was said that his final report card had carried the notation *Will go far, if circumstances permit.*

Thoughtfully Travis looked at the controversial new structure at the north end of the parade grounds. Built for the 1889 Paris World's Fair by the architect Alexandre Eiffel, it was the object of much criticism. It was called everything from a curiosity to a monstrosity, and many people wanted it torn down. Travis respected the Eiffel Tower for what it was: a brilliant engineering feat. The pressure per square inch the tower exerted upon the ground was no greater than the pressure per square inch a man would exert sitting in a chair. At 985 feet, it was easily the tallest structure in the world. There was a nice restaurant there. He and Kitty had dined in it a few times, and . . .

Kitty.

How he loved that woman. He'd never loved anyone so much. All he wanted was to make her happy in their old age, as happy as she made him.

He'd thought that some time in Paris and traveling through Europe was what she wanted. But Kitty was more homesick than she would admit, and she missed Colt terribly.

Travis shook his head. A nagging worry increased

with every day that there was no word from Colt. It had been over three months and, damn it, this wasn't like Colt. Surely he knew his parents would worry.

A knock startled Travis out of his reverie. He went to his desk, sat down, and picked up the document again before calling, "Yes, come in."

His secretary seemed nervous. That, for her, was unusual. Miss Tyrone, an old maid at thirty, detested men in general, but she was an efficient secretary and nothing bothered her. Once, Travis had teased her about the severity of her appearance, good-naturedly joking that she probably scared men away with her drab clothes and overly serious expression. She told him in her usual flawless English that that was how she wanted it. From then on, Travis and Miss Tyrone kept each other at a distance.

As he watched her cross the room, he began wondering what could be wrong. As she held out a yellow telegram, he saw that her hands were trembling.

"For you, sir, a personal matter."

"It's about time," Travis cried jubilantly, taking the paper from her hands. "Do you think now I'll find out what that son of mine has been up to?"

Miss Tyrone's face was filled with sympathy as she said, "It isn't from your son, sir. It's from your daughter. . . ."

And before Travis's eyes could focus on the words before him, he felt his blood turn to ice.

Chapter Twenty-nine

No one attempted to stop Travis Coltrane from entering the convent on Jaune Mountain, which was just as well. He rode through the gates, his eyes narrowed, his back ramrod straight.

He was met by a fluttering nun and refused to listen to her protests, moving politely past her toward the convent. Knowing she was beaten, Sister Marie led him down a shadowy, dim hallway that smelled of old newspapers and wet hair, until they reached the infirmary.

Travis stepped inside silently.

At the far end of the room was a young woman in white on her knees beside a patient's bed, head bent in prayer. Was it the daughter he hadn't seen in fourteen years?

At the sound of approaching footsteps, Dani looked up with tired, burning eyes. A gasp stuck in her throat as she watched the man come toward her.

She was looking at the image of her brother! He was tall, husky, muscular. He had the same smoke-gray eyes as John Travis. The only marked difference was the touch of silver in his raven-black hair.

With pounding heart, Dani gripped the edge of her brother's bed and struggled to stand. Tears began trickling down her pale cheeks from the sharp pain of joy mixed with sorrow—joy at seeing her father . . . sorrow over their long estrangement.

Travis, shaken, held out his arms to her. She moved toward him slowly, and he folded her against his chest. They clung to each other.

When, finally, they drew apart, Travis tersely told the nun on duty to leave them alone. Darting a questioning look at Dani, she left the room.

When they were alone, Dani hurriedly explained all she knew about her brother's condition. Colt was still unconscious. He was no better and no worse than he had been the day before.

After taking a long look at his son, Travis turned back to Dani. He gently cupped her chin and looked down at her with all the love he hadn't been able to give her for fourteen years. "Tell me," he whispered. "Tell me everything."

She nodded and shyly reached for his hand. They sat down, side by side, on the cot next to Colt's.

Dani spoke very slowly, searching for the words. She cried, and then resumed her story. Her father never interrupted.

In fact, Travis was becoming angrier with each word, for he was finally learning a truth he'd never guessed. The depth, the sheer awfulness of what Alaina had done astonished him.

Dani explained about the deception and theft Gavin had perpetrated, and Travis found himself stunned anew. How could Gavin have gotten away with so many lies?

"My friend Briana is missing," Dani finished. "I could hear her screaming far away, but we had no idea where to find her. One of the nuns dared to walk farther down the trail. . . ." She paused, swallowing hard. "She was the one who found Mr. Pope's body. He had been stabbed, but he wasn't dead. He said the name *Hollister* to the sister, and then he died."

Travis got to his feet and moved slowly to the window to stare, unseeing, at the autumn forest behind the convent. The world was dying. His son was dying. A friend was dead. His family had been swindled.

It took all his will to stop himself from driving his fist through the glass.

Finally Travis shook himself. "I'll move Colt, take him to Paris, as soon as it's safe for him to be moved. He can at least be close to me . . . and his mother."

Dani was quick to remind him, "The doctor who came yesterday said he could regain consciousness at any time. You can never predict what will happen with a blow to the head, you know." Then she asked, "Colt? I call him 'John Travis.' "

Her father grinned. "The nickname's obvious. I like 'John Travis' better, but 'Colt' stuck."

As if their discussing him was bringing him back to the living, Colt began struggling out of the nightmare that held him prisoner. His head throbbed terribly, and he felt as though a giant spider had spun a massive web around his brain, preventing him from thinking clearly. Who were the people talking beyond that thick black fog clouding him? What was the matter with him?

Dani got up and went to her father. "I want to go with you, but . . . I must stay here."

"It's what you chose," Travis reminded her softly. "I don't imagine you made your decision hastily. Somehow I feel you aren't an impulsive woman."

She agreed, but she needed to explain. "Had things been different, had I not felt my family didn't love me, perhaps I would not have become a nun. If I'd felt I had a place in life, well . . ."

Travis frowned. Of course he wanted her with him and Kitty, but he did not want to encourage her to throw everything away because of this sudden, emotional upheaval in her life. He embraced her, whispering, "Give it time, sweet one. Think it through." Lord, he thought, she was so much like her mother! He hadn't loved Marilee as he loved Kitty, but he'd respected Dani's mother and loved her in a different, softer way from the way he loved Kitty. Marilee had been one hell of a woman.

As he held Dani against him, time turned backward, and Travis remembered vividly the night Marilee gave birth to Dani.

Weakly, Marilee had lifted her hand to touch his cheek, her breathing ragged as she struggled to speak. "Remember what I told you, darling? Remember . . . I told you that no moment lasts forever?"

Travis relived the anguish of holding Marilee, knowing she was dying. She wasn't fighting to live, not really. He tried to prevent her from talking any more because she needed the little strength she had.

Marilee swallowed hard, looking deep into Travis's eyes. "You said to make more moments," she told him. "*You* make them, my beloved. Make them with the only woman you ever truly loved. . . ."

Pain consumed her then, and blood gushed. It could not be stopped.

He would never forget the agony of watching Marilee's eyes lock in a gaze with eternity.

She had gotten out of the way so that he would be free to love Kitty, his first wife, the wife he had believed dead.

But Marilee's baby had lived, and now he held that baby close. She reminded him so much, dear God, of that tender, loving woman whom he would never forget—would never wish to forget.

A voice broke into the painful remembrance:

"Let's go get the bastards!"

Dani gave a little scream, and Travis whirled around. It was Colt!

And then the three of them were clinging together, there in a whitewashed room in a convent on top of a mountain in France, three who had come so far, from such different places, and who belonged—at least for a little while—together.

They had each been terribly wronged, but by the strength of their Coltrane blood, they were going to make things right.

Alaina could hardly breathe. Each time her lungs struggled to expand, they pushed against her smashed ribs. The pain was excruciating. Not only was her chest cage smashed, every major bone in her body was broken. No one could understand how it was possible that she was still alive three days after a fisherman saw her lying on the rocks.

Dr. Geoffrey Robaire was as puzzled as anyone. He listened to her heart once more, then stepped back from her bed and shook his head. "She cannot last much longer," he said matter-of-factly, seeing nothing to be gained by lying. Surely the woman knew she was dying. He had never been close to the Countess, or, for that matter, to any of his patients. He kept his feelings out of things.

Travis and Colt stood near the door. They didn't want Alaina upset by the sight of them, but they had to find out where Gavin Mason had gone.

"Has she been conscious at all?" Travis asked tightly.

Dr. Robaire shrugged. He had not been around her that much. He had been summoned when she was found, and he'd done what little he could, plainly surprised that she continued to live. In his opinion, she was merely stretching out the inevitable—and causing him the inconvenience of running back and forth to give her injections to ease the pain.

Looking at the wife of the fisherman who had found her, he asked the woman if she'd heard the Countess talk, or whether she'd even opened her eyes.

She shook her head. "She has trouble breathing, Doctor, but even the pain doesn't wake her." She didn't care. The only reason she was sitting in Alaina deBonnett's bedroom was that her husband had said Mr. Mason would be ever so grateful that she had cared for his aunt in his absence. There would certainly be a nice remuneration from Mr. Mason for their kindness, her husband had told her.

Travis stepped forward, eyes glinting. "I'm going to see if I can get her to talk to me. It can't harm her, can it?"

Dr. Robaire shook his head. "But she is heavily sedated, so I doubt she will understand anything you say."

The doctor placed his stethoscope in his worn leather bag and bade them good-day. He wanted to be gone from there. If the imposing-looking stranger wanted to pester a dying woman, that was not his concern.

Travis stared down at Alaina. He felt no remorse at the welling up of hatred within him. She was an evil woman, had been hurting people for years and causing grief to everyone whose path she had ever crossed.

"Alaina," he said harshly, loudly. He did not touch her. He didn't want to cause her further pain by rattling broken bones around. He wasn't a sadist. He just wanted information—and he intended, by God, to have it. "Alaina. Talk to me."

Alaina was in a world of gnawing, white-hot pain. She could feel the flames of hellfire licking at her. The agony was so terrible, it just melded together in one clawing fist that was pulling her down, down toward those hungry flames.

"Alaina. Answer me."

Suddenly the black clouds parted and she saw blue sky. There was warm sunshine. Beneath her bare feet was the cooling bluegrass of her beloved Kentucky. And above, bending over to look at her, was the dear face of a man she had hated and loved.

"Travis," she whispered. The pain in her throat was unbearable. She coughed, tasted blood. "Travis Coltrane. You . . . want me, don't you? Just like . . ."

Travis winced ever so slightly. "Yes, Alaina, I want you," he lied. Where was the harm? "But you must help me. You have to tell me where Gavin Mason is."

She frowned, and that also hurt terribly. Was there no movement that wouldn't cause excruciating pain?

"Mason," Travis said sharply. "Where is he, Alaina?"

The never-ending nightmare was coming back. She remembered the knife slicing through the air, the plunge into the void. Then the all-consuming pain.

"I don't think she's going to tell us anything," Colt whispered. "I can see from here that her breathing is getting shallower. Her color is bad, too."

Travis silently agreed. Death was hovering over Alaina. Her eyes were starting to look glassy. "Where did Mason go?" he urged. "Alaina? Help me, please."

Alaina shuddered with pain.

"Greece . . . He went to Santor . . ." She could not go on, did not want to make another excruciating effort.

She tried to lift her arm, the closest to Travis, but it, too, was smashed. She managed to move her fingers, like the opening and closing of crab claws. Travis saw and understood. He laid his hand on top of hers, hoping it comforted her. Her lips moved, and he leaned closer so as to catch the faint whisper.

"Tell . . . me . . ." She was hardly able to enunciate. Blackness was closing in. ". . . you love me."

Travis leaned over and brushed his lips against her forehead. "Yes, Alaina. I love you," he said firmly.

This time, she was able to smile past the pain. The smile was frozen on her lips forever. In that moment, Alaina Barbeau deBonnett died.

Travis straightened. Glancing at Colt, he saw the faintest glimmer of condemnation in his son's eyes.

"Never condemn a man for leaving a woman happy," he told him.

Colt nodded. It was all right. His father had done what had to be done, and Alaina had died a little less miserable because of it.

Chapter Thirty

THROUGH the mist of despair surrounding her, Briana looked at her small cabin. There was only a chair, a small table, and her bunk. A single porthole offered a view of the endless ocean. The bleak vista suited her. Colt was dead. Charles had been taken away. And she was imprisoned on a ship, Gavin's prisoner—and Dirk's.

The day faded, but she did not stir from bed. As the cabin faded into darkness, there came the sound of her door being unlocked. She tensed, waiting, ready to fight with every ounce of strength.

Suddenly a young Frenchman murmured, "It is so dark in here. Where are you? I have brought your dinner, mademoiselle."

"I'm not hungry," she snapped. "Go away."

She heard him fumbling in the dark, finding the table and setting down the tray. "I have orders, mademoiselle. Wait. I will light a lantern."

A few seconds later the room was flooded with light.

Briana saw her visitor. Still a boy, he was no more than sixteen. He was tall and thin, with dark hair that reached almost to his shoulders. He stared at her, wide-eyed. She decided he was not to be feared.

"My name is Raoul," he said eagerly. "I have been assigned to bring your meals to you."

Then, gravely, he announced, "I know you are being

confined here by your uncle, Monsieur Mason. I must warn you that I will not let you escape. I am strong, so you mustn't try."

He frowned, trying to look fierce, and Briana smiled to herself.

So Gavin had said she was a disobedient niece? That would make the whole ship's crew reluctant to help her if she appealed to them. Whatever she told them about Gavin, they wouldn't believe her. It was a smart thing for Gavin to have done.

"Don't worry," she told him softly. "I won't make trouble for you."

He seemed to relax a little, and he turned to indicate the tray. "It's simple fare, but excellent. Fish. Potatoes. Cheese. Wine. Fruit. If you want more, I can get it."

"That will be fine. Thank you. By the way," she added brightly, attempting to appear friendly, "my name is Briana."

He grinned. "I know. I think it's a beautiful name, just like you—" He fell silent, his face flushing.

He turned to leave, and Briana called softly, "Thank you, Raoul. I hope we can be friends."

He rushed out, locking the door.

Briana smiled.

The next morning, Raoul brought her water for bathing, then left her alone for half an hour before bringing her a breakfast tray of porridge, fruit, and chocolate.

She began to ask him questions, and he stayed for a while—eager, she realized, to tell her all he knew about sailing. He explained that they were in the Ligurian Sea, heading through the Tuscan Arch between the islands of Elba and Corsica. Next, they would enter the Tyrrhenian Sea, eventually passing through the narrow Strait of Messina and into the Ionian Sea.

"You have sailed this route before?" she asked him, glad to see that he was not anxious to leave.

"Oh, yes, many times. I've been at sea since I was twelve, a mere boy."

Briana suppressed a smile.

He told her that he was born in the tiny province of Grasse, west of Monaco. "This ship belongs to my uncle," he said proudly. "And my cousin is the captain. We travel to Greece and back, transporting goods to and from the Cyclades Islands."

Briana nodded, hopeful. If the captain was a relative of this boy's, then she needed Raoul on her side more than she'd thought.

She urged him to tell her about the Greek islands, especially Santoríni.

He grinned. "The real name for that island," he was proud to correct her, "is Thera. It's the farthest south of the Cyclades. It is actually the remains of a volcano that they say erupted about fifteen hundred B.C., the same eruption that destroyed Atlantis.

"There's a lagoon there," he went on excitedly, "over sixty kilometers wide. In the middle of the lagoon are two little islands with volcanoes on them. One is called Néa Kaméni, which means New Burnt Island, and the other is called Palaía Kaméni, which means Old Burnt Island. They still have smoke coming out of them, which means they might blow again."

Briana nodded. "Tell me about Santoríni . . . Thera."

Raoul described the island as having a small settlement along the east coast. The island was made mostly of lava and pumice, and the lagoon was rimmed by red, white, and black striped volcanic cliffs three hundred meters high. "On the top of Thera there is the Mount Profitus Ilías, over five hundred meters high. Not many people live up there, because it's too hard to get there. They use donkeys to carry supplies.

"Then," he went on, eyes shining brightly, for he was enjoying the way she hung on his every word, "there are other settlements to the south, Emboríon and Pírgos. The port at the north entrance of the lagoon is called Oía."

Wanting him to know that she was impressed, Briana gushed, "You certainly are knowledgeable, Raoul. I . . ."

Her voice faded as they heard footsteps outside the door. Raoul held up a hand for silence.

Whoever it was stopped directly outside the door. After a short pause, the steps continued on, their sound fading into the distance.

Raoul quickly got to his feet. "I have other work to do," he said apologetically. He rushed out, locking the door.

Briana lay down on the uncomfortable bunk. He might become an ally. With his help, she could find a way to escape.

And then what?

She closed her eyes. Somehow, she would find the orphanage where Charles was. There would, thank God, be Charles. But the emptiness in her heart would never be filled, the pain never assuaged. For a time, she had loved and been loved. And in that precious instant, when, miraculously, she knew her love was returned . . . it had been stolen away from her forever.

She grieved terribly for her beloved Colt, and for what might have been. And within that wrenching sorrow there burned a rage so hot she often felt as though her blood actually were boiling.

There, in the shadows of the damp cabin, feeling the rhythmic pitch and roll of the ship against the sea, Briana vowed revenge. For taking Colt's life . . . for taking Branch's life . . . for all he had done to her . . . Dirk Hollister was going to die.

When Dirk and his men kidnapped her, dragging her back to the deBonnett château, Dirk had taunted her with the grisly details of how he had murdered Branch. When he and Butch and Artie saw Branch riding alone, they decided not to sound an alarm by shooting. Dirk waited behind a group of boulders, and when Branch passed by, he leaped onto Branch's horse and plunged his knife through Branch's throat, falling to the ground with him.

Briana had died a little bit more with each word, as though the knife that had taken Branch's life was twisting in her soul.

Each time Raoul went to Briana's cabin, they talked. He lingered as long as he dared, talking about the sea, the ship . . . anything to keep a conversation going, obviously hating to leave her. Briana encouraged him, desperate to win his friendship. She had to be warm and kind, aware of what Gavin had probably told the crew about his "niece."

One evening, Raoul brought her a whole bottle of wine instead of the usual single glass. She offered him some, and he shook his head, stammering, "Oh . . . I wouldn't dare. It isn't allowed. I'd be keelhauled, for sure."

She was quick to reassure him. "No, you mustn't break any rules. But what harm is there in your staying a while to keep me company?"

He stared at the floor. "My orders are to bring your trays and then leave. I'm not supposed to spend time with you, because . . ." He glanced at her nervously, then quickly lowered his eyes again.

"Why?" she asked gently. "Why were you told not to stay? What has Monsieur Mason told you about me that makes you think I am so terrible?"

Quickly he said, "I must go." He edged toward the door. "I've said too much."

Briana did not try to dissuade him from leaving. It would not do to frighten him or pressure him. She would just have to be patient.

They had been at sea for two days before Gavin made his first appearance in her tiny cabin. He came in with an arrogant, gloating smile and inquired, by way of greeting, "Well, my dear, have you calmed down?"

She merely regarded him with a look that, she hoped, transmitted all her hatred.

He laughed, delighted. "Oh, if looks could kill, my darling, I would be dead at your feet."

"I only hope," she murmured, "that one day you will be."

A shadow crossed his eyes, "Perhaps," he warned, "we ought to see what a few days without food does to that nasty disposition of yours."

After a silence, Gavin informed her that he was having a terrible time keeping Dirk Hollister away from her. "He wants revenge for your scarring him, and he couldn't do anything about it while he was bringing you back to Monaco. No time. He's also furious that you double-crossed us by telling Coltrane everything."

Briana decided to let herself gloat for a change. "It wasn't me, you fool—though I had every reason to, after *you* double-crossed *me*. It was Alaina who set it up for me to be rescued."

She paused to enjoy herself, watching Gavin squirm. He looked truly mystified at hearing that he was not as brilliant as he'd thought.

"I don't believe you," he said uncertainly, pushing back a clump of blond curls.

She shrugged. "How else would he have known where I was? He had been to the house earlier that day, so Alaina knew he was in Monaco. Colt told me that she went to find him that afternoon and set it up for him to see me."

Gavin looked skeptical, and Briana elaborated on this bad news. "She told him his sister was imprisoned in the cellar. She didn't tell him I was an imposter. She saved that for me. Maybe she didn't want to go all the way in betraying you, Gavin—only *part* of the way."

His eyes darkened to a deep blue. "She was jealous

because of Delia. She thought if Coltrane got his money back, and we were left poor again, Delia would leave me. Then *she* could have me back. She'd never have hurt me otherwise," he said, more to reassure himself than to convince Briana. "When that didn't work, and she found out Coltrane was dead," he went on, "well, I guess that's why she tried to kill Delia."

Briana stiffened. Alaina had tried to kill Delia? She started to ask him what had happened, but he kept talking.

"Served her right. She was a black widow spider . . . wanted to love me, then devour me. She stopped at nothing to get her way. She was always greedy, always conniving and selfish." He shook his head. "My life is so much easier with her dead."

Briana was astonished. He explained hastily, telling her without remorse what had happened to Alaina Barbeau deBonnett. But he left out the fact that she'd been alive on the rocks when he left her. Briana didn't need to know that.

Suddenly Gavin stopped talking. He reached out and took hold of Briana's hands.

"Dirk Hollister will not have you," he said, his teeth clenched, his eyes burning into hers. "I am sick and tired of people interfering in my plans. When we reach Santoríni, I am going to turn Delia over to Hollister to pacify him, and then you are going to marry me. He wouldn't dare touch you if you were my wife."

He tried to kiss her, but Briana twisted her head away. He grabbed her arms and jerked them behind her, holding her wrists with one hand. With his free hand, he grabbed her hair, holding her still as his mouth began to assault hers. When he forced his tongue between her lips, she bit down as hard as she could. Yelping with pain, he slapped her so hard that a shower of stars fell before her eyes.

"Do something like that again, and I will make you very sorry!"

He jerked a handkerchief from his coat pocket and dabbed at his tongue. When he saw the crimson stain, he swore furiously and slapped her again.

Briana tasted blood in her own mouth, but refused to give him the pleasure of hearing her cry out. Venomously she asked, "Are you through?"

"No," he whispered ominously. "I have not even begun, my dear. You will know what real pain is when I have you tied, naked, spread-eagled, and—"

A sound in the hallway outside the door caused him to fall silent. He turned quickly, jerking the door open to peer outside.

No one was there.

Turning back to Briana, he warned, "You will be mine. I wish I did not have to wait until we reach our destination, but I don't want a scene with Delia. Enjoy your solitude." He gave her a look that made her feel as though her flesh were crawling with a thousand maggots. "Soon we will be together . . . me inside you."

He left, locking the door.

Briana's face and mouth felt as though she'd been burned. She lay down on her bunk and waited for sleep to take her away from her nightmare.

Briana awoke to find Raoul bending over her, looking very frightened. "Are you all right, mademoiselle? Who hurt you?"

She struggled to sit up, and some impulse prompted her to tell Raoul the entire story.

He listened, horrified but apparently believing her. "I do not know exactly what they have told you about me," she finished, "but I am telling you the truth."

He nodded very slowly, eyes on her face. "I believe you. You see, I came back here before it was time, to tell you that I know something is very wrong. They lied about you."

He rushed to tell her that he had found it increasingly difficult to believe what he had been told about her. That day, he'd overheard Gavin having a violent quarrel with his ladyfriend in their cabin. He'd known then that Gavin's story about Briana was a lie.

"And what were you told?" she prodded.

He took a deep breath. "Monsieur Mason said you killed his aunt, and he was getting you out of France to avoid a scandal and prosecution. He told my cousin, the captain, that he has political aspirations that would be hurt by something so terrible as a murder . . . by his *mistress*. . . ." His voice trailed away. "First he says you're his niece, and then he says you're . . ."

"Oh, Raoul, I am not his mistress," Briana cried, "or his niece. I'm no relative of his. You must believe me. He and one of his hired killers are the murderers, not me. Hollister murdered the man I loved. They forced me to go to Greece with them, and I was forced into getting involved with Gavin in the first place, and—"

She burst into tears of exhaustion and fury. "Why, I only found out a little while ago that Alaina deBonnett was dead," she added, wiping her eyes.

"Please don't cry, Mademoiselle. . . ?"

Briana smiled. "Briana de Paul. Call me Briana."

He hurriedly assured her, "I know you weren't a murderer. You couldn't hurt anybody."

Briana shook her head. "All I want is to escape, Raoul." She looked at him with pleading eyes. "Will you help me?"

He stared at her, his Adam's apple bobbing. "If I can," he whispered.

She hugged him happily, feeling a glimmer of hope for the first time in a long, long time. "I realize we have to protect you, so that you won't get into any trouble, Raoul. We must be very careful. I need time to think."

"I will help you," he reaffirmed, his tone firm and sure now.

Their eyes locked, held.

Briana told him to go about his regular duties, lest

he be discovered talking to her too much. "I know I can count on you to help me, and I will find a way to get myself out of this."

As it turned out, Briana did not need to find a plan of escape, for one came to her late that night. Delia paid her a secret visit.

Briana had been dozing, but was instantly awake at the sound of a key in the lock. The door opened, then closed quickly, and she could hear someone breathing rapidly, nervously.

"Briana? It's me . . . Delia."

Tense, Briana kept silent, waiting.

"Don't make me raise my voice, Briana. I don't want anyone to know I'm in here. Gavin is playing poker with the captain and some of his crew, on the deck above us. He thinks I'm asleep. He doesn't know I slipped the key to your cabin out of his coat pocket."

Briana remained silent. Delia's tone was conciliatory, but Briana had no reason to let her guard down. Why trust Delia?

"Please." Delia sounded close to tears. "I know you don't like me. I don't guess I can blame you, but won't you hear me out? I came to help you."

Hearing that, Briana sat bolt upright. "If I believed that . . ."

"You have to believe me!" Delia's voice was a mixture of desperation and indignation. "You are my only hope, and I'm yours. We're going to help each other."

"What do you want?" Briana snapped.

Delia gave a sigh of relief, then rushed on. "I was outside your cabin today when Gavin was here. I heard him hitting you."

"Thank you for intervening on my behalf," Briana quipped.

"I couldn't do anything!" Delia cried, then lowered her voice to a whisper. "I could hardly let him know I was out there. But when he came back to our cabin, I just lost my temper and told him I'd heard. To say he was going to get rid of me and marry you was just . . ." Her voice broke.

Delia cried for a few moments. Briana said nothing.

Delia began again. "I know you don't want to marry him. You want to be free of this whole mess and go find your brother. I am going to give you that chance, because if I don't, then Gavin will dump me, and I'll have nothing, after all the chances I've taken. He owes me," she said bitterly.

"Don't worry," she continued in a frenzy to be understood. "You can trust me. I won't hurt you. If I did, Gavin would hate me, and I would never stand a chance of becoming his wife."

Briana supposed that made sense. "What do you have in mind?"

"Hold out your hand."

"Why?"

"Come on," Delia urged. "I have something to give you. Hold out your hand."

Briana did, and was disbelieving as she felt a knife being placed in her palm.

"You must promise not to harm Gavin," Delia said. "I know you hate him, but you must promise you won't hurt him. You will only threaten him with the knife, not actually harm him. Do I have your promise?"

"You have given me this knife," Briana said evenly, "and I assure you that if Gavin tries to harm me again, I will slit his throat . . . just," she added truthfully, "as I will slit yours if you try to take it away from me now."

Delia went on in a rush as though Briana had not even spoken, delighted with herself for having all of this so well thought out. "The first night on Santoríni, I will keep Gavin occupied, no matter what I have to do. Meanwhile, you will have the knife. Use it on whoever is guarding you. The ship does not sail until dawn, I found out. They have to take on goods, and then the crew has free time on the island. That's the way it's always been, I'm told. All you have to do is sneak back on board. By the time Gavin finds out, you'll be safely on your way."

Briana was not impressed. "And if Gavin finds out I'm gone before the ship sails, and comes after me?"

"I will keep him busy until midday. Believe me, I know how," she added. "I will also see that he drinks enough to make him sleep heavily. By the time he wakes up, the ship will be gone, and so will you."

There was a tense moment of silence as the two women thought it over.

Then Delia spoke, warily. "Do you . . . do you think you will be able to kill Dirk, or whoever is guarding you, Briana?"

"I will welcome the opportunity," Briana stated.

Delia moved toward the door then, anxious to get back before Gavin returned. "He's on his good behavior after the fight we had earlier, but still . . ."

Briana was left alone then with her thoughts. And when she felt the cold, sharp blade of the knife pressed against her fingertips, she was able to believe that she really had a chance to fight.

Chapter Thirty-one

GAVIN Mason and his party arrived on the island of Santoríni and found that so many years had passed since Levon St. Clair's coming that no one thought much about him anymore. They were used to seeing his palatial mansion on top of a high peak, used to his being a recluse. Everyone stayed out of his way.

Gavin and the others rode up the mountain on donkeys. Briana, guarded by Biff, her hands bound before her, but not visibly so, marveled at the awesome spectacle. There were precipitous cliffs, over six hundred feet high, made of strata of black rock, russet soil, vestiges of gray lava, and veins of white pumice. Beyond those awesome cliffs stretched an endless blue sea flung all the way to the horizon.

More than once, Briana asked herself why she didn't simply scream for help, tell passersby that she was being kidnapped. But she had spent so much time under Gavin's thumb that she had no faith in a stranger's ability to help her, no expectation of being rescued. Why take a chance on being killed? If she exposed Gavin as a kidnapper, he or Hollister or one of the other American guards might kill her. No, it would be better to wait until she found a chance to escape. These people had killed her dearest love, Colt, and killed Branch. They might very well kill her if she tried to expose them.

They climbed higher and higher. Finally, reaching the top, not one of them failed to be stunned by the great white-walled villa that stood in regal splendor on its own mountain top. Delia clapped her hands in childish delight. Gavin, beneath the attempt to look as if he'd always lived in such places, was clearly thrilled.

A gray-haired old man with an ancient rifle slung over his shoulder did no more than wave them through the gates and into the courtyard when Gavin informed him that he was a relative of Levon St. Clair.

Instead of herding them all in, however, Gavin said he would go alone to meet the master of the house.

He was gone for only twenty minutes before he returned to jovially announce that there was no problem. They were welcome.

By then, Briana's clothes were soaked with perspiration, and her hair hung limp and damp. It had been a long climb, and the weather there was almost tropical. She wanted to go inside the cool white mansion and have a bath, then sleep for a few hours on a real bed, with real sheets, on ground that didn't rock and pitch. She knew she would need all the rest she could get, for she had looked carefully around on the journey upward, and seen how dangerous the journey down would be—precarious, with steep drop-offs. At night, in the dark, she would have to feel her way along very carefully. It would be slow going, and Raoul had warned her to be there on time for their scheduled sailing, at first light.

She watched out of the corner of her eye as Gavin talked with Al, both of them glancing in her direction. She hadn't seen as much of Al's dark side as she had of Dirk's, but she knew he couldn't be anything but bad.

In a moment, Al came over and lifted her off the donkey, then threw her over his shoulder. They moved away from the mansion, toward a rocky bluff nearby, and Briana cried, "Put me down!"

"Oh, shut up!" Al snarled. "The boss wants you locked up so's you won't be no trouble while he gets things organized."

She was taken to a place that was no more than a cave in the side of a large boulder. The entranceway was barred by a rusting gate. "An old hideaway for stolen goods," Al snickered. "And a perfect jail for you."

He set her on her feet and gave her a shove inside. The gate clanged shut with finality.

She scrambled to her feet and ran to grip the iron bars and stare between them. She could not see the villa from there because of the boulders obscuring the view. How was she going to get out of there?

Going inside, she saw that her abode was completely bare. There was not even a rug to lie on.

She took a deep, tortured breath. Delia *had* to come through for her . . . had to find a way to get Dirk or one of the other men to her . . . had to . . . had to . . .

The words drumming in her mind, she reached to her waist, where the knife was tied down flat along the line of her thigh. Raoul had given her enough string to do it.

Tonight *had* to be the night. Raoul had told her the crew always celebrated while they were in Santoríni, drinking and reveling till dawn. Sometimes the ship sailed without a few who didn't make it back in time . . . just as it would sail without her if she didn't get there.

Raoul had convinced the captain, his cousin, of Briana's innocence, for which she thanked heaven. The captain was sympathetic, for he had decided, by the time they arrived in port, that Gavin Mason was not what he had at first appeared to be. Too many card games, too much liquor . . . Gavin Mason had made a few enemies. The captain was not of a mind to interfere, and had ordered Raoul to stay out of the situation, but Raoul was confident that once Briana was on board, she would be safe.

The afternoon wore on, and as the sun began to die in the horizon, leaving a trail of blood on the azure sea, Delia came to the cave. In a frenzied whisper, she told Briana that all was ready.

"Gavin is in such good spirits now that we're here! He told the men to take the night off once the crates are stored, and go back down into the village and raise hell.

"And," she added, "I got to Dirk. I did it, Briana! I fixed everything. I told him that Gavin made arrangements to sell you to a rich merchant from Turkey, that you had brought a good price, and he wanted to get rid of you because you know too much. I told him Gavin wasn't turning you over to him, like he promised, because the Turkish buyer wouldn't take you if you were messed up."

Briana felt panicky. "But what if he goes to Gavin to argue about selling me? Then everything will come out."

"No," Delia assured her. "Dirk won't jeopardize things. He thinks we have a deal. He comes here and gets you, takes you into the village and keeps you down there, all to himself. I don't tell Gavin, and Gavin will think, of course, that you ran away."

Briana had very little faith in Delia, but she had no other choice, either. "You've done a good job, Delia. Thank you."

Suddenly Delia's eyes filled with tears. "Good luck, Briana. Somewhere along the line I started feeling sorry for you. I'm glad it worked out that I could help."

She hurried away before Briana could say anything.

Briana sighed. She sat down on the stone floor to await her destiny. Delia had chosen her destiny, with Gavin, and Briana knew that she would take anything fate held out to her over Delia's future with that madman.

* * *

Despite his head injury, Colt had slept little since leaving France, succumbing only when weariness gave him no choice. He was filled with a myriad of emotions galloping through him like wild creatures.

He kept a constant vigil at the ship's railing, as if he could will the ship to move faster.

Inquiries and bribes at the port in Monaco had given them the information that Mason had procured a vessel to take himself, two women, six men, and cargo to the Greek island of Thera, sometimes called Santoríni. Obtaining that information had not come cheap, for Mason had paid a large sum to keep it from being given out. Travis paid more to receive it.

Travis and Colt departed four days after Mason did. Nevertheless, the captain assured them that they stood a good chance of reaching the island at the same time as Mason, if not actually before. "I know the ship they're on," he had told them confidently. "The ship is old . . . with only a four-cylinder steam engine and a six-mast sail. Its top speed is only eleven knots. We can achieve over twenty knots, because this ship sails entirely on steam.

"If speed is what you want," he finished with a grin, "you've got the fastest ship available."

Colt had winced when his father told him just how much the voyage and the bribes had cost, but Travis smiled. He couldn't resist a good-natured barb. "Did you really think I left my whole fortune in your hands?"

Colt appreciated the lightness, knew that, somehow, his father was hurting for him as much as he hurt. Travis understood how a man can make mistakes. He understood how Colt was feeling, knew the pain, the fury, the burning need for revenge.

And, yes, love for the woman who had been used so cruelly.

Travis watched Colt as they stood at the bow of the

ship taking them to Greece. What, Travis wondered, could he say to his son? He wasn't angry with Colt for having been deceived. They would get the gold back—and, ultimately, the ranch and the mine.

He placed his hand on Colt's shoulder, understanding the pain he was feeling, and the humiliation. Colt didn't take his gaze from the water. Neither did he speak. It wasn't necessary. Both men acknowledged that sometimes silence is the best communication between people who truly understand each other.

Briana huddled on the floor of the cave, trying not to feel the sharp rocks pressing painfully against her body. She pretended to be sleeping, but every nerve was afire.

She had tucked the knife behind a rock, then practiced feeling for it in the darkness until she knew exactly how to reach it from wherever she lay. There could be no miscalculation, for she would get but one chance.

A servant from the mansion brought her cheese, bread, and wine as darkness closed in. Briana tried to speak to her, but the Greek woman stared at her with wide, frightened eyes, backing away quickly after shoving the food through the bars.

Briana ate, needing the strength, then took up her position inside the cave.

As it grew late, she started to feel panicky. What if Dirk didn't come? What if he had gone off with his men to get drunk? What if he had decided not to risk it? What if he had talked to Gavin?

Just as she began to believe the ship would be sailing without her, footsteps crunched against the gravel outside her prison.

She lay very still, forcing herself to breathe deeply and evenly.

There was the sound of a key grating in the lock, and the rusty gate squeaking open.

She tensed, ready, as Dirk crept forward, groping. He laughed drunkenly.

"Hey, little spitfire," he whispered, "where are you? Me and you are takin' a little trip, isn't that nice? You better come along nice and quiet, because you'll be a lot happier with me than with some crazy Turk—"

He bumped into her foot. She stirred, moaning softly, pretending to be asleep.

"There you are. . . ." He ran his hand over her back, and when he felt the swell of her buttocks beneath his fingertips, he breathed deeply, declaring vehemently, "I've waited a long time for this—too damn long. I'm gonna have what's been due me a long time."

She heard him fumbling with his trousers, but she managed to will her body to stay relaxed, as though asleep.

When he had made himself ready to take her, he jerked her roughly over onto her back, pinning her wrists together with one hand while pressing his other hand across her mouth to keep her silent. Her eyes flew open and he grunted, glad to see her awake and looking at him. He reeked of whiskey. "You're gonna give me what you gave Coltrane, damn you," he snarled, "and you're gonna give it to me good. You belong to me now, and I'm gonna teach you how to please me. The day you don't is the day you die!"

He used his knee to spread her thighs, warning that if she made a sound when he took his hand away from her mouth, he would make her wish she hadn't.

Briana made little moans deep in her throat, as though terrified and submissive.

Dirk was pleased. "Hell, I knew once you found out I was boss you'd lose that feisty temper. Now, just relax and it won't hurt. . . ."

He positioned himself between her legs. She continued to whimper and made no move to defend herself, so he released her wrists, moving his hand to fondle her breasts.

"You're doin' good," he gloated. "You know when you're licked, and I think you've also gotten a look at me down here, so you realize how good it's gonna be."

It took all the nerve she had to wait, and not reach for the knife too soon. It was all she could do, too, to keep from screaming aloud with outrage.

He continued slobbering over her, and then, very slowly, she reached out for the knife. Her fingers closed around the handle.

Above her, Dirk Hollister grunted and mumbled. She gripped the knife handle, tensed, then brought the knife down in a deadly arc. But just before it reached the back of his neck, Dirk felt her sudden movement and rolled to the side just fast enough that the blade thrust into his shoulder instead of his neck.

He screamed with pain. Briana knew there wasn't time to try to jerk the knife out so that she could stab him again.

She slammed her hands against his shoulders, pressing her own shoulders back against the ground. With one mighty heave, she raised her hips, bucking him away from her. She lunged to the side and slipped from beneath him, scrambling to her feet while she put as much distance between them as she could.

He was writhing and moaning. Blood was coming in a steady stream, and she could only pray that he was weakened by the loss of it.

She rushed from the cave, pausing outside just long enough to gulp in fresh air and try, for a few seconds, to compose herself and remember the way.

Then she took off, running as hard as she could. She left the rocky plateau and headed down the precarious trail, casting fearful eyes upward every few steps, praying for the miracle of moonlight. But it was a cloudy night, and she could barely see.

Lifting her long skirt, trying to pick her way carefully while moving as fast as possible, she began panting with exertion and fear.

Now and then, when the moon teased her by breaking through the clouds, she made a point of not looking to her left . . . where she knew she would see the sprawling black space down there that reminded her of how easy it would be to slip and plunge down six hundred feet to her death.

Every so often she had to stop and rest, panting. The way was treacherous, and she couldn't afford any missteps. Raoul had said the walk down would take about two hours, maybe a bit more. The trail zigzagged first one way, then another way, for the mountain was too steep for a single trail straight up. If she continued at her present pace, she ought to reach the ship in plenty of time. She was breathing hard now, and hoped the nearness of Raoul and the ship would buoy her flagging energy.

Like a bat swooping in the night, strong hands clutched her throat and forced her down against the stones. She clawed at the hands choking her, felt dizziness overtaking her.

"Bitch . . ." came the guttural snarl. "Die, bitch. . . ."

He kicked her, sending her sprawling forward and down, down into the endless night.

She felt but one sharp pain as her head struck a rock, and then she began floating in that endless sea of night.

Dirk Hollister stared down into the darkness, chest heaving. The knife was still buried to its hilt in his shoulder. He hadn't been able to remove it. But there was, at long last, jubilation at knowing the bitch was dead. He'd sooner have died himself than allow Briana to escape. Well, she'd never escape again.

He began to make his way back up to the mansion, where he would get someone to pull out the goddamn knife. And then, by God, he was going to find out what Briana had been doing with Gavin Mason's knife!

* * *

Briana moaned against the terrible pain clawing at her head. She remembered nothing of what had happened, didn't know where she was, desired only for the clutching fingers of oblivion to take her away again from the terrible hurting.

When Dirk kicked her, she had not pitched off the ledge as he had meant for her to do. The large rock on which she'd struck her head had stopped her fall only twenty feet down.

As she waited for the black fog to waft her away again, a sound reached Briana's ears. But a moment later she was unconscious once more. She didn't hear the clicking of hooves on the trail, didn't wonder who was riding so dangerously fast up the mountain.

Chapter Thirty-two

By the time Dirk made his way to the room their host had assigned to Gavin, pain had driven all vestiges of reason from his consciousness. It had all been a trap, he knew, to get rid of him. Mason, deciding to keep Dirk's share of the wealth for himself, had given Briana a knife and set Dirk up to get killed.

He kicked Gavin's door in. Gavin was asleep, head on Delia's breast. At the sight of Dirk, covered in blood and looking like a bull gone mad, Delia screamed. Gavin came groggily awake just in time to see Hollister lunge for him, a nightmare apparition. It was Gavin Mason's final vision of life before Dirk plunged the knife into his throat.

Delia flung herself off the bed and ran from the room, screaming. Some of Gavin's blood had spattered into her strawberry blonde curls. "You're next, bitch!" Dirk hollered after her. "You were in on it, and you're gonna die tonight, too!"

Delia ran blindly down the unfamiliar corridor, knowing only that she had to run, but not where to run *to*. She screamed on and on.

She turned a corner and started running down the stairs, stumbling and then falling, bouncing against the stairs until she landed hard, on the floor. There was an awful pain, and she knew something was broken, but the maniac was coming after her, the knife held high over his head.

He cackled triumphantly as he scrambled down the stairs, eyes glittering. Reaching her, towering above her, he raised the knife as high as he could, then brought it down.

A gunshot exploded, deafening her, and then Dirk Hollister pitched forward, dead, a bullet between his eyes.

John Travis Coltrane knew joy for the first time since that magical morning in Briana's arms.

There was no time for contemplating Hollister's fate. Travis helped Delia to her feet, demanding she tell them where Briana was. Babbling, she told them what she knew: that Gavin was dead, that Briana was probably responsible for the knife wound in Hollister's shoulder, and that Briana was on her way down the mountain to the waiting ship.

Colt left on the run, and Travis didn't try to stop him. He would catch up.

Ignoring the servants who had appeared suddenly out of nowhere to stare and whisper, Travis went to see for himself whether Gavin Mason was really dead.

Then he would deal with the men who'd helped Gavin steal from him, and get the gold that was rightfully Coltrane gold.

Colt would take care of finding Briana . . . if she could be found.

Briana was sobbing. Time was running out. Her head was bleeding and her feet were torn, but the moment she'd wakened enough to remember what had happened, she'd forced herself up, forced herself to get moving again. Her head hurt unbearably and she was shaking, but she kept going. The sky had lightened, and it was nearly dawn.

She still had another twenty feet or more to climb

down when she paused to wipe her eyes, then stared downward in horror. "No. Oh, dear God, no . . ."

The ship was starting to move!

Panic thrusting her forward, she scrambled over the rocks as fast as she could. She was getting dizzy again, but all that mattered was getting down as fast as possible. The ship would pass directly beneath her, and if she could reach that last ledge, she could jump into the water. Surely someone would see her in the water, wouldn't they? It was her one last chance.

"Please, please, *please* God," she whispered, her body trembling with pain and desperation.

At last, at last, she reached the ledge. Raising her arms, she took a final deep breath, offered up a prayer, and flung herself outward in a smooth arc.

The cool water took her. She went under, then pulled herself up to the surface, taking a deep breath as her head broke through the water.

She swam toward the ship's prow, mustering all her strength and all the control she could impose on herself. Panic would kill her. She had to stay in rigid control of her body and her mind.

Intent on reaching the ship's path, panting with the exertion of swimming so hard after her injury, Briana failed to hear the voice crying out to her from the rocky ledge, did not hear the splashing behind her.

As she swam toward the ship's path, crying out silently for someone on the ship to see her, she sensed movement behind her and to the side, but she didn't dare turn her head to look.

And then Briana began to wonder whether she might be drowning. Her head ached terribly and her limbs were bruised, sore, and begging her to stop swimming. While forcing her tormented body onward, onward, she began dreaming of sleep, and blessed relief. *Stay awake!* she screamed to herself, and fixed her gaze on the ship's prow, which was now a little nearer. Something warm touched her shoulder, but she barely felt it, so intent was she on straining herself forward, forward.

All at once she remembered that, if someone saw his life flashing before him, that meant he was drowning. She must be drowning, then, she realized. Why else would she see her life—her love—before her? Why else would Colt's dear face rise up out of the turquoise waters? How was it that she felt his strong arms around her, guiding her? Why, as she relaxed against him, did she feel herself in shallow water, and then on land?

She felt herself leaving the earthly realm, yet she struggled for consciousness, lest she be denied the joy of her dying vision.

"Briana . . ."

She closed her eyes, yielding to his kiss, felt his strong arms lower her to the sand.

"Briana, I love you."

She opened her eyes. She knew then, praise God, that it was real.

Sometimes, she acknowledged, tears of joy in her eyes, sometimes the dream is real.

She prayed the dream would never end.